UNSEEN DANGER

Bodie dropped down on his haunches to study the situation. Piecing together the sign, he made out that a lone man had squatted on his heels there, rested a long gun against the scrub brush, undoubtedly watching the cotton field out front. The lookout had been active for a time, because he saw old cigarette butts, a faded wrapper from a plug of Brown Mule chewing tobacco.

He straightened to his feet, keened his eyes through the trees, searching out the nearest cotton field, puzzled. The field was at least two hundred yards away. It was obvious that a lone man could do no more than take potshots at the cotton pickers. And that man had to know that the plantation was armed, however poorly.

He was walking toward his horse, still thinking about the direction and method of expected attack, when suddenly he heard a shot . . . then another, followed by two more. Quickly he gathered the reins and swung onto the saddle. Picking his way cautiously toward the sound of the shots, he strained his ears for sound, his eyes for movement.

A grasshopper jumped and landed, rustling the dry underbrush, and from somewhere off on the right a crow cawed. Nothing more.

Then a Winchester exploded, an ugly hiss buzzed by his ear, and a bullet dug into a tree next to his shoulder.

Other *Leisure* books by Hiram King:
HIGH PRAIRIE

DARK TRAIL

Hiram King

LEISURE BOOKS NEW YORK CITY

In loving memory of my parents,
Tom King and Carrie Giddings.

A LEISURE BOOK®

August 1998

Published by

Dorchester Publishing Co., Inc.
276 Fifth Avenue
New York, NY 10001

ISBN 0-8439-4418-8

Printed in the United States of America.

DARK TRAIL

Chapter One

"Don't move, black boy!"

He stiffened at the words hurled at him from the bushes. Somehow he had known there would be trouble. He had seen the two white men earlier when they first came prowling under the trestle where he was squatting on his haunches over a cook fire. He wanted no company; he trusted no white man. All he wanted was to finish eating and move on.

"One wrong move outta you," the man added harshly, "and this gun'll take your head off at the shoulders!"

Maybe he had been wrong, he thought. Maybe one of them was armed after all. And desperate enough to kill a man for a meal like the other three drifters who had made the mistake of attacking his camp, only to find his bedroll empty, and a pistol covering them from the timbers. Or maybe these two had been twisted enough by the war to kill any black man.

He shifted his weight to the other side, bringing his pistol closer to his right hand. "You welcome to the vittles," he said toward the concealed voice.

"You damned tootin' I'm welcome!" the prowler answered. "Now, back away! One wrong move and vittles will be your least worry!"

The black man chuckled lightly. The words were hollow, didn't ring true. Now he was sure the man was bluffing, unarmed after all. Driven by hunger probably.

He stood up, a tall, wide-shouldered, dark-skinned man. "Talk like that won't fill your belly, mister," he said, and flicked aside the butt of his cigarette, the last one he was liable to see in a while. " 'Specially when you ain't got nothin' to back it up with." Just then he saw out of the corner of his eye the bushes move, the other prowler skulking near his tied-up horse. "You!" he shouted. "Touch that hoss and I'll kill you!"

The man who had spoken came out, walking forward awkwardly, grinning oafishly. He was tall, thin-faced, wolfish-looking. Looked to be in his early thirties. Hair the color of wheat straw stuck out from under a gray kepi cap. And he was unarmed after all.

"Come on out, Payne!" wolf-face called out to his partner. "He's onto us!" Payne walked out in the open. He was a smallish man, also in his thirties, and rail-thin, emaciated, sick-looking. Like his partner he wore mismatched, ill-fitting pieces of Confederate army clothes, and had a bone-handled skinning knife stuck in his waistband.

The black man stood off from the fire, watching the two men come into camp. Payne's eyes followed the other man's over to the cook fire where the aroma of roasting rabbit was coming from.

"Food's y'alls," said the black man, guessing they were more starved than dangerous. "Ain't much, but it's fillin'."

The two prowlers broke into a stumbling run toward the sizzling meat. He judged them as just two more discharged Confederate veterans making their way home, if they had a home. He had come across hundreds of such men. Some dangerous, most not. All worth watching, however, considering the unsettled conditions of the country now.

"Man came into camp a while back," he said carefully, "had to break my pistol 'cross his head."

"What for?" Payne asked, lifting the skewered meat from the fire.

"He jumped me. Figured I was scared."

The two displaced men exchanged glances as if that was the farthest thing from their minds.

"Figure to do the same for you two if you got the same notion. Y'all can have at that rabbit or we can have our dustup now. What'll it be?"

"We'll have some of this rabbit," Payne said, licking his lips hungrily. "Won't us, Eph?"

"We'll eat," Ephram Daggett said, rubbing his palms together gleefully. "We ain't et in two days."

"Have at it," the black man said, walking off toward his horse.

"You leavin'?"

"Yep. I was headed down these rails. I better git to it."

Catching up his horse, he swung onto the saddle and guided the horse around the two white men engrossed in tearing hot meat from the skewer. He walked his horse out from under the fire-blackened trestle and angled down into the steep-sided gorge. After splashing across a hock-deep stream of water at the bottom, he topped out on the other side and ranged his eyes down the railroad tracks he had been following for the last seven days.

In the distance loomed a water tower and a train sta-

9

tion. He touched spurs to the bay, lifted him into a shambling trot.

At that moment the agent stepped out the front door of the station, started walking across the wooden platform.

The agent was killing time as usual. More out of habit than anything else, he shielded his eyes with a palm, looked west down the rails. Nothing. Nothing at all except two narrow ribbons of steel stretching away through a brown carpet of wild grasses as far as a man could see. Turning, he glanced east up the rails and looked again. Movement. Unexpected.

He stood still, his eyes fixed on the speck coming toward him along the edge of the rail bed.

The speck grew larger, matured into a man.

"I'm damned if it ain't," the agent said in a low voice. "What in Judas' name is he doin' out here ahorseback?"

He turned over in his mind the remote possibility that some urgent railroad business had required sending a rider thirty miles from town. Usually his orders were received by pouch, or an inspector occasionally showed up among the passengers. At a loss for answers, he scratched at his chin thoughtfully, gave up, put both hands on his hips, watching the rider come.

The man rode his saddle with assurance, like a man who knew what for. Forty yards away, the agent saw he was a black man. His hands fell away from his hips, his mind looked back.

It had been, what . . . two, no, three weeks now since General Lee had surrendered at Appomattox and President Lincoln had walked into Richmond.

As far as the station keeper could judge, and from what he had heard, every pair of black feet that wanted to had already fled the state.

"Howdy," the agent said dryly, his eyes taking in the

jaded mount the black man rode up alongside the platform. "If you followed them rails all the way, that horse's got a right to look like he is." He smiled thinly at his own words.

"How do," the black man replied, saddle leather creaking as he stepped down. "I followed 'em all the way. I'd say he earned his keep." He rubbed a hand over the horse's sweaty neck.

"What brings you this far from nowhere?"

"Name's Bodie. Aimin' to catch up with a train."

The keeper's eyes widened. "You ain't likely to catch it," he said, instinctively looking over his shoulder west down the rails. "She come through here yesterday evening a little bit after four."

"I ain't aimin' to catch up with that one."

The keeper looked suspiciously from under lifted eyebrows. Word had come from the town up the rails that the newly freed slaves were looting and stealing now that they had the chance, hauling out of the state anything that could be carried off.

"Which one you after?" he asked skeptically.

"One that come through here three, four months ago."

"Three, four months ago!" he blurted. Catching himself, he cleared his throat, chuckled lightly. "Train comes through here once a day. I ain't likely to remember one that came through here that long ago."

"It oughta be easy to remember. It was made up of nothin' but stock cars." He narrowed his eyes at the agent. "And every car was filled with slaves."

The agent's face flushed, his lips went white. "I got nothin' to say on that," he said definitely.

"This here's Reams's Station, ain't it?"

"It is. I'm Harry Reams."

"Twenty miles back yonder is Decatur." He pointed in that direction. "That slave train pulled in there, and

11

when it left it came this way or it went south. I'm askin' you which way."

"That's railroad business," Reams said sharply.

Reams was a smallish, clear-eyed man with a clean-shaven upper lip and heavy jaws fringed with whiskers that ran from ear to ear in a wide crescent.

Bodie was better than six feet tall, weighed at least one-eighty, had wide shoulders, heavy muscles, big powerful arms.

"I had kin on that train," he stated firmly.

Reams said nothing.

Bodie unholstered his pistol, an Army Colt .44. "One way or another, you'll answer." And he hefted the gun knowingly.

Bodie and Reams both knew Reams was over-matched. "It . . . it come this way," Reams answered, shaken.

"Where was it headed?"

"I never asked. They's all headed down these rails to the next station, as far as I'm concerned."

"This train was different. Maybe you writ somethin' down about it," Bodie suggested, hefting the pistol threateningly again.

"I'd have to look."

He waved the pistol barrel at Reams. Reams side-stepped away, went inside the station.

The special train was logged there in the agent's log, a running record required of every agent, Bodie had found out.

In January of '65 the Confederacy had been reeling on its last legs. Lee's Army of Northern Virginia had been bludgeoned to the very edge of hopelessness, a dispirited band of ragtag men who had had the means and the will hammered out of them. Every rebel knew the end was near.

But beliefs die hard, whether good or bad. The belief

in using other humans to do their labor wouldn't die with some men. So a half-dozen big planters at Richmond had banded together and financed a special train of one hundred stock cars to transport slaves into the interior of the Confederacy, away from the Yankee line of march and fighting, away from the liberating influences of the steadily advancing Yankees. These men believed that somehow the Confederacy would prevail, they'd recoup their slaves, put back all that the war had shattered, and resume living a life of plenty built on slave labor as before.

But the log, like all the others Bodie had seen, gave no final destination for the train. The ledger simply read: "Richmond Special Arrival 10:30 A.M. Departure 10:44 A.M."

Reams turned the ledger around to Bodie's eyes, looking a question at him.

He read the ledger, confirming what Reams had said. Tight-jawed and stiff-lipped, he turned away quietly, headed for the door.

Struck by the resolute way the man carried himself, Reams followed him out onto the platform. "If you intend to go on, these rails won't do you no good."

Bodie turned, and Reams explained: "Ain't no agent down the line likely to have anything writ down . . . not even what I just showed you. Ain't required to."

Bodie swung onto the saddle. "They'll have to show me, same as you did."

Reams detected uncommon purpose in the man's manner. Looking up at Bodie, a solid mature man of thirty-four, Reams saw quiet determination in the black man's face. Reams's eyes probed for an answer.

"I got nothin' back yonder where I come from," Bodie stated, "and no one of interest. Family is all I got. I don't intend to stop lookin' for 'em till I find 'em."

Looking up at Bodie, Reams saw for the first time a

free black man sitting the saddle, quietly concerned, but with a confident turn to his features. Reams knew this man would never be turned aside, would never move on without answers. He asked respectfully, "What kin did you have on that train?"

"All I got."

Reams lowered his head, studied the platform planks, thinking back. Presently he lifted his head. "Them stock cars was crammed full, hardly breathin' room in 'em. Back yonder," and he pointed in back of the station, "me and the engineer buried four. Three men and a woman. Men suffocated, woman trampled to death. Of course, I have no way of knowin' . . ." And Reams spread his palms helplessly.

"Any one of the men tall, dark-skinned, built along my lines?"

"Nothin' of that sort. Woman was a frail thing, light-skinned."

"I'll find 'em," Bodie said without emotion, touching spurs to his horse.

He was a man without schooling, knew only what he had learned to survive as a slave, and that which a slave mother and father dared pass along. Army life had grown him into a man and had taught him how to kill.

He had been in the saddle close to a month now, and had made his way through some of the worst country for any man, let alone a black man. Hunting for what he ate, sleeping out in the open, he had close to eight hundred miles of rails behind him, following the tracks of a slave train that had hauled away from Huelen Plantation all the family he had.

Huelen Plantation was ten miles south of Lynchburg. Bodie had been brought there from Stem Johnson's plantation in Alabama, as had his two younger brothers and a sister. In '61 when the war broke out, James Norville Huelen rushed off immediately to service in the Confederate cause, leaving his wife to oversee the plantation and seventeen slaves.

In August of '64, when the Yankees had pressed ever closer to Richmond, Bodie escaped from Huelen, made his way north, and had joined the Fifth Massachusetts Infantry, a Negro brigade President Lincoln had reluctantly authorized.

On the third of April in '65, Major General Godfrey Weitzel, with a detachment of the Army of the Potomac, marched into Richmond and took military charge of the fallen city. Sergeant Bodie rode in with the mounted infantry vedettes. Once the city was secured, Bodie was given leave to find out the circumstances of his family, which lived nearby.

He made a hasty ride to Huelen Plantation and found a run-down, weed-infested piece of property. The only slaves remaining were two men and a woman too old and infirm to travel. Uncle Joe, the gray-haired butler, told Bodie, "Me, Willie, and Lukie the only ones left here. Yo' folks, they all gone."

"When? Where?"

"It was a little bit after Christmas. The missus, she done took 'em to Richmond and put 'em on the train before she left. Sent 'em off for safekeepin' for they own good, she claimed."

"Where'd she send 'em?"

"The missus she don't say. And Mr. James, he ain't come back."

Bodie rode back to Richmond sick in his stomach. In two days he had drawn his mustering-out pay after pressing his case all the way up to division headquarters. That same day he took to the rails, trying to find out where the slave train had gone after it left Richmond close to three months before.

His first stop was the Richmond and Danville Railroad at Burksville Junction. There he found that the special train had come through, all right. But there was no written record of where it was going. The agent who had run the place back then had run for his life when the Yankees took Richmond. An old black roustabout still working there remembered the time, and told Bodie, "All I know is, they was loaded up like cows and the train pulled out, heading toward Lynchburg."

So he went to Lynchburg.

Nothing. He headed toward the next station down the rails. And had been heading toward the next station down the rails ever since, following the rails, inquiring at every station. One hundred thirty-two miles of the South Side Railroad was behind him; better than two hundred of the Virginia and Tennessee.

A mild-mannered, deliberate man of purpose, he had ridden on, making the long reach of three hundred seventy-five miles across war-shattered Tennessee, following the East Tennessee and Virginia rails. At Loudon station he had been forced to pistol-whip answers from the agent. And at Chattanooga junction he had to choke the wind out of the agent before he found out the train had taken the rails leading west.

Now Bodie rode away from Reams's Station, following the Memphis and Charleston as he had been doing for the last seven days, scouting the rails ahead.

He rode without urgency, a determined man sure of his objective. Carrying no illusions whatever of what might have happened to his family, he simply followed wherever the rails led him. The shattered country and broken people behind him testified to the unpredictable nature of what lay ahead. Future plans of his own were out of the question until he found his family, wherever they were.

So west he rode.

The bay horse he straddled wasn't his, and the saddle was cavalry issue. The faded blue cotton shirt and the black denim pants he wore had been taken from a clothesline three days before. In his pocket was thirteen dollars left from his mustering-out pay.

The land he rode was a gently rolling sweep of rye grass that fled away into the distance, broken here and there by mottes of hickory and spruce trees. The rails sliced through the countryside, skirting the mottes as a man would a mad dog.

It was coming on to sundown when he topped a low-grade hill, his eyes picking up the rails again as they snaked down into a shallow valley, close to a bunch of spruce trees. And that's when he spotted the trail thirty yards away from the rail bed.

More out of curiosity than anything else, he swung his horse, took the trail, obviously newly made and little used. His eyes picked up discarded objects: a bed frame here, an old stove there, and a dresser yonder. A quarter mile farther on, he came up on the hulk of a busted wagon.

He sat the saddle, studying the wrecked wagon. It was nothing more than a plantation cart, really. Its single wooden axle had cracked, rendering it useless. The grass around it had been trampled thoroughly by three, maybe four people, Bodie guessed. And whoever they were had left afoot.

Bodie touched spurs to his horse, took the trail.

He had been in the trail no more than five minutes when riders charged out of the trees, coming at him at a fast clip.

He checked the bay to a halt and faced around.

Four men clattered up, jerked to a stop in front of him.

"End of the line, boy!" a big man yelled at him.

All four wore floppy hats and loose-fitting shabby clothes, like dirt farmers. The big man had on a home-spun gray coat, black-striped cotton trousers, the cuffs

17

crammed inside square-toed boots. His face was unusually white.

"Free country, ain't it," Bodie answered, making a statement more than asking a question.

The big man smiled crookedly at Bodie and said around a jaw of chewing tobacco, "Country back yonder is."

Bodie turned carelessly in the saddle, scanning the country he had just come through. He turned back around, his face a closed book. Another man, the one sitting his saddle next to the big man, said, "It's free as you please. Country up ahead," and he nodded that way, "it ain't."

"What country's that?" Bodie asked innocently.

"Don't matter. It ain't free." The man grinned devilishly. "Like Dancer here told you, country behind you is free. Was I you, I'd turn right around and head thataway."

Bill Dancer, the big man, cut in, saying harshly, "Niggers can't come in Jason County 'less they prove they ain't carryin' nothin' that don't belong to 'em."

Bodie ignored the insult, reached back, and patted his saddlebags. "I ain't carryin' nothin' but my possibles."

"Well now, let's have a look at them possibles," Dancer said, kneeing his horse toward Bodie's.

Suddenly Bodie jabbed spurs to the bay even as his right hand swept back. The .44 came between his fingers. The bay lunged powerfully, slamming a shoulder into Dancer's horse. The instant the two horses came together, Bodie smashed the barrel of his gun against Dancer's skull, knocking him from the saddle.

The other three men were taken completely by surprise. The scrawny one fumbled at his pistol. Bodie fired, hitting the man's shoulder, slumping him over in the saddle. Jabbing spurs to his horse, Bodie tore out of there, snapping back three wild shots to hold them at bay.

After a dozen or so jumps the bay was in a full-out run, Bodie leaning low in the saddle, his gun holstered again.

The chuffing train that he had heard earlier now whistled its descent, the lonely sound reaching down into the valley. He swung the bay over into the rail bed. The train, with a head of steam up, came at him head-on. At no more than twenty yards away, Bodie swung the bay savagely, raking his spurs at the same time.

The horse vaulted between the rails, stumbling on the cross-ties, kicking back gravel. The engineer jerked angry howls of warning on his whistle. In a scrambling, snorting leap the bay hurtled the other rail, scrambled to footing on the other side. The train plunged on by.

Bodie glanced over his shoulder, checking for pursuit.

None of the white men had dared to cross the tracks.

He swung west, the moving train shielding his disappearance into the tree line.

He rode at trail gait for perhaps ten minutes, then struck a narrow, shallow-running stream. He swung the bay onto the stream's course, knowing all the while he'd return to the rails sooner or later.

Chapter Two

The stream that Bodie had struck in wild country of vine-tangled post oak and blackjack was Wolf River, now a lazy flow of runoff water but at times wild and dangerous, driven by overflows from the Mississippi that would send it plunging torrentially, tearing at its banks.

Bodie followed the Wolf to its confluence with the Mississippi. He paid a Yankee dollar and a half to cross over on Monk's Ferry. He had no way of knowing he was in Arkansas, but he knew the rails were south of him. How far off the rails were was a matter of speculation, so he simply skirted his way along the bank of the Mississippi.

Hours later he was still working his way through briar- and bramble-infested bottomland. Twice he had had to double back to push his way through. Once out, he struck south, casting for the rail bed.

It was late in the afternoon when he came upon two furrows of rank weeds that had obviously once been a wagon road. Following the furrows at a walk, he came to a tumbled-down water tower and burned-out train station. A hundred yards farther on was a small settlement.

He checked to a halt in front of the battle-wrecked train station, surveying the damage. He knew there wasn't a chance in hell those charred remains would yield anything pointing in the direction that slave train had gone. His only chance, slim though it was, was to locate the station keeper Harry Reams had mentioned.

He swung his horse toward the town. And just at that second a timid voice called at his back: "Mister . . ."

Twisting around in the saddle, his eyes searched for the source of the voice.

The girl walked forward shyly, stepping over charred planks that had been the corner of the train station.

"You goin' into town?" she asked meekly.

Bodie faltered at the question, looking quickly toward the town. "Figured to," he answered finally.

"Can we go in with you? Papa's worried."

"Papa . . . ?"

Just then an old man stepped away from the corner and spoke up. "They makin' a commotion down there. I don't know about what."

"This's my papa," the girl said. "Our wagon broke down this mornin'. We walked here. Papa said we ought not to go into town till things quieted down, but things ain't quieted down and it's gittin' dark."

"Name's Jesse . . . Jesse Gone," the old man said. "And this here's my girl Deedee."

"Where's the others?"

"They yonder," Jesse said, his head indicating the bushes behind the station. "Nowdays, you got to be careful."

"Them's words to heed," Bodie agreed.

Jesse ran his eyes over Bodie's horse, peered at the

Winchester riding in the boot, then glanced at Bodie's six-shooter.

"How'd you know there was some more of us?" he asked.

"Seen your wagon back yonder and the trail you left." He swung his horse toward the town and said, "Night's comin' on. Tell your folks to make haste."

Bodie was a quiet, mindful man, not much for initiating talk. With his horse at a slow walk in the lead, he glanced back over his shoulder at the four people and a broken-down nag walking behind him.

The woman was at least fifty years old, maybe Jesse's wife; Jesse looked to be that old himself. The boy leading the nag couldn't have been more than ten or eleven, Bodie figured.

Deedee? She was a tall, slim-waisted, bright-eyed woman of twenty-three, twenty-four at most. A floppy bonnet tied under her chin almost hid her chocolate-colored, slender face. The drab unbleached muslin dress she wore didn't cover the fact that she was all woman.

Marion was a fair-size town that had sprung up in a shallow valley just south of the train station. Four miles to the west the land was table-flat farmland, the land of cotton; and for that reason, Marion was a farming town straddling the rails that led south.

Bodie led the procession down the right side of the rail bed, the town's main street, roving his eyes over the place.

The town was crowded with black folks, the boardwalks looking like a great camp meeting, a carnival atmosphere of activity. Black people were everywhere, slouched on benches along the storefronts, talking animatedly. A jovial atmosphere prevailed, brought on by the wild joy of being free.

On one side they passed a newspaper office, a shoe and clothing store, a general merchandise store, displaying out front the latest in farm implements, and a feed and grain store. On the other side stood two saloons and a hotel, and thirty or forty yards up was a livery. A plank building, obviously newly constructed, was across the street from the livery. A hand-lettered signed proclaimed the new building as the Freedmen's Bureau.

Arkansas, like every other ex–Confederate state, was under federal military rule now. Army officers and civilian men of good Republican standing ran the state, enforcing federal law and looking after the civil well-being of the newly free slaves through the Bureau of Refugees, Freedmen, and Abandoned Lands.

Former slaves took their new freedom as they saw fit. Some left the state altogether; others sought a living by doing plantation work as they had done all their lives. Except now labor had to be paid, hired through the bureau.

Still others flocked into the towns, idling their lives away, much to the irritation of army officers at the bureau.

Although defeated and disorganized, some men fought back, launching guerrilla raids and night attacks against their northern conquerers. The target of their scorn were the white army officers who administered the hated bureau, and their wards, the freedmen.

Every black person in the nation had heard of the bureau and what it stood for. So Bodie swung his horse, crossed the rail bed, headed that way. The procession behind him followed in his horse's tracks.

At that instant a blue-uniformed man stepped through the open door of the bureau and paused on the board-walk, his eyes sweeping the street. He was a tall, lean-jawed, neatly dressed man. The shoulder bars on his blue blouse ranked him a lieutenant.

His eyes shifted back and forth over the half-dozen black men sloughed on the benches on either side of the door. His face went white, then crimson, irritated at what he saw. "I warned you people already," he said angrily. "If you ain't lookin' for work, clear out!"

Nobody moved.

The lieutenant's right hand shot out, grabbed a handful of shirtfront of the nearest black man sitting on the bench. "Clear out, I said!" He jerked the man to his feet and shoved him on his way. The other men burst into motion like thieves caught red-handed, scampering in every direction.

The lieutenant's eyes caught sight of Bodie and the shabby procession with him, coming toward the bureau.

"You people lookin' for work or a handout?" he asked Bodie.

"Neither one."

The lieutenant looked Bodie over carefully, taking in the pistol, the Winchester riding in the boot. At length he asked, "What are you lookin' for?"

"Can't speak for them," Bodie said, nodding his head at the family behind him, "but I'm lookin' for information."

The lieutenant looked over Jesse and his family, taking mental note of the age and condition of the bunch. "You people lookin' for work?" he asked Jesse.

"Yeah, suh, but we works as a family."

The lieutenant swore under his breath. Calming himself with a tight draw of his lips, he said, "Come on inside."

"About that information?" Bodie asked.

"What information?"

"Man used to run the train station . . . any idea where I can find 'em?"

The lieutenant knew that since the war was over revenge killings were commonplace, black and white. And it was the bureau's job to put a stop to just such activity. "You see all these people out here?" He flourished a

24

hand at the boardwalk. "Not one of 'em is armed. Forget about this man who used to run the train station. You want work, come inside. You want trouble, go elsewhere." The lieutenant turned and went back inside.

Undaunted, Bodie swung his horse and clip-clopped over to Grady's Livery, which he had noticed earlier. He swung down.

Grady was a big-faced, heavy-muscled man with thick, shaggy eyebrows and deep-blue indifferent eyes.

"Got grain or oats?" Bodie asked him.

"Corn," Grady answered rudely.

"That'll do."

"Two bits. Bucket's yonder . . . Bones will show you where the corn's at."

Bodie fished in his pocket for money, talking all the while. "Wouldn't, by any chance, know where I can find the man who use to run the tran station, would you?"

Grady paused a long minute, his mind working on the fact that hard feelings ran high in both races. Whom a man knew was best kept to himself. "Nope," he said dismissively, tightening his lips.

Bodie led the bay inside the livery and was met in front of a stall by the man Grady had called Bones.

Bones was a dark-skinned, gray-haired man. He had on loose-fitting apron overalls and a gray flannel undershirt out at the elbows. He limped forward, looking toward the open door of the livery where Grady had headed, speaking to Bodie out of a toothless mouth. "Corn's out back. I'll show you."

Bodie's eyes followed Bones's just in time to glimpse Grady hurrying down the street.

Inside the stall, he stripped off his saddle gear, retrieved a bucket, and fell in step with Bones.

With his eyes straight ahead, Bones asked out the side of his mouth, "You new here, ain't you?"

"Just rode in," Bodie answered, looking over his shoulder at Bones gimping along at his side. "Town seems right touchy. Any special reason for it?"

"Army. White folks here got no use for 'em. Lieutenant Drake, he makes 'em pay fair wages . . . them that wants work done."

They walked through the wide-open rear door of the livery, the gimpy old man pointing to his right. "Corn's in the barrel there. Two bits' worth is one bucket. If you was to git more, I wouldn't notice it."

Bodie smiled to himself. "Much obliged to you, but I'd just as soon take what I'm due."

"Suit yo'self," Bones commented dryly. "Where'd you come from?"

"Lynchburg."

Bones grunted indifferently; Bodie left it at that.

Bodie knew it was a wild shot in the dark when the idea came to him. But it seemed worth a try, since Bones was a talkative sort.

Bodie scooped up a bucket of corn and said conversationally, "How long you been workin' here?" They headed back inside.

"Three years now. Train started comin' through here regular, so Mr. Grady put up this here place. Been workin' for him ever since then."

"Seen lots of trains come through here, have you?"

"More 'n you can shake a stick at. Used to meet 'em all. And there was aplenty!" Bones whistled through his lips. "Them soldiers carried horses on every train, and they always had need for plenty hay and grain. Army paid, so Mr. Grady sold 'em what he could." Bones wagged his head at the thought. "Ain't like that no mo'. You the first one come in here all day."

"Did you hear tell of a train that come through here three, four month ago haulin' slaves?"

"Heard of it, but I never seen it. They come in here off the ferry."

Bodie stopped and faced Bones. "Did you hear where they was headed?"

"You know, I never did."

Bodie's eyes faltered, his lips drew.

"Why you ask?"

"I had kin on that train." Bodie turned into the stall, dumped the bucket of corn into the manger. Bones had stopped outside, scratching at the side of his head.

Bodie found a curry brush there in the stall, started working over the bay.

"Now that I recollect, some folks what got off that ferry stayed put right here," Bones said.

Bodie stopped stroking. "You sho'?"

"Seen 'em with my own eyes." Bones lowered his head, studied the ground. "If memory serves, two men and a woman with a young'un got off, stayed here."

"Where'd they go?"

Bones was struck by the question. He scratched at his head as if digging for an answer. "You know, I never heard," he finally confessed.

Directly, his eyes brightened. "Plenty of folks out yonder on the street. I'd wager there's somebody from every plantation 'round here. If you was to ask the right person, he'd tell you."

Bodie smiled slightly. "Bones, you got the makin's of a right smart man."

Bones smiled broadly at the approval of his brainwork. "Brown Mule Saloon is the best place to ask around," he said.

Bodie tossed the curry brush into the manger and walked out of the livery, heading that way.

The sun in the west was an orange ball flaring on the horizon, casting long shadows over the rail bed, throwing a slight coolness on the late-evening breeze.

The sound of tinny piano music drifted out of the Brown Mule. Raised voices could be heard.

Bodie pushed through the batwings, paused, looked over the room, then headed toward the only vacant space at a corner of the bar.

The Brown Mule was a large cracker-box of a place. It had a dozen crude tables scattered over the floor, each one occupied. A plank standing-room-only bar ran the length of the side wall; it, too, was elbow to elbow. Over in the far corner, a five-cent nickelodeon tinkled out music to the amazement of a half-dozen inquisitive moochers looking at it.

The bartender was about six feet tall with a small head and heavy side-whiskers. His face was swarthy, flushed. The business of serving what had until recently been slaves was new to him, and he had his qualms about doing it.

"What'll you have?" he asked Bodie grudgingly.

"Beer," Bodie answered, and rattled a two-bit piece onto the counter.

A skinny, light-complexioned man standing slack-legged next to Bodie gawked at the quarter, then, looking up at Bodie, drew up attentively. Smiling through small, rat teeth, he said pleasantly, "You must be the feller that rode in today everybody been talkin' 'bout."

Bodie smiled weakly. "I just rode in, if that's what you askin'."

The bartender returned with the beer, set it down in front of Bodie, picked up the quarter.

At that moment the batwings swung open and a man stepped through, then paused, running his gaze around the room.

He was six feet tall, heavy-shouldered, utterly black, his face expressionless. Like Bodie, he had an Army Colt .44 belted around his waist, but his hung carelessly down his thigh. His searching eyes found Bodie, stopped.

Everybody felt the place go quiet. Bodie could almost feel a chill come over his back. The rat-teethed man who had been standing next to him drew off down the bar.

Bodie took up his beer glass, sipped, hearing the thumps of approaching heels. He sensed a body move in next to his elbow.

The bartender hurried down and said in a rush, "Josh, you got to do somethin'!"

Josh looked out over the boisterous, loud-talking, sweaty black men and answered, "Nobody's makin' a fuss."

"I told you, them what ain't buyin' I don't want 'em in here."

"Which ones ain't buyin'?"

"None of 'em is!"

"Come closin' time, I'll have 'em all outa here."

The bartender drew his lips in disgust and moved away.

A heavy voice said conversationally to Bodie, "How do. Name's Josh . . . Josh Gibbons. Who you?"

"Bodie."

"I'm sort of straw boss 'round here. Army depends on me to keep tabs on loafers and slackers. You loafin' or slackin'?"

"Neither one."

"What you doin', then?"

"Lookin' for information."

"About that railroad agent?" Josh smiled at the surprised look that came to Bodie's face. "Man from the stable told the lieutenant who you was lookin' for." Josh pursed his lips thoughtfully, looking at Bodie. "The man who used to work at the station, if he was to come up dead, the army would naturally figure you done it." He smiled wryly at Bodie again and said with conviction, "And I'd have to come git you."

The bartender was fidgety, pacing back and forth uneasily, so Bodie held his words. When the bartender had again moved away, Bodie talked, laying out all the information he had gathered along the way about the slave train, including what Bones had told him.

Josh listened attentively, interrupting now and again to ask questions as to where Bodie was from, how he had come to this place, and suchlike.

Bodie tossed off the last of his beer, set the glass down.

Josh talked freely: "Right around the time them slaves was ferried over here, new hands showed up at Stokely Plantation. Maybe that'd be them."

"I'd sho' like to find out. Even if they ain't my folks, I'd like to ask 'em where the others was headed."

"Them folks what come to town with you, they signed on for work. The army's sendin' 'em to Stokely Plantation in the mornin'. You could ride along with us."

"That'd suit me."

"Maybe not," Josh said, and smiled wanly.

Bodie looked at Josh.

"Might be trouble," Josh warned.

"What kinda trouble?"

"Bushwhackers, guerrillas, nice peaceful folks like that," Josh said facetiously, then continued in a more serious tone: "Stokely Plantation was abandoned during the war. Army took it over and leased it out to a northern man. Now it's worked for wages by freedmen. The man who used to own it, Colonel Stokely, is back in the country."

"And he wants his land back."

"Right. Army won't let him take possession, though. And he won't stand still for nobody else workin' it."

"Not my trouble," Bodie said. "I'm lookin' for my folks."

"Come sunup, I'll have a wagon out front. You be there, I'll take you. Can't promise nothin', though."

"I ain't askin' you to," Bodie said. "I'll be there."

Chapter Three

Early-morning freshness was still on the air. The summer moon and brilliant stars had waned into the slate-gray coming of dawn. The creak of harness gear, the jingle of trace chains intruded on the stillness of the livery. Out back a horse blew, stamped.

Bodie back-stepped down the ladder from the hay-mow where he had slept. His boots touched ground, rustling hay scattered there, and Bones spoke to him from the seat of the box wagon he had just hitched up.

"I waits in front of the bureau. Never know how many folks I'm haulin', so I lets 'em take they time gittin' aboard." He shook the line to a pair of low-grade horses, eased the wagon out, speaking over his shoulder to Bodie. "Come sunup Josh'll be ready. You better make haste. Your horse already been seen to."

Bodie splashed sleep from his eyes with cupped hands full of water from the trough in the stable, saddled up, and trotted his horse over to the bureau.

Josh sat his saddle, his bell-crowned gray hat pulled down tight on his ears, a wrinkle of concern across his forehead and a draw of determination on his lips. He said to Bodie, "Country we goin' through got some good places for ambush. The way I figure it, I'll ride in the lead, you ride behind the wagon. If we come onto trouble, we'll stop and talk it out."

Bodie's eyes took in the hands crowded in back of the wagon: Jesse Gone and his family, plus three more men. Bodie recognized one of them as the rat-teethed man who had been standing next to him in the Brown Mule Saloon the day before. Bodie's and Deedee's eyes met, held for a moment.

"What about them?" he asked Josh.

"Bones know what to do."

Josh heeled out; Bones shook the lines and clucked the team into motion. Bodie fell in at the rear, following behind the kid's nag tied in back of the wagon.

West by north they went.

The sun swung past the overhead. The land they rode was gently rolling, occasionally pocked by mottes of hardwood bordered by fields of lockspur and buttercut. The wagon road they followed was bare earth, litter-strewn and chopped up, beaten by trodding feet of hundreds of freed men and women in search of work, or to leave the country altogether.

Twice that morning Bones had had to leave the wagon road: Once to find privacy for anybody that needed relief, and once to go around a ragtag procession of men, women, and children, some lugging simple possessions tied up in bundles. Most were wide-eyed and confused, not knowing exactly what freedom meant but sensing that a great change had come over the land.

Ten miles farther on another road slanted into the trace from the west. Josh galloped his horse back, and Bones pulled the wagon to a halt.

"Trouble?" Bodie asked, walking his horse up.

"When Bones turn the wagon east yonder, ain't no other place to go but Stokely Plantation. When we've had trouble, yonder is where it came from."

Bodie looked over the indicated terrain. To the southwest the land sloped away gently into a long, ragged tree line.

Josh noticed the sweep of Bodie's eyes and said, "They jumped us from outta there before."

"Anybody hurt?"

"Naw. Gave us some scare talk, though. I was warned if any more hands was brought out here I was to hang right along with Bones."

"Wadn't scare talk," Bones said. "I heard a driver and two hands was hanged on the road to DeVall's Plantation. The army's got to do somethin'!"

Josh patted his pistol and said confidently, "The lieutenant gave me this. And I got permission to use it, too."

"Your trouble," said Bodie. "I'm lookin' for my folks."

"I ain't lookin' to hang, but the army promised these people jobs and protection."

"And you figure to protect 'em?"

"Somebody's got to till the army gits theyself sorted out."

"I'm lookin' for information about my folks up yonder," Bodie said, and nodded his head that way. "I aim to go on, but I wouldn't hold it against y'all if you was to turn back."

The thought hadn't crossed Josh's mind. He turned a blank look at Bodie and swung his horse away, taking up the lead again.

The tree line they skirted was Oak Bottom, a long band of oak trees that bordered Snake Creek, a finger of water that wandered away from the St. Francis River.

The wagon road meandered roughly along with the creek.

The sky was a blanket of pale blue with puffballs of cumulus clouds knitted in. The sun was an hour past the overhead; men and animals walked on top of their shadows. Crows cawed on the wing and blackbirds swooped over wildflowers in search of insects.

The procession moved on at a brisk pace, drawing ever closer to Stokely Plantation.

A while later Josh galloped back to the wagon, and Bodie walked his horse up. "Yonder is where we nooned before," Josh said, pointing toward a spreading pecan tree standing almost alone.

"Seems as good a place as any," Bodie replied.

"We ought to go on," Bones cut in. "Them army vittles eat just as good on the move as settin'."

Just then Bodie's eyes caught movement from the tree line. He lifted himself in the stirrups, focused his eyes, and after a time stated, "We got comp'ny."

Josh kneed his horse around and brought his eyes to bear.

Five men rode out of the tree line, coming at them in a shambling trot.

"Everybody just sit still. I'll do the talkin'," Josh told the people in the wagon.

The man riding the roan, obviously the leader of the bunch, halted the men in front of Josh. Bodie was on their right.

The leader was a slightly built, hawk-nosed man with hard features. Mock surprise was in his voice when he said exasperatedly to Josh, "You agin!"

"Folks got to work," Josh said flatly.

The man didn't say anything but kneed his horse around and circled the tailgate of the wagon, coldly eyeing each occupant. He reined around and faced Bones. Slumping forward carelessly in the saddle, he rested his two hands on the saddle horn. Fixing Bones with arrogant, taunting eyes, he blew a breath of disgust. "I warned you about haulin' folks out here, didn't I?"

"Mr. Henry, these folks goin' to work," Bones said. "They got a right to."

Henry Mason's lips curled into a crooked smile, and he said arrogantly, "You know me, do you?"

"Yeah, suh."

"Who says they got a right . . . you?"

"The gov'ment," Bones answered with conviction.

"The gov'ment?" Mason chuckled derisively. "Your massa Lincoln is dead, did you know that?"

"I knows it, but we still got rights."

"Army sent us," said Jesse timidly.

"Army sent you, huh?" Mason said, shifting his eyes to Jesse.

"Yeah, suh."

"Army says you can work Stokely Plantation?"

"Yeah, suh. Got it all writ down."

"All right!" Mason exploded. "All of you, git outta that wagon!"

"Y'all stay where you at!" Josh said somberly.

Josh's tone brought Mason up short. He became stiff-backed, his eyes bulged. Taken aback at being defied, he reined his roan around deliberately to face Josh. The four men off to the side bucked up in their saddles.

"You barkin' back at me, boy?" Mason asked, taking in for the first time the gun strapped against Josh's thigh. "Army's puttin' mighty big britches on you. You think you can fit 'em?"

"Army says these folks can work. I'm takin' 'em to work."

Mason's face went pale. His gun hand swept down.

The hand never made it to the gun.

Bodie fired twice. The first bullet ripped into Mason's chest on the right side, tearing him from the saddle. Another man reached for his gun, and that's when Bodie fired again. The bullet stabbed the man's shoulder, numbing his fingers. His gun went limp, useless in his weak grasp.

The other three men sat wide-eyed at the sudden turn of events. It had never entered any of their minds that the black man sitting his horse off to the side was a threat. They had all taken him to be just another scared nigger.

"Git 'em, Hawley! Goddammit, kill 'em!" the wounded man said through clenched teeth, straining to bring his own gun to bear. But the effort was useless: His gun slid from his fingers, and a drawn-out groan pushed past his lips.

Bodie had his gun trained on the other three. "These folks can go on to work unless somebody else got somethin' to say."

Nobody said anything.

Bodie shifted his attention to Josh.

Josh's gun was clear of the holster but was canted aimlessly downwind, and Josh had a dazed look on his face.

"These folks want to work, git 'em to work," Bodie said to Josh.

In a stiff wooden motion Josh holstered his pistol. "Let's go, Bones," he said through heavy lips, and heeled out mindlessly.

"Y'all unbuckle them gunbelts and drop 'em," Bodie ordered the three men in front of him after the others had gone.

"Now lookahere, you!"

"Unbuckle 'em!" Bodie snapped.

"You'll hear about this, black boy," one man warned, fumbling at his belt buckle.

Five minutes later, Bodie trotted his horse up in the lead alongside Josh's. He had three gunbelts slung on the pommel and two wrapped around his shoulder bandolero fashion.

Four white men had ridden away back down the trace, carrying one of their own slung across the saddle.

"Where'd you learn to shoot like that?" Josh asked.

"Nobody ever accused me of bein' handy with a gun."

"You beat him to the draw. I never seen the likes," Josh said, wagging his head.

"My gun was practically out already when he started to git his," Bodie said offhandedly.

Josh looked admiringly across his shoulder at Bodie. He had never even heard of a black man handling a gun until lately. Being this good with one was unthinkable. "Where'd you learn that?"

"Army," Bodie said. "Fifth Massachusetts Volunteers." Bodie smiled at the memories. "Had plenty of time to practice."

A quarter mile farther, Josh swung his horse off the trace and rode between the parallel tracks of a wagon road that led to Stokely plantation, looming in the distance.

Stokely Plantation was some three thousand acres of prime farmland in Crawley Valley that formed a crude square with the western edge touching Snake Creek, taking in Oak Bottom.

Radcliff Stokely had had title to the land, but he had been among the States' Rights men who had nudged Arkansas over the edge to secession. When war came, Radcliff joined the Confederate cause and was commissioned a colonel of cavalry. He gained modest military success, drawing name recognition by federal commanders operating in Arkansas, particularly Federal Major General James Blunt.

In late summer 1863 General Blunt marched his troops out of southern Missouri and fought his way from

Fort Smith on Arkansas' western border to Helena on the Mississippi River, taking control of northern Arkansas through hard fighting and heavy losses.

Conquered lands not being put to plow were deemed abandoned land and the titleholder dispossessed. Prominent civilians and high-ranking Confederate officers were first to be stripped.

Radcliff Stokely's land was now a home farm worked by freed men and women in and around Marion, sixteen dollars a month for men, eight dollars for women, food and shelter included.

Bodie followed Josh's lead as Bones guided the wagon into the plantation's wide quadrangle of a yard and angled over in front of the hay barn. At a water trough there, Bodie and Josh swung down from the saddle. Bodie looked the place over.

"Awfully quiet," Josh stated.

"Seems that way for a place like this." Bodie's eyes took in the big high-roofed columned house. Off to the side was a cookshack, and in back seven or eight cabins for working hands. There was a livery and toolshed next to the hay barn. A rough-board corral ran back of the barn, and off to the side a half-dozen chickens and some guinea hens scratched at the earth.

"Bones, find these folks a place to bed down," Josh ordered. "I'll see who's to home."

While the rest of the occupants sorted themselves out, the kid who'd been leading the nag scrambled to his feet and vaulted over the side of the wagon. Gathering himself from a stumbling run, he walked haltingly toward Bodie, his eyes curiously wide. "Deedee said, you shootin' like that, she 'speck you musta been in the army," he said breathlessly.

Bodie's eyes found Deedee. "She said that?"

Deedee's eyes flashed angrily. "Otis, you shut up!"

"Was you? Is that where you learned to shoot?" Otis asked excitedly.

"I'd guess he was army," Jesse said knowingly to his son.

At that instant, Josh beckoned and yelled from the door of the big house, "Bodie! Trouble!"

Bodie took off at a dead run; Otis followed. As he plunged across the doorsill, Bodie's eyes swept the living room. Whirling in his steps, he barked at Otis, "Don't come in here! Just wait out there!"

Two blood-spattered bodies were sprawled on the living-room floor, obviously shot to death.

One dead man, the white one, was still tied up in his desk chair, which had tumbled over. His face was bloody as a beef from a severe beating and two slugs had smashed holes in his chest, knocking him backward against the wall. The other dead man, the housekeeper, was crumpled in the kitchen doorway, evidently struck in the heart as he stepped out to investigate the beating.

"Mr. Tomlinson," said Josh, indicating the dead white man, "the leaseholder of the place."

"Any idea who done it?" Bodie asked.

"I'd guess them five we run into. Mr. Tomlinson was warned like me and Bones."

"He wasn't even armed."

"Not many 'round here is."

Bodie looked at Josh, and Josh said defensively, "Army promised protection."

Bodie had seen enough in his travels to know that the social upheaval created by the war had made it foolhardy for any man to go unarmed. A sick feeling came over him. He clenched his teeth and left the room. Outside he told Otis as he guided the boy off the porch, "Ain't nothin' for you to see in there."

Halfway across the yard, Josh caught up to Bodie's side.

Bodie told him, "There'll be more killin' 'less the army protect these folks out here."

"Way I see it, army can't. Leastwise not this season. They ain't got men to."

"Well, these folks got to protect they ownselfs, then."

"With what?"

"There's five guns hung on my saddle yonder."

"There ain't a man here can hit the broad side of that barn yonder."

"Includin' you?"

"Includin' me," Josh admitted.

Bodie exchanged glances with Josh, and Josh explained, shrugging, "We ain't had guns. We need time to learn."

"You ain't got time," Bodie snapped. "Look, Josh," he said patiently, "I come over a lot of country. White folks I come 'cross ain't goin' to sit still and see the land given to us. They'll fight back. You got to git these folks protection, or git 'em outta here."

"There's another way."

"What's that?"

"You could protect 'em."

"Me!" Bodie waved a protesting hand. "I'm lookin' for my folks."

"The folks you need to talk to about that slave train will come in from the field at sundown. Whatever they tell you can keep till the crop's brought in," Josh said.

"Bodie, you the only one can protect us," Otis said pleading.

"It'd be a cryin' shame for you to ride out of here and leave these folks helpless like they is," Josh said.

"What's the trouble?" Jesse asked when they reached the wagon.

"Two somebodys got shot, Papa," Otis told him.

"New owner and the housekeeper . . . both dead," Josh added.

"That bunch we run into?"

"More 'n likely."

"Jesse, we ought to move on," the old woman said meekly.

"There's more places," Deedee said, her eyes flashing.

"Other places got troubles too," Josh countered.

"If Bodie was to stay, they wouldn't bother us," Otis said.

"Josh!" Bones called, coming out of the lane from the shacks where he had just checked for vacancies. "Hands comin' in." He pointed across the yard. "Looks to me like they had trouble."

At least thirty field hands came straggling across the yard, plodding wearily toward the row of shacks. One man carried a busted arm in a rag sling; another man hobbled, showing blood through a ragged hole in his pant leg; two women stumbled along, played out from the long walk.

A tall, big-shouldered, dark-skinned man broke off from the others and headed toward them at the wagon.

"What happened, Ruley?" Josh asked him.

The question went over Ruley's head; his eyes were riveted on the gun strapped around Bodie's waist.

"Ruley, what happened out there?" Josh asked, forcefully this time. "Where's the wagons?"

Ruley broke his gaze, brought his attention to Josh. "Five white men snuck up on us a little bit past noon. Simon was on lookout, but he seen 'em too late. Nobody was hurt bad, but they run off the mules and broke up the hoes."

Josh swore under his breath; Bodie studied the ground at his feet; somebody in back grumbled discontentedly.

"There's too much devilment here, Jesse," the old woman said in an undertone. "Let's go on."

Josh faced them. "Folks, y'all heard the trouble we got here. Can't say it won't happen again." He slanted his eyes at Bodie. "But you welcome to stay. Anybody

42

that wants to stay, foller Bones and he'll show you where you can bunk. Anybody that wants to go can ride back with me and Bones."

The newcomers shuffled in their steps, each turning the danger over in his or her own mind.

"Who's this?" Ruley asked Josh, shifting his attention back to Bodie and the gun.

"This here's Bodie."

Ruley nodded indifferently, his attention consumed by the gun belted around Bodie's waist. Josh noticed Ruley's preoccupation and said offhandedly, "Them white men that jumped y'all, they come up on us too. Bodie here killed one of 'em . . . wounded another one."

Ruley was astonished. "Well, I'm damned!" he said in awe. Like the others, Ruley had never in his thirty-five years seen a black man carry a gun openly. And more incredibly, shooting a white man and living while others told about it was simply unimaginable. He removed his flop hat, uncovering a big woolly head and exposing a wide face. "Bodie, huh?" He said the name profoundly, like it was a name to be remembered.

"Yep," Josh said proudly, "Bodie Johnson. He's right handy with that gun. Made it look easy as pie . . . ain't that right, Bodie Johnson?"

Bodie was irritated at the prodding. He turned and walked toward his horse, leaving his actions to speak for themselves.

When Bodie was out of earshot, Josh asked Ruley in a low voice, "Them folks that was ferried over here from that slave train, they still workin' here?"

Ruley scratched at his big jaw. "Woman still here. Both of the men lit out a month or so back. Why you ask?"

"Bodie's folks was on that train. He's trying to find out where they went from here."

"I never heard nobody say. Maybe the woman did."

43

"Find out if she did," Josh said confidentially. "And Ruley, tell her don't say nothin' to Bodie, and don't you neither."

Ruley shot a questioning look at Josh, and Josh explained, "Bodie won't leave here till he talks to the woman. If he sticks around, y'all have protection. You see to it he don't talk to her. He's y'all's only hope for protection."

"One man!" Ruley scoffed, making light of it. "That ain't much protection."

"Don't low-rate him. I see'd him use that gun."

Bodie was in the barn stripping off saddle gear when Josh came up, smiling deceitfully. "Feller I was talkin' to is Ruley, Ruley Jones," he said pleasantly.

"And?"

"He says the woman that got off that train is still here."

"Where?"

"Tell you what . . . You want information. These folks want protection. You provide protection, I'll see you git your information."

Bodie stayed silent, his eyes holding Josh's. Then, in a fit of pique, he snatched the saddle and blanket off his horse and flung them rudely in the corner.

Josh shrugged helplessly. "Bodie, these folks got no other choice. It's you or nothin'."

Bodie's eye shifted down to the gun dangling slouchily at Josh's thigh, then lifted to Josh. "You got any cartridges for that gun?"

Josh blinked at the question, impulsively fingering empty loops around his waist. "Just what's here."

Bodie came out of his pocket with a five-dollar piece. "This oughta be enough for a couple of boxes of .44s."

Josh reached for the money even as his lips asked the question: "You'll do it?"

"I'll do it. Leave word with Ruley that everybody'll do as I say, includin' him."

"Ruley's in charge here. He ain't goin' to like it."

"Like you said, these folks ain't got no choice."

"Just don't push him, Bodie."

"We'll need more guns."

"Now, I can't do that."

Bodie's eyes fixed Josh's. Josh said hurriedly, "Okay, okay, I'll try."

"Another thing. Tell that lieutenant about today."

"How come?"

"There'll be more killin'."

Chapter Four

The protection that Bodie provided for Stokely Plantation was nothing more than stationing lookouts and pa-
trolling the perimeter as the army had taught him. To
the south a man stood watch behind a wagon parked at
the turnoff from the trace, another man patrolled Oak
Bottom along Snake Creek bordering at least two thousand acres of cotton, and to the north two men occupied
strategic positions in the shallow hills overlooking the
rest of the cotton fields.

Bodie had scouted the surrounding country, trying to
guess the likely direction of attack, looking for every
possible weakness in their defenses.

Twice Josh had ridden out from town, once to bring
the new leaseholder, a squat, barrel-chested, wide-eared
white man from the north named Sylvester Hoggett. After Josh had introduced Hoggett around the place, Josh
found Bodie and they talked. At length Josh said, "You
know, Bodie, you could settle down right here. There's

plenty of work. Most of us got family scattered around. You ain't no different. How come you to ride all over the creation lookin' for yours?''

"My papa used to say a man ain't got nothin' except his folks when you git right down to it. There'll be time enough for settlin' down.''

"There's precious few families left whole now,'' Josh said. ''You seen all them tracks out there on the trace. People started movin' every which way as soon as they was free. You'll likely never find your folks.''

"I'll find 'em . . . or just keep on lookin'.''

"How come?''

"Only thing we had was family, that was Papa's teachin'. And it stuck with me.''

"Everybody felt that way.''

"Except he lived it. One time he hid out for two months to keep from bein' sold off from us. Took fifty lashes for it, and was on bread and water till he couldn't stand on his own two feet. When Mr. Huelen come around to see about him, he said he'd do it again if he had to.''

"Me, I never knowed no other family except my mama.''

"Most others didn't neither. I count myself among the lucky ones.''

The other time Josh came out he brought supplies. Neither time did he bring additional hands, nor, more to Bodie's distress, did he bring guns. ''There's just no way, Bodie,'' Josh had said. ''Army's got orders against armin' blacks. Don't be for this job I wouldn't have this one.''

"Any word on army protection?''

"Naw. The lieutenant was called away to Fort Smith. While he's there he's goin' to see about gettin' more soldiers detailed over here.

"Mr. Stokely raised hob about that killed white man.

He says if the army won't see the guilty party punished, white folks will. He's spreadin' fear, sayin' we's lawless, shiftless niggers that steal for a livin'.''

Now the country sweltered under oppressive heat. Cotton was better than knee-high, the profusion of blooms turning to flared bowls of cotton. It was only a matter of weeks before the cotton would be ready for picking, and Bodie's every instinct told him that an attack would come soon.

It was a couple of hours after sunup when Bodie came out of the house where he had been taking orders from Mr. Hoggett, a thrifty, skittish man. He stepped off the porch and walked toward his horse tied up at the hitch-rail in front of the hay barn, sweeping his eyes over the farmyard.

The yard was alive with activity: Two women poked at boiling clothes in an iron pot next to the toolshed; another woman scrubbed faded jeans on a scrub board; two men unrolled yards and yards of ducking cloth; and off to the side Deedee was hand-spinning a Throneshuttle sewing maching, stitching the ducking into cotton sacks. Ruley was there, talking to Deedee. And she was smiling broadly, enjoying the attention.

At his horse Bodie swung onto the saddle and turned the bay west. Out of the corner of his eye he caught the turn of Deedee's head, her eyes watching him go. His mind lingered on Deedee as he trotted his horse away.

Did Deedee see something in Ruley?

That she was a woman a man could be proud of he had no doubts. But a home and a family? He had to find his folks, didn't he? Or did he?

Turning off the wagon road, he took to the trace and made a loop south by west. At a shallow depression that Snake Creek touched on, he swung west, riding away from the great flare of sun at his back.

It was hot. The sky was like a great blue oven, and

inside was a pulsing red disk surrounded by whiff-balls of clouds. Not a bird was on the wing, not a breeze stirred. The blue shirt he wore was dark with sweat under the armpits and down his back, the horse sweaty at the neck and flanks.

Presently he swung his horse into a thin motte of oak trees, weaved his way forward, searching the way ahead. A few yards farther on, a clump of scrub brush off to his right drew his attention. He dismounted, led the bay that way, carefully searching the ground. The lay of the grass had been recently disturbed, and at the clump of scrub brush he discovered brown splats of tobacco juice.

He dropped down on his haunches to study the situation. Piecing together the sign, he made out that a lone man had squatted on his heels there, rested a long gun against the scrub brush, undoubtedly watching the cotton field out front. The lookout had been active for a time, because he saw old cigarette butts, a faded wrapper from a plug of chewing tobacco.

He straightened to his feet, keened his eyes through the trees, searching out the nearest cotton field, puzzled. The field was at least two hundred yards away. It was obvious that a lone man could do no more than take potshots at the cotton pickers. And that man had to know that the plantation was armed, however poorly.

He was walking toward his horse, still thinking about the direction and method of expected attack, when suddenly he heard a shot . . . then another, followed by two more. Quickly he gathered the reins and swung onto the saddle. Picking his way cautiously toward the sound of the shots, he strained his ears for sound, his eyes for movement.

A grasshopper jumped and landed, rustling the dry underbrush, and from somewhere off to the right a crow cawed. Nothing more.

Then a Winchester exploded, an ugly hiss buzzed by

49

his ear, and a bullet dug into a tree next to his shoulder.

Bodie cleared the saddle, landed in a rolling heap, and came to rest behind an oak tree, his horse trotting off a ways. He scrunched down belly-flat behind the tree, his gun leveled forward, his eyes keened in the direction from which the shot had come.

Directly, somebody called out, "Bodie! Bodie, that you?"

"It's me!" He kept under cover, waiting for the shooter to show. Ruley shambled into view, walking toward him in the slack-jointed gait of the plowman he had been, a big grin on his face.

Bodie got his legs under him, rose to standing, and walked toward Ruley, holstering his gun.

"Man, I thought you was him done come back," Ruley said sheepishly.

"You seen somebody?"

"Yeah," Ruley said, falling in step with Bodie, heading back toward Ruley's post. "I hadn't been here more'n an hour when I heard somethin' movin' in the brush behind me, and then I saw him." Ruley hefted in his two hands the Winchester Bodie had provided him and said, "I shot just like you showed me."

"Did you hit him?" Bodie asked.

"Naw. He ducked down just in time."

Bodie looked at Ruley and said, "Takes a while to git a steady hand with a rifle."

"I dusted 'em good, though. He knows I wadn't foolin'," Ruley bragged.

When they reached Ruley's lookout post, Bodie saw that it had been turned into a crude camp. In a small clearing behind a dead tree Ruley had scooped out a place for protection, in back of that a small fire burned, and still farther back in the oaks his mule was staked.

Over a tin of coffee they talked, Ruley lying back in the hollow behind the deadfall, Bodie sitting his haunches at the fire. They spoke of odds and ends, Ruley doing most of the talking. Finally Ruley asked, "You figure they'll hit us?"

"The cotton will be ready for pickin' two weeks from now. I figure they'll strike before then."

"I'm ready for 'em. That tree yonder is what I been practicin' on. I'm gettin the feel of it."

"Looks like it," Bodie said, looking out at the pock-marked and barked tree. "How's the ammunition holdin' out?"

"Got plenty left."

Directly Ruley set his cup aside and carelessly picked up Bodie's Winchester propped on the log next to him. Eyeing it enviously, he said solemnly, "They never issued us guns. Not even for drills."

Bodie was struck by the statement. He looked over his cup at Ruley and asked, "They who?"

"You might as well know," Ruley said, averting his eyes shamefully. "I was in the Arkansas Negro Volunteer Regiment."

Bodie dashed out the dregs of his coffee and said flatly, "I heard it said you was."

"You don't think I'm a fool?"

"Knowed some men who'd do anything for one fool reason or another." He rose and walked toward his horse.

Talking at Bodie's back, Ruley spoke loudly and bitterly of the past: "We never done nothin' but dug trenches and toilets." He scrambled his legs under him, picked up the Winchester, and ran toward Bodie, explaining all the while, "We wadn't no fools, Bodie . . . we had promises!"

Bodie turned on him. "Promises to be kept if the South won? That's a fool's promise if there ever was one! If the South had won, you'd still be diggin' trenches and toilets!"

"We had promises of freedom and land!"

"The goddamn rebels lost and you still got your freedom," Bodie countered. He stepped a toe into the stirrup, swung onto the saddle. Looking out at Ruley standing off from him, he pointed a finger through the oaks and said, "There's land aplenty. You want it, fight for it!"

"You stayin'?" Ruley asked.

"Naw," Bodie answered calmly now, "I'm lookin' for my folks." He wavered. "Past is behind us now. You wadn't no different than the rest of us. We done what it took to survive. Country is different now, though. If a man wants land to go with his freedom, he better learn how to use that thing." He indicated the Winchester and flicked his horse away.

Ruley dropped his eyes to the Winchester in his two hands, suddenly aware of the strange feel of the thing.

When Ruley lifted his eyes again Bodie was twenty yards away, weaving his way through the oaks.

"What about Deedee?" Ruley yelled at his back.

Bodie didn't answer. Ruley had no way of knowing whether or not Bodie had heard him.

Bodie had indeed heard the question; the subject had been on his mind lately. He knew that Ruley had designs on Deedee. So what? Ruley had no claim on her. Besides that, he had his folks to find before the thought of settling down entered his head. He touched spurs to his horse, sending him into a lope.

It was coming on to noontime when he reached the bend in Snake Creek. He followed it a half mile, swung back east, heading for town.

On Turkey Mesa where the short grass grows, a lean, hard-eyed man threw on the dying campfire the leavings of the coffee he had just finished. Lake Dawson had been a Texas cowman before the late War Between the States drew him to Confederate service, and four years of war hadn't dulled his skills as a cowman. Now he was again working beeves, hired to move the last of the Confederate commissary on the hoof to Indian Territory for reservation rations.

Through keen, knowing eyes, he looked out over the mesa at the eighteen hundred head of beeves milling on the bed grounds, ready for trail. Turning in his steps, he spoke to the man packing up the chuck wagon off to the side there. "Cookie, eight . . . ten miles west of here there's water and good grass. You pitch camp there. Come sundown I'll send Daks to you."

Andy Fishback was a grizzled-whiskered old camp cook, straight-talking and plain-spoken. "It don't seem right, boss," Fishback said, "runnin' the fat off these beeves for a lark."

"It don't sit right with me neither, Cookie, but this here herd belongs to Mr. Stokely. He calls the tune till we git 'em to the reservation."

"He ought to stick to his politics," Fishback grumbled, "and leave the real work to men who know how."

Fishback watched his boss walk away from the campfire, swing onto the saddle of the roan ground-hitched there, and ride off toward the herd.

Lake Dawson had been one of Nathan Bedford Forrest's hard-riding cavalrymen. He had had his share of unpleasant duties before, and the task ahead of him now was no different. He pulled his roan up shoulder to shoulder with a dapple gray ridden by a slope-shouldered cowpuncher at the point of the restless, low-ing, bawling herd.

"Daks, keep 'em spread out wide," Dawson told him.

"I got you, boss."

"And keep 'em runnin'."

"Whatever you say, boss." Daks Walker was a top-notch hand, and had been left in change of the herd before when Dawson was away. Now Daks asked, "What about you?"

"I'm goin' into town to see Mr. Stokely."

"This don't seem right, boss," Daks commented.

Dawson glowered at Daks and said touchily, "You too? Ain't nothin' 'round here been right to nobody lately."

"Just sayin' my say. I ain't the one doin' the thinkin'."

"That's right, you ain't. Just you see the job gits done," Dawson ordered, and spurred his horse out.

It was afternoon when Bodie rode his horse down the rail bed, Marion's main street. The town was still crowded with people on the move going nowhere.

He weaved his way through foot traffic and pulled to a halt in front of the Freedmen's Bureau. Josh was sitting on the bench, taking in the sorry sight of the town. He stood up, saying pleasantly, "Wadn't expectin' you. Trouble?"

"Naw," Bodie answered, swinging down. "Come for supplies."

"Supplies? Nobody told me."

"Mr. Hoggett says the crop's better'n he ever expected. Figures he'll need another trailer and some more weigh scales, plus other odds and ends." He reached behind his shellbelt and retrieved a note. "It's all writ down here for the lieutenant."

"Lieutenant's busy right now." Josh nodded his head, indicating inside. "Mayor's in there all hot under the collar."

"About what?"

Josh cut his eyes knowingly at Bodie. "White man turned up dead."

Bodie let the statement drop like a rotten load. "Anybody else can take care of this requisition?"

"Next man in line is Sergeant Skillman." Josh scratched his head doubtfully, then said, "He ain't a man to deal with. He wouldn't give a colored man the sweat off his balls."

"Anybody else?"

"Let me clue you in on somethin', Bodie," Josh said seriously. "Most of these army boys don't like what's happenin' here. They only go along with it 'cause they have to. Only square shooter in the bunch is the lieutenant. The rest of 'em eats out of Mr. Stokely's trough."

At that instant Josh's eyes caught movement across the street in front of the Planters Hotel. "Speakin' of the devil . . . Mr. Stokely."

Bodie turned to see Radcliff Stokely standing in front of the hotel, talking to two men. One was a lean, tough-looking man dressed in batwing chaps and a black checked shirt; the other, a tall, heavyset, stoop-shouldered man, wore faded jeans and a gray flannel shirt. Bodie recognized him as the one called Hawley by the man he had wounded earlier.

Josh commented, "Man in the black shirt rode in about an hour ago."

Radcliff Stokely was of medium height, clear-skinned, and looked quick-witted, energetic. He had on black striped pants, a narrow-lapeled Prince Albert coat, and a ruffle-fronted white shirt half hidden by a black velvet vest. Even from across the street Bodie caught the shine of his well-polished boots.

"He looks like a man of means," Bodie observed.

"He is. Throws a lot of weight round here. Lots of folks would kill for 'em. Some have, they say."

Just then Bodie saw the lips of the stoop-shouldered man move and his head nodded across the street. Stokely's and the other man's head came around, looking at them.

Bodie knew he'd been pointed out.

Hawley said, "There's that nigger what shot Morgan."

"He don't look like the rest of 'em," Stokely said oddly.

"That gun he's wearin' makes him stand out," Dawson said. "First I seen of it."

"He's right handy with it, too," Hawley added.

Radcliff smiled a handsome, cynical smile at Dawson and said, "We'll take care of him. Can't have him givin' ideas to the rest of these slope-heads 'round here."

"Ain't my business, Mr. Stokely," Dawson said curtly. "Drivin' beeves is. That's what I'm hired to do, that's what I aim to do."

Stokely smiled again, clapped Dawson's back, and said coolly, "Sure you're right, Lake. A man ought to stick to his business." Stokely spoke pleasantly enough, but the smile fell away from his lips.

Dawson mounted, touched the brim of the black high-crowned hat, and said dourly, "Afternoon, Mr. Stokely."

Radcliff thrust between his teeth the long cigar he had been holding, clenched down hard on it, watching Dawson ride away.

Abruptly a disturbing thought came to Radcliff. A deeper frown came over his brow. "Come inside, Hawley," he ordered the man standing next to him.

When they turned and went inside, Bodie shifted his attention back to Josh. "About them supplies. I could ask around myself, speakin' for Mr. Hoggett."

"I don't know, Bodie. Mr. Hoggett ain't known yet in this town. It'll take the lieutenant's word before them supplies are turned over without cash money."

"Won't hurt none to try," Bodie stated, leading out toward the livery.

They crossed the street, walked through the wide doors of the livery. Grady straightened up from the iron hoop of a wagon wheel he was working over on an anvil, taking in the two men coming toward him, a sledgehammer held carelessly at his side.

"Mr. Grady, Bodie here—" Josh began.

"Note here from Mr. Hoggett," Bodie cut in, "wantin' a cotton trailer and other odds and ends." He reached forward the note he had taken from behind his shellbelt.

"I've got no trailers. None atall." Keeping his eyes on Josh, Grady said smugly, "I doubt if you'll find one anywhere in town." He turned back to his work on the anvil, the ringing blows punctuating his hate.

Josh motioned his head toward the door, and both men headed for the exit.

Outside it was hot. They crossed the street again, Josh's gaze scanning the boardwalks.

Across the street four men slouched on the bench Josh had just vacated in front of the bureau. He had already spent the better part of the morning shooing away slackers. He swore under his breath, then, dismissing that problem for now, brought his attention back to the one at hand: "Mr. Grady had two trailers out back. Did you see 'em?"

"I saw 'em. I guess he got his reasons for not leasing 'em."

"The reason is Mr. Stokely, and you know it."

"Figured that."

"What now?"

"Way I see it, it's up to the army." Bodie handed over the requisition to Josh and said, "Tell the lieutenant Mr. Hoggett needs them supplies mighty bad."

They stepped up on the boardwalk in front of the bureau and Josh stopped, confronting four men on the bench there. "I told y'all this mornin' to do yo' lazyin' round somewheres else. This ain't no place for idle talk and back-scratchin'."

"We ain't botherin' nobody," an older man complained.

"Ain't none of you goin' to feed yo'self sittin' here. Now, move on!" Josh said.

The four men slouched off. Josh told Bodie, "It's been like this every day. Some want to work, some don't."

"Your problem," Bodie said, swinging onto the saddle. "I got my own." He turned his horse away from the hitchrail. "See them supplies git out there. Them folks need 'em."

"If the lieutenant draws 'em, I'll bring 'em."

Bodie kneed his horse out, heading back to the plantation.

The trace he rode now showed new growth of weeds, and rank grass had started to grow where recently there had been only bare earth.

Bodie had the bay at a steady gait, his mind on the situation they faced. Stokely had men to do his fighting. How many? Could poorly armed field hands fight off an attack? And what about Deedee?

Bodie's mind was picking at answers to these questions when his eyes caught the prick of the bay's ears. And ever so faintly his own ears picked up the sound of a distant rumble.

It sounded like the growl of thunder. The bay tossed his head, gathered his muscles. Bodie tightened his grip on the reins, circling his eyes around, looking for answers.

Nothing.

The rumbling grew louder.

What it was, Bodie had no idea. More out of a lack of answers than anything else, he kicked the bay into a full-out run to gain sight of the farmhouse.

By the time he swung off the trace into the wagon road, the distant rumble had become continuous, rolling over the entire valley. And that's when he saw what the rumble was: a stampede!

An unbroken mass of horns, hides, and hoofs at least a quarter mile wide rumbled down the valley, trampling every cotton stalk in its path. Two men rode at the point, keeping the herd at a run, guiding them on. And they were headed straight toward him!

Presently a rapid burst of shots rose above the rumble of trampling hoofs, then a single shot. Instinctively Bodie reached back for his Winchester. But it was gone. Ruley had it.

At breakneck speed, he sheered off to the left, riding for cover in the oaks along Snake Creek. Gaining the oaks, he checked his horse, weaving his way forward, his pistol at the ready, his eyes taking in the damage already done.

The mass of bawling, churning beeves had swept in from the north. Now they wheeled in a loose arc, heading back that way.

There simply was nothing Bodie could do. The drovers were out of pistol range, and the driven beeves couldn't be stopped.

He knew that when that herd finished running, Stokely Plantation wouldn't have enough cotton left standing to make a pillow with.

He sat his horse, looking on helplessly. He knew deep down that his protection hadn't been good enough; the attack was something totally unexpected.

The man he had seen riding at the point was a lanky man wearing a black checked shirt and a wide-brimmed black hat. The other man he had only glimpsed, but he had been wearing a gray shirt.

Bodie holstered his pistol, swearing softly, bitterly.

Chapter Five

Bodie trotted his horse out of the oaks, looking out over the farmland, surveying the damage. The stampede had destroyed the year's cotton crop. What other damage had been done was the question he had to answer now.

A lone rider off to the left came into view. Making out the rider to be Ruley, he pulled to a halt.

Ruley came toward him at a gallop, brandishing the Winchester in his right hand.

"I hit one of 'em! . . . I knows I hit one of 'em!"

"The crop is done for, Ruley," Bodie said. "There ain't one acre of cotton left standin'."

The reality struck home to Ruley. His excitement fell away as his gaze roved over the green carpet of trampled cotton stalks. For the first time the extent of the damage sunk in. "We put in a lot of work on that crop, a lot of work for nothin'."

"Let's go see how the folks made out," Bodie said.

At the parked wagon that had been a lookout post,

they found trouble—trouble in the form of death.

The wagon had been shoved over on its side, the tongue trampled to splinters, the top sideboard smashed off, trampled by leaping hoofs. And a man's legs protruded from under the wagon.

Bodie left the saddle in one motion. Ruley was at his side instantly.

They tipped the smashed wagon upright. Bodie rolled the mangled body over.

"Jesse," Ruley said in a pained voice.

"He's dead," Bodie confirmed.

"That's a dad-blamed shame," Ruley said angrily. "He wadn't here long enough to draw wages."

"I'm the cause of him bein' here," Bodie said.

"It ain't your fault, Bodie. You did all you could."

"Did I?" Bodie asked himself more than Ruley.

Suddenly a scream, an ugly wailing scream, rose up from the trampled field.

Bodie and Ruley both jerked around, searching for the source of the obvious agony.

A hundred yards away, across the carpet of green stalks, a woman was down on her knees wailing sorrowfully, rocking up and down, her two hands clasped together at her breasts.

In one quick jump Bodie mounted and spurred his horse. Reaching the woman, he jerked the bay to a sliding stop, dismounting on the run.

He drew up to a dead stop in his tracks.

When Ruley rode up Bodie was still standing there dumbstruck, speechless over the grisly scene.

The wailing woman was Jesse's wife. What she was wailing over was the mangled, twisted body of Deedee. And no more than a hand's reach away was Otis's mangled corpse.

Ruley dismounted zombielike, walked stiff-legged to Bodie's side. They stood paralyzed with distress, the woman's wails tearing at their insides. "Get the wagon, Ruley," Bodie said through dry lips.

Bodie took hesitant steps over to the woman. Dropping down next to her, he reached an unsure hand to her shoulder. Speaking soothingly through her wails, he told her, "Let's go, ma'am. You can ride with me. Ruley's gone to git the wagon."

The woman rolled the whites of big watery eyes over at Bodie, started wailing again, a long, heartrending wail.

Helplessness swept over Bodie, tugged at his being. He shifted his weight on his knees and said again, "Cryin' won't do no good, ma'am. You can ride with me. The wagon will be here directly."

Bodie's very words lifted the wails even louder.

Helplessly he walked slowly to his horse. Taking the reins in hand, he dropped down on his haunches, waiting.

While waiting, he took in the surroundings, his mind piecing together what had happened:

Twenty yards away from the bodies a tin dipper had been smashed flat, a wooden water bucket trampled to kindling wood. Obviously Deedee and Otis had been taking cool water out to Jesse, who had been standing guard at the wagon. Caught out in the open, they had had no chance whatsoever.

Presently a thought struck the woman. She stopped wailing, caught a breath, stilling her heaving chest. Her lips asked the question, then quivered at the answer: "Where's Jesse?"

"He's dead, ma'am."

The woman doubled over, started wailing again.

Bodie sat his haunches off to the side, listening with heartfelt sadness. There was simply nothing he could do.

A short time later, Ruley careened a wagon over to where Bodie stood next to his horse, and dismounted the seat in one jump.

"Took you long enough," Bodie said curtly, stepping a toe into the stirrup.

"I had to hitch up the team," Ruley answered, surprised at the rude greeting.

"See they git back," Bodie said, meaning the bodies and the woman. Swinging onto the saddle, he added, "Jesse too."

Ruley stood there watching Bodie ride away from him, his mind puzzled by Bodie's queer way.

When Bodie rode into the farmyard. Hoggett was outside talking to the wild-eyed, scared farmhands. Hoggett was saying factually, "That's it, folks, I'm done. The crop's ruined. Those of you that got wages comin', I'll see you git 'em." Hoggett mounted the buckboard and abandoned the farm.

Bodie jogged his horse over to the hitchrail in front of the hay barn, dismounted, and asked Joseph, the man who had been unrolling the ducking this morning, "Joe, who was on lookout over to the west?"

"Refer was. He's in the house yonder."

Bodie strode purposefully that way.

"Wadn't nothin' he could do," Joe called out at Bodie's back.

Reaching the shack, Bodie put a shoulder against the plank door and crashed across the doorsill.

Rafer sprang to his feet from a bunk bed, throwing aside a woman who was dabbing a wet rag to his head.

"Did you see them cows!" Bodie yelled at him.

"I seen 'em, but I didn't know what they was for."

"What did'ya think they was for?"

"I don't know but I fired warnin' shots like I was 'spose to do."

In two quick steps Bodie came face-to-face with Rafer, yanked the pistol from the holster belted around Rafer's waist, stepped back, and spun the cylinder. Three cartridges were missing.

"See, it wadn't his fault, Bodie," the woman said angrily.

Bodie slid the pistol back into Rafer's holster. Sighing futilely, he looked at the woman, then back to Rafer. "I guess it wadn't your fault. We couldn't have stopped them cows nohow."

The woman ran two big accusing eyes over Bodie and said haughtily, "Rafer was almost tromped to death! This protection you providin' ain't worth shit!"

The words stung. Bodie dropped his head, studying the floor.

"Wadn't your fault, Bodie," Rafer said. "You did the best you could. Wadn't nobody's fault."

Bodie turned and stalked out the door.

He was no more than four or five steps from the door when he saw Ruley stop the wagon in front of the cabin where the Gones lived. He headed that way.

Ruley's face was stark and angry when Bodie came up. The sickening job of loading the bodies had driven his mind to dark thoughts, making him want to lash out. "Somebody's goin' to pay, Bodie," Ruley said profoundly. "These folks never hurt nobody."

Bodie reached across the seat, retrieved his Winchester from where Ruley had propped it.

"Where's the woman with information about that train?" he asked him.

"You leavin'?"

"Yeah. Nothin' to protect now. Protection wadn't no good nohow." He shifted his eyes to the bodies in back of the wagon.

Ruley followed Bodie's gaze, conveniently neglecting to mention the woman.

The rest of the hands had heard about the deaths. Now they gathered around the wagon to see the bodies at first hand.

Ruley jumped down from the wagon seat and, looking

across the wagon bed, ordered, "Somebody help me git 'em inside."

Bodie turned away from the ugly scene, walked fast toward the hay barn, his Winchester carried carelessly along his leg.

Two hours later Josh galloped his horse into the farmyard, dismounted at the hitchrail in front of the hay barn, and took off in long, hurried steps, heading for Ruley's shack.

A woman stuck her head out the door of the cookshack, yelled out at Josh, "The men's out diggin' graves," and pointed out back.

They were digging the graves on a hummock in back of the shacks where a half dozen pecan trees grew. The men of the plantation pitched in, taking turns.

Rafer was waist-deep in the hole, shoveling out dirt. He paused momentarily, blew a winded breath and mopped his brow. Glancing up, he spoke to the man waist-deep in the hole next to him, saying, "Bodie, Josh's comin'."

Bodie stopped digging, and along with the rest of the men watched Josh coming toward them.

"He was about as helpful as tits on a boar hog," Rafer said disgustedly.

"He can't do nothin' except what the army tells 'em," Joseph replied.

"I heard what happened," Josh said, walking up, eyeing Bodie's horse tied there to a branch, a bedroll in back of the saddle, a duffle sack hooked over the pommel.

"Army goin' to do anything about it?" Rafer asked.

"The lieutenant got word by wire from Fort Smith them cows was consigned to the Indians over there. How they got off the trail nobody knows. He can't prove it, but he thinks Mr. Stokely was behind it."

Ruley vaulted out of the hole and screamed angrily,

"Mr. Stokely! Mr. Stokely! The army knows dang well Mr. Stokely is the cause of all the trouble! Why don't they do somethin'?"

"Can't without proof," Josh answered factually.

"Yonder is your proof!" Ruled roared. "All the proof needed! . . . Three dead people!"

"Army don't care nothin' about us," Joseph said solemnly. "We ain't got no more rights now than we had when we was slaves."

Bodie climbed out of the grave he had been digging, slapped dirt from his dungarees.

"You leavin', Bodie?" Josh asked.

"Yeah. When the dead's buried, won't be nothin' else to do."

"Wadn't exactly your fault," Josh said.

"I wadn't much help neither."

"Did you git your information about that slave train?"

"Yeah, I got it . . . such as it was."

"You don't believe it?"

"Texas, why Texas?"

"Struck me as odd too, so I made mention of it to the lieutenant. The lieutenant figures that since there wadn't much fightin' in Texas, the owners figured that'd be the safest place for 'em. Wudn't be no place else to run to. You goin' on to Texas?"

"Come sundown I figure to have this place behind me."

"Somethin' you ought to know, Bodie. Regardless of what happened, that crop would have been these folks' last anyhow. Mr. Stokely got back title to the land."

"How!" Ruley demanded. "A while back there was talk of hangin' him!"

"That's what Mr. Hoggett said too. I overheard the lieutenant explaining it to him. The lieutenant said the gov'ment got somethin' now called a Loyalty Oath. All a man got to do is sign it and he's got his rights and property back. But he'll have to pay wages if he wants labor.''

"Wages like before," Ruley said scornfully.

"Ain't my concern now," Bodie said. "I ain't even thinking about labor till I find my folks." And he headed for his horse.

After he had swung onto the saddle, Josh advised him, "Instead of follerin' them rails, the lieutenant said you'd do better to ride west. You'd come to Fort Smith and you could ask about Texas there."

"Worth keepin' in mind." He swung his horse away.

In a loose knot around three partially dug graves in the long shadows of pecan trees, the men of Stokely Plantation watched Bodie ride away. When he was a hundred yards off, they turned their attention back to the business at hand. Josh continued talking, filling them in on the latest news he had heard at the bureau.

He was saying, "Come next month anybody ain't workin' got twenty-four hours to find work, or the law will. Nobody can loaf in town durin' daylight hours."

"Mr. Stokely's doin'?" Ruley asked.

"Mostly him, but there's others."

"Mr. Stokely!" Ruley said scornfully. "Somebody ought to see to him!" He grabbed the shovel and in one sliding step landed in the open grave. Angrily he stabbed the spade into earth and threw dirt over the side. "Somebody ought to see to Mr. Stokely," he grumbled, more to himself than to anybody else.

The long shadows of evening reached their fingers across the land, slowly drawing it into darkness.

The trace west that Bodie had struck grew dark and silent, foreboding under the clip-clop of the bay's hoof-falls. The trail was obviously a chosen freedmen's path leading wherever a man thought freedom lay. It was trodden bare of growth and harrowed like a fine garden patch by footsteps and wagon wheels of those who had moved on earlier today, and the day before that, and each day ever since the war had ended.

At full dark Bodie was over the St. Francis River, chatting amicably with the black ferryman about how it was that he was traveling alone, unlike the others. "Admire your git-up-and-go," the man was saying, "but the country ain't safe for a lone man. I'd make haste and catch up with that bunch that's just ahead of you."

"I'm headed west . . . to Fort Smith," Bodie answered. "Where was they headed?"

"Dunno for sho', but I 'speck Fort Smith. They had a lot of women and chillun in the bunch. Most times that's a sure sign they headed to the fort to see husbands and fathers. Lot of colored soldiers transferring in there now."

For an hour Bodie rode the worn trail without overtaking the people the ferryman had spoken of. Darkness became his enemy, so he swung his horse over to a clump of oaks off to the left and with studied thought chose a likely campsite on flat ground well back from the line of travel.

At the first light of the moon he had his horse staked out, a small fire going, and was sitting his haunches nursing a cup of coffee.

Before his coffee was half finished the snap of a twig perked his ears. Moving methodically, without alarm, he poured the rest of the coffee over the coals, and taking up his Winchester, peered back into the shadows. Letting his eyes adjust to the darkness, he waited.

Ever so faintly, shuffling hoof-falls came to him. He drew back behind a big oak tree, his Winchester held out of sight along his leg.

The hoof-falls stopped in darkness at the edge of the firelight. A voice called out boldly, "Bodie! . . . Bodie! . . . You in there?"

Bodie let out a caught breath. "That you, Ruley?"

"It's me." The hoof-falls started up again. Presently Ruley walked his horse into the firelight.

Bodie stepped into the circle of light, eyeing Ruley skeptically. "What you doin' here?"

"I'm goin' with you," Ruley said offhandedly, dismounting heavily, his eyes avoiding Bodie's.

"How come?" Bodie asked, taking in the played-out condition of Ruley's horse.

"I had to leave."

"How come?" Bodie asked again.

"Any coffee left?" Ruley asked evasively.

Bodie retrieved the cup that he had thrown aside, blew it clean. Taking up the coffeepot, he poured Ruley the last of the coffee. Passing it to him, he asked for the third time, "How come?"

"I killed Mr. Stokely," Ruley said without emotion. Accepting the coffee in his two hands, he drew it to his lips, took a small sip. Looking over the rim at Bodie, he told him, "Army wudn't do nothin', so I did."

"Took it on your own?"

"Yep. Took it on my own," Ruley answered firmly. Clearly wishing the matter closed, he sipped at his coffee.

"How'd you find me?" Bodie asked after a short pause.

"Feller at the ferry." Ruley smiled thinly. "He said I was the second fool he'd seen in the last hour. Said I oughta make haste and catch up with the first one."

Bodie twisted around on his haunches, looked out at the horse Ruley had ridden in on. He had already seen the big "U.S." stamped in the front hoof of the horse. "Army horse, ain't it?"

"Josh staked him out for me."

"The pistol?"

"Josh let me have one of them you took off them

69

men.'' Looking at Bodie out of the corner of his eye, Ruley said, ''Josh's the only one who knows I done it.''

''White man come up dead, you leavin' like that, wudn't take many brains to figure out who done it.''

Ruley sipped at his coffee, thinking the matter over. ''Don't matter,'' he said finally. ''I ain't never goin' back.''

Bodie carried his saddle to the spot he'd picked for his bed ground, adjusted his blankets, and dropped down on them, saying, ''Come first light in the mornin', I'm leavin'. You intend to come, you better see to your horse.''

Ruley looked over his shoulder at the jaded horse standing hang-necked and limp-legged. '' 'Speck I better.'' He set the coffee cup out of the way next to the fire. Scanning the darkness around the campsite, he asked, ''Where's your horse?''

''Hobbled yonder.'' Bodie indicated with his head.

It wasn't long before Ruley had staked out his horse and was back at the campsite. It took even less time for him to prepare his blankets and stretch out. As he rested his head back, his mind wandered back to the events of the past day.

When the men of Stokely plantation had finished burying the dead, Josh was still telling of the worsening lot of the black man. Ruley had had deep convictions all along that the trouble in the county was promoted by Stokely. Josh's talking had convinced Ruley that the army would not act, or could not act.

''Bodie?'' Ruley called over tentatively.

''Huh?''

''It wadn't just on account of them cows.''

''What wadn't?''

''The reason I killed Mr. Stokely.''

''What else was it?''

''He was the one who made us promises of freedom

70

and land,'' Ruley said bitterly. "He was a colonel of infantry, and came around to all the plantations tellin' us how we had to defend our homes and women and children. He said if we didn't we was cowards, and if we did we'd get our freedom and some land.

"We was organized and drilled some, all right," Ruley said disgustedly, "but with sticks! He made like the guns was being freighted in. We laid hands on nothin' but picks and shovels!"

Bodie threw aside his blankets, drew up to sitting, and asked with genuine interest, "How'd you kill 'im?"

Ruley leaned his head back, stared up into the oak leaves shimmering in the slight breeze. "Shot 'im," he stated, "shot 'im twice." He let out his breath in a long sigh, draining away the tension. Unburdening himself, his words tumbled out like a great weight being lifted from his shoulders: "Mr. Stokely kept a room over the Planters Hotel with a balcony on the side. He came out to get some fresh air like Josh said he always did. I shot him from hidin' 'cross the street on top of the bureau. First bullet knocked him against the handrail, next bullet knocked him clean over into the alley."

"Josh have a hand in it?"

"Some. Once he found out he couldn't talk me out of it, he told me how I ought to do it."

Bodie dropped back down on his blankets. "Your doin'. I'm lookin' for my folks."

"I ain't aimin' to bring my trouble on you." Ruley lay back, drew up his blankets.

Nobody said anything. Minutes ticked by.

After a while Ruley called over, "Bodie?"

"What?"

"You know somethin'?"

"What?"

"It wadn't nothin' to killin' a white man."

Chapter Six

The cruel hand of the Civil War had dealt Sam Perry a savage blow. He stood to lose all he owned. Sam was a big man, forty years old, raw-boned and hard-faced. He and four black men had broken camp from among the rocks in the dry streambed of Aqua Creek at the crack of dawn that morning. The sun had been up three hours now, and the prairie trail they had left behind them was obscure.

Riding at the head of the caravan, his high-crowned, wide-brimmed hat pulled down over sun-browned square features, a pelt of gray-flecked hair flopping over lop ears and at the nape of his neck, he rode in studied thought.

In '59 Perry had come from Arkansas to Texas with a handful of slaves and little money in his pockets. He had been among the first whites to settle on good Brazos River bottomland. But the war had ruined him, stripped his plantation of feed and fodder, all its stock except the horse he rode. And war's end had set free his labor.

Sam twisted around in the saddle and swept his gaze down the train of packmules strung out behind him, packmules carrying valuable cargo that he desperately hoped would solve all his money problems. Abruptly he swung his horse off the trail, checked around to a halt facing the oncoming column, sitting his saddle like the Rebel cavalryman he had been before a mostly spent Yankee bullet drilled an eyeball out of its socket, knocking him out of the war for good, marking him forever with a black patch covering an empty left eye socket.

Sam's one good eye looked closely at the riggings of each packmule as it trudged by him, checking to see if anything needed readjusting or retying, leaving nothing to chance. The safety and security of the cargo was paramount to his future.

Without operating capital and no free labor, Sam knew his plantation was on the brink of lapsing back into the rolling prairie of wild grasses and stunted mesquites that it had once been. He needed the cash money this cargo would bring, needed it desperately if he was to have a fighting chance to survive.

"Don't lag, boy! Stay closed up," he said again, warning the black muleteer leading the last tandem of mules at the tail end of the column. "I ain't goin' to tell you again! If you don't keep up, by damn I'll peel hide off you!"

Four days before, Perry and the caravan of four muleteers and twenty-two packmules had left Hempstead on the Texas frontier, heading to Mexico to sell cotton.

During the war the cotton had been sent by flatboat down the Brazos River to Velasco, then clandestinely shipped to Confederate agents in Matamoros, Mexico, for sale to British and French merchants. But the wharves at Velasco had been put out of commission a year earlier, blasted to kindling wood by Yankee spies.

Now in these unsettled times agents refused to buy. Thousands of bales of cotton waited stacked at Boca del Rio, a port city that had mushroomed on the marshy flats on the Mexican side of the Rio Grande because of the cotton trade.

"Mr. Perry, these animals will keel over if we keep pushin' 'em like this," Amos, the lead drover, reminded him.

Sam Perry was at least three inches better than six feet tall, and wore a Smith & Wesson Russian .44 six-shooter. He was a man of long experience overseeing black men, first as slaves and now as free men. He had drawn well the line that a black man was not supposed to cross, and that line hadn't moved much even though blacks were now free.

"You just mind your job and leave the worryin' to me," Perry said angrily.

Sam was a frayed man. The journey was taking its toll. He knew his plantation life depended on the success of this caravan. The cargo had been carefully loaded to command enough profits to bail him out of stifling debt and finance next year's operation.

The black men he had with him to do the manual labor had been handpicked by him from a gang lined up by the sergeant at the Freedmen's Bureau. Strangers to each other four days before, each freedman had his own reasons for being here. They had been warned by the sergeant that this was a chancy journey through wild, dangerous country.

A day before, they had passed twenty miles south of the Outside Settler, the settler who had ventured out farthest onto the plains where Indians regularly came through. Ever since then it had been a vigilant journey, Perry constantly watching their backtrail for marauders and cutthroats, scouting ahead for sign of Indians or

Mexican bandits. At night it was secluded campsites and light sleep.

Perry swung his horse and cantered up to his position some thirty yards in the lead of the column. For hours the caravan moved across rain-scarred prairie, a mere elongated speck in a vast sweep of thin grass under a canopy of blue sky and a red flare of sun. The only sounds were the creak of packsaddles, the jingle of harness gear. Occasionally a jackrabbit jumped up and fled out of the caravan's path, and now and again an animal snorted and blew.

The caravan moved ever deeper into hostile country. Twice that morning they had come across old Indian sign, and the preceding night the picketed mules had been skittish. Whether from Indians, marauders, or from night critters nobody was prepared to say.

The mules were tethered each to the other in groups of five, and each mule's load was two hundred pounds of lint cotton packed in two panniers carefully tied across each mule's back.

The four black men rode worn-out saddles on gimlet-hammed plowhorses, each man charged with tending the load and seeing to the wants and needs of five packmules and his own mount. And in Sam Perry's calculating mind each man was a measure of protection, but only insofar as safety in numbers went: None of them was trusted with firearms.

It was coming on to sundown when Perry checked his horse to a halt atop a low rise, studying the land that swept away to the west.

As far as the naked eye could see, wild grass bowed limp from the wilting heat of the day, and close in on his right a low chain of sandhills rose up to break the monotony of the land. And threading its way across the foot of the hills was the Old San Antonio Road, the trail that Perry was intending to strike.

Hiram King

The Old San Antonio Road, or Camino Real—Royal Highway—was a well established route into Mexico that had been trampled out of wilderness beginning in 1691 by Spanish missionary Domingo Teran de los Rios from Monclova, Mexico. The saving grace of the route was that it touched on places where water might be had, depending on the season.

Perry lifted a finger and, pointing in the distance, said to the lead muleteer, "We'll camp yonder like before, Amos."

Amos was a tall dark man of thirty-five. He had been Perry's slave before this, the groom and general stockman on Perry's plantation. Now free but with no particular urge to move on, he still worked for Perry, but with Perry's agreement to pay wages as demanded by law. Amos knew Sam well and had a vague memory of the route. They had traveled it twice before: once just after the start of the late War Between the States when the Yankees had blockaded the entrance to the Gulf of Mexico, and once when Perry had rightly figured he could make a killing by clandestinely putting his cotton on the market in Mexico rather than have it appropriated with dubious currency by the Confederacy.

Amos turned the bell mule, a tough old Arkansas mule long on trail experience, toward the low chain of hills they had camped in the time before. The muleteer riding immediately behind him, Richmond, turned his lead mule and veered into the trail of Amos's train.

Richmond was heavy-muscled, medium-framed, and had a wide mouth that seemed to smile all the time. He had been a slave all except the last months of his twenty-eight years, and had been trained as a tanner, able to repair saddles and harnesses, make shoes and boots. The X he had put on the work contract at the Freedmen's Bureau had landed him here. The money he would make would set him up in a drummer's wagon to move over the country peddling his harness-repair business as he had seen white men do.

The sun had vanished by the time they found the old campsite, put together a small fire of coarse grass and cedar roots, and dished up regular trail fare.

Perry wolfed down his tin plate of pork belly and beans, and was nursing a tin of coffee, taking his ease away from the black men in the crook of his saddle next to the unloaded cargo some distance from the fire.

The black men lay on horse blankets spread haphazardly around the campfire, each man sprawled back, eyeing the dancing flames, each turning over in his mind thoughts of his own future.

Richmond broke the silence: "How much longer before we git there, Amos?"

"Four more days at most. We cross the river, we'll be doin' good to make fifteen, sixteen miles a day. Trail gits harder, rougher on the mules."

"Damn mules ain't worth worrying over," said Boot, scoffing at the idea of pampering animals. "Just so they git us there."

Boot was twenty-four years old, six feet tall, and weighed a good one-seventy. He was dark and smooth of skin, with thin, tight lips. Where he had come from nobody had asked, and he hadn't said. He had turned up at the Freedmen's Bureau one day leading a played-out horse, and carrying a jute bag that looked mostly empty. Long of arms and slim of muscles, he walked with the gate of a man used to the outdoors. At his word the bureau had signed him up as looking for work, any kind.

"If somebody don't look out for them mules, they ain't likely to git us there," Amos said seriously.

Boot had been playful, talking lightheartedly the whole way. Now a serious question struck Amos: "Ain't you got no concerns, Boot?"

"Yeah. Money."

"We all here for that," Richmond said.

"Ain't none of us likely to git a red cent unless them mules git us there."

"I signed on for money," Boot said, "and I'll git it, one way or another."

Perry had overheard the conversation. He cleared his throat noisily, rolled over in his blankets, and faced them. "Waddy, you got the fixin's to cook up something besides sowbelly and beans?"

"Yeah, suh."

"Good. Come tomorrow we're sure to see rabbits, possibly deer. Either one would be a change for the better from what we been eatin'."

"You kill it, I'll dish it up, Mr. Perry."

Waddy was forty years old, tall and thin-hipped. He had a wide nose and thick lips, and the deep resonant voice of a man of songs, which he was. He had signed up for cook work at the bureau after learning what cooking he knew in a cow camp in the Medina River area. He had been cut adrift when the roundup was over and the herd moved on up the trail.

Perry rolled over on his side, drew his blanket up around his shoulders, and said out of the side of his mouth, "Best you boys get some sleep. Boot, check the animals before you turn in."

Boot didn't answer.

The silence grew.

A draft of wind scurried the flames, and a mule stamped and blew.

Perry lifted his head, his eye searching out Boot. "Did'ya hear me?"

"I ain't turned in yet," Boot replied evenly.

"Do it now!" Perry snapped.

"I ain't no slave no more," Boot said. "I'm supposed to see after five mules, not look after all of 'em."

Perry bolted upright. "Why, you—!"

"I'll see to 'em, Mr. Perry," Amos said hurriedly.

Perry stopped, blew a breath of disgust, and said, "If we don't git this cargo through, none of us'll git a dime."

"You want somethin' done, you ask," Boot said, and drew his legs under him, rose to standing, and sauntered off into the darkness in the direction of the mule herd.

The other muleteers had listened in silence to Boot's obvious indifference to Perry's authority. But Perry knew he needed Boot out here. At least for now. He lowered his head to the crook of his saddle and swore under his breath.

Later, Boot returned to a quiet camp, the men breathing evenly, sleeping peacefully, a snort interrupting somebody's sleep now and again.

He threw a couple of sticks onto the glowing coals, then went to his blanket. Turning his eyes to the star-studded sky, he returned his mind to thinking about his reason for being here.

In the morning the sun at their backs was yet a weak orange flare gathering strength for the day's journey, when the caravan skirted the finger of sandhills and bent west into the emptiness beyond.

The day wore on, the sky high, wide, and blue, the sun golden hot. The gentle prairie had given way to rough broken country, untamed primitive land of nopal and pitahaya cactus, scrub mesquite and greasewood, tarantulas and rattlesnakes. It was a thirsty land, and hot, very hot.

Riding in front of the column, Perry checked his horse to a halt at the lip of a slash in the earth and ran the back of a hand over his sweat-streaked forehead. Twisting around in the saddle, he said, "Amos, we'll noon here. I'll have a look around." He spurred off, following along the rim of the dry wash in front of them.

The slash was Sabinal Draw, the bed of an ancient

stream whose waters had once sprung up from the arid land, gnawed into the earth on its way to the Rio Grande, and had just as mysteriously vanished. Now there was not a hint of water. The gently sloping sides some forty yards apart were the only evidence of its past existence. Greasewood and prickly pear stabbed roots deep into the earth in search of the vanished water.

Amos led the bell mule over the rim. The rest of the train followed, lurching to a trotting halt at the bottom of the draw.

Boot had looked after Perry for a long minute. Now he swung down from the saddle and asked ahead to Amos, "Where's he goin'?"

"Mexican settlement over thataway. He'll go in. He did before."

Boot was uneasily aware that dealing with white men on this new footing of freedom was still all too often on the white man's terms. He rested a careless hand on the rump of the mule that Waddy was untying camp gear from and looked questioningly at Waddy. Then, slanting his eyes back to Amos, he asked, "Knowed 'im for long?"

"Long enough," Amos replied, casually undoing packsaddle gear.

"He a fair man?"

"Fair as the rest. He put his name to the bureau contract. He'll pay us."

Waddy looked up from the packsaddle he was working over and commented, "Bureau guarantees our wages, if that's what you worried about."

"All this time he was in a hurry. Seems strange, now he ain't," Richmond said, mildly worried.

Amos scratched his head under his floppy hat. "As I recollect, a day and a half across that river yonder," he pointed at the Rio Grande, "is where we're goin'. Mr.

Perry needs the money same as us. I 'speck he'll git us there.''

Just then Perry reined his horse over the rim of the draw some twenty yards up, rattled out at the bottom, and came toward the camp at a shambling trot. He swung down from the saddle, and Waddy handed him a tin plate of beans.

"Same as before, Mr. Perry?" Amos asked.

Perry talked around a mouthful of food. "Yeah. I'll ride on ahead into town and pick up what little supplies we need. When you boys come in, drop the cargo at Gunther's and see to the mules." Perry looked across his plate at Richmond and said, "Check over them pack-saddles real good. Anything need fixin', you fix it. I want everything in tip-top shape."

"Yeah, suh."

"Be ready to move out first thing in the mornin'," Perry continued, cutting his gaze over at Boot, who had taken in his every word. "You boys want somethin', see Gunther."

Perry handed Amos his plate, swung onto the saddle, and swung his horse. Almost as an afterthought he wheeled back around, facing Amos, but when he spoke his eye was fixed on Boot: "Don't noon all day. Git yo'selfs a bite to eat, then bring 'em on in, you hear?"

"Yeah, suh," Amos answered.

Boot's eyes faltered, and he tugged at the brim of his hat.

Perry touched spurs to his horse and rode off.

The shade in the dry wash where they nooned was nearly nonexistent, only what a man got when he pulled his hat brim down. And it was hot, so hot a man could only sweat and slap at gnats.

Two hours later, they had finished their beans and bacon and Amos had built the last diamond hitch knot on the packsaddle carrying the cooking gear. "It's hot-

ter'n hell itself down in this here draw,'' Richmond said.
"Let's git where there's some air stirrin'."

An hour or so later the head of the packtrain entered
the hard-packed east–west-running street of Carrizo
Springs. The muleteers looked over the place, sizing it
up.

Carrizo Springs was a small bare-boned Mexican
town. Its narrow street was flanked on the left side by
two square, flat-roofed, sun-bleached adobe cantinas and
a jail. Four stick-and-mud jacals were out back. The
right side was open space that swept away to the Rio
Grande, overgrown with pitahaya cactus, greasewood,
and lechuguilla grass littered through with tequila bottles, rags, paper, and anything else a man had no further
use for.

Gunther's, a lean-to livery, was at the end of the
street, a huge mesquite rail and rider stock pen abutting
the place in back.

"Mr. Perry is yonder," Amos said, pointing out the
second cantina. "Looks like he's got comp'ny aplenty."
Amos had noticed six jaded horses standing slack-legged
at the hitchrail next to Perry's horse.

Just at that instant six shabbily dressed men in mismatched Confederate uniforms filed out of the cantina.
They were all down-at-the-heels, unwashed, unshaven
men, looking as if they had had a rough go of it.

The men were stragglers of the Second Texas Cavalry
and Light Artillery, formerly commanded by General
James E. Slaughter. It had taken two months for word
to reach these men that General Lee had surrendered his
Army of Northern Virginia and that the war was over.
They were bitterly disappointed, and laid blame for their
defeat to every cause. Profiteers and scalawags were at
the top of the list.

The Confederate army in Texas collapsed and dis-
banded on its own without pay—the Big Breakup, it

came to be called. Each man had simply gone home or to an overgrown farm, if such he had. Some men banded together and plundered and pillaged the capital at Austin, stripping factories of uniforms and shoes, raiding armories of rifles and ammunition, and looting the treasury building of what little currency was on hand; General Slaughter had even sold his remaining artillery pieces to a Mexican counterpart for twenty thousand pesos.

These six cavalrymen had had a hand in the rampaging. Now, like so many of their broken confederates, including Generals Kirby Smith, Joe Shelby, Sterling "Old Pap" Price, and Slaughter, they were escaping to Mexico rather than live under Yankee law—or worse yet, face the hangman's noose for insurrection.

Carrizo Springs was one of a half-dozen jumping-off places for those who wished to cross into Mexico. It was also a place of respite for bandits and cutthroats from both sides of the border who wished to go in any direction for good or evil.

The six cavalrymen methodically climbed onto their saddles and turned their horses away from the hitchrail. That's when they spotted the packtrain coming down the street.

The leader of the stragglers, Sergeant Tom Hancock, a smallish man, lifted a hand to the others, and they all sat still, looking at the packtrain coming on.

Even a lowly private in the Confederate army knew that cotton had been a lifeblood commodity, a commodity the Confederacy greatly depended on to sustain itself, to acquire guns and ammunition, medicine and tools, gunboats and cannons.

Tom nudged his horse forward at a walk toward the train, the men following. All their instincts bristled at the obvious profiteering this train, like many before, represented.

"We ought to burn the whole damn lot," Private Frank Tanner said.

Tom stopped the men in front of Amos.

"Your'n?" Tom asked Amos.

"Naw, suh."

Tom looked over his shoulder; his eyes had followed Amos's.

Perry was standing under the overhang in front of the cantina.

"His'n?" Tom asked, turning back to Amos.

"Yeah, suh."

They turned their horses to face Perry. They were six bitter men, men who felt used up by those who had sacrificed little but had profited much.

"You . . ." Tom's voice quavered in scorn. "You damn traitor! You ain't worth spit! And you had the unmitigated gall to drink with us!"

Perry lifted a hand to explain, his lips starting to shape a word. But he never got anything said.

Sergeant Hancock's bullet slammed into Perry's chest, knocking him stumbling in his steps. Before Perry had stopped stumbling, Tanner put another bullet in him. Then four more slugs from the other men ripped into Perry's body, all chest high.

Hancock trotted his horse up and, hovering over the lifeless body, spit a stream of tobacco juice that slashed across Perry's dead face. Another cavalryman, Toby Clark, yelled, "Let's burn the cotton, Sarge!"

The corner of Hancock's eye caught sight of two Mexicans peering out from the open door of the cantina.

"Damn the cotton. Let's git!" Hancock jabbed spurs to his horse and dug out of there; the other cavalrymen threw up a cloud of street dust following at his heels.

The chalk-colored dust had settled. The muleteers and a half-dozen wide-eyed Mexicans stood over Sam

Perry's dead body. Waddy asked, "What we goin' to do now?"

Boot leaned down, unbuckled Perry's shellbelt, and ripped it clear of the body. "Comanches got my brother," he said grimly. "I signed on to git two hundred fifty dollars ransom money." Looping the shellbelt around his waist, he caught up the buckle and cinched it up. "I aim to git it," he stated, adjusting the swag of the heavy gun.

Chapter Seven

So the white man was dead. Depending on him to look out for them was out of the question now. But money was the reason they were all there. And money would take them on.

But first Sam had to be taken care of.

They borrowed a shovel from Hans Gunther and dug Sam's grave out in back of the jacals alongside a dozen other wooden grave markers pointed out by a Mexican whore. Boot emptied Perry's pockets of what little money he had and rolled him into the grave wrapped in his saddle blanket.

Nobody said any words over the body before or after dirt was shoveled over it. Amos and Hans lowered their heads in deference. The whore crossed herself.

They walked down the dusty main street to the livery where the packmules had been relieved of their loads and penned up. In a heavy German accent Hans told Amos, "Sam put up money for feed and board for one night. He aimed to pull out in the morning. You intend to do the same?''

"Don't rightly know," Amos answered.

"I'm pullin' out now," Boot said.

Silence followed, silence Boot took as disapproval, so he continued adamantly: "The cotton that's on five of them mules belong to me. I'm crossin' the Rio Grande and sellin' it."

"It is foolish to go alone," Han advised. "Mexican bandits will only take your cargo, or Indians will lift your hair."

"Besides that," Amos added, "just across the river ain't exactly where Mr. Perry was goin' to sell this cotton. It's a ways further."

"Wherever it is," Boot said, "I'm goin'. I got to git some money." Boot looked over his shoulder and asked Waddy, "What about you? You comin'?"

"I got no use for cotton. I'll come."

"Richmond?" Boot asked.

"Cotton ain't worth nothin' to me like it is. I'll come."

"I say we take the cotton the same place Mr. Perry was goin' to take it," Boot told them. "Amos, you know the way."

"I signed on to git money same as y'all," Amos said, looking at the ground as they walked. "I'd hate to turn back empty-handed."

"Ain't no reason to," Boot said.

"It's two days across dangerous country," Amos warned.

"If Mr. Perry made it, we can too," Boot said.

"You'll have to stay on the lookout day and night," Gunther said. "Every Mexican over there knows the value of cotton. They'll take it from you if you ain't careful."

They walked through the open door of the livery.

Gunther stopped, turned around to face them, and said, "Whatever you decide, you're paid up till morning. If you choose to turn back, we can talk price on the animals and packsaddles. I got no use for cotton." Gunther walked away, heading toward the side door of the livery, where he had a working room.

Money had brought them this far; nobody wanted to turn back.

It was twilight when they waded the packmules across the shallow water of the Rio Grande and came out on the other side in the spot that Amos pointed out. Boot had Perry's pistol and Winchester, so he rode in the lead, liking the feel of the pistol strapped around his waist though he had no experience using it.

They were four black men more at ease walking than in the saddle. The land they headed to was wild, lawless land; only one among them was armed, and he had no skill with weapons.

They slogged across the sandy shoreline, pushed their way through a rank growth of willows skirting the bank, and topped out on flatland. Boot kept his horse and packmules at a walk but twisted around in the saddle and yelled back a question that had been bothering him: "Did y'all have any trouble before?"

"Naw," Amos answered. "We went straight to the customhouse. Mr. Perry was out and about, and I never heard of no trouble."

Amos left the conversation there for a time, but shortly he yelled forward to Boot, "You meant it when you said you knowed how to use a gun?"

"I can some," Boot yelled back.

The gathering darkness crowded in from all sides. The wagon road they had fallen into was of powdery earth that sent up chalk-white puffs of dust with each hooffall. On its way into Piedras Negras, the town up the low grade ahead, the road snaked through dust-covered ocotillo, ash-coated barrel cactus, dwarf mesquite, and occasionally cholla.

Piedras Negras was a lively border town on the Mexican side of the Rio Grande that thrived on pesos spent by soldiers of Maximilian's Imperial Army.

The town's unpaved plaza had big cottonwood trees strategically planted for shade used by fruit and vegetable vendors, and each tree was surrounded by crude wooden benches and three-legged stools. Narrow streets fed onto the plaza, flanked on both sides by shacks.

The town was raw, wide open. Open-air cantinas overflowed into the street, and half-naked women stood in open doors luring customers.

Two days before, French General De Pin's counterguerrillas had occupied the town to collect *alcabala* and *mordida*, or taxes and graft. Major Dublado, a light-complexioned criollo—a man born of Spanish parents in Mexico—and Mexican sympathizers had terrorized the town, hanging the recalcitrant Alcalde and three of the town notables.

Now the town was flush with freewheeling Imperialist guerrillas and sympathizers out for liquor and women. Watching them were shifty-eyed Juaristas, Benito Juárez's liberal revolutionists. Also in the town were Mexican and gringo smugglers and spies, highwaymen, cutthroats, and murderers, and Confederates on the run. It was a town where every man was suspect, where every man watched the other.

Boot led the packtrain into the plaza. Candle lamps burning in the cantinas spread dim light over the plaza, and the heavy smell of perfume and huisache blossoms hung on the air.

Two shabbily dressed Mexican soldiers of the Imperial Army walked sentry duty in the square. The plaintive strum of a guitar came from the first cantina, the lilted voice of a woman accompanying the strumming. Loud *gritos*, or whoops, erupted from the cantina across the plaza, and, visible through the open door, a mariachi band dressed in scarlet, gold, and purple charros uniforms stroked big guitars to the tune of "*El Cielito Lindo*," or "The Pretty Little Sky." From somewhere down an alley a dog barked incessantly.

Boot guided the packtrain at a slow walk down the middle of the plaza.

A gaudy painted woman selling favors from the doorway of the last cantina called out tantalizingly in broken English, "*Pobricitos,* poor devils, you work too long. Soon you come back."

At her invitation a thickset man wearing a felt sombrero stepped into the doorway and glanced out inquisitively. Then he looked again, this time with interest.

Out in the plaza the sentry halted, did a sloppy about-face. His eyes came around, fell on the packtrain. "*Parada! Parada!* Halt!" he yelled, and came running, his rifle at the ready.

Boot and the packtrain came to a jerky stop. They sat their saddles, watching the sentry look up and down the line of merchandise, then briefly inspect the cargo of the first mule.

Widening his eyes at what he discovered, the sentry turned and yelled at his compadre in his own language, "Manuel, they carry contraband! Summon the major!"

Manuel took off on the double, running toward the low-roofed adobe building just off the plaza, obviously the town hall.

Shortly the major came up. Boot had been disarmed, and they all were dismounted, fanned out in front of the sentry, their hands raised to the sky.

The major was a handsome, clean-shaven man dressed in a neat-fitting French army uniform. A Gachupin, a native Spaniard, he had been put in place by Emperor Maximilian to collect Royal Revenues on all commercial transactions. He carried himself with the poise of a proud military man, brandishing a swagger stick in his right hand. As he took measured steps to the first packmule, he asked pleasantly, *"Americanos?"*

"Americans," Boot answered, "free Americans."

The major inspected the cargo of the first packmule, then faced around smartly. "I am Major Humberto Rios, Imperial Army of Mexico," he said in perfect English. Tapping the swagger stick in his open palm, he asked tersely, "What is your business?"

"We come to sell cotton," Boot answered.

The major knew the town was a hive of smugglers. He also knew the handsome taxes the cargo could command, especially the Royal Fifth. He tapped the swagger stick in cadence against his thigh, his mind working at the possibilities. "Senor," he announced finally, "the merchandise you carry is strictly forbidden."

"We sold cotton here before," said Amos.

Major Rios smiled knowingly. "Such was possible during the bandit regime of the peasant Benito Juárez. He is of no consequence now. His Highness Emperor Maximiliano rules now, and his decrees cannot be violated. For this," he pointed his swagger stick, indicating the cargo, "I could have you shot."

"For selling cotton?" Amos asked incredulously.

"Smuggling . . . you are smugglers. And smugglers are put to death," Rios said smugly. He paused for effect, then said with great pomposity, "But I will spare your lives."

Major Rios ordered the muleteers held in jail. Locked up in a small low-roofed bare-earth affair down at the end of the plaza, they sprawled on the dirt floor of the dank room, their backs against the adobe wall, listening to scattered noises from the plaza. Noises mixed with the sounds of carousing came in from the cantinas, loud and boisterous. Occasionally a sentry shouted orders angrily in his own tongue, and was answered.

The moon arced its way through the stars, lifting slightly the darkness over the plaza. Tequila, passion, and exhaustion slowly took hold, the merriment from the cantinas ebbing away, the music staggering to a halt.

The jailer shuffled across the dirt floor, peeped through the slot, checking on his prisoners. Seeing the four black men harmlessly asleep, he shrugged indifferently, went back, and started gnawing at the *cabrito,* or goat leg, he had been eating.

Suddenly the plaza exploded in gunfire. For a long minute the guns went off, then died down and finally petered out to random pops.

At the first shots Boot and the others were jarred alert. Boot scrambled to his feet, rushed over to the door. Flattening himself against the wall, he peeped through the rectangular opening, searching for the jailer.

At that instant a barrage of shots racketed from the plaza. A parade of bullets walked across the desktop, ripping splinters from the wood. The jailer cringed down out of sight, frightened. *"Rendir! Rendir!"* a voice demanded from the plaza. "Surrender! Surrender!"

The cowering jailer eagerly gave up, springing from concealment, clattering his rifle onto the desktop, throwing his hands to the air.

Instantly a rifle bullet smashed his forehead. The bullet exploded his face like a struck melon, knocking him lifeless back against the wall, his face drenched in blood.

A Mexican woman swept through the open door, braced herself in a fighting crouch, her rifle at the ready, her eyes searching the place.

The woman was five feet four inches tall, handsomely built. She had on a sand-colored wide-skirted gaucho outfit she had taken from a big hacienda to the west when her guerrilla band had struck the place to extract a forced loan of two thousand pesos. The expensive boots she wore she had taken from the showcase of a dry goods store in Nueva Rosita. Two bandoliers of shells crisscrossed at her breasts, and the six-shooter at her side had been taken from the French armory at San Luis Potosi.

"Americanos!" she called out.

Boot looked into the flashing eyes under the wide brim of a felt sombrero and told her, "We Americans, free Americans."

Just then two heavily armed Mexicans rushed through the door and joined the woman.

"Juan, the key," she commanded one of them. "Free the *Americanos.*"

She was sitting behind the desk the jailer had been killed at when Juan returned with the prisoners. She took another drink from the tequila bottle left on the desk and bit into the leg of goat meat. "You are not merchants, no?" she asked after swallowing her food.

"No," Boot said. "We just want to sell some cotton."

"But there are no buyers here."

"We sold cotton here before," said Amos. "Sold it to a man named Ramon."

"A criollo pig," she said scornfully. "A traitor to his country, a lackey for the imperialists."

"No buyers atall?" Waddy asked pleadingly.

"None. The men of greed flee for their lives now that the Revolution has destroyed the customhouse and wharf. Without custom taxes and bribes the Imperialists are mere peons, unable to wage war against our people. The Revolution will permit no shipments to come in or leave the province."

Boot exchanged hopeless glances with Amos, then asked, "Can we sell the cotton somewhere else?"

"That is possible. The Revolution also needs pesos to carry on," she confided. "There is a place."

"Where?"

"But you have no merchandise," she said, shrugging with finality. "Your cargo has been taken by the Imperialists. Major Rios ordered it so." She looked challengingly at Boot and asked, "You wish it back?"

"We want it back."

She ran her eyes over each of the black men, assessing their fighting ability. Not one man looked capable. She arched her eyebrows and asked, "You are not afraid?"

"We need money," Boot said, looking around at the others. Nobody disagreed.

She inclined her head, looked along her nose at him briefly, then decided. Opening the desk drawer, she retrieved Boot's pistol and passed it over to him. "Juan, bring their horses," she ordered sharply.

Juan hurried out.

She rested back in the chair, took another drink from the tequila bottle, obviously delighting as it flowed down her parched throat, thinking twice about her decision to let them prove themselves cabable men.

"How they call you?" she asked.

"Boot."

She winced at the rude name. "Boota!" she repeated, a distasteful turn to her lips. Returning herself to the serious business at hand, she leaned across the desk and announced proudly, "I am Captain Lozado. You must follow my orders strictly."

Captain Lozado was a mysterious guerrilla of national fame. On May 5, 1862, an obscure Mexican general, Porfirio Díaz, had routed French general Lorencez at Puebla, Mexico. The stunning victory had been a national celebration ever since—Cinco de Mayo. There was one female that fought that day, and by all accounts her actions were decisive in the victory. She alone accounted for at least ten French deaths. That woman was elevated to the rank of captain, and forces were put at her disposal.

"This you must do, Boota," Captain Lozado said definitely. "Three men leave here. They are traitors, collaborators. They go to Nueva Rosita to sell your merchandise to the Imperialists. You must overtake them and kill them."

"We git the cotton back?"

"That you must do. The Imperialists must be deprived of pesos at all costs. Your merchandise cannot be allowed to fall into their hands."

Boot thought the matter over quickly. "What about my rifle?"

"No," she said emphatically. "The resistance needs modern weapons badly."

Boot looked doubtfully at the pistol she had just handed him, knowing he didn't know how to use it well.

"Jose, give the *Americano* your rifle," she ordered.

Boot looked equally doubtfully at the old French-built bolt-action rifle.

"There is nothing more I can do," the captain said, shrugging her shoulders indifferently. "Shoot them in the back," she said flatly. "It does not matter."

"And the cotton, where do we sell the cotton?"

"The revolution has eyes and ears. We will contact you in Nuevo Rosita."

Hoofbeats sounded outside. Juan rushed across the threshold, breathing heavily, talking excitedly. "My captain, we must go. Time grows short."

She stood and advised Boot, "You have no time to waste." She adjusted the tilt of her sombrero and warned over her shoulder on the way to the door, "If you fail, we will kill the Imperialist at Nueva Rosita, and of course your merchandise will be seized."

The moon had waned and stars were patchy, visible only here and there. Boot led them out past the trees

95

along the south edge of the plaza. They twisted around in their saddles, looking at three men swinging from the last tree: One was Major Rios, his uniform still fitting neatly except that it was now choked up in back from a hangman's noose. The other two were well-dressed civilians. The one swinging next to Rios had a cardboard placard strung around his neck. On the placard was scrawled with large letters in Spanish: "Death to Imperialist collaborators."

A quarter mile on the outskirts of town they veered off the wagon road and lifted their horses into a canter, heading south and a little bit west across broken country as Captain Lozado had told them to do.

Each black man rode worried in his own mind over not being able to use a gun, and what was likely to happen when they came upon the Mexicans with the packtrain. Amos finally said to Boot, "You said you could shoot some. You think you can outshoot them?"

"Not unless they mighty po' shots."

"What we goin' to do, then?"

"Git the cotton back . . . somehow."

Chapter Eight

Whether he was man enough to get the cotton back weighed heavily on Boot's mind. Captain Lozado had warned him that he had to kill the Imperialists to do it. He knew the others depended on him to get the cotton back, cotton that represented money for a fresh start at their new freedom.

It was daylight when they crossed over Arroyo Seco, a dry feeder canyon, and struck open desert country of slate-gray earth, broken boulders, organ pipe cactus, and stunted sage. The sun still had an orange tint to it, the air was still. It was going to be hot, very hot.

Four hours by sun they rode, then walked at Amos's warning that the oppressively dry heat tired the horses fast. In single file, each man walking heavy-footed, their horses plodding hang-necked, they came upon the Rio Salado, just as Captain Lozado had told them they would.

Rio Salado was a steep-sided canyon in limestone

cliffs with a shallow channel of water running down its center. At the edge of the water they let their horses drink.

Richmond wiped sweat from his face and nodded his head toward the trail of chopped-up sand they had seen running along the edge of the cliffs in what little shade there was. "Tracks looked fresh enough. They ain't far ahead."

Waddy lifted the reins, brought his horse's muzzle from the water, and asked, "What's your plan, Boot?"

"I've thought it over. I can't use this gun good, 'cause it ain't like the one I used before." Boot looked at them sheepishly and continued, "No sense in me taking the chance with it." He gathered the men around and told them what he planned to do.

The plan was simple enough. Nobody objected, because none of the others could shoot well either. Boot gave Waddy the pistol.

"Like I told you, I don't know how to use it," Waddy confessed again, looking at the weapon dubiously.

"Just pull the trigger as fast as you can," Boot said.

Boot told Amos, "You catch up them mules as fast as you can, all of 'em."

They mounted up and spurred away from Rio Salado at a fast clip, climbed their horses up onto the mesa, and rode out in the desert thirty yards away from the rim.

For a mile or so they rode at a full-out run, outdistancing the moving packtrain. Their horses in a heavy lather, Boot veered them over to the chasm, checked to a halt away from the edge, dismounted, walked stoopshouldered up to the rim, and looked back down the canyon.

The packtrain was weaving along the cliff-shaded edge of the arroyo. A heavyset Mexican rode warily at the head of the train, his rifle canted skyward and resting on the front of his saddle. Behind him another Mexican rode at the flank of the packmules. The last man rode directly behind the train, looking back every now and again, checking their backtrail. They rode alert for trouble, armed with rifles, a single fully loaded bandolier slung over each man's shoulder.

"They comin'," Boot said, backtracking away from the rim. "Y'all know what to do."

Richmond and Amos galloped their horses off upwind.

"Come on, Waddy," Boot said, retrieving his rifle from the saddle boot.

"If we was to git the drop on 'em, maybe they'd give us back the cotton," Waddy suggested.

"Only one sure way to git the cotton back," Boot said, "and that's what we goin' to do."

The sun was directly overhead, the air hot and still. Nothing moved except the packtrain below.

Lying belly-flat at the rim of the arroyo, squinting out over the barrel of his rifle, Boot wiped sweat from his forehead.

Stretched out a foot away on Boot's right, Waddy held the pistol in his two sweaty palms, a nervous finger on the trigger.

It was very quiet.

A grasshopper landed in the parched grass between them, then, startled, hopped back where it had come from.

Looking down the barrel of his rifle, Boot saw the wide sombrero of the Mexican riding at the head of the train move from side to side. Instantly the sombrero tilted up, the man looking up at the rim of the arroyo.

Boot steadied his aim, blinked, squeezed off his shot. The heavy French rifle exploded with a jolting kickback. A bullet ripped into the Mexican's body, high on the chest. He pitched sideways from his horse, the animal breaking into a startled, wide-eyed trot down the arroyo.

The packmules flinched at the eruption and cowered up in a bunch.

Boot quickly worked at reloading, fingers nervous, clumsy.

Instantly Waddy pulled off a pistol shot at the Mexican next in line. The bullet kicked up a spout of sand five yards in front of the Mexican. The Mexican drew a tight rein on his horse, searching frantically for his assailant, his rifle held at the ready pistol-fashion.

Waddy thumbed off another shot, then jerked off two more hastily.

The Mexican's horse screamed and reared.

All three shots were off the mark, the first two kicking up funnels of sand, the last one scorching the horse's rump, sending him pitching and bucking.

The packmules bolted into a panicked, confused run at the crash of shots compounded by the racket of echoes.

The Mexican riding at the end of the line had spotted the puffs of smoke coming from the rim, but his eyes could find no target. Leaning low in the saddle, he jabbed spurs to his horse, riding for distance down the arroyo.

By this time Boot had reloaded. Now he stood up, braced himself spread-legged, and squeezed off another shot.

The Mexican left his horse.

Hastily Boot worked at reloading again, his eyes lifting now and again to the other Mexican, who had now gained control of his horse.

Abruptly, Waddy's pistol snapped empty.

"Git goin'!" Boot yelled to him.

The Mexican below swung his rifle to bear. Boot saw a puff of white smoke blossom up, heard a bullet whap into the side of the cliff at his feet, whine off angrily to the side.

Realizing his disadvantage, the Mexican spurred for safety down the arroyo.

Boot leveled a bead on the Mexican and fired. But the shot was off the mark.

Boot swore under his breath.

He took off running, slanting down the side of the arroyo in bounding leaps as fast as his eyes could pick a path. Reaching the bottom in a stumbling run, he gathered himself and took off running after the Mexican as fast as his legs would carry him.

Up ahead Richmond and Amos had worked their way down to the bottom of the arroyo and had taken up positions just beyond the bend. "Them mules will come runnin' scared this way," Amos said. "They'll keep away from the rocks. Best chance we got to catch 'em is right out here in the open."

Presently the churn of running hoofs on sand and gravel came to them from around the bend. The rumble grew louder, unmistakable.

"They comin'!" Richmond yelled to Amos.

The packmules wheeled around the bend, an awkward bunch in a loose stampede, slowed by their load.

"Catch up the bell mule!" Amos yelled. "The others will stop!"

The bell mule was an old Arkansas mule that Perry had owned for years and Amos had worked just as long. They knew each other well, and Amos had no trouble catching him. The rest of the mules bunched up skittishly, milling around the bell mule.

They were calming the wild-eyed mules when the Mexican who had escaped Boot's ambush rounded the bend, his horse at a fast gallop. He rode low in the saddle, hell-bent for distance. Suddenly his eyes widened at the sight of Amos and Richmond in front of him, caught completely off guard out in the open.

The Mexican fired his rifle, a one-handed shot, pistol-fashion.

Richmond sagged heavily to the sand. It was point-blank range. Richmond was dead before the echo came back.

The Mexican twisted around in his saddle, fired back where he had last seen Amos. A mule screamed and caved under. The Mexican spurred on, his horse spattering back sand.

Now Boot came running. Rounding the bend, he saw up ahead the Mexican getting away. He came to a stumbling walk, lifted his rifle, and fired.

The shot missed. He stood watching the Mexican ride away from him down the arroyo.

He walked up, gasping for breath, his mind silently counting the number of packmules that had been retrieved.

Above the tramp of milling hoof-falls and the braying and snorting of skittish mules, Amos called out, "Boot!"

Boot saw Amos kneeling in the sand in a small opening the circling packmules made. Hurrying over, he saw Richmond stretched out on the sand, a perfectly round hole in the center of a ragged circle of blood chest high on the left side of his shirt.

"Is he dead?" Boot asked.

"He's dead."

Boot lifted his eyes down the arroyo where the Mexican had gone. "I missed him back yonder," he confessed. Looking disgustedly at the old rifle in his hand, he muttered, "Missed him twice."

Just then Waddy came up at a jog. "I got the rifles," he gasped through ragged breaths, "and what bullets they had." Waddy started grinning, pleased at the way the plan had worked. They had the cotton back, and he had a French-built bolt-action rifle in each hand and two bandoliers of bullets slung over his shoulder, all gathered from the dead Mexicans.

"Where's Richmond?" he asked.

"Dead," Amos said flatly, and canted his eyes toward Richmond's body.

The grin left Waddy's face.

"The one I missed rode up on them," Boot said lamely. "If I'd have got him, this wudn't have happened." Boot looked scornfully at the rifle that had refused to do his bidding. In a sudden burst of anger he flung the unruly gun down in the sand and stalked off toward the strip of shade under the cliffs.

Amos and Waddy looked after Boot for a time, then Amos said, "Let's git these mules under what shade we can, then see to Richmond."

They buried Richmond in a boulder-strewn draw feeding into the arroyo in a hole dug in the sand with fingers and sticks. They positioned the largest rocks a man could carry over the grave to keep out varmints. The men worked in gloomy silence, a silence born of shared guilt. When they finished, no words were said over the body.

All three had the queer feeling that it could just as well have been one of them resting forever under the cold embrace of distant slabs of stone. And all three felt guilty not knowing how to shoot well, something that could mean the difference between life and death out here in this strange, dangerous land.

Boot carefully placed the last stone and they returned to the strip of shade cast by the cliff overhang. While Waddy unpacked cooking gear, Boot said reassuringly to Amos, sitting with his back propped against the cliff wall, "Like I said, I fired a gun once before this. It was a different kind of gun, though."

Amos lifted his eyes to Boot, slipping the bandolier over his shoulder. "You killed two of 'em. That's better 'n me or Waddy could have done."

Boot picked up one of the rifles propped against the cliff wall. "Yet and still, Richmond's dead."

"That he is," Amos agreed, looking out to where they had laid Richmond to rest.

"I should've got all three of 'em," Boot said.

"I seen a man that could do it."

"Mr. Perry?"

"Yeah."

"Next time I will." Boot took off at a fast walk, heading down the arroyo, the rifle at his side.

Amos and Waddy nooned in the thin shade of the limestone cliff. They ate stale venison and dried-out beans washed down with water from the river. The air they breathed was hot and still, fouled with the odor of packmules scattered along the cliff wall. And it was hot. The only sounds a man could hear close in was the occasional stamp of a mule, or a tail swish. Farther out you could hear the gurgle of the river, broken at precise intervals by the explosion of a rifle, the echo rolling away down the arroyo.

Some thirty yards up the arroyo, Boot was braced spread-legged against the recoil of his rifle, target shooting at a small barrel cactus that had taken root on a shelf of the cliff wall on the other side. With studied motions he shouldered the rifle, sighted down the barrel, squeezed the trigger, then reloaded, all in deliberate sequence. With careful motions, he repeated the action again and again.

Amos shifted his eyes to where Boot was and asked Waddy, "Workin' in a cow camp like you was, you never learned to shoot?"

"Never did. There was cause to, but I never did. Rattlesnakes, varmints, and things molested camp from time to time, but me, I never shot at 'em . . . never even had a gun. Cookin' was my chore. The other hands wore guns, though, all of 'em."

"Most white men do. You take Mr. Perry now, I never seen him outside without one kind or another. He was right handy wid 'em, too."

"The hands I cooked for always went armed too. Beatin' the thickets for cows like they was, it would have been crazy not to. Only seen one man, though, that was what you'd call real handy with his gun."

"Mr. Perry had a knack wid 'em."

"The man I knowed worked at it a lot. Fast-drawin', he called it. He worked at it so much, he'd shoot up his wages in bullets."

Waddy shifted his gaze to Boot just as Boot's bullet smashed the last stump of cactus from the cliff. "Boot's gettin' the knack," he commented. "He keep at it, he'll do all right."

Two hours later they rounded up the packmules and got back on the trail to Nueva Rosita. Down in the arroyo where they rode the heat was trapped in a tunnel of rock, the hot air motionless, oppressive.

They had been on the trail less than an hour when Boot, riding in the lead, spotted a body lying at the edge of the water. Even as they rode over they recognized the body as the Mexican who had escaped Boot's ambush.

The dead man had five shots visible through the body; his head had been almost cleaved off from a sweeping machete blow. His rifle and ammunition were gone; so were his boots and sombrero.

"I missed him," Boot commented, "but somebody else didn't."

"Who you reckon done it?" Amos asked.

"No tellin'," Boot answered. His eyes followed tracks in the sand leading away from the body and off toward the cliffs. "He was shot from up yonder, then somebody came down here and stripped the body."

"They didn't leave much," Amos noted.

"Only what the buzzards want," Waddy said.

They moved out at a slow walk, each man turning over in his own mind the danger they faced. Boot had gained some confidence in his shooting ability, but they knew the cargo would draw attention to them like bees to honey. It was likely to draw an attack on them as unseen and unmerciful as the attack they had visited upon the Mexicans.

Boot rode warily in the lead now, his eyes circling the cliff walls, probing down the arroyo just as the dead Mexican had done.

On they advanced down the arroyo that cradled a trickle of water. The high cliff walls gave way to limestone banks no more than six or seven feet high. It was in each man's mind that open country meant less danger.

Seemingly from out of nowhere a Mexican materialized. Boot spotted him sitting a burro in the middle of the trail, his white cotton britches and wide straw sombrero blending in perfectly with the limestone cliffs.

"Somebody's here," Boot said over his shoulder to Amos.

"He don't look bad," Amos said when his eyes found him.

"Maybe he ain't by hisself," said Waddy, looking around skeptically.

"One way to find out," Boot said. He rode on ahead, his horse at a walk, his rifle at the ready, his eyes searching the rocks and boulders behind the Mexican.

He was fifteen yards off when the Mexican removed his straw sombrero and retired it courteously to his side, smiling. "Senor, the senorita wishes to speak with you."

"Who?"

"You are called Boota, no?"

"The woman from Piedras Negras, Captain Lozado?"

The Mexican searched around him as if the rocks had ears, then confided, "*Sí*, she is the one. But please, senor, here she is Dona Guadalupe Flores Esperranza,"

106

he said with dignity. "There are others who must not know."

"Where is she?"

"She is there." He nodded his head to the right. "I am Manuel. I will take you."

They followed behind Manuel's donkey for half a mile east to a cart road, and a mile or so farther on they came to a goat farm. Manuel halted his donkey, and when Boot rode up alongside, Manuel said, "She is there," and pointed.

Under a mulberry tree in the barren yard of the goat farm Boot saw a black jersey wagon drawn by two handsome Spanish ponies and driven by a tough-looking, steady-eyed vaquero.

He rode toward the wagon, his eyes on the vague face in the window next to drawn curtains. When he got closer, the curtain parted fully, exposing the woman inside.

She had a black velvet shawl over her head, framing a slender face with high cheekbones dabbed with a tinge of red, her lips colored deep rose. What he could see of her dress through the window was maroon silk. Her arm rested on the window, revealing white lace at the sleeves. "Boota," she said expressively, "it is good to see you!"

Boot squinted at the beautiful woman and said uncertainly, "Captain Lozado?"

With a smile playing on her lips, she asked teasingly, "Did you not think me a lady at Piedras Negras?"

"A woman, but . . ."

"Do not be unkind, Boota," she said airily. Lifting her chin arrogantly, she added, "Here, I am Dona Guadalupe Flores Esperranza, widow of town councilman Don Antonio Araceli Esperranza, a widely respected hacienda owner murdered by Imperialist general Francisco Mejias."

"Is that why you fight?"

"For that . . . and my country."

"We get the cotton back."

"You have the cotton back," she agreed, and smiling through radiant lips, added in mock disapproval, "but one collaborator you did not kill."

"You know?"

"Sí. We know. Also one of your men was killed too. As I told you, the revolution has eyes and ears. But no matter, the one who escapes you is dead."

Boot squirmed uncomfortably in his saddle and said sheepishly, "I just ain't used to this gun yet."

She smiled at the excuse, then said seriously, "It is an old rifle taken from the Imperialists. It has served its purpose. Now we have new ones provided by your General Sheridan."

She drew forward in the window and said hurriedly with concern, "The Imperialists make plans to attack Nueva Rosita. You must dispose of your cotton immediately. The goat farmer," she nodded her head toward the house, "he will lead you."

"What about you?"

"When the Imperialists attack, our forces will resist them. You alone must safeguard your cargo. Manuel will arm you." In a sharp command, she called up to the driver, "Jose, *vamanos*!"

Jose lashed the lines and they rode out.

Boot galloped back to the packtrain.

Amos and Waddy were astonished to hear that the beautiful woman in the regal coach that had swept pass them, kicking up dust in their faces, had been Captain Lozado.

"Did she say where we can sell the cotton?" Amos asked.

"The goatherd that lives yonder is goin' to take us."

"When?"

"She didn't say. She said they was fixin' to fight some more."

"Us too?"

"She didn't say. She said we got to protect the cotton our ownselfs."

Chapter Nine

Dona Guadalupe Flores Esperranza, also known as Captain Lozado, had ordered Manuel to lead the packtrain to market. Also, the goatherd was told to turn over to them three new Winchesters from the ten crates that General Sheridan had ordered misplaced on the south side of the Rio Grande for Benito Juárez's guerrillas.

Manuel passed out a generous supply of ammunition, and when he showed them what he knew of the weapon Boot immediately started practicing, triggering off round after round at a target in the goatherd's backyard.

An hour or so later, at Manuel's insistence, they took to the trail to deliver the cotton to the guerrillas' village.

The trail they took was the result of Manuel's expert guidance. It sliced through a rugged mountain gap, dipped down into a hot, dry, chalk-white mountain plateau studded with ocotillo, prickly pear, and stunted sage. At a sheer cliff the trail squeezed through a defile barely wide enough for pack animals and entered a shallow arroyo. At the head of the arroyo they climbed their animals up a shallow incline and topped out on a limestone butte.

Hours later the trail led onto a chalk-white tableland covered with fishhook cactus, creosote bushes, and sage.

On they trekked under the scorching sun, the way tortured, the land dry, inhospitable. Manuel constantly searched the horizon, and every now and again looked at their backtrail. He had warned them that this was *tierra paz*, or pacified land, land controlled by Maximilian's Imperialist Army and freelancing bandits of unknown loyalty.

The packtrain got strung out in the open, no concealment in sight in any direction. Not a rock was larger than a man's fist, nothing stood taller than a horse's belly. Their only hope to keep from being seen was the fact that the trail was not often used.

In a scattering of pitahaya cactus Manuel drew up. Boot rode up alongside. "Trouble?"

"No, senor." Manuel pointed. "Puerto Cita is there." He indicated a stretch of low, ragged sierras wandering away to the south.

"We sell the cotton there?"

"*Sí*, senor.

Puerto Cita, or rendezvous port, was the name the guerrillas had given to the hidden village they had established on a spit of land at the bend in the Rio Salado just above its confluence with the Rio Grande. Well out of sight under the lee side of the mountain, the trading post was actually a cave tunneled into the mountain and covered over with brush to throw off anyone of questionable loyalty. The cave doubled as a cantina, and there was a large flat space out front for storage of goods awaiting shipment.

At a signal from the mountaintop, ships returning from legitimate commercial business up the Rio Grande put in at Puerto Cita to take on smuggled goods, if the captain found it profitable. And transactions at Puerto Cita were very profitable. Unlike Maximilian's custom-houses, the guerrillas demanded no *alcabala*, or excise tax, nor did they solicit *mordida*, or bribes. Each deal was strictly cash. And every knowing ship captain returning from upriver looked anxiously for the mountain-top beacon.

It was coming on to sundown when Manuel raised his eyes to the lookout post in a cranny on top of the mountain and got the all-clear signal from the lookout there. Manuel led them into a hidden trail at the base of the mountain, and they drew up at a small brush corral next to the cave.

A heavy-bellied Mexican stepped out under the brush awning over the cave entrance and paused, his eyes relishing the cargo. He whistled under his breath.

Manuel slid from his burro and said to Boot, "Senor, he is the one who will buy your cotton. You wish me to speak?"

"Tell him we want a fair price."

"There is no need. He will know."

Boot exchanged glances with Amos, then asked the goatherd even as they dismounted, "Captain Lozado?"

"*Sí,*" the goatherd replied without emotion.

Looking around the flat ground, they scanned stacks of cowhides, bundles of wool, sheaves of tobacco leaves, barrels of indigo, and kegs of cochineal. The staging area was cluttered with merchandise, and a half-dozen or so *mozos*, or hired men, were there, obviously waiting to load the next ship that decided to dock. "Some place," Waddy commented, awed.

"There's money in this stuff," Amos said.

"Them cowhides yonder," Waddy said, nodding in that direction, "I seen plenty of them lying out there rotting on the *brasada* when I was cookin' for that cow outfit. How much they bring, Manuel?''

Manuel fingered his heavy mustache, thought briefly, then answered, "Four, five pesos. Not so much." Manuel said in his own tongue to the Mexican coming toward them, "Cotton, Diego. My friends bring cotton."

"Sí," Diego said, nodding. "You are expected." He inspected the cargo closely, talking all the while. "Please, go inside. Maria is there. I will join you shortly, and we can talk business."

On their way inside a question came to Boot, and he asked Amos in a low voice, "How much money did y'all git last time?"

"I never heard."

"You got any idea how much we ought to git, Waddy?"

"Never had no truck with cotton before."

Inside, the dugout cave was surprisingly large. The walls, the side of the mountain actually, were pegged and strung with trinkets of silver and gourdes from Monterrey. Crude counters were piled high with blankets from Saltillo and tapestries from Mexico City. Tiles from Puebla were stacked on the floor.

Manuel weaved his way through a scattering of tables in the center of the hard-packed earth. They sat on crude bar stools facing a slim-waisted, sun-browned woman of noticeable beauty behind a bar that ran the length of the rear wall.

The woman smiled beautifully, placed four dusty glasses on the counter, and twisted around for the bottle. At her movement her glossy black hair swept around and fell to rest halfway to her waist.

She turned around with the bottle. The bright calico dress she wore cut low in front exposed smooth flesh in twin mounds.

"For you, amigo," she said after filling Manuel's

glass. Filling the other glasses, she said coyly, ". . . and for your friends," and winked at Boot.

At that instant Diego came in, a satisfied smile on his face.

"Patrone?" he asked Manuel.

"This one is boss," Manuel said, indicating Boot.

Diego shouldered in between Boot and Manuel. "Tequila," he ordered from the woman.

"You buy the cotton?" Boot asked.

Diego lifted the tequila glass to his lips and took a hefty swallow. "I buy."

"How much?"

"Seventy-five centavos a pound."

The black men didn't have even a vague sense of the value of Mexican money. Boot looked across his shoulder past Diego at Manuel, his expression asking for guidance.

Manuel shrugged his shoulders without answering.

"That is a fair price," Diego stated. "Senorita Esperranza wishes it. You can find no better."

They accepted the price offered by Diego, trusting to the fairness of Dona Esperranza, submitting to the veracity of Diego.

Appraised by Diego's shrewd eyes, each of nineteen mules was estimated to be packing two hundred pounds of cotton. At a table in the center of the room Diego stacked five rawhide pouches containing 2,850 silver pesos he and the woman had counted out in the back room. "That is a fair amount, amigos," he said seriously. "You can find no better."

For Manuel's services Boot paid him fifty pesos, looking at the money uneasily. "I was figgerin' on U.S. money," he said.

"Pesos, all right," Waddy assured him. "Down on the *brasada* most anybody will take 'em."

"Seen Confederate money before," Boot said, "but never this kind."

"Me neither," Amos admitted. "Don't know how he come by it, but Mr. Perry had U.S. money the times before."

"American money is possible, *amigos*," Diego said, "for a price."

"How much?"

"That is for others to decide. Maybe a ship comes tonight. For a commission the captain will change your pesos to dollars."

"Let's wait," Boot said, more to Manuel than anybody else.

Manuel shrugged indifferently. "It is your choice, senor. I am at your service."

"Rest where you choose," Diego told them. "I must prepare."

The sun dipped below the mountains to the west, spreading long arms to the far horizon, sending out a spray of bronze color that reached into arroyos, bathed high peaks.

The trading post concealed under the loom of the mountain was instantly plunged into murky darkness. And Diego's hired men went into action.

Like uneasy ghosts in the night, workmen moved goods down to the crude pier that extended out in the deep water of the Rio Grande. The only sounds a man could hear were those of bales being dragged, or the whisper of sandals moving through sand. Occasionally Diego's low voice gave orders.

A wan moon threw out pale light, spreading a silvery glow on the Rio Grande. Boot and the others had talked some, stopped, then talked some more. After that they had withdrawn to the brush corral, each man rolling up in his saddle blanket, sleeping with his own thoughts.

Deep into the night under the frail light of stars the

clip-clop of trotting hoofs disturbed Manuel's sleep. He sat up, rubbing sleep from his eyes, following the vague outline of a rider.

In shadowy darkness the rider dismounted at the corner of the arbor and a heavyset figured stepped forward out of the shadows. Manuel heard the rider say in low tones in their tongue, "Diego, our signal has been answered. A ship comes."

"The *Yazoo*?"

"Yes, that is the one."

"How far off?"

"It is there." Manuel looked where the man was pointing out across the shimmering moonstruck water at two pale running lights gliding stealthily toward them. Diego saw the lights too, and called out excitedly in a slightly louder voice to his hired men, "*Muchachos*, the ship comes! Make ready! *Vamanos!*"

Rushing back inside, Diego lit wax candles and started dusting off tequila bottles behind the counter. Maria started arranging merchandise in its most eye-catching position.

Manuel woke the others and led them through the door.

"Manuel, amigos," Diego announced cheerily when he saw them, "your wait is over. The ship comes. It is the *Yazoo*. She is one of the very best."

"Will the captain come here?" Boot asked.

"*Sí*. He will come." Diego flourished a bottle of tequila. "This . . . and Maria," he said, swatting the woman's ass playfully, "Captain Molloy cannot resist."

Diego came from behind the counter, dismissed himself. "I must greet my old friend. I will speak to him of your wishes."

Diego went out to the wharf. Maria stayed busy arranging trade goods. Boot, Amos, Waddy, and Manuel took seats at a table over in the far corner, sipping coffee given them by Maria.

In the wee hours of night, a black deckhand hurled a rope with practiced precision to a waiting Mexican at the wharf. The Mexican twisted it around a large boulder off to the side; the helmsman shut down the forward thrust of the engine and the ship bumped against the crude wharf.

A double-boarded gangplank dropped into place, and the captain stepped lively, coming ashore.

Captain Finlay Molloy was big, solidly built, with red hair and beard. He spoke heartily and often. "Seen your light," he bellowed when he saw Manuel. "Hope you got something worth my risk."

"*Sí*," Diego answered, nodding vigorously. "Only the best . . . and there is cotton."

"Well, now, you ain't been hunkered down here hidin' from the goddamned Imperialists like every other Mexican I seen upriver at Negras. Let's have a look!"

Diego had noticed the extra-wide gangplank. "What is it you bring?"

"Stinking horses," Molloy said sourly. "Couldn't get my ship under way without the goddamned beasts, or their owners."

Shortly they heard the captain's loud voice all the way inside the trading house: "Diego, you old bandit ass! I ain't a man to swap straight up dollars for pesos! My sense of dickering would be insulted!"

"*Sí.* That is reasonable. What is your commission?"

"Well, now, that depends on how many pesos."

"Twenty-eight hundred."

Molloy looked over his shoulder at Diego and spoke with interest for the first time. "Twenty-eight hunnerd, huh? Well, now, any man with that many pesos warrants my best offer. Twenty-five hunnerd dollars, take it or I'm damned." Molloy was silent only a second, then asked, "Who's the thievin' son of a bitch with the pesos?"

"There." Diego indicated inside.

Inside the dimly lit trading house, Diego slowed his steps, nodded toward the far corner, and said, "They are the ones."

"Them?"

"*Sí*, Captain. They bring the cotton you wish for."

"How the hell did they do that? Ones I seen didn't have sense enough to pour piss out of a boot!"

Diego shrugged noncommittally. "I will tell them of your generous offer."

Six men and their horses had debarked the ship after the captain. They had already said their good-byes, Molloy hoping he had seen the last of them. They followed quietly behind Molloy and Diego, hearing only snatches of the conversation. They tied their horses to the arbor, one man staying behind to stand watch. Now the smallish man led the other five through the door after Molloy and Manuel. He slanted his eyes over to the corner that he had heard Diego mention.

Tom Hancock was startled upon seeing the three black men sitting there. He blurted out of the side of his mouth, "It's them niggers!"

"What niggers?" Toby asked.

"The ones we seen at Carrizo Springs." Hancock put together all the snatches he had heard. And he was astonished. "I'm damned if they ain't done brought that cotton over here and sold it."

The Confederates took chairs around the third table down from the door. Hancock's mind was fuzzed. He was surprised that ignorant niggers had piloted the cotton here; he was stunned the captain was going to lay out to them twenty-five hundred dollars cash money. It was a profitable venture he hadn't remotely considered when they had killed that worthless profiteer. It was even more galling that they were at this moment near penniless.

Frank Tanner, sitting next to Hancock, said angrily, "We shoulda burned that damn cotton like I said, Sarge!"

Hancock pursed his thin dry lips, thinking. "Maybe . . . maybe not. This just might be the stroke of luck we been needin'."

Now it dawned on Amos where he had seen the men who had just come in. "Them's the ones that killed Mr. Perry," Amos said in a low voice, nodding toward the Confederates over at the table.

Boot came forward in his chair, reached for and got the Winchester propped against the table leg. Waddy twisted around, looking. Manuel asked, "They are bad men?"

"Yeah," Boot answered. "They killed the man we was haulin' the cotton for."

"For what reason?"

"For no reason."

"That cotton was the reason," Amos said flatly.

"They hear everything, *amigos,*" Manuel said with certainty. "There will be trouble, I think."

Boot drew the Winchester across his lap with one hand, the other hand clutching the saddlebags he had put the money sacks in. "Money's here," he said firmly. "Ain't nobody takin' it."

Chapter Ten

Tom Hancock relished the unexpected opportunity to get cash money, thinking the black men easy pickings.

Two days before, they had straggled into Piedras Negras flat broke with nowhere to go. Yesterday they had heard that General Slaughter and other ex-rebels were holed up at Monterrey, Mexico. Word was that the general intended to start a colony there built on slavery, as the Confederate States had been.

Hancock had touched the sympathies of Captain Molloy, a former blockade runner, and the captain had transported them here so they could strike out cross-country on horseback to join General Slaughter.

Now, sitting over a bottle of tequila provided by Captain Molloy, Hancock took it as an overdue stroke of good luck that the black men he had seen earlier in Carrizo Springs were here at Puerto Cita and had sold the cotton.

Hancock poured himself a stiff drink from the tequila

bottle and tossed it off. "Toby, go out there and tell Frank to loosen them cinches. We gonna sit a spell."

Toby rose, smiling slyly, and cut his eyes over at the black men. That simple act was like a spoken word. With that sly grin the black men knew some way was being studied to get their money.

Manuel was first to draw conclusions when Toby got up and left. "Senor, I think they make plans to rob you," he said, looking at Boot.

"Let's git our horses," Boot answered in a low tone.

They went outside and casually began saddling their horses.

Tom stepped out under the awning, stretched himself, looking around nonchalantly. Sneaking a quick peek at the black men, he walked casually back inside.

"He comes only to watch," Manuel said.

"I know," Boot answered.

"They intend to jump us," Amos said, worried.

"If they do, we'll know soon enough. We'll do like we planned, right, Manuel?"

"*Sí.* I will go there." Manuel nodded toward the lookout roost high above the trading post. He straddled his burro and, heeling around, warned, "Boota, you must leave Mexico pronto. These who come dressed as soldiers are bandits. There are others."

"Our horses won't take much to wear down once we git out yonder in that heat," Amos said. "Only way to outride 'em is to git a good head start."

"If it comes to the money, we'll kill 'em," Boot said.

"It is your choice, *amigos*. If they follow, I will signal as we discussed." Manuel heeled out. After riding off a dozen paces he twisted around, said loudly, "*Adíos, amigos.* I must return to my flock."

They all stopped what they were doing, turned around, and made an obvious show of saying good-bye. "*Adíos,* Manuel," Boot said. "See you next time."

Waddy had been pretending to work with his cinch but was actually keeping a lifted eye out for Frank. Now Boot turned around and asked, "Did he go inside?"

"He ain't moved," Waddy answered dryly.

Manuel had reached the shoulder of the mountain. "Let's go," Boot said. To a man they swung onto their saddles and walked their horses into the trail along the base of the mountain. They had ridden no more than thirty yards when Waddy twisted around in the saddle, checking on the whereabouts of Frank. "He's gone inside!" Waddy yelled ahead.

"That's it!" Boot said. "They comin'!"

They lashed their horses into a fast gallop and swung north around the shoulder of the mountain where Manual had gone. But Manuel was nowhere in sight. Nobody mentioned it, but doubts entered each man's mind.

On they rode at a fast clip.

They went back the same way they had come. Off to their right the sun lifted over the horizon, sending out the morning's first burst of orange rays over the landscape. The air was still, muggy. Behind them a trail of white dust lingered in the air briefly, then drifted off. It was going to be very hot.

After an hour by sun they checked their horses down to a walk, then after a while dismounted in a scattered stand of pitahaya cactus and led their horses.

"They ain't followin' us," Waddy commented, looking over his shoulder.

"We don't know that for sho'," Boot said. "I'll work my way up yonder and look for Manuel's signal again."

Within thirty minutes Boot had reached the highest point in the rocks. He looked back at the lookout roost above Puerto Cita, where Manuel was supposed to be.

Nothing.

Ten minutes passed, and no signal. Fifteen minutes . . . twenty. Nothing.

Boot lay stretched back against the rocks, his Winchester propped next to him. Down below, Amos and Waddy had loosened their cinches, sitting cross-legged under what little shade a large cactus provided.

Thirty more minutes passed, and no signal. All was quiet. A brown-gray hawk swooped low over the rocks in search of prey.

An hour went by. Still nothing.

Boot came down from the rocks, his pants covered with white dust, his shirtfront sweat-stained at the armpits.

"No signal?" Amos asked, standing up.

"Nothin'."

"Ain't nobody followin' us," Waddy said again.

"Maybe you right," said Boot.

"Manuel didn't go up to that roost like he said he was," Amos said angrily. "He took his pesos and lit out."

"I believed him," Boot said.

"He lied to us," Amos said. "If he'd went up there and flashed that mirror like he said he was, you'da seen it."

"Maybe something went wrong," Boot reasoned. "Anyhow, the sooner we cross the Rio Grande, the better off we'll be."

They cinched up their saddles, mounted, and rode away at trail gait.

Unknown to them, Manuel had kept his word. And that's what had got him killed. He lay dead in the rocks above Puerto Cita.

He had climbed up to the roost, had found the lookout dead, his face bloody as a beef from a machete blow, his pockets turned inside out, his boots gone. Manuel's eyes flared at the sight, and when he turned to flee, a machete blow to the neck ended his life. His pesos and burro went to a roving band of freelancing bandits.

123

But behind them Tom Hancock and his men rode without haste, sure of themselves. Cavalry trained, experienced in mounted pursuit, each man knew that in country like this, horses moving fast would kick up trail dust visible for miles. And each man knew better than to push grass-fed horses too hard.

So they rode easily, perhaps a mile back, following the clearly visible tracks left by Boot and the others.

"Sarge, there ain't no water within miles of here," Toby said. "They ain't likely to stop unless they have to."

"We'll follow 'em till they do stop," Tom answered.

"They keep runnin' them horses, they'll stop sooner 'n they figured to," Frank said.

A little while later they pulled up parallel to the low chain of sierras, studying the ground. "They dismounted now," Tom said, lifting his eyes ahead, seeing no movement or trail dust. "Smart bunch of coons, relievin' their horses like that."

"I say we ride 'em down, kill every damn one of 'em, take the money and head to Monterey," Frank suggested. "Simple as that. None of this cat-and-mouse shit."

Tom sat slump-shouldered in the saddle, his two hands resting on the pommel, his mind mulling over the suggestion. He lifted his eyes ahead again.

Off in the distance he thought he saw a hint of white dust lingering on the blue horizon. He rested his campaign hat back on his head, looked up toward the sun, wiping sweat from his brow. "Its hotter 'n hell itself," he commented.

"And it's sure to git hotter," Toby drawled.

"The longer we take, the worse it's gonna git, Sarge," Frank warned.

"There's truth to that," Toby agreed, wiping a soiled sleeve across his forehead.

"I guess you boys are right," Tom said, coming up-right in his saddle. "Let's git it over with."

Away they spurred, Tom in the lead.

They rode at a hard gallop for a time, then checked down to trail gait. Three times they alternated their pursuit this way, rapidly closing the distance between them and their quarry.

Now they were at trail gait. The white dust they had seen had turned out to be three riders now in a narrow valley studded with ocotillo, prickly pear, and sage. Limestone ridges rose up on both sides.

Hancock reached back and unsheathed his Winchester, the others following his lead. "The next run oughta bring us in shootin' range. We'll cut loose, drop every one of 'em before they know what hit 'em," Tom said.

On they came, rifles at the ready.

More out of jitters than anything else, Waddy turned in his saddle and looked back. Then he looked again. "They comin'!" he yelled out.

A Winchester banged, then five more shots exploded in rapid eruption.

Waddy left the saddle, two bullets between the shoulder blades. Amos let out a startled yelp of pain as a bullet singed a path under his armpit. Boot's neck drew down into his shoulders, the ugly whine of bullets buzzing by like angry bees.

Instantly Boot slapped spurs to his horse. Amos did the same as best he could.

Away they rode as fast as their horses could carry them, Boot's eyes searching ahead left and right for cover, anything.

But there was nothing.

On they sped, bullets whizzing by angrily.

Unknown to the parties in the valley, up in the rocks to the west unblinking eyes of heartless Kickapoo raiders watched with keen interest. In fact, these eyes had been watching ever since the strangers had entered the valley.

The valley was barren, inhospitable land a dozen miles east of Nacimiento, the southern Kickapoo's Mexican homeland, and traversed by Kickapoos on their raids into Texas. And nothing moved unseen by the Kickapoos from Nacimiento to the Rio Grande.

The Mexican Kickapoo were a cunning, savage tribe of tough desert fighters who harbored ancient hatred of whites—and Texans in particular. They lived to take scalps, captives, or loot, preferably all three.

This bunch was led by Wildcat. They sat their horses dispassionately, watching the chase through bloody eyes. By instinct they were eager for battle, on the side of either party or against both parties, it didn't matter.

Bowlegs was there as well. Sitting his horse next to Wildcat, he hadn't moved his eyes from the chase. "We go?" he said impatiently to Wildcat.

"We go!"

The Indians came down out of the rocks, riding like a horde, firing like an army.

"Injuns!" screamed Hancock. To a man they turned in the saddle, returning the fire. But every shot was off the mark.

Up ahead Boot and Amos heard the firing from off to the left. Looking back, they saw Indians attacking their pursuers. They sped on up the valley, looking for cover.

Behind them Hancock and his men knew they had little chance of fighting off Indians out in the open. So they sped on up the valley, looking for cover too.

Wildcat came at them with a special vengeance. He hated anybody wearing anything that reminded him of other butternut-clad invaders who had spoken with a crooked tongue.

In '61, when he and his people lived in the Indian Nation along the Canadian River, Confederate general Albert Pike had ridden into the village with a special commission from Jefferson Davis to raise an Indian fighting force. With cheap trade goods for the women and promises of regular pay and rations for the men, Pike had enticed some starry-eyed young men against Wildcat's entreaties to join a Confederate Indian brigade. Wildcat's son, Kennekuk, had been among the young men who had joined up, eager to prove his manhood. In July of '63 Kennekuk was killed in the battle of Honey Springs when Yankee colonel James G. Blunt defeated Confederate colonel Douglas A. Cooper's Indian brigade. Ever since that time Wildcat carried in his heart one more reason to hate whites, especially those who wore butternut.

Now the chase settled down to a running gun-battle. The firing died down, now only scattered shots echoing across the valley.

Boot swung his horse, headed for the rocks, Amos following, riding slump-shouldered.

The Confederates rode desperately with the Indians so close on their tails. They knew their grab for the black men's money was over. Now they rode only to escape with their scalps.

Boot turned in the saddle, looking over his shoulder for signs of pursuit. There was none—only the trail dust of Hancock and his men, clattering on up the valley, the Indians on their tail, random shots punctuating the air.

Pulling to a halt, Boot turned around and asked Amos, "Bad?"

"Can't hardly breathe."

Boot dismounted and held a canteen to Amos's dry lips. "Ain't nothin' else I can do for you now."

"I know," Amos said, grimacing in pain. "Some shade would feel mighty good."

"We'll find some."

Boot mounted up, and they walked their horses away. They angled back down into the valley.

"Richmond and Waddy dead, me shot like this, money don't seem worth it now," Amos commented sadly.

"We cross the Rio Grande and git back with this money, it'll be worth it. You can buy that piece of land you said you wanted."

They didn't dig a grave for Waddy. In the hot, dry limestone country south of the Rio Grande they left his body lying under the everlasting sun, waiting for the buzzards and coyotes.

They divided up his share of the cotton money, and for lack of better direction they fell into the trail of the chewed-up earth made by the chase that had led up the valley.

"What we gonna do if them Indians come back?" Amos asked.

"Horses ain't in no shape to run no more. We'll talk."

"I heard Indians don't talk much. Put my Winchester in my hand. If they come back shootin', I'll do what I can."

Boot pulled to a stop, and when Amos rode up alongside he leaned out, unsheathed the Winchester from the saddle scabbard, and handed it to him.

After thirty minutes of walking their horses down the valley, a cloud of dust appeared ahead, spreading toward them.

Wildcat and his band swept up in a swirl of chalk dust where Boot and Amos had stopped their horses. Dust drifted away, settled, leaving Boot and Amos looking at stone-faced, hard-eyed Indians.

Wildcat and his bunch had ridden down and had killed Hancock and his men. Two Indians each held the reins of three saddled horses; six pistols and six rifles had been distributed throughout the band; and six bloody scalps hung from saddle pommels.

Wildcat nudged his horse forward, drew up shoulder

to shoulder with Boot's horse. He was silent as a stone, a tight draw to his lips, scorn in his eyes. The other Indians fanned out around them, sullen, tight-lipped too. For a while Wildcat moved his eyes from Boot to Amos and back to Boot again. Abruptly he spit off to the side, mad at what he had seen.

As if on signal, Bowlegs kicked his pony forward, slanted in next to Amos. He snatched Amos's Winchester from his grasp and tossed it to another Indian, who plucked it cleanly out of the air. Then he kneed his horse forward to Boot's, ripped Boot's Winchester from the saddle scabbard, and, raising the gun to his nose, smelled the chamber. An ugly sneer came to his lips, and he heaved the rifle into the dust. Rudely backing his horse away, he looked at Boot, deep loathing showing on his face.

"You coward?" Wildcat asked aloud what Bowlegs and the others only thought.

"Naw," Boot answered.

"You have heart of woman!" Bowlegs snapped.

"We never had a chance," Boot answered.

"They sneaked up on us," Amos added. "Only thing we could do was ride for cover."

Wildcat caught the eye of one of his young warriors, nodded his head toward the rifle lying in the dust.

The warrior swept his leg over his horse's mane and slid to the ground lightly. Walking over, he retrieved the rifle, then looked at Wildcat.

Wildcat nodded his head.

The warrior passed the rifle up to Boot.

Wildcat said something in his own tongue.

Another warrior swung his horse and heeled out at a dead run toward the rocks. At seventy-five yards away the warrior jerked to a stop and faced his horse around.

Wildcat looked down his nose at Boot. "You kill!" he barked.

"Kill him!" Boot said incredulously. "What for?"

"You kill," Wildcat repeated solemnly, "or I kill you."

Boot scanned the Indians arrayed in front of him, resting his gaze on Bowlegs. Bowlegs had a satisfied smirk on his lips. The test Wildcat had given Boot, which undoubtedly he was going to fail, had drawn a knowing smirk to Bowlegs's lips, similar to the smirk Boot could see on the others' lips.

For the first time, Boot realized his courage was being tested. He stepped down from the saddle deliberately. Walking clear of the Indians fanned out around him, he looked at his human target, the Winchester held along his leg. He paused, looking at Wildcat, a slow challenging look.

Wildcat sat haughtily, waiting patiently, his big arms folded across his chest. The other Indians sat motionless, waiting expectantly for Boot to fail.

Suddenly Boot wheeled, swung his Winchester toward Bowlegs, and fired as fast as he could work the action, triggering off shots, exploding sand pebbles at Bowlegs's horse's feet.

The horse screamed, bolted, and pitched.

Bowlegs came unseated, landing facedown in the sand. The horse trotted off wild-eyed.

The Indians to a man whooped in delight. All except Wildcat. He sat unsmiling, but even his old eyes twinkled at the prank.

Bowlegs was furious. He had been shamed in front of the others.

From a kneeling position, he sprang at Boot like a snarling animal.

Coolly Boot flipped the rifle stock over barrel, and drew back for a clubbing blow at Bowlegs's head.

"Stop!" Wildcat exclaimed.

Bowlegs froze; Boot stopped the blow.

"You fight for nothing," Wildcat advised Bowlegs. "There is nothing to gain." He kneed his horse up to Amos and said reprovingly to Bowlegs, "You brave coup chief, but your horse no good. Too scared of noise. Only fit to eat."

An Indian off to the side snickered softly; others twittered a little; one cackled out loud. Bowlegs's scowling glare took the smiles off their faces, then he ran his eyes over the whole bunch, daring them to laugh at his pratfall.

"We go!" Wildcat said, relieving the tension.

Wildcat leaned out in his saddle and looked at the nasty, sweat- and dust-caked wound in Amos's back. "No good," he said. Looking around at Boot, he said, "You come."

Two hours later, they rode down out of the rocks of the Santa Rosa mountains and entered a valley of sandhills called Nacimiento, the Kickapoo Mexican village.

Bowlegs had gotten over being made the object of a prank and had even guffawed at himself for being unhorsed.

Twice they had stopped along the way: once to pack dirt over grass placed on Amos's wound, and once to round up the fifty or so horses they had stolen from across the Rio Grande in Texas and had hidden away in a shallow draw just west of the Santa Rosas when they had first spotted strange riders in their territory.

Nacimiento was a dusty poverty-stricken village of some hundred crude domed shacks made of scrap wood and coarse lechaguilla grass. A goodly number of razor-thin jackasses browsed about on sticks and straw, and most of the houses had a parched-brown garden scratched out of rocky soil off to the side.

There was little activity when they rode in, driving the horse herd. Men of fighting age were off stealing; old men, children, and most women were inside out of the heat of the day. Two women sat on the shady side of a house weaving baskets, and another was making a rug.

The Indians penned the horses with other half-wild horses in a large community corral in the center of the village. The villagers turned out, looking, and after the horses were secured the women joined their mates. Boot and Amos drew curious stares, and one old man spoke harshly in his own tongue, obviously displeased the black men had been brought here.

"He needs care," Wildcat said to one of the old women. "Bring your medicines there," he said, and indicated a lean-to in back of the corral.

For seven days Boot and Amos lived out of the lean-to, their money hidden in a hole dug next to the far wall. By the fourth day Amos's wound was much better, and he was able to work his shoulder without pain. Three times Bowlegs had come to visit, each time late in the evening after returning from a raid across the Rio Grande.

They had talked each time. The first time Bowlegs related to them that his mother's given name to him was Jimmy. Through conversation they found they had little in common except their skin shade: Boot and Amos had been slaves of white men; Bowlegs had been a killer of white men as far back as he could remember first firing a gun.

The thought still lingered in Bowlegs's mind that they were cowards for running from white men. To Bowlegs, whites were implacable enemies to be killed at every opportunity. He couldn't understand why Boot and Amos felt differently.

The second time Bowlegs came by, he told them of his past.

He was the son of a Seminole woman and a runaway slave, and had had to flee the white man's advances first out of Florida, then out of tribal lands along the Canadian River. Now, at the age of twenty-two, he was a tough, seasoned fighter of many raids. He had ridden the plunder trail with numerous bands, starting when he first tended the horse herd for Red Shirt back in '59.

Now living with Machemanet's tribe of Mexican Kickapoo, and raiding with Wildcat's band, he plundered, pillaged, and murdered in Texas with the southern Kickapoo who had migrated from the Canadian River, where part of the tribe still remained, trying desperately to follow the white man's road.

That part of the tribe that was here, Machemanet's band, had come to escape the ever-reaching hand of the white man, here in Mexico on barren, inhospitable land granted by the Mexican government to keep out Apaches. The only means of feeding and clothing their families was to take from others, and the Kickapoo, nursing ancient grievances, gladly chose the white man to take from.

Bowlegs's last visit had been when Cheeno led his band in with two captive white women, driving seventy head of beeves.

They roared in late in the afternoon. Boot, Amos, and Bowlegs were at the horse corral where they had come after target shooting in the sandhills, a child's habit, Bowlegs had said.

Cheeno was a stocky, big-chested, heavy-shouldered man of twenty-three, maybe twenty-four. Visibly mostly Mexican, he had a wide flat face and straight black hair that flopped unbanded just above his shoulders, giving him a wild, savage look, which taken with his reputation was fitting.

While the cattle were being loose-bunched out back, Cheeno trotted his horse over to the corral, leading the two mounted white women by tether ropes around the neck. They both were tattered, chafed, and sunburned raw-red. And both looked to have been violated.

"You buy?" Cheeno asked Bowlegs playfully.

Cheeno and Bowlegs had gained respect for each other when they were first learning the plunder trail together under Wildcat. Cheeno possessed sufficient boldness and cunning, mixed with savagery, to attract other warriors to his side, forming his own band. Bowlegs had not yet achieved this esteem. They still carried on a fighting man's rivalry, boasting to each other of bold deeds, or ragging each other about stupid mistakes.

Bowlegs made a show of looking over the captives, then said distastefully, "Too old!"

"Your eyes deceive you again. They have many sons yet to come." Cheeno grinned; Bowlegs snickered in return.

Grinning down at Boot, Cheeno asked, "You buy?"

"Naw, I don't buy," Boot snapped, squaring around to face Cheeno. "What you take the women for?"

The grin left Cheeno's face. "Money . . . I take for ransom money," he said stiffly. "You no like, you buy . . . take back!"

"Not my family," Boot said, walking off, heading toward the lean-to.

Cheeno swore at him in his own tongue and heeled away. Bowlegs explained to Amos, "We take captives all the time. That is our way. Soon—today, maybe tomorrow—white man send agent with money. Then women go home."

"What if their folks ain't got money?" Amos asked. "Will he kill them?"

"Cheeno no kill. He keep them, or sell to anybody who got money."

"Boot's mad 'cause he's got a young brother taken by Comanches he's got to ransom the same way."

Bowlegs looked after Boot, then said reassuringly,

"Comanches no kill. They sell . . . or make warrior maybe."

Two days later, the first of October, Boot and Amos were sitting out under the overhang, Amos putting an edge on the eight-inch-blade Bowie knife they both had bought and now wore. Boot was fitting on big Mexican spurs he had bought to go along with the high-topped, keen-toed vaquero's boots he had bought earlier from a Mexican he had watched in the corral training wild horses to bridle and spur.

Bowlegs spotted them and came over.

"Wildcat say you leave soon."

"Tomorrow," Boot answered.

"Early tomorrow," Amos added.

"More better you go nighttime. Daytime no good."

"We got nothin' to hide," Boot said.

Bowlegs looked without emotion at Boot and stated flatly, "White man attack Papequah's band, kill women and children. They have nothing to hide."

Here Bowlegs spoke of the Battle of Dove Creek.

In September of '64, Papequah's band of northern Kickapoo had left their camps in southern Kansas to join Machemanet's band at Nacimiento. Trying to avoid a fight while traveling with their women, children, and old people, the band took a route far to the west, then bent south across the Llano Estacado, the staked plains.

Traveling for months without incident, processing meat and hides for later use, the band reached the Concho River deep in Texas. With only a few days' more journey to the Rio Grande and safety, the band camped in a flat valley bisected by Dove Creek, a small tributary of the Concho.

Unknown to the Kickapoo, Texas Confederate scouts led by Captain N. W. Gillentine had come across their trail. The captain sent the alarm to Confederate regulars and militia units throughout the district. Four hundred

Texans mustered for battle, and on January 8, 1865, a frigid morning, they attacked the peaceful Kickapoo camp. Momentarily stunned by the surprise attack, the Kickapoo recovered quickly, scooped up their weapons, and took to the ravines in back of the village. Defending their women and children with a vengeance born of ancient hatred, they laid down a steady stream of withering counterfire. An hour later the Texans withdrew, leaving behind thirty-four dead, sixty critically wounded, and sixty-five horses shot dead from under their riders. The Kickapoo counted fifteen dead. Of all the Texan and Indian battles, the Battle of Dove Creek was the most stunning defeat the Texans ever suffered. For years to come, no Texan would speak of the Battle of Dove Creek. It was legend in Kickapoo lore.

"They attack you because you take women and children," Boot said.

"That is our way," Bowlegs repeated. "That is our way forever."

"That's not our way," Boot countered. "We got nothing to hide. We leavin' in the morning."

At daybreak Boot and Amos threw their saddles on two rank-broke, long-legged ponies they had bought from the bunch that Wildcat had brought in the day before.

After witnessing the vigor of the animals in the corral, Boot had for the first time looked with distaste at the low-grade horseflesh they rode. Bowlegs had told him, "You buy. Your horse no good. Not fit to eat. You buy."

Now they each owned a splendid twenty-dollar horse.

They were cinching up their saddles when the hoof-falls of a rider came to them, the only activity they had heard that early in the morning. They straightened around and watched him come.

The rider was a Mexican apparently of high standing,

judging by the horse he rode and the clothes he wore. He pulled to a stop at Wildcat's house, and before he could dismount Wildcat emerged.

Directly Cheeno, Nokowhat, and Caballo Blanko joined them. Boot and Amos knew the three to be coup chiefs who had at one time or another in the past seven days raided across the Rio Grande and had returned with horses, cattle, captives, and much else a man could use or sell.

Then they saw Bowlegs emerge from his house and gather the reins of a saddled horse tied under the overhang. Leading the horse, Bowlegs came over to join them.

Bowlegs wore a loose-fitting calico shirt, and for the first time they noticed a holstered pistol on his right side, a scalping knife on the left side, held in a scabbard of fancy beadwork and wide leather that had blond scalp-hair woven into it. On his horse was a saddle without blanket cover, obviously one of the saddles taken from the dead Confederates.

In his new outfit Bowlegs looked no part of the heartless killer he was, yet there was something about him that would warn a man.

"No stealin' today?" Boot asked bluntly.

"Agents come today," Bowlegs answered good-naturedly, and nodded toward the corral where the Mexican who had just ridden in was looking over the stock. "He big man from Santa Rosa." Bowlegs was outwardly proud of the amount of plunder their raids had accumulated and which he was now about to barter off. "Another agent comes from Muzquiz. They buy all."

"The women too?"

"Maybe."

Bowlegs looked critically over the new horses and riggings of Boot and Amos. Satisfied with what he had talked them into buying or trading for, he swung onto the saddle and said approvingly, "Now you have good gun, good horse. Nobody bother you."

"We got nothin' to hide," Boot said again.

"Papequah had nothing to hide," Bowlegs countered again. He put his horse in motion and said conversationally, "Agents finish soon. I get money, go with you."

He trotted his horse away, leaving Boot and Amos standing there, perplexed.

Chapter Eleven

Money was what made her hit the trail at daybreak that morning. And it didn't matter that now the forenoon sun was brutally hot. She was a tall, flat-bosomed, loose-jointed woman, jouncing up and down on the seat of a shabby high-seated wagon, handling the lines much as a man would.

She turned into the wagon road, followed it under the portals to Fort Richardson's parade ground, taking in the flurry of activity.

She was slim, dark-skinned, had on heavy high-topped shoes that made her stand eye-to-eye with most men. Her face was heart-shaped, nose snubbed, eyes luminous, alert.

She pulled the team to a halt alongside the unfinished boardwalk and sat the seat, looking at the men lined up there who had gotten word of the fort's activation and, like her, had come to turn a dollar.

She had no way of knowing it, but these men had

been waiting there at the quartermaster's door since a little bit after sunup, anxious to get first crack at federal dollars. Two were looking to sell hay to the army, one was a beef contractor, and the other three were builders wanting to hire on to assist in putting the fort back in operating order.

She was impatient, anxious to be doing. Waiting wasn't in her nature. She swung down lithely, easy as a man, and, removing her gray bell-crowned hat, slapped trail dust from the dungarees she wore, looking carelessly at the men lined up, a waiting line she had no intention whatsoever of joining.

Striding briskly across the boardwalk, she walked right into the quartermaster's open door, breezing by the restless men waiting there, disregarding their scowls.

Distracted by the sound of approaching footsteps, Sergeant Henessy broke off his sentence to the carpenter he was haggling with and, lifting an angry eye, started to say, "The line—"

"My name's Bertha," the woman said hastily. "I brung some vegetables." She tugged down the handstitched ducking blouse she wore, looking from under lowered eyebrows, watching the sergeant for a reaction.

Henessy was a thirteen-year veteran quartermaster with prior years of service on the harsh frontier. An opportunity for fresh vegetables was not to be passed up. He smiled self-consciously, shoved his chair back, and stood up. "This'll only take a wee minute," he said patronizingly in a heavy Irish brogue, excusing himself from the carpenter.

Outside in back of Bertha's wagon Henessy inspected three bushels of tomatoes, two of cucumbers, and a sack of snap beans.

"Madam," he said breathlessly, "it ain't much for an army, but I'll be pleased to take 'em off your hands."

Back at his desk Henessy wrote out a voucher for the

vegetables and handed it to Bertha. "A pleasure doing business with you, madam," he said beaming. "The paymaster will see that you're properly rewarded for your labors."

Bertha had come out of the paymaster's office next door and was tucking her money away when a man who had just stepped out of Major Sturgis's office asked brusquely, "You! You still livin' in Squaw Valley?"

Bertha looked toward the voice, frowning. She recognized the man right away as Ben Putterman.

Putterman was a wide-chested, solid-built forty-year-old man. He had been a Confederate colonel, the adjutant general on the staff of General Slaughter's Second Texas Cavalry.

In the winter of 1864 Ben had reconciled himself to the eventual defeat of the Confederacy, and through devious means had claimed as much abandoned land as he could lay hands on. Now he was the biggest landowner in Squaw Valley, and had a half-dozen other land titles in his sights.

"Mr. Ben, you know where I live," Bertha said airily.

"Now that you people are free, it's hard to keep track of you." Ben smiled thinly at his own wit. "You tell Old Ned my boys'll be cuttin' hay in that valley," he said seriously. "All the way up to Rocky Hill." He paused, cocked his head critically at Bertha. "You think you can remember all that?" he asked mockingly.

"Rocky Hill? What few cows Mr. Ned got, they's up there."

"My boys said there was some Lazy H critters up there. That's why I'm sendin' Ned word."

"I'll tell 'im," she said, running her gaze up and down the length of Ben's frame, giving him a slow, measuring look. She mounted the wagon seat, took up the lines, and her eyes found Putterman.

141

Putterman smiled arrogantly and said, "You be sure and tell Old Ned what I said."

"Don't you worry none," Bertha said, bristling, "I'll tell 'im." She wheeled the wagon around and lashed the lines, sending the team into a trot.

It was late in the afternoon when she guided the wagon from the valley floor and angled up toward the ranch house. From the distance she caught sight of Ned sitting in his crude rush-bottomed chair on the front porch of the semi-dugout log cabin.

Ned Huelen had been too old for conscription when the late unpleasantness broke out. He had sat out the war dodging the confiscatory grasp of Confederate quartermasters, fighting off marauding Indians, and scratching after hard money to keep possession of a hardscrabble, down-at-the-heels ranching operation that could show but few beeves with his Lazy H brand on them. And last year his brother in Virginia had unexpectedly dumped four slaves in his lap for safekeeping. His once-solid, medium-built frame was now hewed down by age and years of frontier struggle to no more than a hundred and thirty pounds of leathery skin, aching bones, and deep wrinkles.

At the sight of Bertha, Ned drew his thin shoulders up and waved a hand, acknowledging her safe return, which he had been worrying about.

Bertha was walking across the yard from the hay barn where she had parked the wagon when Ned's impatience overcame him. "Any trouble, Gal?" he asked as she advanced toward him.

"Not with sellin'," she answered pleasantly. Ned had inoffensively called her Gal from the first. Now between the two of them the old man used the name fondly. "Army's buyin' most anythin'."

"Did you git a fair price?"

"Nineteen dollars for the whole lot." She sat down

on the porch next to him. Looking out over the valley, she said disappointedly, factually, "Nineteen dollars ain't even close to that two hundred and fifty dollars we need. If them Comanches have to keep Berry alive for ransom much longer, they might want more."

"Comanche always have wanted two hundred and fifty dollars' ransom for a youngster. That brother of your'n ain't no different."

"It'll take forever to git that much money."

"Y'all just got to be patient and stash away what you git." Ned scratched at the stubby gray beard on his seamed face. "Army buyin' most everything, huh?"

"Yeah, suh. Hay and everything. Mr. Ben says he's cutting in the valley all the way to Rocky Hill."

"Rocky Hill!" Ned came forward in his chair. "Did you tell 'em I got cows there?"

"I told 'im. He said he 'specked you did. He's goin' to cut anyhow."

Ned tightened his sunken jaws and said, "Putterman's pushed me ever since he come to this valley. By damn, I ain't too old to push back."

Bertha looked at Ned, and Ned said grudgingly, "Well, maybe I am too old to push back anymore." Ned's tireless strength of years ago had been used up. He sagged his shoulders to the back of the chair and asked resignedly, "Army buyin' beef?"

"And salt. The man there said they'd buy all the salt that's hauled in."

"Salt?" He gazed out over the yard, his mind thinking back. "I know where there's salt for the takin' if a man ain't fearful of goin' to git it."

"Where?"

"Injun country. I was out there long before y'all come here. In 1857, Indians struck Henry Putterman's horse herd. Henry was the father of Ben.

"Anyhow, Henry hightailed it over here to raise a scout. Me and some of the boys joined up. We trailed them Injuns for two whole days. The third day we come up on 'em that mornin' in a creek bed feedin' on one of Henry's horses. We killed three of 'em and the rest lit out.

"We buried one of our own out there. He had took an arrow clean through the windpipe. A feller named George Streeter.

"We rounded up the horses and started back. Trouble was, we was all pretty nigh out of water. Henry, he paired us up to keep an eye out for water. First ones to come up on water was to fire a shot. Me and Jim, Moccasin Jim, we found the water. Henry and McCoy, they found the salt."

Ned's old eyes twinkled at the memory. "That lake bed warn't nothin' but salt. Most of it a man could scoop out with his hands, but then there was some you'd have to dig down for. We brung back as much we could haul on our saddles. Salt was always hard to come by out here."

"You reckon there's still some out there?"

"I 'speck so. There was aplenty there then."

"Was you to show me where it is, I'd git some. Salt is sho' to bring good money."

"Like I said, it's in Injun country. It'd be a chancy thing. Nothin' out there but rattlesnakes and Injuns. 'Course, if the army's buyin' there'll be a lotta men out lookin'. They'd likely fight you for it. And I wouldn't be much help to you."

"I got to git more money, and there ain't no other way."

"How long y'all been here now, Gal?" Ned asked thoughtfully. "Nigh six months now, ain't it?"

Bertha lowered her head, studying the ground in front of her. "Seems like longer than that."

"I 'speck it would." Ned studied his shabby outbuildings and sagging corrals. "I guess this place ain't much set against my brother's."

"Don't matter, Mr. Ned. We's here."

"Your brother taken by Injuns and all is partly my fault. I can't change what's happened, but I'll see you git salt to sell to ransom him back."

"In the mornin'?"

"Sunup," Ned said. "We'll leave at sunup."

At sunup they rode out of Squaw Valley. Topping out on the humpback of Rocky Hill, they headed the wagon west and a little bit south. The black woman handled the lines; the old white man sat the seat at her side, his heavy old-style Remington pistol strapped on for the first time in a long time, and his .45 Creedmore Sharps rifle leaning on the seat next to him.

In back of the wagon were two shovels and an ax, a lashed-down barrel of water and a ragged tarpaulin. Ned's saddle was in back, his old range pony trailing alongside the team. "There's plenty of game out there and good graze for the animals," Ned had said, spurning the grub Bertha wanted to prepare. "Only trouble we likely to run into is with Injuns and maybe other salt hunters."

"And findin' the salt," Bertha retorted.

"We'll find the salt, Gal. Don't you worry none about that."

The land they rode was undulating prairie of mesquite grass broken here and there by rocky upthrusts and shallow depressions. The way they made was guided by Ned's vague memory.

They crossed over the main Brazos and late in the afternoon they struck the Clear Fork of the Brazos. Bertha pulled the team to a halt, and they sat the seat looking out at the band of muddy-red water fringed by stunted willow trees. "As I recollect, river all along here warn't no trouble for a horse to cross."

"Don't see no place to," Bertha said, ranging her gaze up and down the rank of willows growing along the low bank.

"That's what we brung the ax for," Ned said, and swung down.

An hour later, Bertha plunged the team through the opening they had chopped through willow saplings. She angled the wagon toward the far bank, Ned's saddle pony splashing alongside. Ned pointed out a likely spot, and she guided the team through young saplings and overhanging branches, lashed them up the sandy bank, and came to a rolling stop on top of the shallow mesa. "That was a fair piece of work, Gal," Ned said delightedly.

"Horses did the work, Mr. Ned," Bertha replied tersely.

They sat, straining their eyes westward at the sweep of rolling prairie studded with sage brush and tumbleweeds, rocky outcroppings and mesquite. "Don't see nothin' that looks like salt," said Bertha.

"It's out there," Ned said confidently. "It'll be another day before we come up on it, though. We best camp here for the night. No use lettin' sundown catch us out in the open." Ned dismounted the wagon with an effort and, reaching back for his rifle, said, "I'll scout the creek for meat. You unhitch the team and put together a fire."

Bertha swung her feet to the wagon wheel and jumped down, landing catlike. "You want me to go for meat?" she asked excitedly. "Wudn't be no trouble."

"You figure to throw rocks at the game?" Ned asked, looking across the wagon at her. "Or learn how to shoot on the spot?"

"I already know how to shoot."

"I figured you did," Ned said bluntly. He came around the tailgate and retrieved his saddle gear. "I ain't so far gone in my old age I can't hunt meat." When he had saddled his horse, he stopped to catch his wind before mounting with care. He swung his horse into the wagon tracks and headed back to the willow thickets. At the lip of the mesa he said over his shoulder, "I won't be long. See the horses get water, then stake 'em out."

She built a fire of mesquite roots and swung the makings for a pot of stew over it.

The red flare of sun was halfway down behind the horizon when the boom of Ned's big gun jolted the prairie.

The sun vanished completely. The lemon light of coming darkness had spread over the prairie when Ned rode in. He undid the thongs and dropped the young deer to the ground from behind the cantle of his saddle. He swung down heavily, his old bones almost creaking aloud.

"Coffee's ready," Bertha told him. "I fixed a place for you yonder." And she pointed at the thick pallet she had made up.

Ned straightened his back, working the kinks out. "I can see to myself. You start on this here meat I nearly kilt myself gittin' us."

Darkness came. A bright moon lit up the prairie. Sagebrush and mesquite bushes showed as dark patches on the land, the willows along the river a dark band that stretched off into blackness. The flames of the campfire danced a jig, heating up venison stew. Crickets chirped in the willows, and from somewhere along the river bottom a bullfrog croaked a mating call.

Bertha fussed over the makings for supper at the tailgate of the wagon. Ned sat on the tarp, propped back on his saddle, sipping coffee and gnawing at the biscuit that

147

Bertha had given him. He broke the silence: "Boot's the one that learnt you how to shoot."

"You knowed?"

"I knowed. A man has a feel when somebody's messed with his gun. Cartridges was missin' too."

"You never said nothin'."

"It wouldn't have mattered. Boot's had his way ever since he got here. Don't know how he carried on with my brother, but I 'speck he was the same." Ned paused, thinking, then said, "I let it go 'cause I kinda figured y'all would be free soon, and anybody in this country better know how to shoot." He stole a look at her. " 'Course, that's if y'all decide to stay now that you're free to go."

"We ain't talked on that yet." Bertha went over and methodically stirred the stew. "Mr. Ned, Papa said you didn't want us when we first come here."

"Your papa was right. I never saw the right in ownin' another man. 'Course, there was some that did."

"Like Mr. James?"

"Yeah, like my brother James." Ned reached out his empty coffee cup to Bertha and continued talking as she came to get it. "I 'speck the South is all wrought up now that they been licked."

She took the cup from Ned and on the way back to the tailgate said, "Miss Sue Ellen was wrought up when she sent us here."

"James's wife?" Ned scoffed. "I'd lay you odds she had no say in it. That was all my brother's doin'. And knowing how I felt, he had to be plenty wrought up to send you to me."

Bertha moved over to the stewpot and dished up two plates. While Ned scooped and wolfed his food, she sat on the tailgate, picking at her own. Directly, Ned said through a mouthful of food, "You reckon Boot'll come back with enough money?"

"Yeah, suh. Boot usually do what he sets out to do. He even gits mad when somebody else don't do what they said they was goin' to do. Papa was the same way."

"I noticed that," Ned said, deadpan. "You the same way too," he added curtly. Ned's spoon scraped over the bottom of the empty tin plate, and he drew the last spoonful to his mouth, then reached the plate out to Bertha.

Cleaning his hands on his pant leg, he said confidently, "Come sunup, we'll strike out. I figure them salt flats to be no more 'n six, seven hours from here." He leaned back in the crook of his saddle and stared up at the starry night. After a while, he asked, "Gal, that brother of your'n what's in the army, where you reckon he's at?"

"I don't know, Mr. Ned. Boot don't neither." She paused, then added, "Boot said if Bodie ain't layin' dead somewheres, he'll find us."

Chapter Twelve

In the morning they broke camp while the sky was still a lemon canopy tinged orange in the east. The air was still, the rush of the river but a slight rustle.

Two hours later, Bertha guided the wagon out of a sandy, sagebrush-studded depression and angled up the hogbacked salient on the other side, turning her eyes toward the distant horizon.

As far as the eye could see the land swept away gently to the west, and nothing broke the landscape except the scatter of low tumbleweeds and sagebrush.

"Don't look like it, but there's dry washes and gulleys all through there," Ned commented. "Water's scarce, though."

"The barrel's full and the horses drunk their fill," Bertha replied.

"Out there where that salt's at, the horses might or might not drink the brine water. Some of 'em would just as soon die of thirst first."

They moved on westward. The parallel wagon tracks stretched behind them like two strands of thread laid out on a tabletop. It was very hot; not a breath of wind stirred; not a bird flew in the sky; not an insect moved. The only sounds that could be heard were the jingle of trace chains and the squish of wagon wheels cutting through sand.

After three more hours Ned had piloted the wagon up to a north–south-running sand bed that had obviously been an ancient river. Years of eroded sand and gravel had lifted its bottom to no more than two feet below the prairie. "We'll let the horses catch their wind here," Ned said. "That salt ain't far from here. A mile or so down yonder," he pointed south, "is where Henry and McCoy found the water."

"Salt that way too?"

"Naw," Ned said, dismounting from the wagon. "Salt's an hour, maybe a little more, out cross yonder." Ned scanned westward, then brought his gaze back to bear on Bertha, who had dismounted. "This's as good a place as any to noon. While you're at it, I'll saddle up and scout a ways west."

Bertha lifted her flopped hat from her forehead and, wiping sweat from her brow, commented, "Ain't no shade nowhere."

"Ain't none out yonder neither, Gal," Ned said factually. "Sun gits to beatin' ya down, crawl under the wagon."

Bertha unhitched the trace chains and dropped the wagon tongue, easing the load on the animals. From the tailgate of the wagon she retrieved an armful of firewood that she had gathered that morning. She dropped the wood at the chosen spot and lifted her eyes after Ned. Far off across the sand flats she could see his back moving away from her.

Bertha was squatting over the firewood, coaxing a

wisp of smoke into flame, when she first heard the rattle of pebbles. She canted her head, peaked her ears, and brought her eyes to bear north up the riverbed.

Without a doubt the sound was that of hoofs crunching sand and gravel, scattering loose pebbles.

Bertha leaped to her feet, her eyes flared wide.

An Indian came toward her, his pony at a walk. And behind him another Indian, then another . . . and others! A dozen Indians rode boldly into view. They were armed but not painted. Her heart caught, raced ahead, throbbing heavily.

She stood stock-still, stiff-legged.

The leader rode his horse majestically, his Winchester resting across his blanket-covered saddlebows.

Bertha had no way of knowing that the leader was Wildcat, a southern Kickapoo. Wildcat was six feet tall, compact, solidly built and powerful. He weighed about one-ninety, and looked every ounce of it.

Approaching his fortieth year of ranging high deserts and wind-swept prairie, he was a tough, experienced leader, now leading this mixed band of marauders.

His straight black hair hung back over his shoulder, tied in place by a two-inch rawhide band. Stolid of features and vicious in nature, Wildcat was a talked-about and feared man in the settlements. The number of his renegade followers fluctuated with his chances of success. The dozen fighting men with him now were all tribal malcontents without affiliation or loyalty.

He checked his black-splashed pony to a halt at the tailgate of the wagon, and the file behind him came to a walking halt. Wildcat's experienced eyes carefully inspected the contents of the wagon, then shifted to Bertha.

"Where you go?" he asked in slow, deliberate English.

"Salt," Bertha said, swallowing nervously. "We lookin' for salt!" Her voice quavered slightly.

Wildcat hesitated, unsure of Bertha's meaning. The Indian behind him interpreted: "Sal . . . sal ah-ray-nah." He pointed to the west.

The Indian who had spoken was six feet tall, weighed about two hundred, none of it fat. He had on blue army pants he'd taken off a dead soldier stuffed inside long moccasins, his breechcloth covering the seat of the pants. Above the waist he was bare, showing big biceps and heavy chest muscles. A deerskin headband held down long, frizzled hair. Other Indians knew him simply as Bowlegs, a Seminole-Negro from the Nation.

Wildcat's eyes had scrutinized Bertha all the while. Now he asked dispassionately, "White man your man?"

"Naw."

"Why you no go? Why you no run away?"

"He's not my master, he's my friend."

"White man no friend," Bowlegs interrupted. "White man lie, cheat . . . no good," he added harshly.

Bertha remained silent at the accusations.

For a long minute Wildcat's and Bertha's eyes held. She could read nothing in his face; he saw the fear in hers, just below the surface. Amused, he silently kneed his horse forward past her. She swallowed the nervous lump in her throat. The Indians behind him began to move. Bowlegs rode silently past her, craning his neck around, eyeing her approvingly. "You got man?" he asked.

Bertha left the question unanswered. She stood in her tracks, speechless, taking in Bowlegs walking his horse away from her, still twisted back looking her over. Ten other Indians—five Kickapoos, four Kiowas, and one Apache—filed past her, gazing curiously. She turned and watched the last one ride away.

It was at least three hours past noon when Bertha heard hoof-falls from across the prairie sands. She crawled from under the wagon where she had taken shade, and stood watching Ned come toward her.

"You find it?" she yelled out across the prairie when Ned was some yards off.

"I found it." Ned checked his horse at the tailgate of the wagon. "It was right where I thought it'd be."

"How far?"

"Two, three hours by wagon." Ned swung down with effort and loosened his saddle girths, talking all the while. "Seen fresh Injun sign."

"Some Injuns come by here," Bertha said calmly.

Ned froze, the saddle he had stripped off held in his two hands. "They see you?"

"They seen me."

"You sho'?"

"Yeah, suh. They talked to me awhile, then rode on down thataway."

Ned looked where Bertha had indicated. "Well, if that don't beat all. Wonder you ain't dead, or worse." Ned hefted his saddle and blanket in back of the wagon, then tied his horse to the tailgate. "No use 'n us takin' chances. We better git the salt and light out."

They wasted no time in loading the camp equipment. Bertha shook the lines and clucked the team west across the sand. Presently Bertha asked, "How come they didn't bother me?"

"If I'd been there, they likely would've."

"They knowed you was here. Knowed you was a white man, too."

"Ain't no accountin' for it, then," said Ned. "Injun's a mighty notional fellow," Ned explained, "but he mostly got reasons. He'll kill ya for no reason or he'll leave ya alone, just depends."

"They killed Papa for no reason."

"They knowed he had somethin' worthwhile in that freight wagon."

They rolled westward in silence, each puzzling at the seemingly whimsical nature of the Indian.

The salt flats lay between two sandhills where decades before water had coursed through two adjacent hogbacks, joining the waters of the Colorado River. Rainfall had steadily declined over the years and the water had become first stagnant, then had evaporated completely, leaving behind mineral deposits.

Bertha guided the wagon up the gentle slope of the hogback and topped out. Suddenly Ned reached over and grabbed the lines. "Hold it, Gal!"

He fixed his eyes southward down the long depression, and Bertha's eyes followed his. "Somebody's beat us here!" Ned exclaimed.

At something like a hundred yards away, two wagons stood parked on the salt flats. Each wagon had obviously been loaded with salt and covered with a tarp. But nobody was in sight, and no animals were present, just two wagons standing alone.

Ned grew uneasy.

"There's trouble down there," he stated at length, reaching for his rifle. "Go in easy-like," he instructed Bertha, searching the surroundings.

Bertha closed to within fifty yards of the wagons. And they both saw the bodies. Two men were sprawled on the sand behind the first wagon. Another man was tied in a sitting position to the spokes of the second wagon, his legs pegged apart. His body had been charred black by a torture fire that still smoldered between his spread legs. His blackened skin was cracked, peeled up; hundreds of blisters oozed clear fluid, pussed over already.

Bertha walked the team up, stopped near the first wagon, her nose turned up at the ugly sight, fighting back a vile feeling in her stomach.

"Injuns," said Ned, taking in the many unshod pony tracks. "And plenty of 'em, too."

They dismounted, and Ned looked closer. The first dead man had been struck by six bullets he could count, all through the body. "They put up what fight they could," he commented, looking over the battlefield.

The other dead man had only one wound, a smashed cheek where a bullet had entered and exploded out the other side of his face. He was probably the first to die, Ned figured.

Bertha looked around, wide-eyed. "You reckon they'll come back?" she asked.

"Them same ones won't, but others might."

Quickly she retrieved a shovel. "Let's git the salt and git out of here."

"Might be we can save ourselves some trouble, Gal."

"How?"

Ned dropped the tarp of the first wagon that he had been looking inside. "Wagon's already loaded. These poor devils got no use for salt now."

"Our horses can't pull these big freight wagons," she stated at Ned's back even as he hurried off down the flats.

Thirty yards away, Ned found the shallow pit he knew all knowing men out there dug for their animals. The pit had about six inches of water in it that had seeped up through the sand.

Hurrying back to where Bertha waited, Ned told her, "If I got it figured right, them Injuns drove off eight, ten animals."

"They mighta kept 'em."

"Ain't likely. They was passin' through comin' from the Nation headin' to Mexico. They'll git good animals over there. Only way they'd keep these was if they was headin' back to the Nation."

"You goin' out to look for 'em?"

"Won't have to. Down yonder is a dug trough them animals drunk from." Ned looked up, checking the position of the sun. "They'll come back here come sundown."

"What if they don't?"

"We'll load our wagon just in case."

It was sundown by the time they had shoveled the wagon full of salt and had stretched the tarp over it. It was pitch-dark when they unhitched the team and staked them out at the dug water trough. They settled belly-flat under the wagon for cover. Ned had his Creedmore rifle craned out to the east, his ears reaching out for sounds of approaching Indians. Bertha was stretched out canted toward the south, her eyes fixed on the dug water hole.

It was quiet, very quiet. Their horses at the water hole had drunk tentatively. Now one blew and pawed distastefully at the briny water; the other wallowed in the cool, damp sand.

The moon appeared in the cloudless sky, and together with the stars threw a bright glow over the salt flats.

Time passed slowly.

"Mr. Ned," Bertha whispered.

Ned twisted his head around to face her.

"Horses comin'."

"How many?"

"Can't say."

They crawled out from under the wagon and Ned cautioned softly, "We got to do this careful-like, Gal. We don't want to spook 'em. Let's git our horses first and lead 'em to where them other horses are at. Then, whilst they's all drinkin', we'll gather up the bunch."

Two by two they secured the dead men's horses to a tether rope Ned had devised between the wagons.

It was late in the night by the time they had hitched the new horses to the two freight wagons, which were bigger and better than Ned's old wagon.

They drove away from the salt flats with Ned's own two horses tied behind the wagon he now drove, his saddle horse trotting alongside. His old wagon was left standing on the flats, loaded with salt. Also, three dead men lay back there in hastily dug shallow graves.

They jounced east through sagebrush and tumbleweeds under the glow of moonlight, Ned in the lead. To their left the polestar guided them like a beacon. Again all they heard was the steady jangle of trace chains and the swish of wheels cutting through sand. Occasionally Ned looked over his shoulder to see how Bertha was holding out.

The moon swung overhead and dipped at their backs. Tumbleweeds and sagebrush gave way to mesquite grass and stunted mesquite trees.

An hour later, Ned pulled to a halt atop the shallow mesa overlooking the cut in the willows they had made yesterday at the bank of the Clear Fork of the Brazos.

Bertha pulled her wagon up alongside.

"I'll feel my way across," Ned told her. "You follow close behind me."

"I oughta take the lead. I remembers the way I come yesterday."

"I seen the way you come," Ned said gruffly. "Besides, these wagons a lot heavier than mine was. You stay close behind me. If I hit a sinkhole, you strike out on your own."

Ned shook the lines and guided his wagon through the willow cut, Bertha following close on his tailgate.

The heavy wagons cut deep into the sandy shore. They made it to the other side without incident but not without a scare. Once Ned's left front wheel plunged below the axle into a sinkhole. Bertha had to guide her wagon around his on the other side as Ned lashed his team unmercifully before they summoned enough strength to pull the heavy wagon out.

It was daylight when they finally reached the other shore, Bertha in the lead now. Her team slogged through loose sand, completely exhausted. She lashed them through the willow cut, pulled to a halt at the spot where they had stopped the day before, and waited for Ned.

"Team's beat," Ned announced when he came up. "We'll have to rest 'em here."

"They ain't the only ones beat," Bertha replied.

They slept, rested some, then slept some more. It was late that afternoon before they pulled onto the parade ground at Fort Richardson. They guided the wagons alongside the boardwalk running in front of the quartermaster's office and stopped, looking around.

Everywhere men worked at construction of one kind or another. Other men were queued up in front of the office in search of army jobs and business.

Ned lifted his aged body wearily and, dismounting the wagon, said, "Come on, Gal, let's see if the army wants this here salt."

"They want it," Bertha stated.

Inside the quartermaster's office Sergeant Henessy shifted his eyes from the man he was talking to there at the desk, and asked Ned, with his eyes on Bertha: "Vegetables?"

"Salt," Ned answered.

"This'll only take a wee minute," Henessy said, begging off from the other man. Following them outside, Henessy made conversation with Ned: "And who might you be?"

"Name's Ned . . . Ned Huelen. Got a small spread a ways up Squaw Valley."

"I've had the pleasure of seeing Squaw Valley, and a beautiful valley it is," Henessy said effusively.

At the tailgate of the wagon Ned lifted up the tarp and gave Henessy a look.

The big sergeant took a pinch of salt between his fingers and drew it to his tongue, assaying its quality. His face registered approval, and he said lavishly, "A bargain is to be had. The army has to feed itself.''

Ned and Bertha exchanged looks, Bertha smiling broadly.

Back inside at his desk, Henessy gave Ned a voucher. ''The paymaster will see that you're properly rewarded for your labors,'' he said, beaming.

''Somethin' the army oughta know,'' said Ned.

''And what might that be?''

''We found three dead men where we got the salt from.''

''Injuns?''

''I'd guess eight . . . ten. They put up a fight but was too outnumbered. One man tortured.''

The man sitting at the desk overheard the conversation. Now he interrupted, asking, ''White men?''

''All of 'em,'' said Ned.

''Any idea who they were?''

''One of 'em was T. J. Harper. Don't know who the other two was.''

''I knowed Harper,'' the man said, surprised. ''He freighted in and out of Weatherford for Mr. Putterman.''

''He's freighted his last. Me and Gal here buried him and two others out yonder on the salt flats.''

''The army will see that the savages are properly dealt with,'' Henessy said forcefully. ''On your way out, if you'll kindly take a wee bit of time to stop by the provost's office, he'd be pleased to take your report.''

At the paymaster's office they redeemed the voucher, collecting a hundred and eighty dollars for two tons of impure salt. Walking along the boardwalk back to the wagons, Ned commented, ''Gal, that brother of your'n was to come up with cash money like you got, you'd be sittin' mighty pretty.''

''He'll git his share,'' Bertha stated.

''Can't say I doubt it.''

"How'd you know one of them men was T. J. Harper?"

"It's writ on the side of them wagons. It's mostly washed out now, but it's there."

"I never seen it."

"That sergeant did."

They parked the wagons around back at the quartermaster's provisions shed and made their way to the provost's office.

Thirty minutes later they had given the provost their report, such as it was, and were back at the empty wagons.

"We goin' to keep these wagons, Mr. Ned?" Bertha asked.

"I don't reckon Mr. T. J. Harper's got any use for 'em now," Ned commented. They each climbed onto a wagon seat, then they wheeled out, heading for Squaw Valley.

No more than an hour after they had gone, two men rode through the gate to the fort. They checked their horses to a walk, looking over the fort's layout. "This is as good a place as any to ask around," one man said to the other. They reined their horse over to the hitchrail in front of the quartermaster's office and swung down leisurely.

The man who had spoken was about six feet tall and narrow-shouldered. He had on batwing chaps over black dungarees, and a khaki waist-jacket over a blue cotton shirt. A six-shooter was belted around his waist. The other man was well under six feet but was stocky. He wore the usual range clothes, and he too was armed.

The tall man led the way into Henessy's office. At the desk he pushed back his black high-crowned hat and started to take off a work glove.

Henessy looked out of the corner of his eye at them

and said, "If you'll kindly wait your turn, I'll be obliged to—"

"Name's Harper," the man interrupted, "Pony Harper. I got urgent business."

"What might your business be, Mr. Harper?" Henessy asked patiently.

"Two days ago, Mr. Putterman sent out two wagons to locate salt for you army boys. Wagons ain't back yet. Mr. Putterman's wantin' answers."

"You'll kindly tell Mr. Putterman there's bad news."

Harper exchanged glances with his partner, Jim Cardine, and Cardine asked harshly, "What kinda bad news?"

Henessy stiffened his jaws and said disgustedly, "Injuns! The savages struck again!" Henessy relaxed his face and said with relish, "It'll be a glorious day when the army puts a stop to their murderin' ways."

"Any survivors?" asked Pony.

"Nary a one," Henessy said, shaking his head sadly. "The provost can give you details such as I don't have."

When the two men came out of the provost's office, they paused at their horses. Harper looked pallid, grim-faced.

From the provost they had gotten details of the Indian attack out on the salt flats, including the name of the man who had buried the bodies and had brought in the salt wagons.

Cardine looked over his shoulder at Pony and said, "The boss ain't gonna like this."

"It don't sit right with me neither," Pony stated. "That story sounds mighty fishy to me. Ain't nothin' to say Old Ned didn't kill 'em hisself for the salt."

"The idea crossed my mind too," Jim confessed.

Struck by anger, Pony grabbed hold of his saddle horn and lifted a toe into the stirrup. "I'll be right interested to hear what Old Ned's got to say for hisself."

"The boss'll want to know first," Jim cautioned, swinging onto his saddle.

"The boss'll get his due, but I'm the one who's got a dead brother buried out yonder. If Ned needs killin' over this, I'll see it gits done."

Pony Harper and Jim Cardine both knew that unpleasant news was best delivered to Ben ahead of gossip, else Ben's queer temper would lash out. They put their horses under lash and spur, hurrying the news to him at Gulch.

Chapter Thirteen

Pony Harper and Jim Cardine ran their horses away from Fort Richardson, going the mile or so into Gulch, leaving a trail of red dust lingering on the air.

Gulch was a small ranching settlement west of the fort on the military road that led from Fort Smith to Fort Belknap and points farther west. The town was a place where farmers and ranchers converged to buy staples and implements, to sell produce, and to deal in beef. The late war had dried up the town's economy, but now that the dispute had ended, townspeople fully expected a revitalizing burst of economic life from the new fort.

Harper and Cardine raced their horses down the middle of the street, scattering freedmen, drawing scowls from those strolling on each side. The lines of dust the two kicked up ended in front of the Bull Head Saloon, fell back to earth as they brought their horses to a running stop at the hitchrail.

Heading into the saloon, Pony Harper stopped at the

batwings and looked back. He swept the boardwalk with his eyes, taking in the throng of black faces in town. In his mind there simply was no living with this; something had to be done, Harper figured.

Those scot-free niggers ate at him, diminished his standing. And he wanted to do something about it.

He pushed through the batwings, veered off to the bar that ran along the side wall. "Beer!" he barked at Bill Holly, the walrus-mustached bartender.

"What's the matter, Pony? All them niggers out there make you nervous?" Holly chided.

"Yeah. Nervous enough to make me want to bust some skulls." Scowling at Holly, he added, "You just draw two beers and keep your trap shut."

Holly chuckled with twisted pleasure at Pony's irritation. "That new governor they put in, Governor Throckmorton, he was a Union man. The work them niggers used to do, you boys likely be doin' it now." Holly grinned at his own words. Moving off, he asked casually over his shoulder, jabbing at Pony one more time, "You payin' or tabbin' Mr. Putterman?"

"Holly, I ain't in the mood for your smart-mouthin'. For two cents I'd break my pistol over your head."

"It wouldn't do no good, Pony," Holly said from down the bar. "It ain't my fault the niggers on top now." He set the beers on the countertop, looking amusedly at Jim Cardine.

Cardine took a sip from his beer, lowered the mug, wiped frost from his lips, and said, "No decent white man in his right mind likes what's happenin'. There's got to be changes."

"Pony!" a loud voice called from over in the corner.

Pony drew up attentively, the half-empty mug frozen on the way to his lips. He shifted his eyes toward the curtained-off nook where the voice had come from.

"Pony!" the voice boomed out again.

There was no doubt in Pony's or Jim's mind who the voice belonged to. They tossed off the last of their beers in one quick gulp, then hurried toward the voice.

They stepped around the curtain and drew up stiff-backed, face-to-face with Ben Putterman.

Putterman withdrew the thick cigar from between his teeth, his eyes flaring angrily. "You boys do your drinkin' on your own time! What about them salt wagons I sent you to find out about?"

"They ain't comin' back, boss."

"Why the hell not!"

"Injuns."

"Injuns? Who said?"

Pony related to Putterman the story he had heard of the Indian attack on the salt wagons. Putterman listened with keen interest and, when Pony finished, asked with a curious edge to his voice, "Old Ned, huh? You figure the story's doctored up?"

"Doctored up or not, my brother's dead. Ned's the one who brung in them wagons. If his story don't stand up, he'll answer for it."

Ben narrowed his eyes at Pony. "Nobody'll answer to nothin' unless I say so!" he said sharply. "And I ain't sayin' so. You leave Ned alone, you hear?"

"You mean I ain't to do nothin' about it?"

"You'll do somethin' about it when I say so. And I ain't sayin' so right now." Putterman calmed down some, then added mildly, "There's plenty of time to take care of Ned. Right now there's bigger fish to fry. You boys go on out and finish your drinkin'. Tell Holly to set 'em up."

Ben pulled on his high-crowned, side-creased Stetson and went outside on the boardwalk. He paused, exhaled a rich plume of cigar smoke, scowling out at the displeasing street scene he had come to detest.

Everywhere he looked were black men, their coming

and going unhampered by white men, each black man's work, or lack thereof, a matter of his own choosing. And as far as Ben and other white men were concerned, the lack of work was the rub.

In Ben's mind, and in the minds of many other white people, free black people in their midst was an insult, a disgrace beyond the pale. The thought of these people managing for themselves, moving over the country without being watched, was unacceptable. The practice simply had to be crushed, smashed in its infancy before it took hold, Ben figured. The business with the salt wagons could wait.

With a quick motion Ben shoved the cigar between his teeth and clamped down on it firmly. He took off at a fast walk down the boardwalk, weaving out of close proximity to black men. Four doors down, next to the newspaper office, he pushed through the belled door to the land office. The door banged shut behind him, unleashing a flurry of sharp jangles.

District Land Commissioner Henry Parker looked over his desk from under a green visor through horn-rimmed glasses, his face expressionless, his mind trying to think of a reason why Putterman had come. They exchanged greetings, then Ben made light conversation. "Town's swamped with niggers. Ain't hardly room for a white man to move around."

"It's been this way ever since the nineteenth of June when General Granger got off that damn Yankee boat in Galveston and told them they was free," Parker said disgustedly.

"Now that we ain't got slaves to do our labors it's sure to cripple us, if not ruin us completely," Putterman said. "Most of my land is layin' idle, goin' to wilderness while good labor is goin' to waste."

"That's a fact. No white man can last this way," Parker said.

"Won't have to. If I know them boys at the statehouse, we'll have our niggers back before long."

Parker was shocked at the thought. "Slaves again!" he gasped. "You're crazy! The federal government wouldn't stand for it."

"Not exactly slaves. Black Codes, they're callin 'em. Soon as they come down, them sluggards you see out yonder won't be around. They'll be put to work or run out of town. And any young'uns old enough will be apprenticed out."

"It's high time they send down them codes, then. The land'll be wilderness before long."

Ben softened his tone, said conversationally, "Speakin' of land, did you check on Old Ned's like I asked you to?"

Parker switched his eyes from side to side as if the room had ears, then said confidentially, "Like most folks, the war threw him in debt. He's mortgaged to the hilt. Ain't paid taxes since before the war."

Putterman smiled knowingly. "He come into one hundred and eighty dollars from salt. That ain't likely to bail him out, is it?"

"Not by a long shot. He's delinquent close to two thousand dollars."

Now Putterman's suspicions had been confirmed. He left the commissioner's office, a satisfied glow on his face. Outside on the boardwalk he paused, idly fingering coins in his pocket, his right hand holding the heavy cigar in his teeth, his eyes taking in the languid, unenterprising look of the town now that freedmen had started hanging around all the time.

But Putterman was satisfied. Things were falling into place. Just as he had thought, the right man could prosper in these chaotic times. The fact that a man had been on the wrong side of the late war need not be a hindrance if he played his hand smoothly, quietly.

Now all he had to do was wait for the enactment of the Black Codes Governor Throckmorton was poised to sign into law and he'd have all the coerced labor he needed to make profitable his present landholdings and others he was working craftily to acquire.

He blew a satisfied stream of smoke out toward the street.

A week later, Putterman was standing in front of the station when the Butterfield stage came through Gulch and dropped off a bundle of *The Ledger,* the weekly newspaper from Austin. On the front page of the top paper the headline screamed: NEW BLACK CODES!

Putterman worked the top paper from the bundle and hurried off to his saloon office. In the quiet of his nook amid foul odors of stale beer, tobacco smoke, and heavy perfume, he read with relish the new laws. On the second reading he licked his lips at the prospects opened up by the contract labor law: Laborers who desired to contract their services for periods longer than thirty days must record the contract before magistrates and witnesses.

Putterman knew this statute cleverly undercut the authority of the Freedmen's Bureau. And that's exactly what he and other prominent white men had been clamoring for.

But just now the last code had more immediate importance for Putterman. It declared: "Anybody convicted of vagrancy shall pay a fine of ten dollars, or work at a dollar a day until the fine is paid off."

Putterman put his cigar between his teeth and rose, gingerly folding up the paper that had brought him the news he hoped to build a fortune on.

Weaving his way through dusky, ill-clad freedmen, he ducked into the open door of the sheriff's office.

Sheriff Roy Willis looked up from the newspaper he had been reading and swung around to face Putterman.

"You seen the new laws, Roy?" Putterman asked.

"I seen 'em. Fact is, I've already talked to the mayor about 'em. Tryin' to figure out what it all means."

"They're plain as day. Come the first of the month you're to clear the town of shiftless niggers. Them that ain't got work, you've got to put to work on somebody's place."

"Law's clear on that part, all right. The question me and the mayor is wantin' an answer for is how in Judas' name am I goin' to do it. There ain't but one of me, you know."

Putterman relaxed, said offhandedly, "I figured you'd be needin' help. I might be able to chip in along those lines."

"Who'd you have in mind?"

"Pony."

"Pony Harper?"

"The way I figure it, you could use him as a sort of unofficial deputy. Like I told the mayor, it wouldn't cost the town nothin' and he'd be under your orders. And there's other hands at the ranch to draw on if need be."

So Pony Harper, Jim Cardine, and three other ranch hands rode under cover of law.

In late July, under sweltering heat, Gulch's main street billowed with dust kicked up by scurrying feet of freed men and women, dodging trampling hoofs and the swinging clubs of Sheriff Willis and his men. Any act by blacks of disrespect, insolence, or idleness, real or perceived, brought on assault. And any man, woman, or child of age unable to show proof of employment was considered a vagrant and jailed, or hired out for labor. Ben Putterman got his share of those hired out.

By the first of August, Gulch had been cleared of freedmen. Those who had escaped forced labor had hidden out in makeshift shacks thrown up in prairie gulleys and oak hollows. A town of crude shacks of the most miserable sort came into existence across the prairie near the fort for army protection. Only the most courageous of blacks dared venture into Gulch, so wanton and vicious were Sheriff Willis and his men.

Under a high, wide overcast September sky when the leaves had started to change, a box wagon turned off the browning prairie and swung into the wagon tracks that led into Gulch's main street.

Sheriff Willis was in the Bull Head killing time with Pony Harper and a few other men when he saw over the batwings the wagon pass by. Willis said over his shoulder, "Pony, Old Ned's here. I wonder what brings him." Willis walked up to the batwings, and Pony joined him at his side, looking after the wagon.

Bertha was at the lines, Ned sitting the seat next to her.

"That's T. J.'s wagon that wench is drivin'," Pony growled.

The wagon pulled up in front of the sheriff's office.

Willis looked at Pony and said, "I'll see what they want."

Bertha and Ned were on the boardwalk when the sheriff walked up. "Howdy, Ned," Willis said. "Ain't seen you in a while. What brings you?"

"Gal here got business."

Willis looked without care at Bertha and asked, "What kinda business you got?"

"Y'all hung two colored men. I come to ask who it was."

"How would I know? Vigilantes hung 'em."

"A bunch of cowards, that's who hung 'em. You wouldn't do nothin' about it even if you knowed who done it. Least you could do is say who was hung."

"They had fair warnin' to stay out of town. Ain't no use 'n you makin' a fuss over it."

171

Ned could sense the conversation was leading to no answers, so he interrupted. "Roy, Gal here got a brother that went off somewhere and ain't come back. She's worried."

"You too?"

"Me too."

Willis chuckled lightly at Ned worrying over worthless niggers. "I wouldn't know her brother from any other coon 'round here, but them that was hung, they still out yonder. You welcome to look."

"Come on, Gal. We'll look."

They mounted the wagon, and Bertha took the lines. She had the last say. "We don't have to look. Boot wadn't one of 'em."

"Who says?" Willis asked.

"If one of 'em had been Boot, you'da knowed it."

Willis chuckled again.

"Knowed what?" a voice asked from behind the wagon.

"Pony, these folks askin' about them two niggers what was hung," Willis stated seriously. Then, smiling knowingly, he said, "You got any idea who they was?"

"I got no idea and don't want one," Pony retorted. "Only thing I know is this here wagon was my brother's before he was killed. Ain't that right, Ned?"

"That's right, Pony. Killed by Indians."

"So you say."

"I gave the army my statement."

"That don't make it so."

"Gal here was with me. She seen what I seen."

"Her word ain't worth spit and you know it. You'll answer to me when the time comes."

"You figure to do some more night ridin', Pony?"

"You watch your tongue, old man!"

"Ten years ago, I'da beat you to a cripple for callin' me a liar . . . or more'n likely put a bullet in your brain.

Like I told the army, Indians killed your brother. Wagons're rightfully yours. You can ride out and git 'em anytime you've a mind to.'' Ned's spare, leathery face was flushed red. And through a weak smile, he added scornfully, "That is, if you can tear yo'self away from scaring unarmed men, women, and children.''

Pony stiffened as if from a ringing slap to the face. "Someday, old man—"

"Let's go, Gal," said Ned.

Bertha shook the lines, clucked the team into motion.

Willis and Harper looked after them for a time, then Pony said, "Someday I'm goin' to kill that old buzzard.''

"You notice he's come to wearin' his gun again.''

"Yeah. I hear tell he used to be a man to reckon with.''

"Did you see that old Creedmore propped next to the woman? He came prepared for trouble.''

"He'll git it, too, next time he smart-mouth me like that, Mr. Putterman or no Mr. Putterman.''

They found the two hanged men still swinging from an elm tree just at the edge of town. Bertha breathed a sigh of relief. Neither one was Boot.

After the hangings, Brazos County became like its old self before the war. Huge plantations and small farms were stocked with blacks drawing meager wages or none at all. The Freedmen's Bureau was powerless at getting fair contracts, written or verbal. White men got what labor they wanted at what price they wanted to pay.

Fall came on.

Gulch purred with economic activity. Hardware stores did steady business in farming tools and implements for the coming planting season; army contractors freighting between the fort and Weatherford constantly moved over the road; a handful of buffalo hunters made Gulch their jumping-off point; and the Bull Head Saloon thrived off

173

free-spending soldiers from the fort. During the last days of September, a second story atop the Bull Head was nailed together and turned into a whorehouse, and was doing good business.

Ben Putterman had forty freedmen and had gotten seeds and implements to work the land. Putterman was a big man now, the biggest in the valley. In addition to four hundred head of longhorns he had slapped his Slash P brand on, he had abundant cheap labor to command. Now all he needed was time, springtime, so he could start planting. Then he could sit back and watch the cash roll.

But one thing still rankled Ben. And that was his inability to get his hands on Old Ned's choice land in the valley.

The Black Codes had come with a little-noticed companion law that simply stated that no homestead of two hundred acres or less could be repossessed or sold to pay off a public debt.

Ned's yearly taxes went unpaid on the books. Legally Parker could do nothing about it.

Putterman went to the commissioner's office to discuss the matter. "Anything on the horizon that suggests he's goin' to come up with the money?"

"Not as far as I can see, and he ain't dropped a hint. But Old Ned don't strike me as a man to run away from debt."

"What's he up to, then?"

"Can't put my finger on it, but I'd swear there's somethin'. He don't seem worried like he ought to be." Parker looked helplessly at Ben and suggested, "If you laid your cards faceup on the table, maybe he'd sell to you for a good price."

"Tried that. That stubborn old fool said he wouldn't sell for any price."

"That's all she wrote, then," Parker said, shrugging

his shoulders helplessly. "Land stays on the books just like it is, unless Ned changes his mind."

"Or dies?"

"Or dies," Parker stated flatly.

Ben left Parker's office, his mind reaching out into the future. If that stubborn old goat didn't get out of the way, he'd have to be shoved aside, Ben thought.

As he stood outside on the boardwalk, thinking, Ben's mind slowly came full circle. It had to be done. So be it.

Just as he stepped off, his eyes caught sight of a buckboard coming down the street at a fast clip.

The sorrel horse pulling the buckboard glistened with sweat. Mayor Joseph Speed was handling the lines. The mayor was in a hurry and had come a long way, that much was obvious.

The mayor, fitting the key into his office door lock, looked up and saw Ben dodging across the street coming toward him. He pushed through the door, turned around, and said, "Come on in, Ben. There's news."

"Trouble?"

"The worst kind. Comin' out of the blue like it is, it's a blow." The squat, round mayor took off his bowler hat, exposing a fat, pumpkin head, bald except for a fringe of hair around the sides. He dropped down in the swivel chair behind his desk and indicated a chair to Ben. Looking defeated, he said wearily, "Them Black Codes ain't goin' to stick, Ben. Pure and simple."

"What you mean?"

"Governor Throckmorton's being pressured to get rid of 'em."

"Who's doin' the pressurin'?"

"Federal government. Word come up from Austin this morning. I rode out to Fort Richardson to find out first-hand. It's fact. Major Sturgis has it from army brass that

175

if Throckmorton don't give the niggers some civil rights, the army's going to take over the state.''

"Niggers got their freedom. What more they want?''

"Civil rights, voting rights, the whole shootin' match, same as any white man got. The federal government is demanding Throckmorton give 'em property rights, and the right to vote.

"The thing of it is, them big-shot Republicans at Washington figure we elected too many ex-Confederates to the national legislature. The way they see it, we ain't properly regretful and willin' to live with our defeat.''

Putterman was aghast. "They can't tell us who to elect!''

"My words exactly to Major Sturgis. But like the major said, we can send anybody we want to to Washington, but them radical Republicans up there ain't got to seat 'em.''

"What about President Johnson?''

Mayor Speed blew a breath of disgust and said scornfully, "Hell, he's got no standin'. None atall. There's talk of impeachin' him.''

"Ain't nothin' Throckmorton can do?''

"Not a thing, the way I heard it. General Sheridan has appointed General Griffin as military commander of the district, and General Griffin is the one who told Governor Throckmorton the state ain't in a good light at Washington. Throckmorton was warned directly to make things right as far as the niggers is concerned.''

"Throckmorton was a Union man,'' Ben said in disbelief. "One of only seven to vote against secession.''

"That don't cut no ice now. The way they see it, Throckmorton was a live-and-let-live Union man. He don't show sufficient will in reinin' in ex-rebels. When he insisted on votin' rights for Orin Roberts, the loudest-mouthed secessionist we had, the people at Washington got distrustful. When we elected Orin a senator and sent him to Washington, well, that kind of broke the camel's back.''

''We ain't the only state that's sendin' ex-Confederates to Washington. There's Arkansas, Mississippi, Georgia . . .''

''They're comin' under federal military rule, too. The way I see it, if a man ain't a Republican in good standin' . . . or a nigger, he's got little chance. And mighty few of us qualify.''

''Them tryin' to put the niggers over us ain't right.''

''Republicans got the whip hand now, that's all there is to it.''

''One thing about it, Mayor, a whip hand can be chopped off just like any other.''

''What're you sayin', Ben?''

''Every white man in the state got a gun of some sort, and most of us killed before, in or out of the war.''

''Kill out the blacks!''

''Won't have to,'' Putterman said smugly. ''Kill a few of 'em, the rest'll forgit about this equal-rights business and git back in their place.''

Governor Throckmorton at the statehouse was a tough, seasoned politician, canny. Against overwhelming odds in the secessionist convention of '61, he had stood against seceding in the face of public scorn and ridicule. But when the vote had gone against him and the state went over to the Confederacy, he followed out of patriotic duty, joining the army and being made a commissioner to the Indians.

Now his political courage was being tested again, tested severely: The federal government was demanding that he see that Texas guarantee equal rights for blacks. Throckmorton knew this would raise holy hell all over the state. The only thing he could do for now was go along and hope to change things before the state erupted in blood. In the meantime, he'd soften the blow in his own way, as much as possible.

The first ex-Confederate Throckmorton fired as a show of compliance left Austin on a swift horse, carrying news of the governor's new hardfisted policy as fast as he could ride.

The word of Throckmorton's action reached Gulch and struck Ben like a mule kick to the solar plexus: Freedmen had been granted civil rights; high-ranking ex-rebels and prominent civilians had been denied the same. Ben knew that most of the land he had acquired, and every labor agreement he had, written or verbal, wouldn't stand up under law.

Putterman knew he had to act with haste, move while he still had room to maneuver. He emptied his safe and rode on a fast horse out to his Slash P ranch house, where he retrieved from the wall safe the choice delinquent land deeds that Commissioner Parker had put in his possession. Shuffling through them hastily, he laid aside three he coveted most: Ned Huelen's and two others with good water on choice land.

Pony Harper knew something was up when he rode into the ranch yard at the head of six other Slash P riders and saw Ben's horse standing slack-legged at the hitchrail next to the porch.

"Boss is here," Pony said. "I'll see what he wants."

At Ben's answer to his rap on the door Pony entered the parlor, walked back to Ben's working office, and found Ben sitting long-faced in a rocker-armed chair at his desk. "Didn't expect you, boss," Pony said, a worried look on his face. "What brought you?"

"Somethin' come up. We've got to move up our plans."

Pony smiled at the thought that leaped into his head. "I git to kill Old Ned now?"

"If need be," Ben said solemnly. "Fix yo'self a drink, Pony," and he indicated the wet bar over in the corner. "It's time you boys earn your wages."

Chapter Fourteen

Over at the wet bar in Ben's working office Pony Harper poured himself a generous shot of rye. Dashing it down, he turned around, listening as Putterman gave orders.

Ben finished talking. Pony splashed himself another stiff drink, tossed it off in one quick motion, and left the room hurriedly.

Outside, Jim Cardine and five other Slash P riders waited at the hitchrail, anxious to hear why Putterman had made the unusual trip out to the ranch. Pony spoke to them as he walked up: "Jim, you and me got ridin' to do. The rest of you boys git them beeves moved like we started to do."

Harper and Cardine mounted their horses and tore away from the ranch yard at a hard ride. A half mile north they swung off the trail and rode into Elm Thicket, a motte of elm trees on the south side of Rocky Hill. Even in broad daylight Elm Thicket looked sinister. It was a hideout for former draft evaders, army deserters, stock thieves, murderers, and various other unsavory characters of dubious background dodging the law for one reason or another. And they all had one thing in common: They were open to anything that promised money.

Pony recruited five men for this job. He rode away from Elm Thicket with Bud Monroe, a tall, thin Confederate army deserter of heavy beard and little conscience; Tim Snowden, a heavyset beady-eyed man; and Ed Blount, a lean-faced, spare man. Also riding with him were Lafe and Tish O'Callahan, two immigrant Irish brothers of little ambition and much viciousness gained on New York's waterfront.

Pony Harper led the men west out of Elm Thicket. They swung south at the foot of Rocky Hill and, riding on the other side of the valley, skirted Lazy H land. Two miles south they angled back across the valley, drew rein at a squatter's camp down in the bottom of a gully. Pony scouted the miserable dwellings of cloth lean-tos and scrap-lumber shacks.

Speaking in a tone of twisted pleasure, Pony gave them orders: "We gonna bust up this nigger camp. Anybody git in your way, shoot 'em down like varmints."

The seven riders struck the camp hard and swift like a prairie tornado, swirling in from the north, firing their pistols, yahooing like wild men, sending the squatters into a burst of motion.

It was over and done with in minutes. They roared out the south end.

Behind them there wasn't a structure left standing. Flames licked at two plank shelters that Tish O'Callahan had touched off with a burning brand.

Three black men lay dead, two children trampled to cripples. Every person in the camp had taken to heels and lay cowering behind what cover they had found.

Billowing smoke twisted up from the gully, floating

away on the wind. Pony led his men at a gallop on a wide swing, then turned back toward the Lazy H. They swept up to Ned's place in a cloud of dust and pulled to a hard stop. The dust swirled, settled. Pony searched around, looking for somebody.

Nobody was in sight. Nothing moved. Not a horse, nor a cow. Not a hog, nor a chicken. The only sounds he heard were the windmill cutting wind and water trickling into the horse trough.

Pony rose in his stirrups, looking around more closely.

"You got business, Pony?" Ned called out to him from behind the edge of the barn.

Pony lowered himself back down into the saddle and straightened around to face Ned. Ned stepped away from the edge of the barn. Pony's eyes caught on the pistol strapped to Ned's side.

"I got business," Pony answered stiffly.

"Speak it, then."

"Mr. Putterman says you oughta think again on that offer he made you."

"Already did. Answer's still no."

"He's willin' to sweeten the pot some. You oughta take it, Ned. You'd save yo'self a lot of trouble."

"And if I don't?"

"Mr. Putterman's got ways. You know that."

"Burnin' and killin'?"

"You got no call to talk like that, Ned."

Bud Monroe looked impatiently across his shoulder at Jim Cardine and said what the others were thinking: "Cut the rot, Pony! Let's git on with it!"

"I'd think twice if I was you," Ned warned.

At that instant Bertha craned the old Sharps around the corner of the barn, and at least a dozen black men appeared in the barn door brandishing pitchforks, shovels, hoes, and anything else a man could possibly fight with.

"You old fool!" Pony snarled contemptuously. "This'll get your grave dug for sure!"

"Your wagons're yonder, Pony," Ned said, and gestured. "Take 'em . . . and you got no reason to show your face around here again."

"Wagons ain't what I come for," Pony stated.

"I'll just bet!" Ned said. "And you can tell Mr. Putterman he can stop sniffin' after my land. I'd as soon sign the place over as see it go to him."

"Figured you for more sense than that," Pony said. He scanned the black men arrayed against them. Raising his voice, he warned, "You better clear out now while you got a chance! You're free now! Move on! You got nothin' here!"

Nobody moved. A dozen or more stone-faced, tight-lipped black faces glowered sullenly at Pony.

Pony's eyes came to rest on Bertha. She tightened her jaw, thrust the Creedmore forward menacingly, the black hole of the bore pointed at Pony's belly.

"Damn slope-heads," Pony muttered. He jabbed spurs to his horse and wheeled out. The other men followed.

It was coming on to sundown by the time Pony and Jim had dismissed the men from Elm Thicket and galloped their jaded horses into the Slash P ranch yard. Putterman was waiting for them on the porch, a questioning look on his face.

"No dice, boss," Pony told him.

"Did you tell 'em I was willin' to up the ante?"

"I tole 'em. Still no dice."

"Did you bust up the place like I told you to?"

Pony slanted his eyes at Jim and shifted uncomfortably in his saddle. "Well . . . naw, boss. He had a gaggle of niggers there who woulda seen things. Wadn't nothin' we could do out in the open like that."

Putterman glanced at Jim, who spoke up hastily:

183

"That's right, boss. Them niggers there wid 'em was mostly from Gulch. They seen me and Pony before."

"Old Ned made fool talk about signin' the place over rather than see it defaulted," Pony said.

Putterman looked sick to his stomach, his face pale. "To who? He's got nobody!"

"Maybe that winch he calls Gal. Treats her like she's more 'n a nigger."

Regaining his composure, Ben said with authority, "You boys get into town. Ned shows up, see he don't sign over nothing. No more pussyfootin' around!"

"What about Sheriff Willis?" Pony asked.

"You tell Willis I said he's to go fishin' . . . anywhere. Just keep his mouth shut."

At Gulch, Sheriff Willis walked his rounds under a gloomy autumn sky, weaving his way through his own people, who had drifted back in since blacks had been driven out.

He crossed over the alley next to the bank, broke his gait, looking distastefully at a heap of trash the wind had whipped up against the building.

He moved on.

In front of the Bull Head Saloon he paused on the boardwalk, eyeing the four horses standing slack-legged there, the same Slash P horses that had been hitched there every day for the last few weeks. Willis reflected back on the day Pony Harper had told him of Putterman's order to get lost if Old Ned ventured into town. Willis shook his head at the lawlessness and killings that had come to the country lately. He lifted his eyes out toward Squaw Valley, and admitted to himself resignedly that there was nothing he could do. Old Ned had brought it all on himself.

And at Squaw Valley two men swung their horses from the valley floor and took the wagon road leading up to Ned's place. Ned watched them come, struck by their appearance: One was a white man, the other black, apparently working as a team. They pulled to a halt at the edge of the porch.

"Somethin' I can do for you?" Ned asked, stepping into the doorway.

"Hope so," the white man answered. "Name's Seth . . . Seth Poole. This here's Charlie Pierce."

Ned nodded, and Poole continued : "We come from the county seat," and indicating the ledger he had under his armpit, he added, "to register voters."

"Register voters! What for?"

"Convention delegates and a new state constitution," Poole said proudly. "Its been four years now. The state's puttin' in a whole new gov'ment."

Ned wagged his head from side to side in disbelief. Catching himself, he said hurriedly, "Y'all git down, come on in. There's coffee."

The two men dismounted, brushed dirt from their clothes. Ned took a couple of steps down the dog run and yelled toward Bertha's door, where he knew she was listening anyhow. "Gal, come on out here, there's comp'ny!"

At a crude table in what served as Ned's kitchen the men from the county seat explained the reasons and rules for the coming election, Poole doing the talking. Now he looked from under lifted eyebrows and said, "One thing, though, there's an oath you got to take."

"What kinda oath?" Ned asked.

Poole produced a registration certificate, showed him the Loyalty Oath printed at the top.

"You got to swear by it," Poole said, "then sign it."

"Had no hand in the war," Ned said, "saw no use in it."

"Good," Poole said honestly. "Gov'ment's lookin' for good loyal men like you."

"Well, I'm damned," Ned said in disbelief. "I never thought Governor Throckmorton would come around to riddin' hisself of the ex-rebels he was surrounded with."

"He didn't," Poole said. "You ain't heard?"

"Heard what?"

"Throckmorton's out. Like you said, the federal government figured he had too many ex-rebels hangin' on his coattails. Now he's out, removed by General Sheridan. We got ourselves a new governor."

"Who?"

"Feller named Pease, Edmund Pease."

"The one who was governor back in '57?"

"He's the one. He was a Union man but took no hand in the fighting, so the federal government figures he's the right man to bring Texas back in the Union."

"He did a fair job back then. First thing he ought to do now is bring some law and order. Country's overrun with outlaws."

"Mr. Huelen," Poole said, repeating the name he had seen written down on the certificate, "you vote in some good loyal Republicans, you'll get law and order."

"It's what the country needs," Ned said firmly.

Poole canted his eyes over at Bertha, who was acting as if she were occupied at the coffeepot but was actually listening in. "She got a man?" Poole asked. "Every man over twenty-one gits to vote."

"Coloreds too?" Ned asked, dumbstruck.

"Coloreds too. Gov'ment orders."

"I signs up colored folks," Pierce said, speaking for the first time. "If there's any here, I'll see to it."

"There's some here kind of temporary-like," Ned said to Pierce, then, turning his eyes to Bertha, told her, "Give Mr. Poole here some more coffee, then show this here feller where the colored folks at."

Bertha led Pierce across the yard, Ned watching until they disappeared from his view through the open door.

Turning back to Poole, he lifted his coffee cup and said decidedly over the rim, "Mr. Poole, I don't envy you this job."

"There's been trouble," Poole admitted. "Whites don't cotton to us schooling the coloreds in their rights."

"You been to other ranches in the valley?"

"We come by the Slash P."

"Any trouble?"

"Mr. Putterman was right touchy about the whole subject. Wouldn't even consider the oath for hisself, and threatened Mr. Pierce with horsewhipping if he spoke to the coloreds there on the place."

"I expect he would," Ned said. "He made hisself quite a record with the Confederacy. Lotta men 'round here look up to him."

"That explains it, then," Poole said.

"Explains what?"

"Seen only one man all day who could rightly take the Oath, and he refused. Scared of Putterman, I figure." Poole closed his ledger, gathered it under his arm. "Mr. Huelen," he said with conviction, "I don't rightly know which side you really stood on, but the country's changed now. The war settled that. The federal gov'ment says these people got a right to vote. Gov'nor Pease and General Sheridan intend they get that right."

"Mr. Poole," Ned said with equal conviction, "I stood where I said I stood. I figger coloreds got a right to this country same as white men."

Out across the yard Bertha pulled the heavy barn door open and stepped inside the cavernous building. The racket got the attention of Joe Ben, a lanky, middle-aged black man working bear grease into saddle leather a couple of stalls down. Joe Ben stepped out into the shaft of light and, seeing Bertha, asked irritably, "What you want out here?"

"There's a man wants to see y'all," Bertha answered testily.

"About what!" another man asked from down near the middle of the barn.

"He got somethin' important to tell y'all!" Bertha told him, looking out the corner of a fixed eye at Joe Ben.

"Important about what?" Joe Ben asked mildly.

"About votin'," Pierce cut in, stepping forward from Bertha's side.

"Votin'!" the other man repeated. "What we got to vote on?"

"That's what I come to tell you about," Pierce said. Lifting his voice, he announced loudly, "All y'all come on down here. I got somethin' to tell ya!" Turning back to Bertha, he said dismissively, "Thank you, ma'am."

Lifting her chin haughtily, Bertha rolled her eyes at Pierce and grudgingly edged off to the side a couple of harmless steps. A dozen or more black men and at least half a dozen women and children whom Ned had given refuge in his barn fanned out in front of Pierce in the center of the barn where four walkways met and formed a square. They listened with interest as Pierce told them of the upcoming election in which colored men over age twenty-one were qualified to participate for the first time.

Pierce was a northern freedman of some education and had come south on his own to teach at one of the schools the Freedmen's Bureau had set up. He was a short, heavyset man, dark-skinned, and between heavy lips two rows of perfectly white teeth showed. He was of indeterminate age, and wore a bowler hat a size too small for his ample head. A store-bought gray coat covered a blue checked flannel shirt.

Pierce said to them, "All you got to do is sign your name and I give you a certificate. You show up in town on election day, show your certificate, and vote."

"Some of 'em can't write," Bertha said from off to the side.

"Then they can make an *X*," Pierce said tersely, obviously annoyed at men's business being butted into by a woman.

"They won't let us go into town no more," Joe Ben said.

"They who?" Pierce asked.

"The sheriff. He calls it loiterin'. Says we goin' to jail or farmwork."

"He ain't got no right to do that," Pierce said. "There's a white man with me up to the house right now. I'll tell him what you just said, and he'll see somethin' gits done about it."

"How we know who to vote for, anyhow?" another freedman wanted to know.

"You got to vote for Republicans. They the ones who set you free. They the ones will see that you git land and jobs to take care of your families.

"We's called the Loyal League. Remember that . . . and we goin' to meet with you every week. I'll tell you who the good Republicans is. Now, let's sign up here."

Two hours later the new registrars, Seth Poole and Charlie Pierce, had registered every man on the place over the age of twenty-one. They mounted their horses at the porch. Poole looked down at Ned and asked, "Any more folks up the valley?"

"Not as I know of, but there's some colored folks live in a gully south of here—Gullytown we come to call it. There's colored men there old enough to vote if you can git 'em to."

"Mr. Huelen, its our job to get 'em to," Poole said, and swung his horse that way.

The registrars walked their horses away from Ned's yard heading south, each man carrying his ledger under his arm. Two miles farther on they came upon the rebuilt lean-tos and plank shanties once destroyed by Pony Harper and his riders.

There at Gullytown Pierce lectured again, then registered every man over twenty-one. They promised to return in a week to give further schooling on how to vote.

Late that afternoon the registrars walked their horses down the main street in Gulch and passed in front of the Bull Head Saloon.

At the sound of hoof-falls and the sight of movement, Holly lifted his eyes from the glass he was idly polishing. Looking out over the batwings, he caught sight of two strangers riding by, one white, one black. Holly spoke casually over toward the table where four men sat killing time playing penny-ante poker: "Pony, you said Mr. Putterman chased off two men ridin' the county signin' up voters?"

"Yeah. He wants 'em run clean out of the country if we come up on 'em anywhere."

"They just rode by."

"Where?" Pony asked, bolting out of his chair.

Holly jerked a thumb, indicating down the street.

Pony rushed over to the batwings, pushed through.

Poole and Pierce had just swung their horses to the hitchrail in front of the sheriff's office. Stepping out onto the boardwalk, Pony brushed past two pedestrians, stood spread-legged, and announced to them, "Move on! We got nothin' here for you."

"We come to register voters," Poole said uneasily.

"We got no niggers here for you to register," Pony said, and smiled devilishly.

"We register any man that's qualified," Poole answered. "White or black."

"Trouble is, you more interested in votin' niggers than white. Look around you," Pony said, flourishing a hand. "Town's got no niggers . . . and ain't no white man cares. Now, move on!"

Poole studied first one white face, then another. He found no sympathy whatsoever. Suddenly he wanted to be somewhere else, doing something else. He looked toward the sheriff's door. No movement. He swung his leg over the cantle, dismounting to notify the sheriff.

Pony shot him.

The bullet struck Poole in the chest, dead center. He was dead before his other foot cleared the stirrup.

At the sound of gunfire three men charged out of the Bull Head and joined the other white men lining the boardwalk. Sheriff Willis ran out his door and stopped on the boardwalk, his eyes taking in first the dead man lying next to the water trough, then the group of men standing off from the saloon.

Pony had holstered his gun now, so Sheriff Willis asked, "Who did it?"

"Who gives a damn," a man answered. "Any white man roaming the country promoting niggers over his own kind deserves no better."

Willis ran his eyes over the solemn white faces watching him, waiting to see what he'd do. He couldn't bring himself to disagree with what had been said. "I guess it was bound to happen," he said halfheartedly.

"He was from the county seat. You think there'll be questions?" Cardine asked.

"None that can't be answered," another man said. "Any one of us woulda done the same thing."

"With so many bushwhackers and robbers roamin' the country," somebody else suggested, "he's just one more man shot down for his belongings."

"What about him?" Pony asked Willis, indicating Pierce, sitting petrified in his saddle.

Sheriff Willis deliberately walked around to Pierce's side and looked up at him. He stated flatly, "You can take him and ride out of here, or you can join him."

"I takes him," Pierce answered, shaken.

"You ain't been in this town, and you ain't seen nothin', you hear?"

"I hear," Pierce said weakly.

Joe Ben was working at the front of the barn. He was first to see Charlie Pierce turn off and enter the wagon road leading up to the ranch house. Joe Ben took off at a run to summon Ned. Bertha heard the clamor too. All three stood solemnly at the edge of the porch, watching Pierce come on, a body dressed in clothes they all recognized slung over the saddle of a led horse.

Even as he walked the horses up across the yard, Pierce declared shrilly in shocked disbelief, "They killed him!"

"Who?" Ned asked.

"Man in town," Pierce said, pulling to a stop.

"Sheriff do anything about it?" Ned asked.

"He didn't do nothin'. Ain't nobody else goin' to neither, and I ain't to tell nobody."

"Mr. Ned, you know that sheriff ain't no 'count," Bertha snapped reproachfully. Calming herself, she said resignedly, "Git down, Mr. Pierce." Bertha looked forlornly at the body and said to Joe Ben standing there, "Git po' Mr. Poole off that hoss."

Ned looked at Bertha. "Gal, you ain't got nobody 'round here to boss. Ain't you got somethin' to do in the house?"

"Coffee," Bertha said, smiling. "I'll make some coffee."

Inside the house over coffee, Ned grilled Pierce on the shooting. Bertha listened intently off to the side. After Pierce had explained in detail, Ned asked, "What you goin' to do now?"

"Git Mr. Poole home. He had family."

"I mean about votin'. You still goin' to sign up coloreds?"

GET FOUR BOOKS TOTALLY *FREE*—A VALUE BETWEEN $16 AND $20

"Got to . . . ain't nobody else."

"Can't the army give you protection?"

"The army!" Bertha scoffed from over where she was working at the stove. "They can't even protect they ownself!"

"Army's been told to stay out of it 'less there's some law broken," Pierce said.

"A man's been killed," Ned said. "Won't that bring them in?"

"Maybe. Only thing I can do is make my report to the bureau when I git back. They'll likely look into it."

"Because Mr. Poole was a white man?"

"Yeah, suh."

So winter came on, short bleak days of overcast skies and chilly winds that kept most men inside pondering their future. Word went throughout the state that coloreds were qualified to vote. Everybody knew that ex-rebels who couldn't or wouldn't take the Loyalty Oath were disqualified from voting, barred from elective office from highest to lowest, and couldn't even hold appointive positions. Influential ex-rebels howled all the way to Washington but got little relief, because General Sheridan, Governor Pease, and the federal Congress nullified the promises of a weakened President Johnson.

The common white man scrambled for a living, the outlaw trail gathering its share of reluctant riders. Stock thieves and stage robbers flourished; revenge killers and paid assassins were on the hire. Every man in the country knew that the only law now was what a man carried in his holster. And most men packed a gun and a fighting knife.

No man was safe. Racial and revenge murders became commonplace. Through it all justice was a farce, the civil courts a mockery: White jurors refused to convict white men for fear of retaliation, but convicted black men for frivolous offenses. Fear became a part of every man's daily life.

Law-abiding citizens petitioned Governor Pease and the army, clamoring for justice and protection.

And election day drew nearer.

Chapter Fifteen

Bodie and Ruley broke camp in the early hours of a crisp October morning, heading for Fort Smith. The land they rode was blanketed with golden-brown leaves, covered over with a clear blue sky. Long hours in the saddle proved Ruley to be a blunt, plainspoken man of easy manners, with an affable disposition. Harsh experiences as a slave hadn't dulled his good nature.

In early morning and late evening two old double-breasted blue army coats Josh had sent along stood them in good stead against the autumn chill, and with one hand in his coat pocket, the other handling the reins, Ruley talked ruefully of the past, hopefully of the future.

At Cache River Bodie paid the last dollar of his army mustering-out pay to cross over horses and riders, and for three days they followed the trace west, overtaking colored people all along the way, some afoot and some riding a conveyance of one type or another. They tarried along the route, making conversations, Ruley mostly, but never staying long enough to claim friendships.

They traveled with no urgency about them, loafing along the trail, moving at their own pace. Ruley was taken with the six-shooter he had gotten from Josh. He drew it to hand at every chance, cleaning it, firing it at rocks and things.

Fort Smith was their destination, and their progress was steady. Most folks they talked to along the way said they were heading to Little Rock or Fort Smith to see army relatives. A few were headed to unknown parts, parts where freedom felt like freedom.

Each day they left the trace where game had been killed out and rode cross-country in search of table meat. Each time they worked their way back to the trace with full bellies of stick-roasted rabbit. Twice they encountered bear but rode shy of the beasts. "Meat's mighty tasty," Ruley had said the first time, "but ain't no use in killin' it if we ain't got time to pack in the meat."

In late afternoon of the fourth day, they reached Teele's Crossing on the White River. Lacking cash money to cross over horses and riders, they searched a mile or so downstream, found a shallow-looking point, and swam their horses across.

On the other side they made night camp under copper-leafed oaks and gnawed at the last of the rabbit, both men mildly aware of their down-at-the-heels condition. Ruley admitted peevishly, "This here freedom sho' makes you worry about where yo' next meal's comin' from."

"Been thinkin' on it," Bodie answered. "Come morning we'll strike out for a town. See if we can't scare up some travelin' money."

"How?"

"Wages. Work ought to be easy to come by."

In the morning they broke camp and struck south,

feeling their way toward a place where Bodie had heard there were settlements.

Arkansas, like the other ten ex–Confederate states, was in upheaval. Lawlessness prevailed. Homeless, drifting men moved over the country, searching for a living. Returning veterans and displaced men of every race hired out at whatever labor they could find: ranch hand, tenant farmer, or freighter; saloon roustabout, liveryman, stage driver; anything for a dollar.

More than a few took to the outlaw trail.

The settlement they rode into was Picayune, a fair-size town any way you looked at it. The east–west-running main street was eight buildings long on the north side and six long on the south side, with a high-roofed courthouse sitting in the middle of the six. The half-dozen stores, telegraph office, bank, post office, hotel, and four saloons all took on double importance as a crossroads to Little Rock to the south and Fort Smith farther west.

Like most other towns in the vicinity, Picayune had seen most of its white folks drift back in now that freedmen and their women and children had been finally driven out.

But unlike most other towns in the vicinity, the army, if such it could be called, was here at Picayune.

Of the meager 124 federal army officers scattered throughout the whole of Arkansas to administer the Freedmen's Bureau, Major Armstrong and First Lieutenant Cross had been detailed at Picayune, put up at the Statesman's Hotel across the street from the post office.

And like other federal army officers throughout the South, local whites hated them.

Standing on the boardwalk in front of his office door, Lieutenant Cross, a hardworking, resolute young man, read the telegraphed message from Fort Smith again:

DEPUTY MARSHAL SAM BOWMAN HAS MINGO SANDERS

CORNERED AT BEAR CREEK. SEND HELP IMMEDIATELY. MAJOR ARMSTRONG.

Major Armstrong, his commanding officer, and the sheriff had been called away two days earlier to testify at Fort Smith in a bank-robbery case, and ever since then the lieutenant had received from the major a steady stream of telegraphed orders and instructions.

Lieutenant Cross tipped back his campaign hat, exposing a sun-browned, angular face topped off by shaggy brown hair. He swept his eyes up and down first one boardwalk and then the other, seeing nothing but townspeople who hated his guts, southerners who loathed any white man who'd help coloreds gain equality with them. Cross had come to expect nothing from these people; he hadn't been disappointed.

He swore softly under his breath and stepped off hurriedly, heading toward the courthouse. In the middle of the street he broke his stride, looking at two colored men riding toward him.

Lieutenant Cross noticed with keen interest that they rode better-than-average horses and, more important to Cross, they were armed.

Walking slowly across the street, Cross turned, his eyes following the two men walking their horses toward him. He felt sure these were cavalry mounts they rode. His eyes shifted to the Winchester riding in the boot of one of them. By the time the riders drew abreast of him, Cross was certain at least one of the two was a drifting army man. He had seen enough come through Picayune to know.

Working on an educated hunch, Cross called out, "Sergeant!"

And instinctively Bodie twisted around in the saddle. "Come over here."

They checked their horses to a stop. "I ain't goin' nowhere," Ruley said. "I ain't army."

"Wait here," Bodie said, and heeled away from Ruley.

"Guessed you for army," the lieutenant said pleasantly when Bodie walked his horse up.

"Was, till the war ended."

"A sergeant?"

"Yeah, sir, but only for a few months."

"Well, Sergeant, I'm Lieutenant Cross," and Cross glanced down again at the telegram he carried in his hand. "You lookin' for work?"

"Only for a day, two at most. I'm lookin' for my folks, but run short of travelin' money."

"Wherebouts you lookin'?"

"Texas."

"Job I got wouldn't take a day. The money you'd make would help some. You'd be doin' the army some good, and I'd see you get a rightful share of the commission on the warrant, whatever that is."

"What kinda work is it?"

"Posse work. About five miles out of town. The marshal's got a wanted man pinned down at a place called Bear Creek. The marshal can't flush 'im, so he's callin' for help."

"What about him?" Bodie asked, indicating Ruley.

"Fine," Cross said, giving Ruley no more than a cursory glance. "Take him along. The marshal's named Bowman. You'd both be under his orders."

"I took 'em before," Bodie said, and swung his horse away.

They rode south from Picayune. Bodie explained the job to Ruley as they rode. Ruley was uneasy working for the army. He said, "That Lieutenant Drake likely done reported by now that Mr. Stokely was killed. Whole army probably heard about it now."

"The sooner we git travelin' money, the sooner we travel," Bodie reminded him.

"When a white man is killed, word travels fast," Ruley advised, "and the way Josh tells it, the army's the first to git it."

The sound of random gunshots drew them to Bear Creek. They drew up forty yards off, surveying the situation.

On a rise a ways from the creek a cabin had been burned to the ground, ashes still smoldering. From all indications the wanted man had taken refuge in a log smokehouse just at the water's edge.

One lawman was concealed behind a dead tree just up the rise, banging away at the heavy structure with shotgun blasts that did little damage.

At that moment the man sighted over the log and let loose another blast that racketed over the creek bottom, sending a load of buckshots harmlessly into the heavy logs.

A pistol shot answered, knocking bark from the log the lawman was shielded behind, the shot answered by another shotgun blast from off to the left at the creek's edge.

"Marshal Bowman?" Bodie called, walking their horses up at the back of the lawman lying behind the log.

The man jerked around, startled, leaving his shotgun craned out over the log.

"Marshal Bowman?" Bodie asked again, then said mildly, "Lieutenant Cross sent us."

The man looked without care at the two black men and, gritting his teeth in pain from a bloody gunshot wound at the leg, nodded his head toward the creek and said, "Marshal's down yonder."

They found Marshal Bowman under cover behind a big oak tree near the water's edge.

Bowman was a middle-aged man, short but wide-built and strong-looking. Just now he was in a sour mood. He and two other possemen had had Mingo Sanders pinned down for more than six hours. One of his possemen had been wounded; another had been sent off to get help.

Bodie explained their presence there.

Bowman didn't disguise his displeasure over the help that had been sent him. "How in hell did the lieutenant come to send you two!" he asked exasperatedly.

"Guess he figured we could help you," Bodie answered mildly.

"I'll just bet." Looking them both over critically, seeing nothing to his liking, he asked hopefully, "Is the lieutenant sending anybody else?"

"Not as I heard."

Bowman turned away sharply. Speaking out toward where the outlaw was holed up, Bowman said more to himself than to them, "I got the most ornery critter in the county pinned down yonder, and that snot-nosed lieutenant sends me two field hands!" He lifted his eyes to the sun, guessing at the time. "Maybe somethin' will give before sundown." Facing where the outlaw was, he cut loose another shotgun blast, peppering the smokehouse.

The marshal had a clear field of fire at the back of the low-built house, and back there the logs had been peeled bare from repeated shotgun blasts.

Ruley gave Bodie an uninterested, to-hell-with-it look.

"I got a Winchester," Bodie said at the marshal's back.

"Can't hurt none," Bowman said without interest over his shoulder. "Pick a spot and have at it." An afterthought came over Bowman and he said distrustfully, "Just make sho' what you shootin' at."

They backed off to the sounds of shotgun blasts and answering pistol fire as Marshal Bowman and the other posseman continued to fire random shots at Mingo, protected behind the heavy logs of the smokehouse.

Bodie retrieved his Winchester from the saddle boot.

Ruley's doubts had steadily mounted. "This here ain't right. That feller down there ain't done nothin' to us."

"We just goin' to help drive him out, that's all."

"You done this kind of thing before?"

"Naw. I done guard duty, movin' prisoners, but nothin' like this."

"How you goin' to drive him out?"

"I figure them oak logs'll turn aside a bullet if hit just right. When lead gits to flying around his head, maybe he'll give up without gittin' hisself killed."

Bodie explained the idea fully to Ruley, who went to the pointed-out firing position at an angle into the door frame of the smokehouse.

At Bodie's first shot Ruley cut loose too. Together they laid down a solid blanket of rifle and pistol fire into the smokehouse door of heavy logs as big as a man's thigh.

The whine of lead told them of ricochets, and there were many.

They held their fire. There was no answering pistol fire.

"Maybe he's hit!" Bowman yelled over at them.

"Wouldn't chance it," Bodie yelled back.

Bowman leaned out and cut loose with another shotgun blast.

No answering fire.

"Marshal, I think he's hit," the posseman yelled from up the rise behind the deadfall.

"Can you walk?" the marshal yelled back.

"Naw, leg's broke, I think."

Bowman studied his thoughts for a quick minute, then told them, "Cut loose on him again. I'm gonna work my way down there."

In the racket of gunfire and the whine of ricochets, Bowman weaved and darted his way closer to the smokehouse. Twenty yards away Mingo stumbled out the door, his gun pointed carelessly into the ground.

Marshal Bowman shot him.

At point-blank range Bowman triggered off a load of buckshot into Mingo's chest, sweeping him back inside the door frame.

Whether premeditated or otherwise, they couldn't say. Ruley gave a questioning look at Bodie; Bodie's look was one of equal puzzlement.

They reached the smokehouse just ahead of the posseman, dragging his broken leg along. Bowman had dragged Mingo out of the door frame and was looking him over.

Mingo Sanders had been a tall, solidly built man with a cold black mop of hair now disheveled, partially hiding his square-jawed face. His chest was a bloody mess, and a scalp wound showed at his forehead.

Bowman flicked back his suitcoat, exposing a bloody wound at his side. "Ricochet got him there," he said, then, lifting his shoulder at the back, he added, "and here."

"What'd he do?" Bodie asked, looking at the disfigured body.

"Last thing he done was robbed the payroll at Fort Smith, killed a guard doin' it. He was a bad one. He earned a hangin', and he knowed it."

On the way back to Picayune Bowman and the posseman rode in the lead, Bowman with Mingo's body slung in back of him. Success had dampened Bowman's hostility toward the black men. Now as they rode he talked freely, complaining of the lawlessness around, inquiring of Bodie's and Ruley's situation—where they were going, where they had come from. He was struck by Bodie's having been in the Union army. "From Virginny?" he asked incredulously. "How'd you wind up in the Union army?"

"Wadn't easy," Bodie said dryly, and warming at the memories, added, "Ran away. Spent three months hidin' out, duckin' the patrols before I got to Philadelphia."

"How'd you come to wind up there?"

"Just kept goin' towards where I figured north was."

After a time Bowman fell silent, riding with his own thoughts. Later on he said to the posseman, "Guess you'll be laid up some with that leg."

" 'Speck so, Marshal."

Bowman grunted an acknowledgment, asked over his shoulder, "How long the lieutenant said y'all was to take orders from me?"

"Pay's only promised for today," Bodie answered.

They rode into Picayune, drawing all eyes to them, the dead man dangling at the back of the marshal's saddle. Somebody from the boardwalk yelled out, "Who's that you got there, Marshal?"

"Mingo," the wounded posseman answered proudly. "We got Mingo Sanders."

Townspeople followed along, buzzing incessantly. At the courthouse a crowd built up, everybody wanting to hear details. And not a few furtive eyes took in the two armed black men. Off to the side on the boardwalk a short, red-faced man said, "It ain't right . . . niggers got no right to hunt down white men."

"Mingo was a bad one," a man said, disagreeing. "A killer. He got what he had comin'."

"That don't matter," the red-faced man answered. "He was a white man."

Lieutenant Cross came up. He was pleased with Bodie's and Ruley's actions when he got details from Marshal Bowman of what had transpired. Shortly after, Bowman hurried off to the telegraph office and reported to District Judge Caleb Stanhope at Fort Smith: MINGO SANDERS RESISTED ARREST AND WAS SHOT DEAD. REQUEST AUTH TO PAY TWO COLORED POSSEMEN PART OF

WARRANT COMMISSION. MARSHAL BOWMAN.

Bowman had been back in his courthouse office less than thirty minutes when the telegrapher rushed over with a reply: REQUEST DENIED. BRING IN SANDERS BODY AND COLORED POSSEMEN. JUDGE STANHOPE.

Bowman thought the telegram over, looking first to Bodie and then Ruley, who were there because they had arranged temporary room and board at the courthouse with Lieutenant Cross.

"Looks like you boys'll have to wait on that warrant money. I got orders to bring in Mingo's body first. You're to come with me if you want that money."

"What's that mean?" Bodie asked.

"Means the lieutenant will pay you only regular wages now . . . two dollars a day and expenses for the use of your own animals and ammunition. You want a share of the commission on that warrant, you'll have to collect it at Fort Smith same as me."

Ruley blew a loud breath of displeasure and said to Bodie, "Army again. . . ."

"Any trouble collectin' at Fort Smith?" Bodie asked the marshal.

"None that I see. Mingo resisted arrest, was killed. Happens all the time."

"Ain't no trouble that he was killed," Lieutenant Cross said from across the room where he had just walked through the door. "The trouble is, who killed him." The lieutenant crossed the room and told them, "There's ugly talk startin'. The sooner you travel, the better off the town'll be."

"Nothin' holdin' us but the marshal here," Bodie said. "The sooner he git ready, the sooner we travel. That right, Marshal?"

"That's right," Bowman told the lieutenant. "Mingo's body will be on the next train to Fort Smith."

Word spread rapidly of Mingo's killing. The under-

205

taker mistook the ricochet bullets and reported that Mingo was cut down by Winchester fire. From his report the story stretched, until by sundown Picayune seethed with the rumor that two colored killers in town had gunned down a white man. The red-faced man, who had been steadily agitating loafers in the Bobtail Saloon, told anyone who would listen that they ought to do something about it, now.

And the train wasn't due in until sometime late the next day.

Chapter Sixteen

In the morning the ugly talk in Picayune had mushroomed into talk of lynching. The town was surly, ready for a hanging if the right words were uttered.

Three heavily armed, shabbily dressed men rode into Picayune, looking like trouble-hunters. The three had kept their horses under whip and spur for the last day and a half, coming in from the Buzzard Roost, a notoriously bad outlaw den west and north of Fort Smith.

Dulin Sanders, his younger brother Edner, and a first cousin, Curly Tatum, had taken only a day and a half to reach Picayune after news reached them that Mingo had been shot dead by two colored men.

The grim-faced undertaker peered out from his parlor work shed at the three trail-hardened men, walking beat-out horses down Main Street about two o'clock in the afternoon. The undertaker looked out of cheerless eyes at the three men switching their heads from side to side as they rode along, sizing up the town through cold eyes that matched every bit those of Mingo.

At the clip-clop of horses passing, Lieutenant Cross glanced out the doorway, looked again with concern as the three strangers pulled up at the hitchrail across the street in front of the Bobtail Saloon. Appraising them to be no-account drifting men on the make, Cross retrieved his wide-brimmed campaign hat and headed for the saloon to make the army's presence known, as he always did when trouble-hunting men on the loose turned up in town.

The three men sat their horses in front of the saloon, looking in over the batwings, hearing tinny music coming from inside. Dulin, the middle-aged, broad-shouldered leader, had his two palms stacked on top of the saddle horn, slumped forward in the saddle, his mind thinking ahead. Directly he gave his partners a mild warning: "We go in there, remember we come to see after family matters. We got no reason to hunt needless trouble. You hear, Edner?"

"I hear," the youngest of the three answered. Edner had cold, black, mean eyes. Now he flashed them at Curly, spit a stream of tobacco juice out toward the street, and commented, "Town don't seem like much."

"If he had a say, Mingo might disagree," Dulin deadpanned. Casting a sideways, cockeyed look at the lean, hawk-faced man sitting the saddle next to him, he said, "We ain't come all this way to wind up like Mingo did. We'll see to what we come for and move on."

"No call to git skittish," the hawk-faced man said. "Like Ed said, town don't seem like much." The man twisted around in the saddle, scouted up the street, then down. Facing back around, he stated, "Town ain't likely to give us no back talk. I say we kill them two niggers outright and be done with it."

"We'll do it my way," Dulin declared flatly. He

stepped down out of the stirrups and ordered, "Curly, you git over to the undertaker's. See what he's got to say."

Curly and Edner swung down as one. Curly went on his way; Dulin and Edner pushed through the batwings, Dulin going first.

Inside the saloon men glanced up casually, then looked again with misgivings at the two rough-looking strangers who'd just walked in. The two hardhanded men looked like the kind used to taking their own way, both looking uncurried, as though they could stand up to the worst of it.

"What'll it be?" the bartender asked.

"Whiskey," Dulin answered, looking at the bartender slantwise through cold, ruthless eyes crossed so plainly it made the bartender want to turn away.

The bartender hurriedly sat out two glasses and fumbled behind him for the whiskey bottle. Dulin rattled a silver dollar on the bartop and said loudly with effect, "Name's Sanders . . . Dulin Sanders." He made the name heard throughout the place. Taking time to let it sink in, he deliberately reached for the whiskey glass and continued talking with purpose. "This here's my brother Edner."

"Kin to Mingo?" the bartender asked, nervously slopping whiskey into one of the glasses.

"Brother," Edner said. "Cousin's 'cross the street."

"Heard Mingo had kin somewhere in the Nations," the bartender said. "Didn't expect you this soon."

"We come soon as we heard. Damn nigh killed three good horses gittin' here, too," Dulin said. "We don't aim to be disappointed."

The Sanders boys both picked up their whiskies. Dulin tossed his off in one quick motion and returned the empty glass to the bartop. Eyeing the bartender coolly, he asked, "Niggers what done the killin', they still in town?"

"Last I heard they was. Sittin' there at the courthouse just like nothin' ever happened."

Dulin exchanged a sideways glance with Edner. "Courthouse?" Edner repeated. It sank in, and Edner smiled knowingly at their apparent good luck. "That oughta make the job real easy."

"Maybe not," Dulin said dubiously, shifting his attention to the bartender. "Lawman over there protectin' 'em?"

"Marshal's there, if that's what you mean."

"Marshal or no marshal," Ed growled, "town's gonna have to start a nigger graveyard."

Just then Curly pushed through the batwings, brushing sideways past a man going out in a hurry. Curly gave the man a dirty look, then came over to where Dulin and Ed were at the bar.

"You find out anything?" Dulin asked him.

"You ain't goin' to like it," Curly said, then told the bartender out the side of his mouth, "Whiskey."

"Try me," Dulin snapped, irritated at being made to wait.

Briefly Curly related to them what the undertaker had told him: Mingo's body had been loaded aboard the twelve-o'clock train to Fort Smith. The marshal had also boarded, standing guard duty in the car carrying the deceased.

"What about them two darkies?" Dulin asked.

"Undertaker said they hadn't showed up when the train pulled out." Curly tossed off his whiskey. "They ain't been seen all morning. Undertaker figures they lit out."

"Runnin'?" Dulin asked.

"That was my guess too," Curly said, "but the undertaker don't figure so. He said they both was armed better 'n most white men, and didn't seem like the kind to scare easy.''

"Undertaker got a mighty high opinion of 'em," Dulin said, scowling across his shoulder at Curly. "He ain't one of 'em, is he?"

"He ain't one of 'em. He just figures them for stand-up fighters. Says we'd be makin' a mistake to low-rate 'em. The marshal and the lieutenant both tried to rush 'em out of town when talk started, but they wouldn't be rushed. Something to do with travelin' money.''

Dulin looked at the clock on the wall behind the bartender, saw it was a little past three in the afternoon. Shoving his empty glass across the bar toward the bartender, he ordered, "Hit me again." Dulin swallowed the stiff drink the bartender slid back to him, then told Ed and Curly, "Let's go. We got business at the courthouse. We'll see what kinda stand-up fighters they is.''

Just as they turned away from the bar, Lieutenant Cross entered the door way, paused, his two hands holding the batwings apart, his eyes searching and finding the three hard cases.

The lieutenant picked Dulin for the leader, crossed over to him, and asked pleasantly, "You men passing through, or you figure on staying?"

"It ain't army business," Dulin said stiffly to the neatly dressed army officer.

"Army ain't askin'," the lieutenant countered. "I am.''

"Ask all you want, bluebelly, you'll get nothin' from me.''

"If you've got ideas about avenging Mingo's death, forget it. He wadn't worth it. Besides that, the marshal's on the train, so's Mingo's body.''

"Marshal's got his comin'," Dulin promised, "but right now we got a score to settle with them two niggers what done the killin'.''

"You got it all wrong. They didn't kill him. The marshal fired the fatal shot, double-ought buck."

"That ain't the way we heard it," Curly said.

"Listen, soldier boy!" Dulin cut in harshly. "Maybe you Yankees sit by and see white men killed by niggers, but ain't no Sanders goin' to stand for it!" He shouldered his way past the lieutenant and said out of the side of his mouth as he went by, "You stick to your army business, we'll stick to our'n."

Dulin led them outside. They mounted up and walked their horses up the street to the courthouse. The place was deserted.

At the livery they found out that the marshal had checked his horse out three hours before. Without looking directly at Dulin's cocked eyes, the liveryman asked, "You kin to Mingo?"

"That's right," Dulin said.

"You lookin' for them two sambos?"

"That's right. We find 'em, we're gonna do the town a favor and git rid of 'em permanant like."

"You ain't likely to. They come got their horses an hour before the marshal did. Seen 'em ride out south."

"South? Ain't nothin' for 'em thataway."

"I figure that was only for show, to throw you boys off the trail. They was to collect warrant money at Fort Smith."

"They heard we was comin'?"

"They heard. Whole town did."

The Sanders boys were no strangers to sniffing out and following a trail, nor were they tenderfoots to man-hunting. South they rode. Relying on considerable tracking skill learned from renegade Indians in the Nations, Dulin's trained eyes found prints made by hoofs that had been neglected so long they now grew over the front plate of the shoe, the same telltale prints he had seen back at the stable.

He picked up the trail of the two black men where it left the wagon road five miles south of Picayune.

Edner and Curly followed at a gallop.

The land they rode was dormant land of winter, trees reached gaunt fingers to high, cloudless skies, and the ground was carpeted with brown leaves.

Dulin kept to the trail by following the distinct hoofprints as they turned a leaf here, disturbed a rock there, snapped a twig farther on. It was coming on to sundown when they drew up in a shallow draw. Dulin sat the saddle, looking over the surroundings, scratching at the side of his stubbled jaw, eyeing the serrated peaks of a low ridge of rocks off to the left. "I'd lay odds that's where they's headed," he finally guessed.

"You figure they lookin' for a hole to hide in?" Ed asked.

"Don't seem like it. They ain't run their horses none. It's like they don't expect comp'ny . . . or they intend to fight."

Curly didn't believe they would fight, was taken aback at the mere suggestion. "Niggers I knowed would just as soon run as fight."

"Niggers you knowed wadn't armed neither like these two," Edner said.

"Either way, they're dead meat," Dulin said firmly. "The sooner we finish 'em off, the sooner we git back to things more to a man's liking."

A mile or so farther west along the trail, at the foot of the ridge Dulin had been looking at, Ruley puttered around a small campfire in a portion of the runoff draw shielded from open country by bare branches of stunted live oaks and low embankments on two sides.

Ruley paced back and forth uneasily. Abruptly he retraced his steps over to the fire, picked up the coffeepot, refilled his half-empty coffee cup. Clumsily returning the coffeepot to the coals, he started pacing again.

Like Bodie, Ruley was worried. Both were painfully aware of the fight that was shaping up. At that moment Bodie came toward the camp from among the rocks where he had been hunkered down behind a rock at the peak of the ridge, looking at their backtrail.

"They still comin'?" Ruley asked.

"They still comin'. You knowed they would be, same as me."

"It don't make good sense," Ruley said. "Mingo is dead. Ain't nothin' can bring him back. That posse work you was so taken with don't look so good now, do it?"

"I still say it beats stoop labor," Bodie repeated.

"It beats stoop labor if you live to tell about it," Ruley said.

"I doubt every warrant served leads to a killin'. Mingo was different. He needed it."

"Too bad his kin don't see it that way. Now nothin' will do 'em but to have at the two niggers what killed their brother."

"That's what don't make no sense. By all rights, we ain't the ones that killed him."

"They don't know that."

"Guess there ain't' no help for it, then." Bodie focused his eyes at Ruley and said facetiously, " 'Less we run like the scared niggers they figure us for, forgit about Fort Smith."

"The hell you preach!" Ruley growled. "I ain't above runnin', but I want my warrant money. The way I see it, we kill them or they kill us."

"Right here's as good a place as any. We can't dodge 'em forever."

"There's cover here," Ruley said, looking around at the jumble of broken rocks. "How many of 'em is it?"

"Three."

Ruley studied his thoughts for a quick minute, then asked, "What about findin' your folks?"

"What about it?"

"You ought to ride outta here, see it gits done."

"What about them?"

"I'm already runnin' from one killing. No use 'n you too."

"There's three of 'em."

"Way I'm goin' to do it, it don't matter."

"Ambush?"

"Killin's killin', I told you that," Ruley retorted. "That marshal didn't give Mingo no chance. I ain't givin' these one neither."

"From up there?" Bodie asked, nodding his head toward the rocks.

"Good a place as any." Ruley started off.

At that instant a harsh voice shouted out to them: "All right, you buggers up there . . . your runnin's over!" The voice came from thirty yards down the draw, from the other side. "Come on down here, face up!" the voice demanded angrily.

"Too late!" Bodie said softly to Ruley.

"It ain't too late," Ruley said over his shoulder, weaving through the rocks. "They still got to be done away with!"

"Maybe I can talk some sense into 'em," Bodie said. "I'm goin' down and try."

While Ruley was searching the rocks for a position from which to bushwhack them, Bodie was working his way down the draw, his Winchester in his two hands, keeping to what rock cover there was.

The Sanders boys waited below, Dulin resting forward in the saddle, waiting, amused. Bodie moved in and out among the rocks, his body visible one instant, invisible the next, each time reappearing with the Winchester first to come in sight.

Now he disappeared from view twenty yards up the draw.

Suddenly he didn't reappear where they expected him. Seconds passed.

They squirmed uneasily in their saddles, shifting their eyes from rock to boulder, worried.

From out of nowhere Bodie's head popped up from behind a rock fifteen yards away from them. "We didn't kill Mingo," he announced loudly.

"That ain't the way we heard it," Dulin drawled. "Word in town was, you boys was right proud of what you done."

"Where's the other one?" Curley asked, twisting around in the saddle, searching.

"No need for nobody to git killed," Bodie said. "We didn't kill Mingo."

They sat their saddles confidently, insolently, carelessly dismissing his words out of hand. Right then Bodie knew nobody was going anywhere without somebody getting killed. Casually he shifted his Winchester to his left hand, freeing his right hand for close-up pistol work.

"Talkin' won't do you no good," Dulin said. "We come too far to be put off." Dulin's lips hadn't stopped working for a second before a pistol shot sounded from behind Bodie.

Dulin left the saddle, a neat red hole in his chest. Before his body came to rest in the dirt, the gun exploded again. A bullet ripped into Edner's throat, tore him from the saddle, his gun hand clutching his sixshooter.

Bodie was dumbstruck.

Curly was too. His mind wasn't prepared for it, couldn't believe Dulin and Edner had been shot out of the saddle in front of his very eyes.

Bodie knew it was a hard thing for any white man to take. He drew his pistol, leveled it at Curly. "What's done is done. You could ride," he advised.

Curly didn't say anything, he just sat there, looking sick.

"Just let it lay, and ride," Bodie repeated with conviction, looking over his pistol barrel at Curly. He hoped his warning would be an invitation, a nudge for Curly to ride from under his gun on up the trail.

Curly was white-lipped, sick to his stomach. Nothing in his southern upbringing had conditioned him to accept defeat from black men. He was utterly incapable of riding away, carrying the dishonor in his mind.

Staring down the dark muzzle of Bodie's drawn six-shooter, he tightened his lips like a man knowingly playing to long odds. He went for his gun.

Bodie's eyes bucked at Curly's bad judgment. And then the gun muzzle winked. He knew right away Curly was dead from the clumsy way he left the saddle, landed hard, grotesquely.

Bodie went down to the lower part of the draw and was looking over the bodies when Ruley came down and joined him, breathing hard from working his way down out of the rocks. He, too, looked over the white men they had killed.

Dulin died from a gaping wound in his back where the bullet had exited. Edner, shot through the windpipe, no doubt had died instantly. Bodie had hit Curly in the chest on the left side, just below the heart. He died with a froth of blood on his lips.

"They never had a chance," Bodie said, lifting his eyes to Ruley.

"Didn't intend 'em to have one," Ruley answered. "This ain't like the army. Only rule we got is to stay alive."

Hastily they dragged the bodies out of plain sight, broke camp, and spurred away from the draw, putting distance between them and the dead men. A mile or so

217

up the trail they checked their horses down to a shambling trot.

"You still figure posse work don't suit you?" Bodie asked.

"There's drawbacks, but it beats stoop labor. . . . Pay's better, too."

"If you live to collect," Bodie stated.

"Oh, I'd collect. I wouldn't take no chances. Not even a little bitty one. Killin' is killin'."

They rode on. After a time Ruley said, "This'll make you a wanted man too," looking across his shoulder at Bodie.

"Don't feel no different," Bodie stated flatly.

So they rode on, neither man talking much as they rode, each man turning over in his mind what lay ahead at Fort Smith.

Chapter Seventeen

So Boot and Amos left Nacimiento. They dug up their cotton money buried in the earth floor of the shed and, with Jimmy Bowlegs unexpectedly joining them, rode away the first week in October on a cloudy overcast morning.

They had been in the saddle only a couple of minutes when Amos started chiding Boot again about his dress as he had done earlier when Boot first put on the gaudy Mexican outfit: "With them clothes on, you'd fit right in at that whorehouse Bowlegs took us to."

Bowlegs turned around in the saddle, smiling, amused at Boot dressed like a Mexican rodeo rider gone mad, wearing a maroon Bolero-style jacket over a black cotton shirt, and tight-fitting, narrow-legged pants of gray Mexican fabric with green stripes down the sides stuffed inside intricately designed high-heeled boots.

They rode north and at the south bank of the Rio Grande at the Grande Indian Crossing, a much-used portion of the Chihuahua war trail from the Nations, they crossed at a dangerous swift-running point considered impassable by soldiers but used often by Indians. On the other side of Painted Gap Boot looked back with a sense of respect at the rugged land they had entered as doubting freemen, but leaving now as men of some proven fighting ability, men who had stood up to the challenge.

At Boot's action, Amos turned around too, and after looking over the country behind him for the last time, he commented, "Never really figured we'd do it. Never counted on a cent after Mr. Perry was killed."

"I had my doubts too," Boot said, straightening back around. "But we done as good as any man, black or white."

"Wish Richmond and Waddy was here."

"They ain't," Boot stated flatly, and tugging down his new wide-brimmed ten-gallon hat with the concho-studded band, he kicked his horse into a trot, taking up the distance between them and Bowlegs, who was riding in the lead.

Riding easy in the saddle, they traveled through rugged country of the Pecos valley, following faint game trails, wild longhorn cattle paths, and mustang traces.

For eight days Bowlegs led them through dense chaparral, over rocky ravines, and across wide stretches of desert flats, taking obscure trails, skirting sandhills, and bisecting cactus patches. It was dry, inhospitable land dotted with prickly pear, cactus, and sagebrush. For long hours in the saddle nothing moved, then suddenly a roadrunner would dart away. Occasionally buzzards could be seen swinging lazily in the sky, searching for the dead that would surely turn up.

Bowlegs rode in the lead, and they talked little, only a hand signal from Bowlegs now and then. At each night's secluded campsite talk invariably settled on a man's particular circumstance.

The conversation at the first night's dry camp had been about Bowlegs's decision to join them. "I go home," he said. "Kickapoo have another home long way," he swept his hand to indicate many miles, "on Blue River in the valley of the Washita. I go there with message from Papequah."

"What message?" Amos asked.

"Papequah wishes Pecan to join him."

"What for?" Boot asked.

"Soon winter comes. Pecan must bring his people now or wait till spring. Winter no good there. Women and children go hungry."

Chief Pecan was headman of the only band of Kickapoo still north of the Red River. In spite of numerous couriers having been sent back to plead with Pecan to bring his starving, decimated band south, the old chief still refused. In the face of encroaching settlers, dwindling game, and almost no buffalo to be had, Pecan stubbornly refused to leave his valley of the Washita.

Now, in a last-ditch effort before winter set in, Bowlegs was being sent back to plead with the chief once more. Wildcat had given Bowlegs his share of plunder money and had instructed him to show Pecan the money as proof of how they subsisted here in Mexico: They would plunder and capture across the Rio Grande in Texas, sell and ransom at good prices to Mexican agents operating under cover of Mexican law. Pecan would surely understand that this way of life was better suited for Kickapoo warriors than having his young men roaming the streams of Washita, Kiamiche, and Canadian rivers looking for trapped-out beaver, venturing out on Comanche/Kiowa-infested western plains in search of killed-out buffalo. Or worse yet, having his women and children beg the soldiers at Fort Washita for weavilly flour and scrawny beef.

"How come you to go?" Amos asked.

"Long time ago Pecan's lodge my lodge. He know I speak from heart." Bowlegs smiled knowingly of the silver pesos he carried in his saddle pockets. "And I show him good proof."

Yesterday's camp talk had been mostly of Boot's captive brother. The talk revolved around whether chances of getting him back were better with trade goods or cash. Amos thought trade goods; Bowlegs didn't care one way or the other. He said, "Money, trade goods, same same. Comanches take either one. Maybe kill you first."

"Trade goods," Amos repeated. "I heard it said so."

"Traders come all time," Bowlegs said. "Sometime trade good, sometime trade not so good. You got guns, trade good."

When they started to break camp Bowlegs asked. "How much you pay ransom your brother?"

Word had gotten around that most captives could be bought back for $250 if kept alive. That's why Boot had signed up at the bureau and had jumped at the muleteer's job with Sam Perry. Now he had more than enough money. But he had no intentions of revealing this to Bowlegs. He looked skeptically at Amos and said evasively to Bowlegs, "Depends on how much my sister got."

"You got sister?" Bowlegs asked, arching his eyebrows.

"Yeah. Bertha."

Bowlegs was silent, reflective, while they continued saddling up. First to finish, he swung onto the saddle, looked down at Boot tightening up his cinch, and said, "Your sister, maybe I see. She tall woman, dress like man?"

"That's Bertha, all right." Boot dropped his stirrup.

Stiffening his voice, he asked, "Where'd you see her?"

Bowlegs related to them how the band had come up on a black woman and an old white man far out on the plains in Comanche territory.

"You didn't bother her, did you?" Boot demanded.

Bowlegs smiled benignly. "We no bother. Wildcat say no."

"Would you have bothered her?"

"I bother," Bowlegs answered without emotion, swinging his horse away.

"What you reckon they was doin' out there?" Amos asked as they mounted up.

"Woman say lookin' for salt," Bowlegs said over his shoulder.

"Salt!" Amos repeated incredulously.

"To git money, I betcha," Boot guessed, "ransom money. We was penniless when Comanches took my brother. Mr. Ned, that's the old white man Bowlegs seen with Bertha, said we could go anywhere we was of a mind to but it wouldn't be no use 'n us goin' to Indian country without ransom money or trade goods, so we set out to git money."

"Her goin' out there like that," Amos said reproachfully, "wonder somebody ain't got to ransom her too."

They caught up to Bowlegs's side.

"You go to Comanche lands?" he asked.

"Yeah," Boot said. "Amos here is comin' with me."

"Maybe you both die," Bowlegs said. "You shoot good, him not so good."

Bowlegs led the way out of the hidden draw they had camped in and took to the arid plains.

They rode north by a little bit east.

They crossed the shallow waters of the Pecos River at Horsehead Crossing and before sundown arrived at Twin Mountains, two utterly flattopped mountains, if such they could be called, with a cleft between them.

223

The gap through the mountains was a well-established route used by the Butterfield Stage Line before the war. The route was yet marked by broken water tanks half buried in windblown sand.

They kept to rock cover along the north edge of the gap, and here Bowlegs ventured a conversation about their eventual separation, a subject they had already agreed on and hence was little discussed. "We come to red waters soon. Tomorrow I sleep daytime, go nighttime. You do same same. Soldiers no come nighttime."

"We got nothin' to hide," Boot said again. "We'll rest at night same as we been doin'."

"You have good horses, no need rest."

"Horses might not, but we will," Boot said with finality.

Darkness had gathered by the time they had ridden through the gap and had cleared the detritus at the foot of the mountains. Bowlegs pulled up easily, looked out over the wide expanse of alkali flats now ghostly pale under the frail light of stars. When Boot and Amos rode up alongside him, Bowlegs jestured at a jumble of boulders over to the side. "You find camp there, I find water."

"Tonight?" Boot asked.

"Tomorrow no water. Must find water tonight."

Amos looked out across the star-struck alkali flats. As far as his eyes could see, the bald, flat land offered nothing, not a tree nor a shrub, not a sandhill nor a gully. "We shoulda gone back the way we come," Amos muttered, more to himself than to the others.

"This way more better," Bowlegs stated again.

Boot twisted around in his saddle and, scanning the rocks at his back, asked, "You sho' there's water up there?"

Bowlegs indicated the goatskin canteens carried on

their saddle horns and said, "You drink, I bring more."

An hour or so later, carrying three full canteens in his two hands, Bowlegs joined them on a small piece of flat ground that Boot had picked out in the rocks. Looking around approvingly, Bowlegs said, "This good place."

"How'd you know there was water up there?" Amos asked.

"Black rock keep water long time . . . you find black rock, you maybe find water. Same same fire rock."

Bowlegs unsheathed his fighting knife and picked in the sand. Striking stone, he swept aside the sand, heaping it up into a crude berm. "You put more sand, bring horses. I bring water."

From an oval-shaped sand berm perhaps four feet across they watered the horses, the solid rock underneath absorbing only a little of the water Bowlegs had brought. He made four trips up to the *tinajas*, a small concave depression in the rocks where rainwater had been trapped and some still remained. On the last trip he told them, "You drink now, then sleep. Tonight we go." Bowlegs's argument about the danger of traveling in wide-open Comanche country in daylight had prevailed for now.

They slept. Bowlegs woke them up somewhere around midnight. They started their horses across the alkali flats.

They began their crossing at a canter, walked some, then cantered some more. Twice they stopped, watered the horses from the canteens, each time wiping alkali dust from the horses' nostrils.

In the wee hours of dawn the alkali flats gave way to rough, hardscrabble ground, flat as a pancake but showing mesquite-covered sandhills in the near-distant east.

Two hours later, the great disk from the east appeared. They crossed over a brush-choked, north–south-running ravine. Topping out on the east side, Bowlegs said,

"River there," and he indicated the Concho to the northeast. "Water not so good there. We get water here, then go."

On they went over flat rocky ground bisected by a stream of clear-running water bordered by a clump of scrub timber on the east and on the south by zigzag slashes of shallow ravines so briar-choked they were almost impassable.

Bowlegs checked his horse to a slow walk, searching the area, seeing holes where tepee stakes had been driven into the ground, the outlines of many circles where lodges had once stood, camp debris scattered all around. He rode past dead campfires, half-burned sticks of mesquite roots, and buffalo bones of past meals.

Looking around wide-eyed at what had obviously been a big Indian village, Boot asked, "What place is this?"

"This Spring Creek," Bowlegs answered. "Papequah camp here before go to Dove Creek." Bowlegs swung his horse over to some boulders at the edge of the abandoned village described to him in detail by subchief Pashagon, and where Pashagon had said his daughter Ahteewat had been buried after the ordeal of the long journey from southern Kansas had brought on premature childbirth and sudden death.

Bowlegs stopped and sat his horse, looking without emotion at the grave at the edge of the rocks that he had stopped by to honor at the request of Chief Pashagon. When Boot and Amos checked their horses to a halt alongside him and saw what Bowlegs was looking at, Bowlegs said bitterly, "White man disturb death sleep."

Boot and Amos looked with horror at what Bowlegs was talking about: The grave of Ahteewat had been opened. The slab of limestone that had been placed over it had been moved aside, the shallow grave scooped out, exposing the body to sunlight and predators. The buckskin dress Ahteewat had been buried in had rotted, stiff ribbons of leather clinging between bleached skeleton bones scattered by predators.

"Who'd do a thing like. this?" Amos asked disgustedly.

"Kickapoo bury dead with sacred ornaments," Bowlegs said. "Now ornaments gone."

"They dug her up for trinkets!" Boot said unbelievingly.

"Now she have nothing to hide," Bowlegs said. "White man take." He swung his horse away rudely and said without emotion, "We get water, go."

At Spring Creek they drank cool sweet water, filled their canteens, then watered the horses. Bowlegs took only minutes, then mounted up and rode away. When all traces of the abandoned village were behind them, Bowlegs led the way down a steep ravine, into a feeder canyon partially hidden by dwarf mesquite and prickly pear. They stripped off saddle gear, hobbled their horses, and each man took to his saddle blankets. They had all plunged off to sleep even before the sun probed its rays into the ravine's bottom.

Bowlegs slept a little, woke up, slept some more. For no good reason, he woke up again. This time he silently crept away. While the other two slept he worked his way up the slope of a nearby sandhill, and as far as his eyes could reach scouted the surrounding country.

Nothing moved out there.

Returning to where the other two slept, he sat his blankets, chewing on jerked beef, turning over in his mind the thought of their going out into Comanche country. Bowlegs knew it was a dangerous undertaking even for an Indian. Every tribe had renegades roaming the plains, killing and scalping for reasons of their own, not least of which was the queer notion of pleasure.

It was in the cool of sundown that they took to the trail again, men and animals well-rested. Under a wan moon and pale stars they rode thirty miles without incident over hard-packed earth with no water and little grass. What grass there was was a tawny brown from lack of rainfall and the coming of winter.

At Colorado River—or Red Water, as Bowlegs knew it—they let their horses drink the brackish water, each man thinking about the implications of their parting.

Bowlegs lifted his eyes into the slate-gray vastness to the east, reassured them of their direction: "Four, five hours is fort, maybe soldiers there. One day maybe more is another fort, no soldiers there. You find fort, you no get lost."

Here Bowlegs spoke of abandoned Confederate Fort Chadbourne on Oak Creek, a small tributary of the Colorado, and farther north Fort Phantom Hill. Chadbourne was the only one that had been occupied from time to time by Confederates and Texas Militiamen, but both forts had been ineffective in checking Indian raids and were now under review for federal usefulness by General Sheridan.

"We'll keep goin' east like you told us," Amos assured Bowlegs.

"Which way you go from here?" Boot asked Bowlegs.

"I follow Red Water to Big Spring," Bowlegs said, lifting his horse's muzzle from the water. He stepped up to the stirrup, swung aboard, and continued, "I join other Indians there, make talk."

Boot and Amos mounted up but lingered there in the saddle, making small talk, each man reluctant to leave.

"Daytime come, you rest," Bowlegs told them again.

"We got nothin' to hide," Boot repeated.

"Ahteewat had nothing to hide," Bowlegs countered again.

Bowlegs instructed them: "This time year Indians come from all around to Big Spring. You travel daytime, Indians see. Daytime no good, you sleep. Nighttime more better, you go."

Bowlegs was speaking of the raiding season of fall, the time of the harvest moon when Indians of every affiliation came from as far away as the Platte River in Colorado, gathered at the Big Spring on the Colorado River in Texas. After a time of war talk and feasting the Indians split up, took to the plunder trail, taking the route that offered the best chance for success: To the west they struck at Chihuahua, Mexico; to the south they marauded lower Texas and Coahuila, Mexico; and to the east they ravaged Texas settlements lightly defended.

And since Boot and Amos were heading east, Bowlegs told them about a little-known thing only Indians with respect for enemies observed: "Indian see you, you ride circle." He weaved his finger in a small circle. "Means no fight. You talk, maybe Indian listen."

"I heard Indians don't talk much," Boot said, cutting his eyes at Amos.

"Maybe, maybe not," Bowlegs said flatly. "You try."

Bowlegs knew that although they had demonstrated some skill, they had no chance against skillful, veteran fighters out there, as the Indians they were likely to meet would surely be.

Finally Amos led out reluctantly and Boot followed, plunging his horse into the knee-deep chocolate waters of the Colorado. On the other side they twisted around, looked back across the water.

Jimmy Bowlegs had his horse in a shambling trot up the west bank of the Colorado, barely visible in the obscure light of early morning.

"Probably the last we'll see of him," Amos said sadly.

"No tellin'," Boot said, and touched his horse into a trot, heading north by a little bit east.

Chapter Eighteen

Boot and Amos had better than six hours in the saddle now since they had crossed the Colorado River, and Jimmy Bowlegs had gone his own way. Each man rode slump-shouldered, their horses walking hang-necked. The land they rode was flat, arid country. The only thing that distinguished one spot from another was the occasional appearance of a gully or a low hogback. Nothing showed them the way except a sense of where the east lay, and a weak sun, which was scudded over regularly by cumulus clouds.

Two more hours they rode under a canopy of gray sky before checking their horses to a stop at a long roll of the land, ranging their eyes as far ahead as the horizon. Up ahead the same cheerless terrain stretched into the unknown. "We shoulda gone back the way we came," Amos said ruefully.

"Too late for that now. We's here."

"No tellin' where that fort is Bowlegs mentioned."

231

"Don't see how a man can rightly judge distance out here nohow," Boot said, looking all around.

"Bowlegs was right about one thing. A man stick out like a swole head out here. Ridin' at night like he said makes a whole lot more sense now."

"We'd see anybody the same as they'd see us."

"Might be more of them than us, though," Amos said flatly.

"Might be," Boot agreed.

Later, thinking the matter over, he relented, saying, "We find a good spot, we'll stop till night."

On they rode, their horses at a walk. An hour later the land was still disheartening to look at, tiring to ride across. There wasn't a hint of shelter between them and the horizon. Their smallness stood out starkly in the vast sweep of land, making them feel helpless, vulnerable.

Around noontime they struck the dry wash that had been Oak Creek, once upon a time a north–south-running stream that had carried water to the Colorado during times of abundant rainfall. Now it was powder-dry, nothing but fine sand that a man could blow away with his breath.

"No sense in pushin' on," Boot said. "Let's find some place to rest."

"You won't git no argument from me on that score," Amos said.

Weary in the saddle, they walked their horses up the wash, each man aching down in his bones, ready to give up the search for the fort that Bowlegs had told them about.

Directly the dry wash turned between two low sandhills, and in the middle of that desolate wasteland crouched the tumbled-down walls and dilapidated buildings of abandoned Fort Chadbourne.

"There it is!" Boot blurted out.

"It sho' ain't much," Amos commented, roving his

eyes over the broken adobe walls and caved-in buildings.

"It's better 'n nothin'," Boot said, flicking his horse into a faster walk.

They rode through the open space that had been the gate into the old fort. They pulled up, dismounted next to an adobe wall partly covered with banked-up wind-blown sand, a log roof slanting from it. "You reckon there's water here?" Amos asked, looking around as they both stripped off saddle gear.

"Maybe a dug well somewhere. I'll look around."

Shortly Boot returned, telling Amos even as Amos positioned his saddle, spread his blankets, making a bed: "No sign of a dug well nowhere. We'll have to make do with what water we got."

"Soldiers musta hauled in water," Amos guessed.

In a sweep of some thirty miles of bleak, barren land two beat-out black men sat on their blankets, chewing smoked goat meat, making idle talk. Boot said, "We git to Indian country, we could ask around for Bowlegs. He'd be a mighty big help to us."

"Who we goin' to ask?" Amos wondered.

"Mr. Ned said there's friendly Indian villages just across Red River before you git to wild country. He says if you was to give 'em tobacco or something like that, they'd tell you what they know, maybe even show you for a price. Maybe they'd know Bowlegs."

"Way Bowlegs tell it, they'll know him, all right."

"Way he tell it, we might be sorry we asked about him."

"I 'speck Bowlegs's talk is mostly brag," Amos said, chuckling lightly.

"I wudn't be so sho'. Bowlegs's seen a lot. Nothin' bothers him, not even killin' and kidnappin'."

"Like you said, he'd be a big help if we was to find him."

Shortly they lapsed into silence, their heads on their

saddles, their chins resting on their chests, their horses standing slack-legged off to the side.

Around them nothing moved. No breeze stirred the sand; nor did a fly appear. No leaves rustled; nor did animals move about.

But the buzzards came.

Three swung serenely overhead, searching the ground for a meal.

Boot and Amos had been asleep about three hours when wagons topped the sandhill from the east, dropped down into the depression.

The loud crack of a whip jerked Boot out of his sleep. His right hand grasped the rifle propped there against the wall. He stood up, holding the Winchester alongside his leg, searching out toward the jingle of trace chains that he heard.

He saw the wagons coming. Startling Amos awake with a jab of his boot-toe, he told him in a low voice, "Somebody's comin'."

Amos collected himself, stood up next to Boot, both watching the outfit come on. Amos said, "They colored!"

"Yeah," Boot grunted offhandedly. "Ain't them bones they haulin'?"

"Them's bones, all right."

Boot looked questioningly at Amos. "Bones good to sell . . . nine dollars a ton, last I heard. People up north make fertilizer out of 'em."

"They got a plenty of 'em," Boot commented.

The scavenging outfit consisted of a freight wagon with a trailer wagon behind it, drawn by four mule teams. Each wagon was heaped high with bleached buffalo bones, and a man was walking on each side of the lead wagon. A lean man with gray whiskers rode the seat of the lead wagon, all three shabbily dressed with shapeless hats flopped down like sunbonnets. Each looked to be in his late thirties, or possibly early forties.

The outfit turned into the open space leading onto the parade ground. Out of the corner of his eye the man riding the seat spotted Boot and Amos for the first time. Looking at them skeptically, he hauled back on the lines and drew the team to a rolling stop just inside the fort. Smiling broadly from under the brim of his hat, he said through gapped, tobacco-stained teeth, "Well, I'm damned if y'all ain't chillun of my own soul! What in hell you doin' out here?"

"Headin' east," Boot said, bringing the Winchester innocuously into view.

"Headin' east!" the man blurted out, lowering his eyes to Boot's Winchester. "That ain't sayin' much, boy!"

"Sayin' enough," Boot answered.

"Why hell, there ain't nowhere else to head 'lessen you was Mexican or Indian. Then it wudn't be no tellin' where you was headin'. You ain't Mexican, is you?" he asked, finally taken by the outfit Boot was wearing.

Amos spoke up pleasantly. "We headin' to Gulch . . . Squaw Valley, to be exact. Name's Amos; this here's Boot."

The man shifted his eyes to Amos. "Squaw Valley, huh?" he repeated deliberately, leaning out, spitting a stream of tobacco juice out across the sand toward Boot. "Guess you ain't heard. Squaw Valley ain't a fit place to go." He brought his eyes back to bear on Boot but kept his words directed at Amos. "Name's Thompson, Rattlesnake Thompson most folks call me." Keening his eyes at Boot, he asked hopefully, "You heard of me, ain't you?"

"Naw," Boot answered.

Thompson's face went slack, his feelings hurt at not being heard of. Looking at Boot with a fixed eye, he asked, "Can you hit what you aim at with that long gun you got there?"

"I do fair."

"Uh-huh," Thompson said, nodding his head, disbelief coming through in the way he did it. Twisting around on the seat he said to the man standing on his right, "Bozy, tell 'em about Squaw Valley."

"There's a race war goin' on over there," Bozy said, dragging his words out. "If I was y'all, I'd pass the place by. Heard there's shootin' and hangin' every day over there."

"Coloreds too?" Boot asked.

"Them what got guns," Bozy drawled.

"How'd it start?" Amos asked.

"The way it was told to us when we stopped at Gullytown was two fellers come in there, started signin' up coloreds to vote. One of 'em, a white man, was killed in Gulch. Townspeople spread word that ain't no nigger goin' to vote in Gulch.

"Coloreds banded together in the Union League, said they was goin' to vote, take over the county." Bozy's voice was slow, tiresome to listen to, but that didn't lessen his meaning. He shook his head sadly. "Squaw Valley and roundabouts ain't a safe place for no colored man. Whole county's gone crazy, and ain't nobody doin' nothin' about it."

"What's this Union League?" Boot asked.

"Some outfit from up north," Thompson answered. "Hear they teaches what rights we got, the Constitution and all.

"They say it's led by a right smart colored feller. Him being new to the county, he'll git a lot of folks killed over this here votin' stuff."

"I got a sister waitin' for me in Squaw Valley," Boot said. "I got to go back."

"Better keep your eyes open, then . . . and hit what

you aim at," Thompson warned, "or leave your gun out of sight."

"Where y'all headed?" Amos asked.

"Anywhere there's bones. You seen any?"

"None to speak of," Boot answered.

"We come in from Mexico," Amos volunteered.

"Mexico," Rattlesnake repeated. "Thought you was from somewhere else," he said knowingly, looking closer at the way Boot was dressed. Then he looked again at the fine horses and saddle gear off to the side. He focused his narrow eyes at Amos and asked, "You got any of that Mexican whiskey with you?"

"None," Boot answered.

Rattlesnake looked disgustedly at Boot. "Didn't figure you did." He continued cheerily, "Mexican whiskey is the only whiskey I know that's as good as mine." Rattlesnake shook the lines, got the team in motion, then said out the side of his mouth, "We puts up in the old officer's quarters yonder. You welcome to join us if you care to jaw a spell. We got coffee, hog meat, and beans . . . and whiskey of my own makin'."

"Might take you up on that," Amos yelled out to him.

Amos wanted to join them, but Boot didn't trust the scavengers. However, he was eager to hear more of the troubles at Squaw Valley. Before he agreed to join them he and Amos stashed the money in a dug hole in the banked-up sand there, saddled up, and was ready to light out at the slightest hint of trouble from the unsavory characters.

They walked across the parade ground, filed past the unhinged door, and stepped inside the old officers' quarters.

"Come on in," Thompson said good-naturedly from a crude plank table down in the middle of the room. "Was hopin' you'd come." Rattlesnake looked down to the end of the room where a man was working over a broken fireplace, and said, "Clubby, dish up two more plates for these here fellers." Turning back to them, he said, "Whiskey's good, and I'm talked out with these two knotheads."

"Rattlesnake, I ain't never seen you talked out," the man called Clubby answered. "Or heard of it. You, Bozy?"

"If Rattlesnake was to git talked out he'd drop dead on the spot," Bozy drawled from over next to the wall where he was busy sweeping back dust for bedrolls. "Only man I know got somethin' to say about everything."

"That's 'cause I took time to think on 'em," Thompson said. He blew sand from two tin cups rummaged from the camp gear spread out on the table and set them out.

Boot and Amos sat down at the table on a bench opposite Rattlesnake, took turns pouring a drink from the jug there. Amos tasted a small sip from his tin, took another, sat it down. "Whiskey's right good," he told Rattlesnake.

"Whiskey's sort of my trade," Rattlesnake said proudly. "That and bones."

Boot sat his tin down after taking a drink, let his eyes follow Clubby, who was walking by, swinging a bucket in his hand, obviously going somewhere for water. Bringing his attention back to Thompson, Boot asked, "About this trouble in Gulch, is it spread all over?"

"Everywhere! There's race killin' everywhere now. Around Gulch is just the worst. You musta been in Mexico not to have heard . . . or dead." Rattlesnake took a long drink, sat the cup down, and explained: "We got the right to vote now, but white folks tryin' to scare us into not usin' it. Scared we'll vote 'em out."

"Vote 'em out of what?" Amos asked.

Even Rattlesnake was surprised by their ignorance. He

exchanged looks across the room with Clubby. Clubby said, "We can vote on everything now. There's a whole new gov'ment. We got the same rights a white man got."

" 'Course, they'll kill ya to stop you from votin'," Thompson said. "That's what the trouble is at Gulch. The Union League is pushin' the coloreds to vote, the whites pushin' to stop 'em from votin'. It's a mess. Any stranger, black or white, suspected of being in the Union League is horsewhipped out of town or shot."

"Gulch that bad?" Boot asked, his eyes following Clubby, returning with a bucket of water.

"That bad," Thompson confirmed. "There ain't a single colored man left in Gulch now, and two men who dared to come back was hanged."

"At least a dozen been whipped," Bozy said ponderously. "And half that many been shot."

"Some big rancher," Thompson said confidentially. "They say he got hired men to rid the county of colored folks. Even got colored men on his payroll, I heard," he said disgustedly. "If that don't beat all, ain't nothin' will." Thompson took another sip, set the cup down. "We skirted the place on the way out here. Was I y'all, I'd do the same."

"Can't," Boot said. "Got a sister waitin' there."

Rattlesnake took a long drink this time, lowered his tin, and said, "You go back there, you better figger to do some killin', 'cause that's what white folks'll be doin'."

Bozy walked down from the fireplace, slid three tin plates of beans and fried pork on the table, and said cautiously, "Y'all go back there, don't trust nobody. Not even colored folks."

Boot and Amos ate. Thompson resumed talking: "A lot of homeless men, white and colored, roamin' the country lookin' for work. Any one of 'em will kill you for money, or maybe just for the hoss you ridin'."

"That's the truth," Clubby droned. He studied his thoughts for a minute, then said something that had been bothering them all: "Rattlesnake, we sell these bones, we ought to buy us some guns. We naked as jaybirds out here. Anybody was to jump us, we couldn't fight gnats from in front of our faces."

"Hell, you'd likely shoot yo' ownself," Rattlesnake scoffed, "or me or Bozy."

Amos smiled knowingly. And for no good reason whatsoever, Amos asked Thompson, "How come they call you Rattlesnake?

Thompson smiled, looked over at Bozy. "Tell 'em, Boz."

"Well," Bozy drawled, catching his breath. "That whiskey you drunk, when it's just about ready, Thompson here catches one of them rattlesnakes he keeps, cuts off the head, and puts it in the brew. He says it gives the whiskey a good bite like no other. That's his brag. And it's true. Ain't that right, Clubby."

"That's right. Once you taste Thompson's whiskey, you never forgits it. Anybody wants good whiskey, they ask around for Rattlesnake Thompson."

Thompson had smiled with pleasure while Bozy had told the story. Now he sipped his own whiskey, making a show of it, and said proudly to Amos, "You live to git out of Squaw Valley, you ask around about old Rattlesnake Thompson. They'll know me."

"We'll live," Boot said, talking around the last mouthful of food. Taking up his Winchester, he tossed off the last of his whiskey and started for the door, saying over his shoulder, "First we got to git there."

On their way to the horses Amos said in a low voice, "There's water here somewhere."

"I know," Boot said. "It won't be hard to find. When Clubby came back carryin' that bucket his boots was covered with wet sand. That water's hid somewhere close by. We'll find it."

They dug up the money bags from the sand next to the wall, led their horses across the parade ground, and found Clubby's tracks leading away from the officers' quarters. They followed them to the back of the old hospital building, and found a dug well partially concealed by a wooden door put in place over it. They drew a bucket of water, drank their fill, topped off their canteens, and let the horses drink from the well bucket.

They mounted up and started across the parade ground. Rattlesnake spoke from the door where he and Clubby had been watching them all the time: "If you'da asked, I'da told y'all where that water was."

"Wadn't no trouble," Boot said. "Tracks plain as day."

"Right smart-alecky, ain't he?" Clubby said.

"Yeah. He's careful to a fault," Bozy said, dragging out his words.

"Or plain scared," Rattlesnake retorted.

Boot and Amos walked their horses across the old parade ground leading out of the fort. Rattlesnake yelled out to them, "West of Gulch you'll come to Gullytown. If you was to ask, colored folks there could tell you more about the goin's-on at Squaw Valley than I can."

"Heard all I need to," Boot answered, and kept on riding.

Exiting the fort's gate, they touched their horses into a canter and headed out onto the plains, riding for Squaw Valley and whatever danger lay ahead.

Chapter Nineteen

Abandoned Fort Chadbourne and Rattlesnake Thompson were three days behind them now. They rode in daylight hours, feeling their way east by sun and shadows. Wild country was grudgingly giving way to gently rolling prairie land dotted with sagebrush, mottes of scrub mesquite, and dwarf pines.

That morning they had skirted the first settler's cabin they had seen since crossing the Colorado River, a low-roofed log cabin on the other side of the valley.

That afternoon they topped a low rise as they had done many others, but beyond this one across the prairie they saw the ruins of the other fort Bowlegs had told them to look out for.

Fort Phantom Hill had been built in 1852, but for lack of drinking water had been abandoned in 1854. Every building inside the fort had been mysteriously burned, some said by prairie fire, others said by overjoyed soldiers to prevent its reoccupation. Now sentinels of weathered brick chimneys stood watch over forty-six overgrown mounds of ashes that used to be building foundations.

They nooned in a shaft of shade cast by a lonely chimney at the edge of the fort, and between chews of jerked goat meat Boot told Amos, "Brazos River ain't far off now. Once we cross there, home's only a hop and a skip away."

"You know the country from there?"

"Pretty much."

"Gullytown?"

"Never heard of it before. From what Rattlesnake said, we can't miss it, though."

"You figure to stop?"

"See no reason to. If there's trouble, Bertha will know about it. And take my word on it, she'll tell us all about it when we git home."

From Phantom Hill they worked their way by intuition toward Squaw Valley. Two days later, just at sundown, they struck the line of endlessly shimmering willows that marked the Brazos River. "No use 'n tryin' to cross tonight," Boot said, and they skirted the willows, searching for a place to camp.

"We ought to cross now," Amos advised. "Like Bowlegs did. If somebody was follerin' us, we'd have the river between us."

"River's too risky to cross at night. Even in the daytime you got to watch out."

"Wadn't no trouble crossin' the others."

"This one ain't like the others. It's full of quicksand and suckholes, and there's snakes, water moccasins. I heard tell of a man ridin' into quicksand and his whole hoss just disappeared. Another man got halfway 'cross and a suckhole pulled 'em under, hoss and all. Safest thing for us to do is wait till daylight. That way we can see what we doin'."

They weaved their way through second-growth willows, and on a swath of sandy shore next to a lightning-struck willow they stripped off saddle gear, staked out their horses, and went into night camp within hearing distance of the babbling water.

Kneeling over a bunch of twigs and dried leaves, Boot coaxed flame while Amos got out the cooking gear, as had become their routine.

"Coffee would go right good 'long about now," Boot said.

"It sho' would. Seems like we been out of coffee a month instead of two days." Amos dropped a skillet and a slab of stiff goat meat down next to Boot's leg. He positioned the empty coffeepot near the small flame Boot had started. Since they had run out of coffee they had started drinking just the boiled water. Amos said of the tasteless, insipid substitute, "Hot water ain't gettin' no tastier. A man ain't likely to mistake it for coffee."

"Ain't tryin' to," Boot said. "Just makin' do."

Amos walked away to search for firewood, as had also become the routine. Boot warned him, "Don't look for no driftwood. You might step in quicksand or run up on a snake down by the water."

The sound of Amos's footsteps had barely faded away when wild thrashing came from the bushes and a shaken voice cried out in shock, "I'm bit!"

Boot sprang to his feet, grabbed his rifle propped on the deadfall. The water moccasin that had bitten Amos was slithering for the water when Boot came up on the run. He fired on the move, braced himself spread-legged, fired again.

The first shot parted the snake in two; the second one took the head clear off the body.

"He bit me!" Amos screamed, looking wide-eyed at Boot from down on his knees.

"Where?"

"Got me on the wrist!" Amos said, holding up his right wrist for Boot to see. "Them kinda snakes don't kill you, do they?"

"Young'un might," Boot said. "Old one ain't likely to."

"Which one was he?"

"Can't say," Boot answered, laying his rifle aside. "He got you good," Boot said, inspecting the puncture marks. "Swellin' set in already."

"What we goin' to do?"

"First thing we got to do is tie it off, stop the poison from spreadin'." Hurriedly Boot stripped off his shirt, and he was about to rip off a strip when they heard footsteps crashing through the brush. They both brought their eyes around.

A white man was standing over near their campfire, his Winchester pointed generally at them, a youngster standing behind him.

For a minute nobody spoke, each side sizing up the other.

Boot glanced uneasily toward his Winchester lying on the ground where he had thrown it aside.

"Heard your shots," the man said mildly. "Trouble?"

"Snake," Boot answered. "Water moccasin."

"I'm bit," Amos stated flatly.

The white man moved the rifle alongside his leg and ordered the youngster, "Go back to the wagon and tell your ma. She'll know what to send."

When the youngster had gone, they started back to the campsite, Boot carrying the firewood Amos had gathered. The white man introduced himself: "Don't guess names mean much out here, but mine's Gillespie, Ed Gillespie. That was my boy what left."

"Mine's Boot, his'n is Amos."

Gillespie was a tall slim man of medium build. He

wore dark homespun trousers, a store-bought gray flannel coat. He had a friendliness about him but kept his rifle close at hand and moved carefully. At the campsite he swept the surroundings with his eyes, saw nothing offensive, and said conversationally, "Saw you come in off the prairie. Figured you'd ford the river before dark. Where you headed?"

"East," Boot answered, stooping to build up the fire.

"Man usually fords a river in front of him before he beds down," Gillespie said questioningly.

"Figured to wait for daylight so we could see what we was up against."

"That's sound reasonin' . . . but misplaced this time. We crossed no more 'n half an hour ago. No trouble." His rifle held pistol-fashion, Ed walked casually over to the deadfall where Amos sat, lifted Amos's wrist, and looked at the wound. "Swellin's bad. That wrist'll be as big as a man's leg come mornin'."

"I'm feelin' mighty poorly, too," Amos said. "Ever knowed anybody to die from this kinda snake bite?"

"Knowed some," Ed said. "And some that wished they had. Fever comes on. Without proper doctorin' it'll kill you."

At that moment the rustle of undergrowth and the swish of willow branches came to them. The youngster rushed up out of the shadows. "Here, Pa," he said, reaching over a tied-up bundle. "Ma said be sure and git it tight."

Working hurriedly, Ed untied the bundle, bathed the punctures in coal oil from a jar he found inside, then plastered them over with baking soda that was also there. Quickly he wrapped the wrist tight with rag bandages, then drenched the bandages with more coal oil. "This'll keep till you can see a proper doctor," he said, capping the peach jar of leftover coal oil. "Take this with you. That bandage starts to dry out, soak it again real good."

On Ed's advice Amos took to his blankets, lay back in the crook of his saddle. Ed told the youngster, "Go back to the wagon and look after your ma and sister. I'll be along directly."

Boot and Gillespie talked while Boot prepared rations of warmed-over goat meat and flour bread.

It turned out that Gillespie and his family were refugeeing to Mexico to escape the wrath of staunch exrebels who had accused him of contriving and promoting their political and social disabilities. Derisively called a scalawag, Gillespie was a native southerner who believed in equal rights for all men, and had lived that way.

Gillespie had accepted a job as a registration board member. Word had gotten around that the mild-mannered scalawag was actively promoting coloreds over whites. Gillespie was warned to quit the job, but he refused. In the last two weeks his store was sacked, his kid was beaten to embarrassment, and his wife was hooted at in town.

Gillespie knew that another scalawag had been shot down in broad daylight, and two days earlier the county judge in the adjacent county was shot dead at his office after insisting that a colored witness be brought in to testify in his court against a white man who was later convicted.

Word came to Ed by night rider that unknown parties were out to get him. He was next. So Gillespie was getting out now with his family, joining other scalawags in Mexico.

Sitting cross-legged on the deadfall, Gillespie hitched his leg around and commented, "Country ain't safe for a fair-minded white man." He sipped from the cup of tepid water that he had accepted out of courtesy after Boot had protested against having the youngster bring back real coffee.

"Bone scavengers we run into out on the prairie said

247

it ain't safe for colored folks neither," Boot said.

"It's been that way all along," Ed confessed, "especially in and around Squaw Valley. But this's the first I can remember when white folks turned on their own kind so viciously." Gillespie gazed forlornly into the crackling fire. "It's worse 'n '61 when the country broke apart." Looking across the fire at Amos, who had dozed off, he said to Boot, "Best you git 'em to a doctor as soon as possible. Town called Gulch is west of here, but I wouldn't recommend it."

"Gullytown?"

"You're welcome to try, but I doubt they'll have a doctor. Place ain't nothin' but a bunch of homeless coloreds livin' in shelters of sheet tin and scrap lumber."

Gillespie sat his tin cup down on the deadfall and stood up. "Any trouble west of here?"

"None. We traveled mostly at night."

"Well," Ed said resignedly, "can't say the same for east of here. You'll have trouble with white folks for sure, coloreds too maybe."

"Heard some coloreds turned on their own. What's behind it?"

"Power . . . political power. Who's to run the county. It's all tied up in votin', civil rights, and such. Colored outfit called the Joe Jones gang ridin' the country terrorizing coloreds not to vote, or if they do vote to vote like they're told."

"Leaving whites in charge of the county?"

"Just as sure as they are now."

"How come Joe Jones and his gang do it?"

"Money . . . and power. Not many coloreds got guns to defend themselves, so a feller named Putterman pays the gang wages, puts guns in their hands, and sends 'em to do whatever pleases him.

"Well," Gillespie said finally, "I better git back. Got a long day ahead of us tomorrow."

248

In the morning Boot discovered a wide band of quicksand just off the campsite, so they forded the Brazos without incident a hundred or so yards upstream where they saw Gillespie's wagon tracks. They struck the open prairie, and four hours later they spotted wisps of smoke rising up seemingly from out of the prairie itself.

"Gullytown?" Amos asked.

"Got to be. Wadn't nothin' else out there." Boot studied his thoughts, then asked Amos, "How you feelin'?"

"Poorly."

"We'll see if they got a doctor," he said, and swung his horse toward the columns of smoke.

They came in off the prairie, riding into Gullytown among their own kind. But they looked nothing of the sort.

Maybe it was the Mexican bolero jacket and big hat one of them wore. A man watching them snickered at the queer way Boot was dressed, then grinned wide. "Ain't never seen nothin' like it," he commented.

"Seen Mexicans down in Rio wearin' stuff like that," another man said.

A half-dozen or so men were watching them come, and they all knew these two were different.

Maybe it was the pistols they wore, balanced by a fighting knife on the other side; maybe it was the long-legged ponies with the Mexican saddles and a Winchester riding in the boot; maybe it was just the feel of them, but the squatters knew there was something about these two.

They came to a tin-roofed lean-to first. Out front a tall, thin-shouldered man with a kinky gray beard was selling whiskey from a plank countertop. Like the others, his shifty eyes had followed the two strangers coming in from the wrong direction. Now that they had gotten within talking distance, he made his sales pitch good-

249

naturedly. "Got good whiskey . . . ten cents a shot, or you can belly up for four bits."

They checked their horses to a stop, looking over the counter merchandise: canned tomatoes, chewing tobacco, coffee . . .

"Coffee," Boot told him, "just coffee."

The man came from behind the counter with the coffee, his eyes taking in the crude bandage on Amos's wrist. Passing the coffee up to Boot, he asked, "What ails him?"

"Snakebite."

"How long ago?"

"Twelve, fourteen hours."

"He ain't dead, whiskey's good for it," the man advised. "All he can swaller."

"Anybody here trained to doctor?"

"Well, I don't know about the trainin'," the man said, scratching along his jaw, "but there's a woman named Maude, Maude Tilly. Her place's just the other side of the gully yonder," and he nodded his head that way. "She's got a fortune-teller sign out front, but she doctors most ailments."

They rode away from the drummer's counter, questioning eyes following them. Along their way women pulled children to them, ducked out of sight.

They rode past a loose knot of men working over a slaughtered hog hung up for butchering in a vacant lot. They swung their horses, crossed over the gully, came out on the other side where a woman behind a counter was selling sweet-potato pies and cookies.

At the far end of the poverty-stricken village they pulled up in front of a tin shack no taller than a man's head. Before they could dismount a middle-aged woman stepped into the curtained-off doorway. She was heavy-breasted, and gray stringy hair hung limply from under a blue headrag framing a dark, round face. She asked boldly, "What y'all want?"

"You Maude Tilly?" asked Boot.

"Yeah, I'm Maude Tilly," she answered firmly, and thrust small pudgy hands on her ample hips.

"Snake bit him," Boot said, nodding toward Amos. "Heard you doctor some."

Maude's hands fell away from her hips, and her shoulders sagged in relief. "Git down," she invited. "I thought y'all was some of them," she said, obviously relieved.

"Some of who?" Boot asked, swinging down.

"Some of Joe Jones's devilish men. They been comin' 'round here every day now shootin' off them guns, scarin' the chillun!"

Amos had hung back in the saddle, not liking the looks of witchcraft about the woman, or her uninviting quarters. "What kinda doctor is you?" he asked.

"What kind of doctor you think I am!" Maude said irritably. "You can git down or keep on ridin', don't matter none to me!"

Maude's large frame filled the doorway. Her small pudgy hands went back on her hips. Amos reluctantly dismounted. She ordered Boot, "You wait out here." And to Amos she commanded, "Take off that pistol 'fo' you come in here!"

Amos took off the thirty-dollar Army Colt he had bought back at Nacimiento. Boot watched Amos disappear behind the curtained doorway, then killed time while Amos was getting looked at.

Ten minutes went by, fifteen minutes, then half an hour. He heard voices murmur, the splash of poured water, and twice Amos gasped in pain. He had been waiting close to an hour when he heard hoofbeats drumming from across the prairie. Turning, his gaze found five black riders and followed them.

251

The man in the lead rode a great black horse. His bell-crowned white hat made him appear even taller in the saddle than the six feet two inches that he was. Four of them wore pistols; one was unarmed and looked and rode like a schoolteacher.

Somehow Boot knew the man on the black horse was Joe Jones.

Jones and his gang swept across the gully, climbed the other bank, and headed for the vacant lot where the hog was being butchered.

More out of curiosity than anything else, Boot walked back the fifty or so yards and was standing off to the side next to the pie shop when the whiskey bottle made the rounds and came back to Joe Jones, standing in the hollow of the U-shaped gathering. Jones made a show of taking a big drink. He capped the bottle and passed it over to the man next to him. "Here, Skeeter, finish this off." Looking over the men gathered in front of him, he smiled broadly and said, "There's more for all of y'all . . . compliments of Mr. Putterman. He said you boys deserve it."

Joe Jones was a dark, solidly built handsome man, thirty years old. He wore a tall side-creased white Stetson ten-gallon hat, and he had on black dungarees held up by wide canvas suspenders over a long-sleeved cotton jersey undershirt. A big Colt Peacemaker was strapped around his waist.

Chewing on a bite of sweet-potato pie he had bought from the woman, Boot leaned back against the countertop, listening to Jones talking glibly, smiling handsomely.

Jones was saying instructively, "Now, y'all listen here. The last time I was out here, I told you you didn't need to vote. Well, Mr. Putterman's had a change of mind. You need to vote now." Joe smiled handsomely, clapped the man standing next to him on the back, and added, "Ike here is gonna tell you how."

The man called Ike was Ike Scales, a quiet, bookish man of middle age, with some formal education. Of northern background, he wore a once-fashionable, store-bought outfit of gray wool trousers and brown coat. Scales was from a Philadelphia organization called the Freedman's Alternative Society, a social organization that followed the Democratic party line of gradual black rights.

Ike adjusted his horn-rimmed glasses, squared up his shoulders, and started his speech.

For fifteen minutes Boot listened to Scales telling the freedmen of the benefits to be reaped if they voted against Republicans. "I know the Loyal League is tellin' y'all the Republicans is your friends," he said. "And that they gonna look out for you. Well, they ain't!" he shouted. "As soon as they take office they'll forgit you and your families. You got to vote for Conservatives, for Democrats!"

Low grumbling rippled through the gathering, and men shuffled uncomfortably. One man, thinking differently, shifted his weight to the other foot and said, "Democrats ain't no good. They won't give us no rights."

"If you don't vote like Mr. Scales here says," Jones said, smiling, "don't show up." Jones grinned sinisterly at the men in front of him. None of them found courage enough to disagree, as Jones knew they wouldn't. He smiled briefly, then looked across the way again at the obvious outsider he had seen leaning on the pie counter while Scales was giving his talk. "What about you?" he asked Boot. "You intend to vote?"

Boot had started to move off, but now he turned around and said mildly, "Hadn't thought much about it."

Jones smiled slightly and said through perfectly white teeth, "You think about it . . . then do like Mr. Scales here said."

"I git a mind to vote, Mr. Scales won't tell me how . . . Mr. Putterman neither."

Jones knew the other men were listening. And this kind of talk undermined all Mr. Putterman had him working for. Worse yet, he figured, this kind of talk if not stopped might give backbone to these men he had already cowed. Jones's smile left. "You callin' me and Mr. Scales here fools?"

Boot knew whatever happened next depended on his answer. He also knew the Winchester, the gun he handled best, was in the saddle boot back at the fortune-teller's shack. He had practiced some with Mr. Perry's Russian .44 six-shooter now strapped around his waist, but he hadn't had time to get a good feel for it as he had done with the Winchester.

He knew what his answer was, but he had doubts, the same as before. He hesitated, weighing the consequences.

Then from out of nowhere Jimmy Bowlegs came to mind—and all that Bowlegs stood for. Seemingly on their own his lips made the words: "Y'all damn fools. The biggest damn fools I ever seen."

Joe Jones stiffened as if from a ringing slap to the jaw. He switched his eyes from side to side, checking to see if the men of Gullytown had a reaction.

Somebody behind him said in a low voice, "Joe's gonna kill that show-off for that."

Jones knew they all had heard. He returned his attention to Boot, his handsome face stiff and ugly now. He knew there was simply no way he could take such an insult in front of these people he had already spent so much time putting fear into.

Jones's shoulder dipped and his hand swept down, reaching for the Peacemaker.

For the slightest instant Boot's eyes flared wide, surprised at Joe's obvious intent to shoot him down on the spot in broad daylight in front of witnesses. But as quick as lightning Boot's right hand darted down, leaped back up, and exploded.

And a man stumbled to his death in front of him, froth on his lips.

Joe Jones's mouth worked briefly, then life went from him, his body crashing into the carcass of the half-butchered hog hanging there from a scaffold.

The suddenness of it all left Boot standing bent-legged, his gun leveled forward, his mind shocked at what had just happened.

Somebody whispered in a stunned voice, "He killed Joe Jones!"

Seconds dragged by; blue gunsmoke drifted away toward the prairie. And then the woman working the pie stand screamed, "Look out!"

Boot's attention snapped back to reality. Out of the corner of his eye he saw the other man's hand moving. He was swinging his aim when a Winchester erupted in back of him. The man in front of him went spinning. And even as he did, Boot fired anyhow, fired into his body as he went down.

Boot looked behind him to see where the shot had come from.

Amos was coming, leading their horses, his Winchester carried in one hand in shooting position. Amos took one look at Boot's ashen face and asked, "Joe Jones?"

"Joe Jones," Boot answered, holstering his gun.

Amos looked closely first at Jones's body, then the other man's. Lifting his eyes to the other two armed men who had their hands raised chest high, Amos asked, "Joe Jones's gang?"

"What's left of 'em," the woman said. "They wadn't no 'count nohow."

"Y'all better git outta here!" shouted the fortune-telling woman, who had rushed out with Amos at the first shot.

Quickly Boot and Amos mounted up and rode out.

Nobody much cared about the death of Joe Jones and the other man. Ike Scales was left standing there, shaking with fear. The other two survivors felt lucky Joe hadn't gotten them killed too, and were glad to be rid of Joe.

They crossed over a hogback divide and took to dormant prairie of sandhills and scrub mesquite. They rode with the confidence of men who had proved themselves, men made stronger by the death of others. But they were worried some, one man with a first killing on his conscience, the other man with three to his credit.

And they were heading to a place where there was likely to be more killing.

Chapter Twenty

Election day hovered ominously in the future like a crouched cat ready to spring on Brazos county at the appointed time. White men looked into the uncharted future and saw social upheaval and economic ruin. A spate of racial and revenge killings was the response. Colored men traveled in numbers for safety or not at all. Intimidated into paralysis, town officials failed to uphold the law, turning a blind eye to the violence and bloodshed that racked the county. Talk of renewing the rebellion reached all the way to the statehouse.

Governor Pease was railed at daily by law-abiding citizens and staunch Rebublicans for protection and justice. The Freedmen's Bureau was sending him every week stacks of reports of unfair labor schemes, of killings and lynchings of colored men. And Pease was not a man to sit still.

On a clear, blustery day a tall thin man swung his horse off the prairie, cantered up the wagon road, and rode down Gulch's windswept main street. He kept his eyes straight ahead, oblivious to those watching him. When he got to the sign indicating the mayor's office, he swung his horse to the hitchrail.

He dismounted smoothly, the wind whipping at the tails of his sand-colored trailduster. A pearl-handled Peacemaker six-shooter peeped out from under the flap of the coat as he stood there. He ran his eyes up one side the boardwalk, then the other. Turning, he crossed the boardwalk, opened the door to the mayor's office, and walked through.

"What can I do for you?" Mayor Speed asked, looking up from the newspaper he had been reading.

"Name's Semester, Goodwill Semester," the man answered thr ugh thin white lips. "You're Mayor Speed, I take it?"

"That's right."

Reaching a hand into his shirt pocket behind the satin vest he wore, Semester withdrew a folded sheet of paper, unfolded it carefully, slid it onto the desktop, and said candidly, "Been two weeks getting here, but I'm here."

Mayor Speed scanned the sheet, started at the top again, reading more carefully this time, lifting his eyes now and again, assessing the man standing before him, the man the credentials charged with bringing law and order to decent citizens of Brazos County.

Judge Goodwill Semester was six feet tall, a spare, frail-looking man. He had been a district judge before the late unpleasantness, and had built a reputation as a tough-minded, no-nonsense judge, a careful practitioner of the law who dished out his justice with uncommon vigor. Uncommon vengeance, some said. He had been stripped of his judgeship when he refused to forswear allegiance to the U.S. government and switch it to the Confederacy when Texas went Confederate. But now Governor Pease had restored him.

"Welcome to Gulch, Judge," the mayor said, coming to his feet and extending a hand. "Is this a look-see visit, or business?"

"Both. I'm sort of familiarizing myself with the territory, and at the same time leaving word of the governor's displeasure with the amount of violence in the county."

"We have our troubles same as the rest of the state, but you'll find Gulch a peaceful town."

"The report at the county seat tells a different story."

"What's it say?" Speed asked, lifting his eyebrows.

"Practically nothing good. The whole of Brazos County is rife with lawbreakers, yet prosecutions are unheard of." Leveling his eyes at the mayor, the judge stated, "Especially Gulch."

"Judge, that's talk mostly from them carpetbaggers over at the Freedmen's Bureau. They see things different."

"Ain't but one way to see wanton killings. And there's been too many of them without convictions turning up on the governor's report."

"Granted, we've had our share of killings, but there just ain't been no witnesses. The sheriff's doing the best he can, though, under the circumstances."

"Sheriff strikes me as a man almighty slow to act."

"How's that?"

"Colored fellow over at the county seat swore out a complaint against a man named Pony Harper. Says Harper killed a voter registrar, man name Seth Poole. Sheriff witnessed the killing but did nothing about it."

"Judge, you ain't taking a nig—a colored man's word!"

"Any man that swears out a complaint got a right to have it looked into."

"Taking a colored's word against a white man! Now, Judge . . ."

"Brazos County has been lawless too long, Mayor," the judge said sternly. He leaned over the desk, rested his two palms on the desktop. "I aim to see the law enforced. From now on it's going to be swift and sure. I suggest you call a town meeting, get that word around." The judge straightened up, drew his duster over the Peacemaker that had been showing, and said offhandedly, "I hear there's talk of interfering with the coming election."

"There's some talk," the mayor admitted. "Most folks don't like it."

"Like it or not, it's the law. I intend to see the election is held fair and square. You can drop word, any man that starts trouble, I'll finish it in my court." The judge narrowed his eyes at the mayor and concluded, "or out in the street."

When he left the mayor's office the wind tugged at his duster as he strode across the boardwalk. He mounted up and rode away, the mayor watching from the boardwalk. He could see the Peacemaker showing where the duster had caught on the butt.

Within the hour a hastily called town meeting was assembled. They all had heard of the urgent meeting by word of mouth or a swift rider. City councilmen, interested merchants, and the banker was there; a few ranchers and two farmers turned up; Land Commissioner Henry Parker and Sheriff Willis showed up, both uneasy over what the meeting meant.

Ben Putterman rode in at the head of six men after Pony had made a fast ride out to the ranch and had given him news of the new judge's promise to bring law and order to Brazos County.

At the meeting Mayor Speed repeated what Judge Semester had said and implied. Men grumbled to themselves and to each other. The mayor pleaded for each citizen to let the election come off peacefully. He fortified his plea with the threat that "if we don't make a showing, the army will come in. None of us want that."

"Damn the army!" a man shouted back angrily. "Niggers got no right to vote!"

"They outnumber us!" another man yelled. "It ain't fair!"

"No white man oughta be ruled over by niggers!" yelled another.

"I say we stop 'em!" the banker cried. "They own no property! They got no rights!"

"Now . . . now, men!" the mayor cautioned. "That kinda talk will bring in the army."

"To hell with the army!" a storekeeper screamed. "I say we hang any nigger that shows his face around here!"

"Yeah!" half a dozen men yelled in unison.

The meeting broke up with angry men swearing to themselves and to each other, each man seeing himself as standing up for his own rights.

But some men knew there was something more at stake.

Commissioner Parker lingered on the boardwalk. When he got his chance, he told Putterman, "Ben, things have changed." He switched his eyes from side to side, said confidentially, "We've got to talk."

"I'm listenin'," Ben said irritably. Ben knew Judge Semester's coming had not only changed his circumstances but had changed those of a lot of other men in Brazos County.

"Not here," Parker said, looking around suspiciously. "At my office."

They walked quickly across the street to the commissioner's office, where Parker hastily withdrew a letter from his desk drawer.

"This came yesterday," he said anxiously. "I'm being removed as land commissioner, Ben."

261

"Means nothing," Ben said, lifting his eyebrows, surprised at Parker being so concerned. "There's always something else."

"You don't understand, Ben. This means I'll have to square my records. Every one of them . . . including the arrangements you got."

"Arrangements I got?" Ben fought back his rising anger at the bumbling commissioner, the stupid fool. Smiling cunningly, he played along, saying, "Why sure, Henry. Wouldn't want you to have trouble on my account. I'll have Pony return the deeds to you first thing in the morning."

"Glad you understand my predicament," Henry said, relieved. "The new man will want to see all he's accountable for."

"Any word on when he's due?"

"Any day now."

"You've nothin' to worry about, Henry. The deeds will get back where they belong and nobody will be the wiser."

At his home on the outskirts of town Commissioner Parker worked that night by lamplight to square his books. At an unknown hour, a bullet was fired through his window, striking him down. His home was ransacked.

That morning Sheriff Willis investigated but found no clues. With no one able to name a single known enemy, speculation spread that Parker was killed by penniless freedmen looking for anything of value, possibly one of the riffraff at Gullytown, or maybe one of the rabble holed up at Ned's place.

Later that morning, Putterman and his hands came into town. Pony Harper took the boys to the saloon while Ben walked the boardwalk, chatting. Every citizen he met grumbled about colored thievery and violence, and made suggestions about what ought to be done about it.

A surly merchant suggested angrily, "The sheriff oughta clean out Gullytown."

"Only sensible thing to do," Ben agreed. "And Ned's place, too. Old Ned's shelterin' a bunch of no-'count thieves over there for no good reason." Putterman made the rounds of the businesses along the boardwalk, listening to complaints and promoting discord wherever he got the chance. At the last hardware store he listened to Hans Stover's complaints against the colored, then told him, "If there's any bunch that needs to be run off, it's them coons at Ned's place."

"All of us went along when you told us not to sell them guns," Hans said, "but they've got them somehow."

"Like I warned, guns in their hands is like guns in children's hands. Parker's killin' prove that," Putterman said self-righteously.

"Ain't no white man can sleep peacefully at night after this," Hans said.

Satisfied that he had done all he could to keep the trouble stirred up, Putterman walked down to the mayor's office. He pushed through the door, and the mayor told him right off, "Town's mighty unsettled, Ben. There's trouble's brewin'."

"It's plain as day, Mayor . . . it's the coloreds. All this fuss over the election's got 'em worked up."

"I'm worried, Ben."

"Any sensible man would be, Mayor. Every white man in the county got a stake in this. If the coloreds take over the county, we've got nothing left. One other thing," Ben told the mayor, "colored feller I had working for me, Joe Jones, him and some of his boys was keeping an eye on the goin's-on over at Gullytown."

"I heard there was a bunch of coloreds over there . . . and at Ned's place," the mayor said. "Any trouble?"

"Not so you'd know, but this Loyal League's right

263

busy fillin 'em with political nonsense. Tellin 'em how the constitution works, and how to vote and all.''

"This colored feller you brought in to counter them, he show any results?''

"Mighty little. Joe Jones was killed over at Gully-town. Scared the others witless. They're near useless now.''

"It ain't surprisin','' the mayor said. "Even illiterates got sense enough to look out for their own interest.''

"If they know their own interest,'' Putterman countered.

"You sayin' they don't?''

"I'm sayin' this new man, Ike Scales, is goin' to git some backbone and convince them our interest is theirs too. And Pony Harper and his boys goin' to make it stick.''

"The less killin', the better,'' the mayor cautioned. "Judge Semester can cause us a lot of trouble.''

"He won't,'' Ben said. Turning to leave, Ben asked the question he had been wanting to for some time: "Mayor, about this election . . . you didn't really expect it to come off, did you? Fair and square, I mean?''

"I don't know, Ben,'' the mayor said doubtfully. "Judge Semester is a stickler. There might not be any other way.''

"There's always a way,'' Ben said, and walked out the door.

The mayor sat at his desk looking at his palms as if he were reading the future in them. He knew the county was set to explode, that Gulch was at the center of the explosion. He knew Ben Putterman would plunge Brazos County into a shooting fight rather than see colored voters.

Chapter Twenty-one

But Ben Putterman was stymied. The cover of law that he had depended on to work his will had been removed by Judge Semester's arrival.

The judge had made it clear that law in Brazos County was no longer a sham as it had been before. He would not look the other way while men broke the law or made their own.

Putterman was coldly furious. But there was nothing he could do except hold his forces in check, rely on the fear and intimidation he had already instilled to keep blacks away from Gulch and the voting booth. Outright beatings and killings were out of the question for now.

So Putterman lay low at his ranch, fuming over his loss of advantage, yet still sending his henchmen over the county making noisy showings, letting it be known that any black man who wanted to live to see next planting season had better not set foot in Gulch on election day.

*   *   *

From the flank of Rocky Hill, Boot sat his horse, Amos at his side, their eyes circling around Squaw Valley, taking in the stark beauty of the place now under the lean hand of autumn. "We here," Boot told Amos. "House's just up the valley yonder."

"Mighty nice country," Amos said. "It don't look like much for cotton, though."

"It ain't. Only planting done 'round here is feed crops."

From the high ground they occupied Boot looked out over the the valley that he had been away from for months. He was glad to be back on familiar ground. Something off to the east caught the corner of his eye. He rose in the stirrups and narrowed his eyes, looking closer at the movement.

He made out a loose bunch of riders, seven he counted, headed west at a fast gallop. Amos followed the riders with his eyes, saying, "They in a hurry to git somewhere."

"They headed towards the Lazy H."

"Trouble?"

"Might be," Boot said, and nudged his horse off high ground, angling down into the valley.

"Could be friends," Amos suggested after catching up to Boot.

"Mr. Ned ain't got that many friends in the whole state," Boot said. "We better figure strangers as trouble. We'll circle around and come up on the place from the back way."

Boot and Amos had no way of knowing, but the riders they had seen were possemen led by Sheriff Willis. Mayor Speed, at Ben Putterman's insistance, had ordered the sheriff to the Lazy H to bring in Parker's killer. Putterman had insisted he had reliable word that that's where the killer was holed up.

Sheriff Willis and seven possemen swept into the hard-packed ranch yard and jerked to a stop at the front porch. Pony Harper and Jim Cardine were there; the riff-raff from Elm Thicket had now become the sheriff's regular henchmen, and they were there as well—Bud Monroe, Tim Snowden, Ed Blount, and the O'Callahan brothers, Lafe and Tish. They sat their saddles behind Sheriff Willis, waiting for word to start earning their pay.

But things were unusually quiet for this time of day. Not a sound could be heard except the forlorn creak of the turning windmill.

The ominous stillness troubled the sheriff.

His fears grew with each creak of the windmill. Something just wasn't right, he thought. In addition to Ned and the wench called Bertha, the place was known to shelter at least thirty more blacks.

So where were they?

Willis's mind jumped to conclusions. He grew wary. He stole a peek out of the corner of his eye at Pony, at Cardine. Finally he said what they all were thinking: "Place's mighty quiet. They musta got word we was coming."

"Or seen us," Pony said, looking over his shoulder at the barn, the most obvious place from which an ambush might come.

"Could be a trap," Cardine warned, looking around uneasily.

"Niggers ain't that crazy," Sheriff Willis said, more to convince himself than anyone else. Nerved by his own brave words, Willis scanned the outbuildings.

Nothing. No movement whatsoever.

Sudenly he felt like the place had a hundred black eyes, all watching him. A queer shudder came over him. He licked his dry lips nervously, ran his eyes over the outbuildings again. Finding nothing to his liking, he stiffened in the saddle, drew up to full height, and ordered, "Tish, look around. See what you can see."

Tish grinned with pleasure at the opportunity and shifted his weight to dismount. Before his right foot could even clear the stirrup, a measured voice stopped him cold:

"I wouldn't if I was you!" Ned spoke through a slit in the shuttered window of the room that Bertha occupied on the other side of the dog run where he had been watching and listening all the time.

"That you, Ned?" Willis asked.

"It's me. You got business, Sheriff . . . or did you come out here to throw your weight around?"

"I got business. There's been a killin' in town."

"Anybody I know?" Ned asked sarcastically.

"Henry Parker. He was gunned down at his home, his house ransacked."

"And you figure some trifling nigger from out here done it?"

"That's right," Willis agreed.

"And you and this bunch of thieves and killers come out here to git the one who done it?"

"That's right," Willis agreed again, but this time he squirmed uncomfortably in the saddle, not liking the fool Ned was making him out to be.

Ned chuckled scornfully.

Bertha called loudly from inside, standing next to Ned, "Ain't none of us been to town in a month of Sundays! You know we ain't killed nobody!"

"I aim to find out," Willis answered.

"How?" Ned asked.

"Line 'em all up out here in the yard so I can see 'em, talk to 'em. Somebody'll tell me what I want to know."

"Just like in the old days, that right, Sheriff?" Ned scoffed.

Willis disregarded the remark, looking over his shoulder at the barn where he knew the freedmen were holed up.

Nothing stirred, not a hint of life showed.

Willis heeled his horse around, clip-clopped across the yard, drew up twenty yards off, facing the barn door, the possemen at his back.

"All right," Willis yelled at the closed doors, "all of you, git out here now!"

Two strangers who had just ridden in off the prairie nudged their horses into view from around the corner of the barn. One of them said mildly, "Ain't nobody in there."

Sheriff Willis and the possemen shifted their eyes to the two black men, both strangers to the valley. The one who had spoken was a slim-built, dark-skinned man, looked to be all of six feet tall, sitting the saddle of a long-legged Mexican pony, the same as the older man sitting next to him. Sheriff Willis and the others looked twice at the pistol and fighting knife each man wore and the Winchesters riding in the boot.

"Who're you?" Willis asked. "What you want here?"

"I live here," Boot said. "That is, I used to." Boot looked them over, then brought his eyes back to Willis. "I could ask you the same thing . . . what you want here?" Boot changed the tone of his voice at the last, and none of them missed the implication.

None of the possemen had seen or heard of freedmen openly standing up to white men. It was simply not done. These men had been mere chattel only months before. It had been certain death then. And no white man had changed his mind.

Every white man in the posse took Boot's words and actions as an affront. Pony Harper took exception the most. He saw no reason whatsoever to take it, and was going to do something about it. He looked disgustedly at Sheriff Willis and said flippantly, "Freedom's made these boys mighty forgitful, Sheriff." Pony smiled crookedly at his own words.

The smile fell away abruptly, replaced by an ugly sneer. Pony said bluntly, "I say they still ain't nothin' but dirty, ignorant, cotton pickers and we oughta put 'em in their place!"

Pony Harper didn't live to get a second older.

A gun went off up in the hayloft where a freedman was hidden, listening. A clap of gunfire racketed across the yard, and a bullet tore at Pony Harper's chest. Pony jerked sharply, then slumped forward. After hanging there precariously for a split second, he tumbled to the ground heavily.

Horses flinched at the sudden explosion. The thought of an ambush flashed through every man's mind. And right in front of Sheriff Willis's eyes the posse turned into an uneasy bunch of men thinking they were under attack from unseen enemies. To a man they thought that the ambush they had suspected all along had been sprung, that they were under widespread attack by hundreds of savages lurking everywhere.

Jim Cardine had reached for his gun when Harper dropped from the saddle. Now Cardine fired at the wisp of smoke that he had seen rise from the loft where the shot had come from. And instantly Cardine's shot was answered by a killing bullet fired from over by the corral. The bullet struck him in the back of the neck just as his horse pranced around.

By now Sheriff Willis knew Harper and Cardine had been shot from the saddle. However, he didn't know who else had been hit. Scattered shots made the already confused situation even more confused.

Willis kept his pistol ready in firing position, watching the hayloft, wanting to shoot the man who had started it all.

270

Ever since Boot and Amos had first showed themselves the two O'Callahan brothers had paid them close attention, sizing them up with eyes for their eye-catching belongings. At the sudden gunfire Boot and Amos had lunged from their saddles, scrambled for cover behind the corner of the barn where they now looked out.

Suddenly Ned and Bertha ran across the yard toward the possemen, Ned leading the way, yelling, "Hold your fire! Hold your fire!"

The din of battle died away. Quiet slowly came over the yard and the confused situation calmed down, with Ned and Bertha standing out in the middle of the yard.

"Boot! That you, Boot?" Bertha called toward the barn, where she had seen a familiar black man, although he was dressed in funny-looking clothes.

"Yeah, it's me!" Boot yelled back, and stepped into view from the corner of the barn, followed by Amos.

Tish O'Callahan, hidden in the crowd, had had his mind made up all along. Now he saw his chance. With a smirk on his lips, he drew and fired past the man in front of him.

The bullet whipped past Boot, ripped into Amos's chest, knocking him back to the edge of the barn.

An answering shot came from over by the corral, and another bullet fired from the other side of the barn spattered dirt at Willis's horse's feet. Everybody drew their pistols again, ready for more action.

"Hold your fire!" Ned screamed. "All of you, hold your fire, dammit!"

An uneasy quiet came over the yard once more. Sheriff Willis kept his pistol ready, looking around uncertainly at his broken posse.

The sheriff knew the only reason he had been ordered out there in the first place was to harass the blacks and get them away from Ned's place. First isolate Ned, Putterman had figured, then drive him completely out of the valley.

But now that he was out there, Willis wanted something tangible to show the town folks. "The one who fired that shot from the loft, I want him turned over," Willis demanded. "And this'n too," he insisted stiffly, looking at Boot, down on his knees cradling Amos's head, straining to make out his dying whispers.

"You're crazy!" Ned said to Willis in disbelief. "Plumb loco! They just now rode up."

"I want him," Willis said sternly.

"I wouldn't push it if I was you, Willis," Ned said. "There's men hid out watching you right now who'd like nothing better than to run a pitchfork through your guts, or put a bullet in your brains. You take this bunch and ride out of here!"

Willis sat very still in the saddle, doubt tugging at his mind. His eyes scanned the outbuildings, lifted up to the loft, then dropped down to rest on Pony's body.

"If I was you, I'd ride," Ned warned again. "Some of these folks already figger they owe you a debt. They'd like nothing better than to light into your hide."

At that minute Amos's weak voice in Boot's ear fell off, stalled, then said hoarsely, "Like Bowlegs said . . . don't trust 'em."

Boot gently lowered Amos's shoulders to the ground and stood up. Looking out at Willis, he said grimly, "Amos here never laid eyes on you or this place before this. Now he's dead." Boot knew Willis by reputation. He had heard bad stories about him.

But this was the first time he had laid eyes on Tish, the man who shot Amos. And Boot was going to see that nobody laid eyes on him alive again.

In one deliberate motion his right hand swept down and came up, gripping a pistol that exploded, smashing Tish from the saddle. There was no effort at speed in his draw; it was simply a deliberate motion to accomplish a definite purpose, as straightforward as shooting a barn door.

Unknown to Boot the dead man's brother, Lafe, was sitting his saddle on the other side of the posse, out of Boot's view. Lafe's gun hand started forward.

"Don't do it!" Bertha yelled from over on that side. Lafe froze, and his gun hand stiffened where it was.

Fixing an eye on the black man who had just shot his brother from the saddle, Lafe weighed his chances.

Bertha eared back the hammer on the Creedmore, the click sending a cold shiver down everybody's spine.

For a long second Lafe looked at Boot, his lips resolutely tight, his mind weighing the chances that the woman would shoot at point-blank range.

"She'll shoot," Ned said grimly. "Take my word on it. There wouldn't be enough left of you to fuss over."

Nobody wanted to see the damage the big gun would do, least of all Lafe. Ned offered him a way out: "Let it alone. There's worse things than your brother getting hisself shot."

Lafe's eyes wavered from Boot. He looked around at the woman who had thrown down on him. He stared into the dark cavernous bore of the big buffalo gun, the tight-jawed woman looking back at him through keen eyes down the barrel of that same gun.

Lafe knew he'd be cut in two if that hammer fell. He turned red-faced and white-lipped, ashamed at being bested in front of white men by low-life blacks. Suddenly Lafe felt sick to his stomach. He looked uneasily across his shoulder at Sheriff Willis for answers.

"The law'll handle this," Willis said bravely. "Somebody'll answer."

Lafe's gun hand fell aside, his shoulders slumped. Sheriff Willis turned to Ned and said, "It ain't over, Ned. You and these niggers got the upper hand now, but

273

it ain't over, not by a damn sight. Somebody'll pay for this.'' Willis glowered at Bertha, holding the big gun.

"We ain't done nothin'," Bertha said stiffly. "And we ain't payin' for nothin'."

"I seen a lot of you lately," Willis said, looking at her. "Too much. You Bertha, ain't you?"

"That's right, Bertha Johnson ... and that's my brother yonder, Boot Johnson," she added, lifting her chin proudly.

Willis craned his neck around, looked out with renewed interest at the man dressed in gaudy Mexican clothes who had just shot Tish from the saddle. "He's a killer," Willis said. "He'll answer." He swung his horse away, leading what was left of the broken posse out of the valley.

So they dug four graves on a low rise in back of the ranch house. The freedmen took turns digging the graves, each man knowing in the back of his mind that big trouble was bound to come over the deaths of three white men. It had been that way before. A worried man asked Joe Ben, the lanky dark-skinned man who had fired the first shot from the loft, "Why'd you shoot that feller? We was to keep 'em covered, not kill 'em."

"He was one of them that hung my brother. I promised myself I'd kill the man who hung him if I ever got the chance. I got the chance."

"I seen that rascal in Gulch before too," another man said. "He wadn't no good."

"He was the leader when they came to Gullytown that time," somebody else remembered.

"I'm glad he's dead, then," the worried man said.

Nobody thought much about the dead colored man who had ridden in with Boot, but Amos was just as dead as the white men. Boot dug his grave alone and buried him in a lonely place far from where he intended to be.

* * *

With Pony Harper shot to death Bud Monroe stepped forward and took his place as the leader, even though he was at first uneasy about facing Putterman. He knew it would set off Putterman's explosive temper when he was told that the posse had been surprised and men had been killed by a bunch of ignorant, ill-equipped former slaves.

They rode behind Sheriff Willis down Gulch's main street, swung their horses to the hitchrail in front of the Bull Head Saloon. The sheriff rode on down to the courthouse to tell the mayor the appalling story of what had happened out at the Lazy H.

Bud Monroe led the men through the batwings, ordered beer across the bar as he had seen Pony do.

"You doin' the tabbin' for Pony now, Bud?" Holly asked playfully. "Or is Mr. Putterman got hisself a new moocher?"

Hearing that kind of talk, Putterman looked up quizzically from over at his usual corner table, his ears pricked.

"Pony's dead," Bud replied loudly enough for Putterman to hear it. "I'm takin' his place."

Putterman's interest flared. "Bud, you got something you ought to tell me?"

"Yes, sir, Mr. Putterman."

"Get over here and do it, then."

"Bad news, Mr. Putterman," Bud said clumsily, walking up.

"What happened out there?" Putterman demanded. "Where's Pony? Where's Jim?"

"Dead."

"Dead? Both of 'em?"

"Yes, sir."

"That can't be!"

"It's true, Mr. Putterman," Bud confirmed. "We rode

out to Old Ned's place like you told us to. Niggers got the drop on us. We never had a chance.''

"Got the drop on the lot of you!'' Putterman said unbelievingly. "All of you was well-armed,'' he shouted angrily, looking past the curtain at the pistols belted around the waists of the other three men standing at the bar.

"They was armed too, Mr. Putterman . . . at least a dozen of 'em, hid out too,'' Bud said firmly. "Except two of 'em . . .''

"Except two of 'em what?'' Putterman asked.

"Two of 'em that just somehow turned up. Nobody never seen 'em before, but one of 'em was that smart-mouth wench's brother.''

"You sayin' Old Ned's done turned them field hands into fighters?''

"I don't know about that, but both of 'em was well-armed, looked like they knowed what for.''

"They did, huh?'' Putterman said, pursing his lips pensively.

"Yes, sir, Mr. Putterman. Tish shot one of 'em, and that Johnson feller dropped Tish from the saddle as smooth as any gunfighter you ever seen and never batted an eye. Wadn't no scare in him atall.''

"What about the sheriff?''

"What about him?'' Bud asked contemptuously.

"He all right?''

"If you want to call it that.''

Putterman toyed at the corner of his puckered lips with a finger, turning over in his mind the possibility that blacks had banded together to fight. In which case, Putterman knew they could strike back any day in superior numbers. It was a dreaded thing that brought back to Putterman's mind the old fear of insurrection. The thought sent a cold shiver down Putterman's spine. He knew that having things his way in the valley depended on fear and intimidation. If that was gone, so was his control.

Putterman would leave to chance nothing so vital to his interests. He smiled cunningly and said to Monroe, "Now that Pony's dead, I'll need a good man. The job's yours if you want it."

"I want it, Mr. Putterman."

"All right, it's yours," Putterman said, and brought a fine cigar between his teeth. He stood up and said around the cigar, "You start earning your keep right now."

"Yes, sir."

"There's some ridin' I want you to do."

"Where?"

"Arkansas."

"Arkansas!" Bud echoed, looking around, surprised.

"That's right," Ben said. "A place just over the line called New Hope. Pick one of the boys and get yourselfs the best horses we got.

"There's an old friend of mine there named Forrest, General Nathan Bedford Forrest. He's organizing an outfit called the Klu Kluxers, and they're in the business of convincing niggers they ain't as free as they think.

"I want you to ride over there, tell General Forrest that Brazos County got need of his services."

"Yes, sir."

"And Bud, you tell General Forrest the enemy's getting bolder by the day. Tell him I need first-rate soldiers to take the field right away. He'll get my meaning."

Chapter Twenty-two

Exactly one week after killing Mingo Sanders's kin west of Picayune, Bodie and Ruley rode into Fort Smith, a thriving frontier outpost thrust out to the end of civilization from the east and marking the beginning of wild country to the west.

The federal government had invested time and money to refit and resupply Fort Smith after reoccupying it without a fight in September '63 when Yankee Maj. Gen. James Blount put to flight Confederate Brig. Gen. William Steele, whose forces had been unable to defend the place because defective gunpowder had turned into paste and would not fire.

Now the fort was garrisoned to protect immigrants, homesteaders, and railroad tracks against hostile plains Indians. The town that had sprung up across the street from the fort had been built up by a mixture of rude, tough men and solid law-abiding citizens who had stuck it out and now thrived off lucrative government contracts

278

carried out with the protection of the well-garrisoned fort sitting atop frowning red bluffs in a bend of the Arkansas River.

The killings west of Picayune were not far in the back of their minds when Bodie and Ruley rode their horses down Fort Smith's Garrison Avenue, the main street that came up before them when they stepped off the flatboat they had crossed the Arkansas River on.

Garrison separated the fort from the town, and just now the street was bustling with hundreds of unsettled men who saw Fort Smith as a drawing card for seekers of opportunity, lawful and unlawful.

At the second intersection they swung their horses over to the civilian side of town and headed toward the courthouse where Bowman had told them to meet him.

The civilians at Fort Smith had had their loyalties tested severely as the fort shifted hands first from North to South, then back to North again. Every man in town knew it paid for a man to keep his loyalties to himself, and where a man had really stood during the war was best left unsaid.

They pulled their horses up to the hitchrail in front of the two-story plank courthouse, heeling in next to two mounts already tied there. "Hope the marshal's in," Bodie said. "I'd just as soon collect that warrant money and go on 'cross town to the fort."

"Funny thing about money," Ruley said, "seems like a man ain't got none if it ain't in his pocket where he can git at it. The quicker I git that warrant money in my pocket, the better I'll feel."

They swung down, crossed over the porch, and walked inside the high-roofed courthouse.

Nobody was in sight, but presently a tall, spare man emerged from one of the back rooms. Spotting Bodie and Ruley, he asked curtly, "Something I can do for you boys?"

"We looking for Marshal Bowman," Bodie answered.

"The marshal's out right now. Maybe there's something I can help you with. I'm Judge Stanhope."

"We was wantin' to see the marshal hisself," Ruley said, fending off the stern-featured man.

"Personal," Bodie added, seeing the doubting look the sober judge was giving them.

"You must be Bodie . . . and Ruley," the judge said, shifting his eyes from one to the other. Judge Caleb Stanhope was Bavarian by birth, a humorless, unbending man of law and order.

"You heard of us?" Ruley asked, looking at Bodie, worried.

"Marshal Bowman talked some of you two." The judge folded the sheet of paper in his hand. "It didn't take you as long to get here as Bowman figured it would. You had no trouble, I take it."

"You'd be taking it wrong," Ruley said. "We had some."

"What kind?" the judge asked, arching his eyebrows, then quickly searching their faces.

"Like the marshal figured, we was jumped," Bodie said. "West of Picayune . . . three men."

"The marshal mentioned the town was stood on its ears over Mingo's killing, you two being colored and all. The men that jumped you . . . kin of Mingo's?"

"One of 'em was his brother. Can't say about the other two."

"You killed Mingo's brother?"

"We killed all three of 'em," Ruley said. "All three of 'em come at us."

Judge Stanhope looked slant-eyed at Bodie, his eyes

registering doubts that two colored men could somehow kill three armed white men.

"We wadn't particular how we done it," Bodie said.

"You ambushed 'em," the judge said, more a statement than a question.

"We wadn't no stand-up match for them with guns," Ruley said.

"It was them or us," Bodie stated.

The judge looked at them again, in a different light. "Marshal Bowman told me you handled yourselves right well down there at Picayune, and Bowman ain't a man to toss around praise when it come to posse work." The judge turned on his heels and said over his shoulder, "You men come into my office."

Stanhope led them back to his small, well-kept office and withdrew from his desk drawer a half-dozen or so warrants. After looking through them carefully, he announced, "Seems Mingo was the only Sanders with money on his head." Looking across his desk at them, he said sincerely, "There's no warrant money for none of his kin, but the state owes you boys a debt for ridding the country of the likes of them."

The judge relaxed his sober countenance and, looking with renewed interest at Bodie and Ruley, said conversationally, "Bowman spoke well of you two. I see no reason to disagree with his opinion." Speaking in a formal, official tone, he said, "As the federal judge for the Western District of Arkansas, I'm gratified to see colored men willing and able to perform their civic duty."

"Warrant money kinda nudges a man forward," Ruley said, smiling knowingly, looking at Bodie.

"Speaking of warrant money," Bodie said, "we'd just as soon collect what's due us and be on our way. Like I told the marshal, I'm looking for my folks."

"Warrant money's right here," Stanhope said, retrieving from his desk drawer the envelope Marshal Bowman had turned over to him before leaving. "Marshal Bowman said there's twenty dollars a man there." The judge slid the envelope across the desk to Bodie. "That's ten percent of the warrant, same as any white posseman earns." Watching with keen interest as Bodie tore open the envelope, the judge said, "There's money in serving warrants, for the right men who're willing to earn it. I'm offering you two the opportunity."

"I ain't interested," Bodie said instantly.

"Same kind of work we done at Picayune?" Ruley asked.

"Mostly the same. The governor's been after me to commission colored men to serve warrants on their own kind. That's what you'd be doing."

After a minute Ruley said thoughtfully, "It beats stoop labor."

"I'm lookin' for my folks," Bodie answered, stuffing the envelope containing the warrant money behind his shellbelt. "You do what you of a mind to."

"I ain't got no folks to look for, and I'd be doing something other than stoop labor."

"One thing you ought to know, Bodie," Judge Stanhope said. "District court is in recess now and Judge Semester, the judge who sits on the eighth district court down in Texas, was up here. He's one of the few Texans who always had eyes and ears for the Union. He'd know the ring that was crossing slaves into Texas.

"At that time it was a natural enough thing to do, but that slave train coming all the way from Lynchburg was a mighty big surprise that drew a lot of attention. Most folks had faith in the Confederacy. Wouldn't believe the war was going badly. When that train of slaves showed up it was like dynamite went off. Politicians and generals couldn't deny it. What few Union men that was still left here took hope. Judge Semester was one of them."

"Did he tell you where the slaves off that train went to?"

"There's a respectable businessman who used to run a regular freight line between Fort Smith and Fort Richardson. Seems he had an overseer who went into business for himself and was one of a half-dozen or so characters who used legitimate freighting business to cash in on hauling slaves to working plantations at night."

"Where's this man?" Bodie asked.

"He's set up permanently now as post sutler out at the fort. His name's Yetter, Edgar Yetter."

"You take the job if you want to," Bodie said to Ruley. "I'm going to see Mr. Yetter."

"Not many people like their past brought up nowadays," the judge warned Bodie. "And Yetter's no different. You mention to him what I just told you, he'll either kill you or help you, and I wouldn't put money on it either way."

Ruley looked at Judge Stanhope, and the judge said to him, "Job's yours if you want it."

"I want it," Ruley said, "but . . ." Ruley's words trailed off, his eyes looking after Bodie.

"Nothing says a man can't work alone," the judge said. "Fact is, Marshal Bowman works alone most of the time."

Ruley shrugged noncommittally, falling in step behind Bodie, leaving the question unanswered.

An hour later, they were back at Judge Stanhope's courthouse.

The judge was sitting at his desk with the door open when his ears picked up a sound. He lifted his eyes and spotted them, surprised they had returned so soon. Before he could shape a question, Ruley asked, "That job still open?"

"It's still open," the judge said, looking quizzically at Bodie. "What happened over there?"

"We found Mr. Yetter."

"He talk to you?"

"Yeah. Like you said, though, he was right touchy at first. Figured we had revenge in mind."

"Did he remember where your folks went?"

"He's pretty sure the man who used to trail for him and did the actual delivering of slaves will remember where he took my folks to . . . a feller named Choctaw Bill."

"Choctaw Bill? He's with the marshal, and they've gone to Choctaw Nation to serve warrants on a killer and some whiskey peddlers. I don't expect them back for at least a couple of more days."

"That's what we heard," Ruley said eagerly. "And while we waiting for them to come back we figured we'd serve some of them warrants and collect some of that warrant money." Ruley smiled sagely.

"That's good thinking," the judge said. Shuffling through the warrants again, he withdrew one and slid it across the desk. "He's in Choctaw country. Job should take two, three days at most . . . a day's ride there, a day to get the lay of the land and stake out your man, and a day's ride back with the prisoner." The judge relaxed back in his chair, saying encouragingly, "You two working together, that's fifty dollars apiece . . . plus expenses."

"A hundred dollars," Ruley repeated wonderingly, and they both looked at the warrant poster for the first time.

The poster was an artist's hand-drawing of a heavy-lipped, bold-faced, obviously mixed-blood Negro with long frizzled hair held in place by a headband. Judge Stanhope told them what he had heard about the renegade they were to bring in:

"Bowlegs," the judge said distastefully. "Nobody knows his real name, but that's what he answers to. He's part Negro, part Seminole, and I hear all spiteful. He lives off the land, knows the country like the back of his hand from the North Canadian River to Nacimiento in Old Mexico."

"A hundred dollars for bringing him in. What'd he do?" Bodie asked.

"Drove off twenty head of prime horses."

"That don't seem like much, considering the unsettled way things is," Bodie commented.

"It ain't much to most folks," the judge said, "but the man he stole them horses from . . . Bill Colbert, he ain't your average man. He thinks differently.

"South and west of here there's a crossing into Texas at Red River called Colbert's Ferry. It's owned by Bill Colbert, a mixed-blood Chickasaw Indian. Colbert sees himself as white as any white man, and before the war he owned a two-thousand-acre plantation called Valley Forks, running upward of three hundred slaves. He sided with the Confederacy. It cost him his wealth.

"Since the war he's built a substantial living running the ferry and trading with wild Indians out on the plains, mostly in guns and whiskey through Comanchero middlemen. At any one time he's got on hand trade goods and stock valued in the thousands of dollars."

"If I was him," Ruley said, "twenty horses wouldn't mean nothin' to me."

"Stolen horses ain't what's bothering him."

"What is?"

"Bowlegs shot his right ear off . . . for spite. Colbert knows Bowlegs could just as easily have put that bullet in his brains."

"Why didn't he?" Bodie asked.

"There's no explaining Bowlegs. No other Indian, for that matter. But before others get the idea he's gone soft,

Colbert wants Bowlegs brought in and punished, or he wants him dead.''

"This Bowlegs . . . where's he likely to be?" Ruley asked.

"When he ain't off raiding somewhere he makes the closest thing you'd call home at a Kickapoo village a day's ride west of here on the Washita River."

Judge Stanhope stood up, circled from behind his desk, satisfied that he had finally recruited two able colored men to do peace officer's work against colored and mixed-blood offenders, as he had been urged by the statehouse to do now that so many freedmen had joined the criminal element roaming the territory.

Passing the warrant to Bodie, the judge said, "I got no qualms about how you killed Mingo and his kin back there at Picayune." Hooking his two thumbs in his coat lapels, the judge shifted to a more official tone. "Now that you're warranted by the court, I got some sound advice for you." Stanhope's face took on a severe look. "Don't gun down a wanted man from ambush. Word gets back to this court, you'll be treated same as any other bushwhacker.

"Another thing. This court insists that you treat the wanted man with respect. I claim no knowledge of how you ought to go about doing this job, but the court demands that you do it honestly and fairly. Granted, that won't be easy . . ." the judge conceded, his voice trailing off.

Reviving himself, the judge continued: "You turn off Garrison Avenue and head south, you're in Choctaw Indian territory, a no-holds-barred country picked over by killers, robbers, rustlers, thieves, and cutthroats, and none of them care much about human life. For the horse you're riding any one of them will cut you to shoelaces and never think twice. And this Bowlegs, he has the credit of being one of the worst of the lot.

"But they're all human beings," the judge said soberly, "put on God's green earth for God-only-knows-what. You'll give them the respect due all God's children."

So they rode away from Fort Smith, heading south by a little bit west, following the old Butterfield Southern Overland route that the judge had told them about. The country they rode was red land of rolling prairie broken by occasional low sandhills, populated with leafless dwarf mesquite and sand oaks.

It was unsettled land. Broken water barrels and rotting timbers showed where the old stage route had been. Here and there a sod house or log cabin marked the presence of Indian farmers.

They traveled down the Poteau some distance, left it, returned to it, and crossed over at Mclean's Crossing, a shallow ford nine miles southwest of Fort Smith. They nooned in the foothills of Poteau Mountain and, taking up the trail again that afternoon, skirted rude Indian farmhouses and outbuildings, speaking to no one. Judge Stanhope had told them what Bill Colbert had told him: Questions asked about Bowlegs were likely to be answered with lies or silence, because Bowlegs was feared by many and trusted by few.

Careful not to be seen by others so as not to raise suspicions among the scattered Indians, they felt their way down the southern slope of Poteau, wending through bare-branched post oaks that dotted this poor excuse for a mountain.

In the shank of the afternoon they struck the valley of Boggy River, a reddish-brown stream that wandered down from the north.

"River's right where the judge said we'd find it," Bodie commented. "That settlement ought to be just around the bend if he's right about that too."

"He's been right as rain about everything else," Ruley answered. For no good reason he shifted his attention from the way ahead to the canopy of sky, as a traveling man will do from time to time. "Buzzards circling yonder," he said to Bodie. "Something's dead."

Pulling to a halt, Bodie lifted his eyes to the sky, then he searched the trail and noted, "It's right over yonder. Let's have a look."

They walked their horses along the fringe of the timber, and from fifty yards off they made out the body of a man stretched out in the middle of the trail, his location pointed out by two buzzards that had left the circling bunch and perched nearby on a low bush, waiting with whetted appetites for the right moment.

"Figured our luck was too good to hold," Ruley said sourly.

Not until they got within twenty yards of the dead man did the two buzzards flap clumsily to the sky. Warily they drew up, inspecting the dead man from the saddle.

"Shot in the head, looks like," Bodie commented.

"Shot more 'n once," Ruley added, spotting the bullet holes in the man's chest. "Whoever done it made sho' he was dead."

Looking more closely at the body, they were both impressed by the three close-spaced bullet holes in the man's chest, holes that a man could cover with a palm. "Whoever done it is a dead shot," Ruley commented.

"He ain't been shot long, neither," Bodie said, looking around uneasily. "Whoever done it could still be 'round here somewhere."

"That place we heading to . . . Boggy Depot. We ought to tell them about this."

"We better keep what we seen to ourselfs. No use 'n buttin' into somethin' that don't concern this warrant."

They followed the trail for another hour, then left it, riding toward loud, raucous sounds, the sounds of jubilant people and occasionally gunfire. Drawing near, they cut across a narrow neck of timber, rode across a hundred yards of rolling prairie, and rounded a bend of Boggy River. Boggy Depot burst suddenly upon the eye.

Boggy Depot was situated in a picturesque clearing that had been an ancient trading location in a beautiful, finger-shaped piece of land surrounded by a post oak grove that jutted down from the prairie into a horseshoe bend of Boggy River. Because of its pleasant location, the place had once been the site of the Fusk, the yearly ceremonial gathering of the Choctaw Nation.

In modern times the Fusk had been allowed to peter out, the location evolving into an Indian bartering and trading site and yearly annuity pay ground. A two-story building had been put up by the Riddles and Towers Company, run by two questionable merchants who had joined together to provide twice-weekly beef rations at exaggerated prices to the removed Indians, and to hand out yearly annuity payments to Chickasaw, Choctaw, and Kickapoo families.

A log cabin council house and meeting room had been added to the location, and off to the side a sutler had put up a lean-to trading post to sell the Indians goods banned by the government.

Bodie and Ruley swung their horses toward the two-story building, riding down the natural trail created by Boggy River on one side and a gentle sweep of post oaks on the other. They cast their eyes around, taking in at least three or four hundred whites, blacks, Indians, and mixed-bloods—in every imaginable skin shade and every conceivable variety of dress style. They had all come in early for annuity day, which was only one day away.

It was obvious some Indians had been camped there for days. Tents and brush arbors ringed the depot itself and dotted the timbers nearby. At the wagon park that had been established up at the edge of the woods, a dozen or so tailgates had been swung down and enterprising men and women indulged themselves buying, selling, trading, and swapping, all in a sideshow atmosphere.

Bodie and Ruley advanced under the uninterested side glances of a loose bunch of raucous men busy swapping stories, betting, talking, laughing; others were fiddling, eating, drinking, smoking. Men rolled in blankets lay around campfires, sleeping off the effects of "busthead," prohibited whiskey bought from the tailgate of more than one wagon parked up in the timbers. A great carnival atmosphere prevailed, masking the commonplace violence that lay just below outward appearances.

"I ain't seen such goings-on since freedom day," Ruley said. "Wonder what they celebratin'?"

Just then the pop-pop of two quick-spaced shots drew their attention to a rider fogging it out of the timbers, coming down the slope to their left and running his horse at breakneck speed toward the two-story building ahead. At his reckless riding, catcalls and whoops of encouragement swelled up from the Indians scattered along the edge of the timbers in his path, urging him on.

Bodie and Ruley came on at a walk, their eyes following the rider. He raced up to the hitchrail in front of the main building where they were headed, jerked to a hard stop, leaped from the saddle at a dead run, dashed across the porch, and disappeared inside the building.

After the war, the five civilized tribes removed to Indian Territory had been compelled by the federal government to free their African slaves, just as the white southerners they had emulated had had to do. Now there were hundreds of full-blooded Negroes in Indian Territory.

As they rode through, nobody paid much attention to them. They swung down from the saddle next to the sweaty mount that had just been left there.

They crossed the porch, and Bodie led the way through the first door, toward the counter along the back wall, his eyes searching for somebody inside the dimly lit room.

At the sound of their approaching footfalls the curtains in back of the counter parted rudely and a ruddy-faced man of less than average height and build burst through the space, shouting angrily at them, "If you've come begging for annuity money this early, you'll get none! I ain't passing out no payments till sunrise in the morning. That's final! Now, git!" The man's voice was surprisingly heavy for someone built along his thin lines.

"We ain't here for no payments," Ruley said, annoyed.

"We lookin' for Mr. Riddles," Bodie added. "Judge Stanhope sent us."

Composing himself, the man said, "I'm Jesse Riddles. What can I do for you?"

"Bodie! Ruley! That y'all out there?" shouted a voice from the room behind the curtained-off door in back of the counter.

Bodie and Ruley questioned each other with their eyes, then looked at Riddles.

"That's Marshal Bowman back there," Riddles said. "You two know him?"

"You damn straight they know me!" Bowman roared to Riddles. "Now, send 'em in here!"

Riddles led them into the back room. Over in a dark corner Bowman was sitting on the edge of a rumpled bed, his right arm in a sling, a heavy bandage across his chest. Bowman was pale, drawn, a dark growth of whiskers covering his face.

Bowman looked them over wonderingly, shaking his head in disbelief. "What y'all doin' out here is beyond me, but I'm damned glad to see you. I need possemen. Need 'em bad. Men I can trust."

"We already doing posse work," Ruley said.

"For who?"

"Judge Stanhope."

"Serving a warrant," Bodie added. Judging by the looks of Bowman, they could tell he had been badly wounded and was in no shape to carry on. "But we can git you back to Fort Smith if that's what you wantin'," Bodie offered.

"Hell no," Bowman said stiffly. "That ain't what I'm wantin'. In a day or two I'll git myself back."

"What you need posse work for, then?" Ruley asked.

"The man that done this," Bowman said, nodding his head, indicating the wound in his chest, "rode in here and lorded it over to the rest of them folks out there. Riddles just rode in and says he's just killed Choctaw Bill, the posseman I had on his trail after I was put out of commission."

"Musta been Choctaw Bill we seen dead back yonder," Ruley said, ". . . three bullets in his heart."

"The man who done it dumped Choctaw's body back there and come in here bragging that Choctaw was made an example of. He warned when he rode out that if anybody else was to come after him, he'd give 'em the same treatment."

"We didn't see no torture marks on Choctaw," Ruley said, "but he was mighty dead."

"Choctaw was tortured, all right," Bowman said. "Indians got subtle ways of doing it. And I got no reason to believe he won't torture the next man. But I want you boys to go after him."

"Us?" Bodie asked.

"Y'all! And right now!" Bowman insisted. "He crosses Red River into Texas like he's headed, we got no jurisdiction. I'll see you get the warrant money. All of it.''

Ruley jumped at the offer. Turning to Bodie, he said coaxingly, ''It wouldn't take long.''

''Where's he now?'' Bodie asked reluctantly.

''Riddles here says he seen him south of here. He's riding with a moving band of Kickapoos led by old Chief Pecan.''

''What's his name?'' Bodie asked.

''Bowlegs,'' Bowman said grimly. ''A mixed-blood son of a bitch called Bowlegs.''

''Bowlegs!'' Ruley repeated, looking sharply at Bodie.

''That's who we lookin' for,'' Bodie said to Bowman.

''You ain't got far to look,'' Bowman answered grimly.

Chapter Twenty-three

They rode away from Boggy Depot late that evening at Marshal Bowman's insistence, putting their mounts back on the trail without feed and rest, leaving behind them a wounded marshal and a dead man as Bowlegs's warning to those who might come after him.

Bodie's deliberate nature was quickened now. Bowman had ordered them angrily: "Y'all go after that half-breed bastard now! He cross into Texas, the law'll never lay hands on him!"

"We goin'," Bodie said.

"Right now!" Bowman yelled again.

"We'll git him," Ruley promised.

Bowman desperately wanted Bowlegs, but doubts kept forcing themselves into his head. Finally he cautioned them, "Y'all watch yo'selfs, though. He's trickier 'n a cat. Don't take risks with him. Either one of you git the chance, empty his saddle first and ask questions later."

"We'll be on the lookout," Bodie said.

"Expect trouble," Bowman said again, " 'cause he'll give you some."

"We find him," Ruley said. "And when we do, we ain't takin' no chances."

Outside at their horses, Bodie said to Ruley, "Sounded to me like you and Bowman forgittin' what Judge Stanhope said about treatin' the prisoner fair and square."

"I ain't forgittin'," Ruley said touchily. "But Judge Stanhope ain't the one out here to git shot at."

They rode south and a bit west, following the old Shawnee Trail over a land of little timber and dormant buffalo grass stirred by a low prairie wind. Just as Bowman had thought, at no more than an hour's ride out, they came into a wide swath of freshly made pony tracks, interspersed with many footprints and cut earth from two lodgepoles being dragged.

"Back home we done a lot of hunting," Ruley said, looking ahead along the swath of chopped-up earth. "Rabbits mostly. Tracks a rabbit leaves can tell you a lot, if you know what you lookin' at."

Ruley glanced slyly at Bodie. But knowing Bodie didn't talk much, he continued: "I'd say these here was the tracks of thirty-five, forty people travelin' together, some ahorseback and some afoot. And they ain't in no hurry. Wouldn't you say so?" he asked innocently.

"Yeah."

"And I'd guess Bowlegs was in the bunch. Wouldn't you?"

"Yeah," Bodie said flatly, flicking his horse into a trot away from Ruley's annoying chatter.

At a ford of Blue River, they sat the saddle, looking out over the water.

"We've come about as far as daylight will let us," Bodie said, aware that it was less than thirty minutes before dark. "Country's too dangerous to ride at night." In the dim light of falling darkness, they slumped tired in the saddle, looking out at the normally placid water that now rushed past them toward the Red River, spurred on by the first high-up winter rains.

"River don't lack much from bein' out of its banks," Ruley said. "It took some doin' for them Indians to cross."

"They likely know the place," Bodie said. "We'll need daylight to cross safely."

Ruley cast his eyes over to the other side, saw a dangerous-looking shoreline and uninviting underbrush, if they lived to scale the frowning, slick red bluff. He said halfheartedly, "Ain't as bad as it looks."

At Bodie's scowling, sour look, Ruley said seriously, "If we was to cross tonight I betcha we'd catch old Bowlegs with no trouble atall."

"Or git killed in the doing. Ain't no use 'n gitting shot or drowning ourselfs in the dark trying to sneak up on Bowlegs. Like the marshal said, he ain't hurrying like a man scared. My guess is he's camped real close on the other side."

Bodie had no way of knowing it, but he was exactly right.

At that very moment a smooth-faced, light-complexioned half-breed was sitting his haunches on the other bank as motionless as the lightning-struck forked tree masking his presence. He had been watching the two men ever since they had appeared on their backtrail out on the prairie more than two hours before, and had positioned himself as rear guard after Pecan's band had crossed Blue River. When Bodie and Ruley rode up he put aside his Winchester, his interest piqued by the two black men obviously in strange country, off the trail and out of place, just like the other two blacks he had come to know.

Bodie and Ruley sat their horses for a minute, un-
aware that they were under Bowlegs's patient gaze.
Bowlegs's eyes narrowed in studied thought when Bodie
and Ruley turned their horses away from the water's
edge, heading upstream.

In the cool of an October night under the frail light
of a waning moon, instead of crossing over as Ruley
wanted to do they unsaddled on the east bank of the
river under the dead branches of a leafless hackberry
tree, and went into night camp.

Bowlegs sat still, thinking quietly. Through a rank
stand of leafless timber, he focused his gaze back across
the water again, studying the campsite, his ears sorting
through night sounds, his mind working at what must be
done.

Sleep fell away from Bodie. He woke up with a start.
Yet he lay there snugged warmly in his blankets, listening to early-morning sounds: The river gurgled along,
birds twittered somewhere close by, a horse stamped on
a dry twig. Nothing more.

Suddenly he threw aside his blankets and bolted upright. A quick look around the camp confirmed what he
had suspected the silence meant: Ruley was gone!

Thinking back on what Ruley had said just before he
dropped off to sleep the night before, Bodie guessed
right away that Ruley had crossed the river alone, going
after Bowlegs. Ruley had mused aloud, "We was to
cross tonight, I betcha we'd catch old Bowlegs with his
pants down."

"Maybe," Bodie had said. "But from the way he's
talked about, Bowlegs ain't one to git caught with his
pants down."

"We might have to kill him, then," Ruley had stated,
and drawing his blankets up, had rolled over and had
gone to sleep. Or so Bodie had thought.

Now Bodie looked out across the water for any sign of Ruley, first up, then down the opposite bank. Nothing showed.

Working quickly, he gathered up his belongings, saddled up, and within minutes rode away from the campsite. In the early gray of morning, he followed Ruley's tracks upriver to an easily fordable place that Ruley had evidently stumbled onto, a place where beeves for Indian rations had regularly been crossed over, Bodie guessed.

Without incident he swam his balky horse across Blue River and scrambled him up the slippery mud bank on the other side. Following Ruley's tracks leading away from the river through naked timber and through the Kickapoos' abandoned camp of the night before, he struck the open prairie where Ruley's tracks fell in with those of the departed Kickapoos. Standing in the stirrups, he strained his eyes ahead, searching the prairie for movement.

And he spotted Ruley's horse off to the left.

The horse was standing ground-hitched and partially concealed in the fold of a prairie dry wash, his ears like two cones pricked forward.

Bodie checked his horse down to a walk and circled away, moving warily through the stirrup-high wild hay, his eyes searching for what the horse was looking at.

Suddenly he reined up, his eyes flared wide at the sight before him.

Ruley!

Bodie jumped from the saddle. The bloody wound high on Ruley's left breast and the ugly tilt of his head told Bodie that Ruley was dead, or near to it.

Kneeling, he lifted Ruley's shoulders, brought his head around. Through empty eyes Ruley saw it was Bodie. "Almost had him," Ruley said, smiling weakly.

"Whyn't you wait till morning?"

"Figured to catch him with his pants down."

"You figured wrong," Bodie said curtly, looking down at the bloody, mangled flesh left by a bullet that had torn at Ruley's heart.

"He didn't give me no chance," Ruley said, red froth bubbling on his lips. "Seen me comin' . . . musta been watchin' all night."

"Did you see him?"

"I seen him," Ruley said feebly, and coughed back blood. "He come down here, stood over me just as bold as you please."

"He say anything?"

"Wanted to know how come we following them. They figured us for army."

"You tell him about the warrant?"

"Yeah. He just laughed. Said stealing horses was only a big thing to the white man. Indians do it for fun."

Bodie shifted his kneeling position and lifted his eyes south, the way the tracks led. Ruley felt the movement and brought his weak eyes around to Bodie, saying, "He already knows you here . . . said for you to quit followin' him . . . or else."

"Or else what?"

Ruley chuckled without humor low in his throat. "You ask me that after seeing what he done to me?"

Bodie looked up, toward where Bowlegs had gone.

"You still going on after him?"

"After I git you back to Boggy Depot."

Ruley's lips shaped a weak smile. He knew he didn't have a prayer to make it back to Boggy Depot. A prairie gully would be his grave. A serious frown came to his face, and he said admonishingly, "Go find your folks, Bodie . . . let Bowlegs go."

"Let him go!" Bodie repeated, shocked at the suggestion. "You was the one itching to serve warrants, remember?"

"Still say it beats stoop labor," Ruley said weakly,

"and it was something I figured I could do good."

Bodie looked down into Ruley's eyes, a penetrating, searching gaze. "You right. It beats stoop labor," he agreed.

Ruley's eyes stared back, empty.

After a time Bodie said in a low, meaningful tone, "I'll see the warrant gits served."

"Leave him be," Ruley said, his voice a whisper now. "He'll kill ya without warnin'."

"Can't," Bodie said. "Warrant's got to be served now."

"Go find your folks . . ." Ruley's words trailed off. A drawn-out hoarse breath pushed past his lips, an ugly grating breath that had the sound of death to it. His fingertips pulled Bodie's sleeve, his eyes fell off to the side. He tried to form words but produced only thick guttural sounds. Then his head sagged back, his life gone.

So Bodie rode away at a hard ride, in a hurry now, leaving Ruley's body lying out in the prairie dry wash where he had found it. It was a lonely place even for a blunt man without pretensions, as Ruley had been. But he wasn't alone. Remains of the Old Ones had been scattered there long before Ruley deposited his.

Bodie followed the Indian's trail south, riding hard. He wanted Bowlegs, and he wanted him now. All his deliberateness was gone now. Something new was pushing him on, driving him like never before.

Over prairie land of buffalo grass and dwarf timber he rode, over slashes of dry washes and rents of runoff rains.

The sun climbed overhead, the tracks grew fresher, dung heaps appeared only lightly crusted over, bent grass almost straightened up. Using what common sense he had and what little cavalry tactics he had learned, he swung off the backtrail and took to the open prairie, making a wide loop around the moving band to outflank them.

Two hours later, he had headed the Indians and was closing in on their flank, coming in carefully from the west, the sun at his back.

But Bowlegs was not deceived. He sat his horse still as a rock, quiet as camp smoke, his eyes squinting, blunting the sun's ray's, watching Bodie coming out of the sun toward him.

Bodie topped a low sandhill, searching ahead, expecting to see the moving band.

He was shocked when he saw a rider sitting his horse impassively, watching him.

He knew right away it was Bowlegs.

Bowlegs knew right away this man still intended to force on him the white man's silly paper that meant nothing.

Bodie knew from what he had heard that Bowlegs could have killed him already. Checking to a halt, he reached back, unsheathed his Winchester. Bringing it to bear in his right hand, he fixed his eyes on Bowlegs, waiting for Bowlegs's next move, expecting the worst.

But Bowlegs just sat his horse boldly, his chest held high, looking along his nose at Bodie, his chin lifted arrogantly, as if he could conquer the world if he chose to. His point made, he heeled his horse into motion and expertly pranced in a loose circle out in front of Bodie, a circle of warning, yet a circle of friendship.

Rounding the imagined circle, Bowlegs swung his horse and cantered off across the prairie, pompously turning his back to Bodie. Dipping down into the shallow wash he had materialized from, he rode away, all but his moving shoulders concealed.

At a low spot made by a feeder dry wash Bowlegs's full body came into view.

Bodie jerked his Winchester up, snugged it to his

shoulder in firing position, and curled a finger, taking up trigger slack.

At that instant a Winchester cracked from up the wash.

A bullet whipped pass Bodie's head, startling him, spoiling his aim, his bullet singeing a furrow across the hip of Bowlegs's horse. The horse screamed, bolted suddenly, violently, tumbling Bowlegs from the saddle.

Bodie had no idea who had fired the shot. But he knew Bowlegs was doubly dangerous now.

Bowlegs scrambled to his feet. Moving cat-quick, he dived behind the lip of the wash, his pistol ready. Parting a bunch of tall grass, he lifted his head cautiously, peered out, searching the prairie in front of him.

Instantly a spate of bullets crashed in, kicking up spouts of dirt at the spot where his head had just been.

Bowlegs's head went out of sight in a shower of dirt, his eyes somehow catching the loom of the rider coming at him, his Winchester still in firing positon.

Bowlegs ducked aside, fired blindly, a quick shot triggered off with only general aim at the horse coming at him in a full-out run.

At that instant Bodie dug in his spurs, sending his horse into a rip-snorting leap, the horse's hoofs leaving the ground where Bowlegs's face had been just an instant before.

Bowlegs fired again at the flash of iron hoofs soaring over him, his pistol exploding just as the horse's underbelly glided by.

The horse bellowed painfully, landing on the other side in a snorting, clumsy stumble, pitching over on its side finally, pinning Bodie in the saddle.

Bodie was unarmed now, his Winchester lying out on the prairie, his pistol gone, lost in the dirt somewhere under him.

Working the reins urgently, he exhorted the animal to

gain its feet. The horse whinnied feebly and flailed his legs wildly, lifting his head, trying to see the rider who was asking too much of him.

Abruptly Bodie's efforts stopped, his attention drawn by a long-haired, wide-mouthed man who had just appeared at the edge of the wash, visible only from the waist up, a gun in his right hand.

It was eerily quiet. The horse blew a subdued snort, eyes walled helplessly, giving up the effort to get to its feet.

Bodie saw the pistol muzzle come up higher, pointing to his chest, saw the muscles clench in the half-breed's clean-shaven jaws. Unfeeling eyes fixed him, squinting noticeably, and a curved finger started to tighten on the trigger.

Bodie knew he was a dead man. At any instant he expected a bullet to break into his body.

"Don't!" somebody screamed. "Don't shoot him, Jimmy!"

Bowlegs's finger froze on the trigger. He swung around, trying to find where the voice had come from.

The swishing sounds of moccasins running over gravel came to him, and then a man bounded out of the wash, showing himself to Bodie for the first time. He was an unwashed, wild-looking youngster. And he drew up spread-legged when he saw Bowlegs's pistol still aimed at Bodie, pinned under the horse. His eyes keened guardedly at Bowlegs, his Winchester coming around not so subtly in Bowlegs's general direction.

Bowlegs eyed the young man uncertainly, aware that the black kid he had ransomed from Comanches just days before had for the better part of the past year lived the savage ways of his Comanche captors and would kill him in the wink of an eye if he had learned anything at all from them.

303

Bowlegs glanced at Bodie, searching for a brave way out.

Bodie was looking in wide-eyed surprise at the wild-looking thing dressed in ill-smelling buckskins that was obviously the younger brother he hadn't seen in close to three years and more than half a country away from this place. "Berry!" he said incredulously. "That you?"

"It's me," Berry answered quietly, still watching Bowlegs.

Bowlegs was shocked that the two knew each other. He looked questioningly at the youngster.

"He's my other brother I told you about," said Berry. "The one me and Boot told you would come sooner or later."

"What in God's name you doin' here?" Bodie asked Berry. "I heard y'all was in Texas."

"We is—"

"Comanches took him captive," said Bowlegs. And reminding Berry again of who his deliverer was, he added boastfully, "I get him back." Bowlegs thumped his chest manfully with his fist, for Bodie's benefit.

"You'll get paid back," said Berry.

Bowlegs held his chin high, looking out indomitably at Bodie, his gun still leveled forward, making the point that Bodie's life was his if he wanted to take it.

"If my brother is followin' you," Berry said firmly, "he's got good reason." Keeping his eyes riveted on Bowlegs, his Winchester positioned for a quick shot if need be, Berry asked out of the side of his mouth, "That right, Bodie?"

"That's right, I got reason."

"You have white man's reason," Bowlegs said scornfully.

"That . . . and a dead partner back yonder," said Bodie.

Bowlegs slowly lowered his pistol, eyeing Bodie

boldly all the while. To Berry he said, "Maybe this brother same like other brother."

"How's that?" Bodie asked.

"Scared of white man. Maybe I teach you too."

"I told you he'd come," Berry interjected brightly, breaking the tension.

"Maybe you scared white man too," Bowlegs accused him. "Maybe I give you back to Comanches . . . Comanches teach you good." He turned and walked toward his horse standing off to the side. He caught up the reins, gave a casual inspection of the burn mark the bullet had cut across the horse's hide, then swung onto the saddle.

"What you after him for?" Berry asked Bodie.

"He's wanted by the law at Fort Smith. I've got a warrant here that says he's a horse thief."

"Horse thief!" Berry said in disbelief. "He traded horses to the Comanches for my freedom. That's the only reason I'm here."

Bodie glanced out at Bowlegs, who had just kicked his horse into motion, coming toward them. Looking at Berry, Bodie removed the folded warrant from his shirt pocket and turned it between his fingers, watching Bowlegs's reaction all the while.

"White man's paper means nothing to me," Bowlegs said indifferently from the saddle.

Bodie crumpled the warrant in his palm and threw it in the dirt. "Let's go home," he said to Berry.

Chapter Twenty-four

The sun was completely up when they rode away from the dry wash heading south. Bodie and Berry were going home to Squaw Valley to reunite with what family they had left and hadn't seen in months. In Bodie's case, years. Bowlegs was riding to intercept Pecan's band and pilot them to Nacimiento.

Berry Johnson was afoot, a gangling, lean-at-the-shoulders, rawboned kid of sixteen walking with the cat-like grace of the Comanches he had been forced to live with for the last year or so.

Berry was without a mount because Bodie's horse, which Bowlegs had wounded, had been put to death by Bodie—a pistol shot to the head. And Bowlegs changed his mind and gave Berry's Indian pony to Bodie, telling Berry, "I take back horse I steal for you. You good Comanche, you walk."

The kid made no comment. He had come to accept

Bowlegs's whimsical nature. Besides that, he would have done it anyhow for Bodie.

The land they traveled was a wide prairie of dry grasses, sagebrush, and stunted mesquite, low sandhills, shallow gulleys, and dry washes.

Walking alongside Bodie's horse, Berry did most of the talking. Right off he told Bodie in hushed tones, "We saw Mama only once after they put us on the train. Next time we saw her was a week later when the train stopped to clear the cars of the dead. Mama was among them."

"Papa?" Bodie asked.

"Dead too."

"How?"

"Papa had a good freighting job hauling supplies for the army between Weatherford and Fort Richardson. He was doing real good, me helping him most of the time. Then, one day last fall, Comanches jumped us.

"We only had one old army rifle Papa had picked up at the fort. Papa put up a good fight with that, but he couldn't hold out. After a while they got two arrows in him. When he couldn't shoot no more they rushed in on us and shot six more arrows in him. They done it mostly for spite, 'cause Papa had killed five of them, four I seen myself.

"They was fixing to kill me too, but the brother of one of the dead Indians saved me. He told the others he wanted me to slave for his dead brother's family and the families of the others Papa had killed."

"Where was Boot?"

"Boot?" Bowlegs said, interrupting "I see him in Mexico."

"Mexico?" Bodie repeated. "I heard army talk about Mexico. What was he doing down there?"

"Money. He get money, go home get sister, then come get brother."

Now they moved across the dry lifeless prairie where a man could see for miles. A little bit before noon they fell into the tracks of the moving band.

Off in the distance to the south a stark wandering line of bright green willows stood out against the brown prairie, marking the presence of Red River and Texas on the other side, a line the Kickapoos knew marked the presence of the hated Texans, a line that piqued the vigilance of Bowlegs and the Kickapoos, and any other Indians headed in that direction for any reason.

"There," said Bowlegs, checking his pony to a halt, pointing in the direction of the stand of acorn trees growing in between the building at Colbert's Ferry. "You cross river there, go home."

"That right?" Bodie asked Berry.

"He says he knows. Boot told him what part of the country we live in."

"I listen good," Bowlegs said. "Your home that way two days more, maybe three you no hurry."

"Boot was at home when we was attacked," Berry explained to Bodie. "But Bowlegs here says he came from Mexico with Boot and a man named Amos. He says Boot had money to ransom me. That's how he heard about me and the country we was from."

"You tell Boot pay me for horses I steal give to Comanches for you, everybody happy," Bowlegs said. "You tell Boot soon I come . . . you tell sister, too."

"What about Bill Colbert, the man you stole the horses from?" Bodie asked.

"He got heap plenty more."

"You think Boot got ransom money in Mexico?" Bodie asked Berry.

"He may have. Mr. Ned, Mr. James's brother, where we was sent to, and Boot, they mostly stayed at home, looking after the place while me and Papa did the freighting. Mr. Ned didn't have no cash money. Boot

308

had to leave home to git some if he wanted some."

"Your sister, she get money too," Bowlegs commented, to their surprise.

"Bertha did the cooking for the bunch of us," Berry explained to Bodie. "But Bowlegs says he seen her out on the salt flats with Mr. Ned gittin' salt to sell."

"Your sister, she got man?" Bowlegs asked suddenly, shifting his eyes from Berry to Bodie and back again.

"You seen her since I have," Berry said, annoyed, and left the question there.

Bowlegs heeled his horse into a canter; Bodie did the same. Berry trotted, keeping up with the horses, holding on to Bodie's saddle skirt.

They cantered their horses awhile, walked them some, then cantered them some more. After the walks, when Berry had caught his wind, he filled Bodie in on what had happened with the family since being shipped off to Texas, and answered as best he could questions posed by Bodie, occasionally interrupted by a question or comment from Bowlegs, who thought he knew Boot well since they had traveled the country together from Nacimiento.

"Now he no scared of nobody," Bowlegs told them, taking the credit. "He got good gun, good horse. He good fighter."

The sun was directly overhead and they were walking on their own shadows when they caught up with Pecan and his followers camped in a brush-choked ravine skirting Bill Colbert's land. The Indians had pitched day camp to gather strength to travel at night, as Bowlegs had told Pecan they must do to avoid unprovoked attacks from the Texans.

A young Kickapoo warrior who had been posted as rear lookout took them across the prairie to see Chief Pecan, who had picked ground to rest on at the head of the ravine. At their approach the thin, leathery man of surpassing stubbornness rose from his cross-legged sitting position with the aid of a willow staff curved at the end.

His ancient eyes looked out unwaveringly from cavernous sockets, inspecting Bodie for the first time, taking in the way he rode his saddle and the campaign hat he wore, both bitter reminders of the yellow-legged horse soldiers he had fought all his life and had come to despise like death itself. "Why did you not kill him too?" he asked in his own tongue.

"He is the brother of the captured one," Bowlegs told him.

"He is a soldier!"

"No more."

"Why did he follow us, then?"

"White men sent him to capture me."

"Hah!" Pecan exclaimed, showing a mouth with missing and broken teeth. "He is clumsy like a buffalo. He could not capture a Kickapoo, not even an old squaw."

"That is true, Old One," Bowlegs said seriously. Slanting his eyes at Bodie, he added tauntingly, "He is frightened of white men."

"About that horse . . ." Bodie said.

Bowlegs smiled, amused at Bodie's discomfort. Turning to the young Kickapoo who had led them there, he told him in the Kickapoo language, "Bring the Comanche horse, the big black one."

The young warrior eagerly swung his horse away and soon came back at a gallop, leading a fine black stallion. When he started to pass the reins to Bowlegs, Bowlegs nodded toward Bodie and said, "Give it to him." In English, Bowlegs told Bodie, "This good horse. You take . . . go home."

"We'll pay you back for him," Berry said.

"I come your home collect. You tell Boot soon I come . . . you tell sister soon I come."

"Tell her yourself," Berry said curtly, and swung his horse.

Bodie and Berry rode away from the Kickapoo camp carrying traveling rations of jerked beef and full canteens of water for the uncertain journey south to Squaw Valley. Two hours later, they pulled to a halt within sight of Colbert's Ferry at the crest of a hogback on a long sandhill that swept away to the south. They sat the saddle quietly, watching two men at the pole corral training to bridle a rank mustang. Presently a man came out of an outbuilding up the slope from the tied-up ferry, and Bodie commented, "Ferry don't seem in use."

"Never rid one before," Berry confessed. "Swam my horse across or didn't go."

"It's safer. Cuts the time, too," Bodie said flatly, and flicked his horse into a shambling trot. Berry followed.

They slanted in off the prairie and joined the wagon road, walking their horses toward the tied-up ferry.

Across the road opposite the ferry a false-fronted, high-roofed building had a sign on it that said "General Merchandise" and below that the word "Whiskey" in smaller letters. Next to this was a livery barn with stock pins off to the side and a rail and rider fence circling the whole setup. A big ranch house sat way up in a saddle at the highest point of the swell that they had just ridden over, looking every bit the house of a prominent man, a man such as Bill Colbert was credited to be, Bodie guessed.

They had passed in front of the livery and were walking their horses across shady ground provided by a grove of acorn trees used for a wagon park when a man of medium height, thin shoulders, and indeterminate age stepped over his wagon tongue and said, "You boys looking to catch the ferry?"

"Was," Bodie said, and they checked their horses around to face the man. "Headin' to Texas."

"If you was to cross you'd be in Texas, all right," the man said earnestly. "But you can't . . . ferry's out of service."

Bodie looked toward the heavy log ferry.

Dull-red water plunged wildly, churning up a rooster tail at the stern of the tied-up vessel. The ferry strained at its rope lines, thumping clumsily against the wooden moorings.

"Red River's kinda finicky this time of year," the man said. "Mr. Colbert left word the ferry stays where she is till the river dies down some."

"When's that expected?"

"Hard to say. Been operating this rig now longer than I care to remember, and that river's taught me never to predict. She just kinda do what she's of a mind to."

Bodie looked without emotion at Berry, and before Berry could say anything the man told them, "Two days' ride downriver there's another crossing, Spanish Landing it's called. Water might not be near so rough there. You welcome to try."

"We'll wait," Bodie said dryly.

"Suit yo'self," the man said. "You can wait yonder." He nodded his head in the direction of the false-fronted building and warned mildly, "Wouldn't go in the saloon if I was you. Might start trouble."

"Ain't looking for trouble," Bodie said.

"Most men ain't, but there's some is. Gov'ment says you're free, but that don't mean white folks got to sit over drinks with you. There's plenty whiskey in there, and whiskey makes a man careless of his words and reckless in his doing. Was I y'all, I'd steer clear of the place."

"Sounds like good advice to me," Bodie said, looking at Berry for agreement. "Never was much for whiskey."

Berry kept silent, so the stranger advised them, "There's hay and grain in the barn. No telling how long you'll have to wait. Name's Biggers . . . Eli Biggers. Ferry don't run without me. I'll see you get word when Mr. Colbert says she's back in business."

Not wanting to draw attention to themselves, they quietly stabled their horses, forked down some hay, and put out a bait of grain. When Berry complained about the wait Bodie told him, "No help for it."

"Seen the Brazos on the rise once," Berry said. "Stayed that way three days. Hope this don't last that long."

They gathered up their stripped saddle gear and headed around the barn, looking for shady ground on the other side.

"We ain't got no choice but to—" Bodie's sentence broke off as they rounded the corner. They both drew up short in their tracks, their eyes taking in three white men directly in their path sprawled back on blankets against the side of the barn, their saddles serving as pillows, their hats serving as eye shade.

One of the men, Jim Riggs, carelessly tipped back his black, wide-brimmed, low-crowned hat and brought his eyes around toward the sounds of the footfalls that had disturbed his sleep.

At the sight of two black men standing near him holding saddles in their hands, the man's whiskey-reddened eyes widened contemptuously. "Jake!" he called, jabbing awake the man lying next to him.

"What the—!" Jake Spooner exclaimed, coming upright, startled. Jake's eyes were drawn to the two black men Jim Riggs was looking at, his gaze shifting from Bodie to Berry and back again. Anger came over Jake, deep long-held anger. He narrowed his eyes, slid his gun hand down next to his pistol, and barked sharply, "Ground's taken! Clear out!"

Berry looked across his shoulder, expecting a fitting response from his brother, who had seen different things, things up north.

Bodie showed no anger, his face calm, unmoved, his eyes unoffended.

Berry looked down, disappointed. And just as quickly his own temper rose. A tight draw came to his lips, and his eyes flashed. Dropping the saddle in the dust in front of him, he set himself spread-legged, hovering his right hand over the handle of the skinning knife belted at his side.

But Berry had no gun.

A twisted smile came to Jake's lips when he saw the Winchester still in the boot of the dropped saddle. Jake gathered himself, sprang to his feet.

Jake Spooner was a hard, slab-sided man of better-than-average height. He wore his gun low and tied tight, and had the reputation of a man who wouldn't hesitate to kill if the odds were in his favor. "I said," Jake repeated with emphasis, "the both of you take your foul-smelling hides somewheres else. You got objections?"

"He ain't got none," Bodie interrupted, looking across his shoulder at Berry.

"That's right, Jake," Eli Biggers said loudly from behind Jake, where he had just stepped from around the corner of the barn. Jake turned sharply, looking around for the voice.

"What objections could the likes of these two have?" Biggers asked incredulously when Jake's eyes found him. Shifting his attention to Bodie and Berry, Biggers lied reproachfully, "You boys go on up in the loft like I told you to. These fellers want privacy. Ain't that right, Jim?"

"Jake here takes it real personal when his sleep's disturbed," Jim answered. " 'Specially by niggers," he added tauntingly. "Last nigger what disturbed him, Jake shot his ear clean off." Jim Riggs grinned at his own mischief and asked, "Ain't that right, Jake?"

"That's right," Jake said grimly. "I got a notion to—"

"They meant no harm," Biggers cut in, "they was just—"

"Ain't no use, Eli," Jake said. "I been bothered now . . ." Casting a sinister look at Berry, Jake stated ominously, ". . . and I don't like it."

Suddenly Berry felt helpless. He was facing a gun with only a skinning knife. He looked uneasily at the Winchester still in the boot, then out the corner of his eyes at Bodie.

"Home's waitin'," Bodie said quietly. "Let's go."

"We ain't—" Berry started.

"We ain't what?" Jake interrupted with an ugly smile.

"We ain't got nothing here," Bodie said stiffly to Jake, speaking for Berry. "We'll go."

"I wadn't talking to you," Jake said to Bodie. "I was talkin' to that there wild man. You got business elsewhere . . . go see to it!"

The instant Jake shifted his eyes to Bodie, Berry jerked his skinning knife clear of the scabbard.

Jake's right hand swept down, going for his gun.

Bodie's two hands fell away from the saddle, the saddle plunging toward the ground, his right hand darting for his pistol.

Bodie's hand came up first, holding a pistol. The gun spit a ball of fire that flamed away from the muzzle, licking out savagely at Jake, slamming hot lead into his chest.

The bullet smashed Jake to his toes. He tottered there, a shocked look in his eyes, a pained expression on his face, looking wide-eyed into the dark bore of the six-shooter held by a man he assumed to be unarmed, as the other man plainly was.

Now Jake tried desperately to summon enough strength to steady his aim and trigger off the shot his dying fingers strained for.

But it was no use. Tottering on tiptoes till the last, he collapsed sideways, crashing down hard next to Riggs, who had goaded him into spending his life blood for a lark.

Jim Riggs was shocked too, mouth open. The other man lying there, Elliot Norton, had bolted upright, jarred out of his drunken sleep by the crash of gunfire. "What the—" Norton exclaimed, his right hand automatically reaching for his gun, his eyes searching for the trouble.

Norton's gaze came to rest on Jake's dead body crumpled next to Jim Riggs. And while his mind worked to sort out what had happened, Riggs told him, "He done it," nodding toward Bodie.

Norton looked at the black man standing there, gazing at him over the barrel of a pistol.

"It was a fair shootin'," Bodie said. "He seen it." He nodded his head toward Riggs and, switching his eyes quickly at Biggers, added, "He seen it too."

"That's right," Biggers said hastily. "There's no call to push it further."

"None atall," Bodie said.

"This don't sit right," Norton said, unsure of himself.

Bodie looked without emotion directly into Norton's bleary eyes, his pistol level.

Norton knew he'd be a dead man before the gun now under his palm cleared leather. He blinked involuntarily, soberly. His gun hand came away from the gun butt.

"Let's go," Bodie said to Berry.

"Hay barn's as good a place as any to wait," Eli

Biggers suggested. ''Ferry starts to running, I'll see you git word.''

They back-stepped away, disappearing around the corner of the barn, Berry lugging the saddles he had retrieved. Bodie twisted around as he retreated, keeping his gun trained in case of foul play.

When they were gone Norton cast a sickly look at Jake's body, then said to Riggs, ''Jake never done nothing to deserve this. Word git out we was outdone by a couple of niggers, we'll be the laughin'stock of the whole of Texas.''

''Don't you worry none about that,'' Riggs said. ''Word ain't goin' nowheres.''

''How come?''

''Them two niggers'll be dead before the river goes down.''

Chapter Twenty-five

Bodie stood slack-legged in the open door to the hayloft where they had retreated after he had killed Jake Spooner. Berry was still sleeping on the pile of straw where Bodie had woken up and had quietly edged away, taking in the full measure of the place, gathering his thoughts.

Now in the cool of late evening he looked out thoughtfully, listening to the dull thumps of the ferry steadily bumping against the crude dock. Long shadows stretched away from the false-fronted building and high-roofed hay barn. Willow leaves shimmered in the cool prairie breeze sweeping the riverbank.

The saloon was noisy. Now and again somebody swore loudly. Presently Bodie's attention was drawn by two more men some hundred yards out, trotting their horses in off the prairie. The two men fell into the wagon road, coming on. Bodie watched them with interest, struck by the coarse, down-at-the-heels look about them. These two were not at all like the last four who had ridden in together dressed in store-bought pants, suit coats, and wearing low-heeled boots as most townsmen did. Upon reflection, Bodie counted these last two to be the fifth and sixth men to come in within the last hour to board the ferry. They would have to join the others holed up in the saloon waiting for the river to die down.

Bodie knitted his brow, thinking.

Berry tossed in his sleep and mumbled something.

The angry voice rose from the saloon again, drawing his attention, even though his mind was still sorting through facts.

He knew at least ten men were holed up in the saloon, waiting for the ferry to start running, six he had seen ride in. The talking had grown louder, more forceful, as the whiskey took hold. He knew, as Eli Biggers had warned, that trouble was brewing.

Propping his Winchester against the door, he squatted on his haunches, looking out reflectively over the rushing waters of Red River.

An hour went by. A lone rider came in off the prairie from the direction of the fine house up on the hill. He was a big man with chiseled, square jaws. He wore a high-crowned white hat and rode a fine palomino horse. Eli Biggers rushed out to meet him near the ferry.

Bodie watched them.

They talked animatedly for a while, then the big man mounted up and rode back up the swell toward the house. The big man had to be Bill Colbert himself, Bodie guessed.

Fifteen more minutes went by quickly. A man and a woman came up in a ranch wagon, both neatly dressed in store-bought outfits.

The evening wore on. Bodie kept mostly to his watchful perch, with nothing to do but wait for the water to go down, like the others. Twice he saw Biggers go down to the ferry. Both times Biggers inspected the moorings and looked out inquiringly at the roiling chocolate water. The last time, Bodie thought he detected a hopeful nod to Biggers's head when Biggers lifted his eyes to the hayloft where he knew Bodie and Berry were waiting.

About thirty minutes before sundown Berry finally woke up. He joined Bodie at the door, looking out over Bodie's shoulder.

Two more men rode in off the prairie. When he first saw them Bodie's glance was casual, but looking again, he drew up attentively, studying them more closely.

One of the men, tall in his roan's saddle, had on a black, high-crowned, wide-brimmed hat and a black checked shirt. The flutter of batwing chaps was visible. The other man was a heavyset, pudgy, slope-shouldered man. They both rode with the look of experienced horsemen about them.

At Bodie's obviously hightened interest, Berry asked, "You know 'em?"

"Seen 'em before," Bodie said, standing, taking up his Winchester. "Both of 'em."

"Where?"

"Stokely Plantation. A while back I was at a big farm just over the line in Arkansas called Stokely plantation," Bodie said, moving away from the door space. Shaping up a place to lie down in the hay, he continued conversationally, "Them two men that just rode in, they was with a bunch that stampeded a herd of cows down on us." Bodie paused in his work, lifted his eyes, looking blankly past Berry, remembering the ugly sight of Deedee's mangled body. "Them cows trampled down every stalk of cotton standing," he said, "and killed three people in the doin'."

Exhaling audibly in resignation, he sprawled back in the pile of hay, resting his head on his saddle. "What's done is done," he said. "River goes down tomorrow, we go home." He turned on his side, putting his back to Berry.

Berry turned around and watched night come on. The only sounds he could hear through the open door were the plaintive coos of doves, the eternal shiver of willow leaves, and Bodie's even breathing.

Sleep suddenly fell away from Bodie. He flinched awake with a start, his eyes snapping open. Yet he lay perfectly still, adjusting to his strange surroundings. Slowly his eyes settled contentedly on Berry, who had resumed lookout duty in the loft's open door after being relieved twice by Bodie during the night.

Bodie stood and walked groggily to where Berry was looking out, rubbing sleep from his eyes.

"Wind's down," Berry told him without looking at him. "River's calm too."

Drawing the door open fully, Bodie looked out.

The tender light of sunup was creeping up the sky. Red River's chocolate waters flowed along calmly, lapping gently at the ferry bobbing quietly at the dock. Birds chirped from the motionless oaks nearby.

In the gray light of early morning he saw a man step through the saloon door, stand in the middle of the boardwalk, and pan his eyes over the surroundings. Presently another man joined him and they both stood talking for a time, looking out over the abated waters. Then they turned, went back inside.

Judging by what he had seen, Bodie knew that if conditions continued to improve the ferry would operate today. He said as much to Berry.

He forked hay down from the loft, and while Berry busied himself gathering up their gear, Bodie backstepped down the ladder with a half sack of corn on his shoulder. He was distributing the corn to the horses in the manger when voices came to him from the center of the barn.

"We could do worse," one voice said.

"Not by much," the other said disapprovingly.

The voices were mingled with the creak of saddle gear, the jingle of spurs. Men saddling up, Bodie figured.

"The war's over," the second voice continued. "Ridin' the countryside terrorizing darkies ain't goin' to change the outcome."

"Job's only temporary," the first voice responded, pained. "It ain't like this is our life's callin'."

Bodie was struck by the second voice; he had heard it before somewhere. Cocking his ear, he came around the partition and stepped away from the stall out into the walkway, looking toward the voices.

Bodie came eye to eye with the tall man in the black checked shirt, the same one worn by the rider who had led the stampede that had trampled Deedee to death back at Stokely Plantation.

Lake Dawson recognized Bodie too. Dawson knew this was the black man who had witnessed the intentional stampede, the one who had chased after them for a while.

They made no effort to conceal their recognition of each other. Each man stood watching the other, both expecting trouble, alert for action.

"You a long ways from where I seen you last," Dawson said finally, his eyes holding Bodie's. "Hope I ain't the cause of you being here."

"You ain't."

"That's good to hear," Dawson said. "You come with a name?" he asked pleasantly.

"Johnson, Bodie Johnson. . . . Your'n?"

"Don't care to leave one," Dawson said mildly.

"Your choosin'."

"Your partner?" Dawson inquired.

"Dead," Bodie answered tersely.

"Him?" Dawson asked, lifting his eyes to the loft where he had seen Berry looking out when they first rode in.

"My brother."

"Don't look it," Dawson said.

"Can't disagree with that," Bodie said, remembering how wild Berry looked now.

"Yet and still, it don't seem logical you here by chance," Dawson probed, unsure of Bodie's intentions.

"I got business," Bodie answered. "I got no bone with you worth pickin' over."

"What about them fool cow critters that took a notion to run on their own?" Dawson said shamelessly.

"Not even that," Bodie said honestly. "If it was that."

Dawson knew Bodie was accusing him of starting that stampede. Seconds ticked by; neither man backed off. More seconds ticked by. Finally Bodie said mildly, "I got kin waitin' 'cross the river. Figure to go see 'em as soon as the ferry's workin' "

"Wind's down," Dawson said. "She'll be operatin' shortly." The corner of Dawson's eye detected subtle movement over in the next stall. He made out a man hiding in the shadows there, skulking as he had suspected when they first came in.

Facing Bodie head-on and averting his eyes slowly, perceptibly, toward the concealed man, Dawson issued a veiled warning: "A man would have to watch his back if he wanted to live to board that ferry."

At the subtle movement of Dawson's eyes and his warning words, Bodie's eyes followed Dawson's. Bodie made out the darker shadow of somebody crouched in the next stall.

"Fact is," Dawson continued conversationally,

"nowadays it'd pay a man to watch out for back-shooters wherever he went."

Considering his warning given, Dawson turned, said down the stalls to his partner, "Daks, git them horses down to the ferry."

"It'll be a minute, Lake," Daks answered back, irritated at being pushed.

"Now!" Dawson said firmly. "Take 'em down now!"

"Sure," Daks said, blinking at Dawson's inexplicable urgency. "Sure, Lake." Daks gathered up the reins clumsily.

"See you don't miss the next ferry over," Dawson said easily to Bodie, back-stepping out of the barn, watching first Bodie, then the stall where the man was lurking.

Bodie knew he was being deliberately left alone to settle his own troubles with at least one man hiding in the stall down the way. How many others there were, if there were others, he had no idea.

Unholstering his pistol, he flattened himself against the near wall and crept forward, his eyes on the darkened stall where he knew the ambusher was. Abruptly Berry's moccasins swished, walking through hay up in the loft above him. Bodie realized Berry was descending the loft and had no way of knowing that a killer was waiting just below him.

Suddenly there was no time for stalking, no time for guile. Bodie knew he had to act now.

From a running start he vaulted over into the next stall, landing on his feet next to a bay horse that shied away. Slapping the horse's rump, prodding him out of his line of movement, he dived, doubled over into a somersault, and came to a roll stop in a pile of hay in the next stall.

And he came up shooting.

Firing as fast as he could work the trigger, he searched his bullets down the back wall and into the far dark corner, each bullet a probing finger of death.

The first three bullets stitched a path down the wall. The fourth bullet whined angrily only inches from the man's head.

The ugly-sounding bullets had paraded too closely for comfort. The ambusher suddenly bolted from cover, his face ashen, his eyes wide. He froze in his tracks for a split second, searched for a way out, found it, then dashed frantically for the hidden door no more than three paces behind him.

Bodie's next shot took him.

His chain of hammering shots never broke, never stopped. The fifth bullet broke into the man's rib cage just as he turned to run, knocking him sideways. A sixth bullet drilled a neat hole in the man's back, exploding out his chest, propelling him out the door into the hard-packed barnyard.

Bodie stood in the open doorway, his gun held in his hand, his fingers ejecting empty casings.

"That you, Bodie?" Berry yelled down, worried. "What's all the shootin' 'bout?"

"It's finished now. Come on down here so we can git on that ferry," he said, hurriedly reloading cartridges into the empty chambers.

"Y'all again!" somebody said unbelievingly at his back.

Bodie whirled at the sound, his pistol sweeping around to bear. Eli Biggers's eyes flared at the pistol bore he was suddenly looking into. "It's me!" Biggers blurted out, lifting his empty hands to Bodie's view. His eyes found the dead body lying outside the door. "Now there'll be hell to pay," he warned. "I told you to steer clear of these folks," Biggers added disgustedly, dropping his hands.

"Wadn't my fault," Bodie said flatly. "He was layin' for us."

"That won't cut no figure with this crowd," Biggers said. "They ain't likely to take this lying down, that white man shot in the back and all." Hurriedly drawing the barn door shut, Biggers told Bodie, "Y'all stay in the barn, let me do the explaining. The wind dies down enough, I'll see you git on that ferry."

At Biggers's obvious worry, Bodie looked out toward the false-fronted building. He saw a loose knot of white men gathered in front of the saloon, looking toward where the shots had come from. Just then a man came running from around the side of the building, shouldered his way through the men gathered on the boardwalk, and ducked into the saloon.

Bodie noticed the black checked shirt and high-crowned black hat in the bunch.

He had no way of knowing it, but Lake Dawson and Daks Walker had turned over the herd at the Indian agency, and like so many other unsettled men were moving on in search of a place to put down roots. They had come there to Colbert's Ferry hunting up a man named Bud Monroe, who they had heard was hiring hands for a riding job for a prominent man over in Texas.

Dawson looked at Monroe and said of the dead man, "He's the one I mentioned was hid out in the barn. Seems he got what he deserved."

"You didn't mention it was just a nigger he was fixing to kill," Bud said, eyeing Dawson coolly. "That woulda made a whole lot of difference, you know." Bud Monroe had with him half a dozen other white men of the newly formed outfit called the Ku Klux Klan, being sent from New Hope, Arkansas, by General Forrest at the request of Forrest's former comrade-in-arms, General Ben Putterman of Texas.

The Klansmen had been talking over drinks at the

table with Monroe when Dawson came up and inquired about the riding job. Dawson was hired on, joined them over drinks, and told them of the shooting scrape shaping up out in the barn.

Now Dawson looked around at the shiftless-looking bunch of Klansmen watching him accusingly.

"If you'd told it straight," John Rowan said, "that nigger would be lying out there with a hole in him instead of a white man." Rowan was a sallow-faced drifter out of Missouri. He had drifted into New Hope and joined with other rootless Confederates doing General Forrest's bidding.

"He was a back-shooter," Dawson said. "He deserved no better."

"Any decent white man would've stepped forward with him against that nigger," another Klansman, a big man named George Tucker, said brashly. "Mister, you got a lot to learn."

"Maybe you'd like to teach me?" Dawson said coolly. The Klansmen drew back expectantly, watching Tucker.

"You lop-eared jackass," Dawson said. "You couldn't teach your mama to suck eggs."

"You no-account, nigger-loving son of a bitch!" Tucker roared, and lunged at Dawson.

Monroe and a man named DeBow caught him and held him at bay. Keeping a restraining arm across his chest, Debow told him rudely, "Take it easy, Tuck. Ain't no use 'n going off on this here feller."

Hinton DeBow was a tall, solidly built, ruddy-faced man. A blunt-talking, coldhearted killer, he wore two Navy Colt .44s, butts hanging away from his body, and was utterly ruthless. Like the other ex-Confederates there, he had been mostly without wages since the war ended. General Forrest had provided him and numerous other enlisted veterans the only steady work they could find, and that was terrorizing freedmen in and around Van Buren and Fort Smith.

"That's right," Monroe said soothingly to Tucker. "Yonder across the river is plenty niggers you can take your anger out on."

DeBow now took charge of the scene as he always did. He stepped back from Tucker and, looking at Dawson, warned, "You was lucky, cowboy. Don't be for Mr. Venable, you'd be dead meat right about now."

DeBow smiled crookedly, turned away slowly, and swaggered back into the saloon, his two palms resting over the butts of his Colts as he walked away. Three other men dressed in town clothes that he had ridden in with followed him inside.

"Who's this Mr. Venable?" Dawson asked the only man left standing out on the boardwalk with him.

"Mr. Charlie Venable is that tall white-haired gentleman sitting over in the corner. He's said to be General Forrest's right-hand man. The general's sending him to Texas to organize. Any good Confederate is welcome to go along. There's a job waiting."

"Fightin' job?"

"You know any other?"

The man walked back inside the saloon, Dawson following behind him, searching for the white-haired Charlie Venable.

Venable was only forty years old, his hair prematurely white but still thick and curly. He had been Chief of Staff in Forrest's cavalry regiment, and when the war ended in defeat he headed up a guerrilla band operating out of the Missouri Breaks. When word reached him in his hideout that General Forrest had organized a bunch called the Ku Klux Klan to overtly carry on the war of politics, and covertly the war of terror, Venable came out of hiding and joined his former commanding officer.

Now he was being sent to Texas to organize and become the Grand Wizard of his own Conclave, as General Forrest had designated it.

Venable's fine features were set off by his immaculate clothes: a gray Prince Albert coat, a white ruffle-fronted shirt, and a black string necktie.

As Dawson looked at him, Venable lifted a finger and carefully stroked a thin spade-shaped mustache. As if struck by an afterthought, Venable motioned DeBow over and whispered something in the man's ear.

DeBow lifted his eyes out toward Dawson while he replied in a low tone.

Just then the man Dawson had moved next to at the bar tossed off his second drink and said accusingly to Dawson, "You seen it, didn't you, mister? You seen that nigger shoot Jim in the back, didn't you?"

"You mean when he turned tail and ran?"

Elliot Norton's windpipe twitched up and down nervously. He grabbed his glass again, finished off the last of the drink. Swallowing hard, he said anxiously, "I told Mr. Venable that nigger killed Jim for no reason. You'll back me on that, won't you?"

Dawson sat his drink down from his lips and said scornfully, "Did you tell Mr. Venable that Jim was a low-down, sneaking back-shooter?"

"That's a lie!" Norton blurted.

And before his words died away, a ringing blow to the face stunned him. It was a vicious backhanded slap that turned his head.

"Mister, any man call me a liar better have good cause," Dawson said, "and you ain't got one." Dawson turned around to face Norton.

Norton was flustered, his face cherry-red from the sudden rush of blood the ringing blow had brought on. His gun hand trembled, wanting to take exception. But his mind couldn't persuade the hand to move against the tall-hatted stranger facing him.

Bud Monroe had been looking on with other men from down the bar. "Leave it be, Norton," Bud said, ". . . for now."

"He's sidin' with that nigger," Norton said angrily. "He's got no business with white men."

"Best you leave it be," Bud said firmly.

Norton's shoulders sagged. He turned away grudgingly. Dawson faced back around, belly to the bar, and took up his drink.

Bud Monroe and Hinton DeBow moved in on each side of Dawson. Leaning over the bar, Bud said in low, measured tones, "Dawson, you still got in mind taking that riding job?"

"Maybe," Dawson said, aware of the veiled anger in Monroe's tone.

"Like I said, Mr. Putterman is looking for good men," Monroe said mildly. "Men who's choosy about who they side with."

"Most men are," Dawson replied.

"You siding with niggers and all, well—"

"He had no business, Bud," Norton interrupted from down the bar, "none atall. That nigger ought to be hung . . . and him, too, if he butts in again."

"Yeah!" Tucker agreed. "We ought to hang us a coon this morning, and anybody else that gits in the way."

"Seems you in the wrong company," Hinton DeBow said, picking up his drink and smiling amusingly at Dawson's discomfort.

The day wore on. The sun climbed up the sky; the wind abated; the river calmed.

Bodie had looked out from the upper door of the barn numerous times. Each time he had heard loud talking, swearing mostly, coming from the false-fronted building. Also each time he noticed increased activity about the place, activity that made him hopeful the ferry would operate soon, before all hell broke loose.

At ten o'clock Eli Biggers quietly pushed through the saloon door and stood unnoticed at the end of the bar, listening to the talk of drinking men getting madder and madder at having one of their own killed by a black man.

Bud Monroe sat at the table with DeBow, Norton, Tucker, Rowan, and Ellwood Goodloe, all ground-floor members of the newly formed Ku Klux Klan. DeBow was saying frankly, "That nigger killing Riggs like that, that's just the thing we got to put a stop to. If we don't, others will git up nerve to try it."

"Like I said, we ought to hang him," Norton said again loudly, looking down into the bottom of the whiskey glass he had just emptied.

"I seen a few nigger hangings since Mr. Venable organized us," DeBow said. "This'n wouldn't be no different."

Bud Monroe looked enviously across the room at the cool, calm Charlie Venable, taken by the man's poise and good looks. "Mr. Venable," he asked DeBow, "you think he'll do some hangin' when we git to Brazos County?"

"If niggers in Brazos County is half as uppity as you make it out to be, there'll be hangings. And if I know Mr. Venable, them smart-alecky Johnsons you told him about will be the first ones to hang."

"Sounds like just the thing Mr. Putterman intends," Bud said, pleased with his trip.

Eli Biggers had heard what he suspected. Trouble was here, he could feel it. Moving to the middle of the room, Biggers announced loudly, "Folks, I just got word from Mr. Colbert the ferry'll be runnin' shortly. Anybody got animals to cross over better see to 'em now."

"It's about time!" a drunken man said from the other end of the bar.

Lake Dawson had overheard DeBow's conversation too. He tossed off the last of his whiskey and said out of the side of his mouth to the man next to him, "Let's go, Daks."

"Horses already seen after," Daks answered. "What's the rush?"

"Comp'ny we keepin' is mangy," Dawson said, and moved out.

Chapter Twenty-six

Colbert's Ferry was nothing more than a large raft with five-foot-high rails running around its edges. The log raft was carried by current downriver some fifty yards to the landing on the other side, then poled back, guided by ropes each way. When Red River was on a rise, as it was from time to time, the heavy raft lay idle, lashed to its mooring, covered with a tarp, too heavy for a man to pole back against the stiff current.

Word had spread that Eli Biggers was down at the raft throwing off the lines, removing the tarp. Men straggled alone and in groups from the saloon, belongings slung over their arms and shoulders, making last-minute preparations to cross.

Half concealed in the door to the loft, Bodie unobtrusively looked out at the activity that had come over the place since word had got around that the ferry would get under way shortly. Men were coming to and going from the barn, retrieving their horses and gear, and talking.

Unnoticed up in the loft, Bodie had heard talk about the new outfit called the Ku Klux Klan. The outfit had been put together to terrorize coloreds, he had heard, and to kill, if need be. Where the terrorizing and killing was to take place, it chilled him to speculate.

The last two men he had heard talking—Bud Monroe and Tish O'Callahan—had walked their saddled horses away from the barn, heading toward the hitchrail in front of the saloon. Monroe resumed the conversation that Bodie had heard only parts of: "Mr. Putterman will be right pleased with the men General Forrest is sending him. If what Mr. Venable says is true, them niggers holed up at Ned's place will be sorry they wadn't long gone come election day."

"And me brother Lafe, God rest his soul," Tish added reverently, "will be joined by the darky that perpetrated his passing."

In the middle of the yard Bud and Tish met Hinton DeBow and three other Klansmen striding purposefully toward the barn. Elliot Norton was walking shoulder to shoulder with DeBow, and Norton had a length of rope in his right hand.

"Venable know about this?" Bud asked, surprised since Venable had earlier rejected the notion of hanging.

"He knows," DeBow said. "Only thing he wants is to git it over with. He says the ferry waits for no man."

"Them boys ain't goin' to sit still while you fit 'em with a necktie," Bud said.

"They ain't goin' nowhere," Norton said. "Their horses're yonder." He jerked a thumb in the direction of the hitchrail in front of the saloon. "Tucker seen to it."

Monroe exchanged glances with Tish O'Callahan. They both turned and headed back toward the barn with the hanging party. "Now's as good a time as any," Bud said.

Tish smiled with pleasure, the seven men walking somberly toward the barn intent on a hanging. Tish said gleefully, "Glory be! Now me dead brother can rest in peace!"

Just then Berry ascended halfway up the ladder to the loft, raised his head up the rest of the way, and announced, "Bodie, our horses gone!"

Bodie knew what it meant. Looking out at the activity in the yard, he picked them out immediately from the others, seven men in a loose bunch. Taking up his Winchester, he said to Berry without taking his eyes off the advancing men, "Trouble's comin'."

With calculated purpose Bodie stood spread-legged back in the open doorway, the unlighted loft at his back making him a dim target to men down below. With Berry looking on at his back, he leveled out his Winchester and fired.

A spout of dirt leaped up at the feet of Hinton DeBow, the man he took to be the ringleader. As a group, the seven men drew up sharply, startled, their eyes lifting to where the shot had come from.

"That's far enough!" Bodie called down to them. "We ain't lookin' for trouble. Ferry's runnin' . . . me and my brother will be out of your sight as quick as we can git on it."

Norton looked doubtfully out of the corner of his eye and saw that Bodie's words had had effect. Nobody was really in the mood to push for a hanging except him. Fact was, DeBow had agreed at first with Venable that they had bigger fish to fry over in Texas. But Norton didn't intend to let the lynching party pull back, not after seeing his partner killed.

"You killed a white man," Norton said with emphasis, letting his words sink in on DeBow and the others. "You didn't figure we'd stand by and see you kill a white man and git away with it, did you?"

"Didn't figure to kill no white man, period," Bodie answered. "He come after us."

Just then running hoofbeats sounded behind them on the hard-packed yard. Twisting around, they saw a rider coming at them bent low in the saddle, slapping spurs to his horse, holding the reins to two led horses.

The bunch of them parted in a wild leap out of the path of the churning hoofs. The rider screamed a blood-curdling "Yahoo" and sped his horse through them, heading for the barn door standing open.

Even as Dawson and the horses sped through the door below him, Bodie recognized the man in the black checked shirt, and the led horses as theirs.

They dashed over to the ladder leading down from the loft, scurried down, and landed just as Dawson jerked his mount to a skidding stop inside the barn.

"Johnson!" Dawson called out. "Johnson, git out here!"

They ran toward the horses, saddle gear in hand.

Dawson threw Bodie the reins. "Ferry's your best chance! Git a move on!" he said, wheeling his own mount to face the oncoming hangmen.

He reached the door just as DeBow and the others sorted themselves out and started running toward the barn.

Dawson threw a quick shot, sending them diving to the ground again.

Glancing back, Dawson saw that the Johnsons had saddled up. First Bodie and then Berry swung aboard, and Bodie brought his horse around, faced Dawson, a questioning look in his eyes.

"Never liked owing nobody," Dawson said. "Debt's paid for turnin' them critters on you . . . now, git!"

Bodie wheeled his horse and took off after Berry, racing out the back door of the barn.

Throwing out random shots every now and again, Dawson held the lynch party at bay.

Out at the ferry, Eli Biggers had looked up at the sound of gunfire. Now he heard running hoofbeats. Recognizing the two riders blistering the breeze toward him, Biggers's temper flared. When they jerked to a stop at the ferry, he exploded, "You two again!"

"Can't help it," Bodie said. They stepped their horses over the landing gate and boarded the ferry.

"What the . . . what's the meaning of this?" Biggers demanded. "Ferry ain't ready yet!"

A shot sounded from up near the barn, then another.

Bodie's eyes found the only remaining rope holding the ferry in place. "Untie it!" he ordered Biggers.

"Ferry ain't ready!" Biggers said again.

Bodie drew his pistol and, leveling it at Biggers's belly, ordered, "Cut it!"

Berry's skinning knife flashed from the scabbard even as he swung from the saddle. Keeping a grip on his reins, he took two quick steps over and parted the rope with one swift stroke.

The ferry jolted against the wooden mooring and floated slowly away from the landing, the stern breasting out first.

Just then two men came riding hell-bent along the riverbank, men afoot chasing them, firing as they came. Bodie shifted his eyes toward the sound of gunfire as he dismounted. It was the man in the checked shirt again, and his partner. And they needed help.

"Git these rails down!" he ordered Biggers.

Biggers looked at the chased riders coming toward them, puffs of blue smoke blossoming away from pistol barrels of the men chasing them. Biggers wanted no part of the running gunfight coming his way. He took cover behind the stout logs of the poleman's shelter.

"Help me git these rails down!" Bodie yelled at Berry.

They unhanded their reins, leaving their horses snorting and prancing nervously at the unusual surroundings. Working hurriedly, they removed the poles that held the side rails in place at the stern.

By the time the last pole had come down, the raft had drifted at least ten feet away from the landing.

"Jump!" Bodie yelled when Dawson galloped up. "You can make it!"

Dawson twisted in the saddle, threw back one last shot at the men chasing them. Then he jabbed spurs to his horse, sending him lunging onto the ferry. The horse landed with a skidding, scrambling stop on the wet deck.

Dawson leaped from the saddle, the horse fighting for footing. Flogging the horse's rump and hauling around on the reins, Dawson cleared a space and Daks's horse soared aboard, scrambling for footing on the moving craft, coming to a skidding stop barely before plunging into the water.

The raft caught the current, picked up speed, and moved away from the bank, closing on the other side. The running men pursued along the bank, swearing loudly, firing wildly, the last bullets landing harmlessly in the water.

Eli Biggers came from behind the shelter, staring apprehensively at his uninvited passengers. Tentatively he inspected the condition of the ferry, his eyes coming finally to rest on Bodie. "Ever since I laid eyes on you two," he scolded, "you been nothing but trouble."

"Wadn't our choosin'," Bodie said. "We ain't the kind to go out of our way to make trouble for others," he added, eyeing Dawson suggestively.

"Trouble don't care who makes it," Biggers retorted. "Anyhow, the place'll be a damn sight better off without you."

The current hurried the ferry down and across Red River. They neared the landing on the Texas side, and Dawson asked Bodie, "You got kin this side?"

"Another brother and a sister."

"This'n looks mostly Injun," Daks said, looking critically at Berry.

"I ain't," Berry said stiffly.

"He was taken captive by Comanches," Bodie said.

"Y'all them Johnsons from Brazos County?"

"Squaw Valley," Berry answered. "Gulch."

"Heard of y'all," Dawson said. "Whole country has. Your pa Britt . . . Boot, Bertha." Dawson looked again at the youngster dressed in buckskins and moccasins. "Mighta guessed it," he said. "You'd be Berry, the one them Comanches took."

Dawson looked back and said reflectively, "It figures now, y'all being Johnsons and all."

"How's that?" Bodie asked.

"One of them fellers that was itchin' to hang you was coming back to Texas with organized Ku Klux men. Bragged they had some Johnsons to hang when they got back."

"Which one done the braggin'?"

"Bud Monroe . . . the thin feller with the beard."

"Seen him before?" Bodie asked Berry.

"Naw."

"Ever hear tell of a man named Putterman, Ben Putterman?" Dawson asked.

"Naw," grunted Berry again.

The ferry bumped against the dock on the Texas side, and after a mild struggle with the balky horses, they debarked without incident. Dawson and Daks walked their horses over to the side, and had started cinching up when Bodie and Berry led their horses through the thick sand away from the landing toward them.

Dawson lifted his eyes from the stirrup he was working under and looked at them thoughtfully for a time. Then he said to Bodie, "Johnson, Mr. Venable and that Ku Klux bunch I told you about figure to run you clean out of Brazos County."

"Like I said, some men'll go out of their way to start trouble," Bodie said, cinching up his saddle.

"There'll be hangin's," Dawson stated. And watching Bodie for a reaction, he asked, "Y'all goin' on to Brazos County anyhow?"

"Just as fast as these horses will take us," Bodie said, lifting a toe into the stirrup.

"Well, I'll be hanged," Daks said in a low tone. He added in a louder voice, "Heard y'all was slow to anger." Pausing for effect, he spit off to the side, then added disdainfully, "And even slower to fight."

"Two dead men 'cross the river might disagree," Bodie said mildly.

"That ridin' job General Forrest promised," Dawson said, looking up at Bodie, "we was thinkin' on passin' it up."

"What you figger to do, then?"

"Heard the country 'round Durango had promise. We figgered to have a look."

"Luck to you," Bodie said, and turning his horse, he rode away.

"Luck to you too, Bodie Johnson," Dawson said quietly to their backs.

Berry didn't say nothing when he rode up and joined Bodie's side, but he twisted back twice to look at Dawson and Daks.

They rode away from Colbert's Ferry. They went south by west. The land they rode was of broken prairie and leafless timber.

Two hours behind Bodie and Berry, Charlie Venable and Hinton DeBow rode in the lead of Bud Monroe, Tish

O'Callahan, and four other Klansmen. Venable had threatened Biggers with a pistol-whipping if Biggers didn't immediately ferry them across Red River after Eli had poled the raft back.

Now Venable and DeBow pulled to a halt, the men closing around them. "They still ain't split up into pairs yet like Monroe figgered," DeBow said to Venable.

"Maybe they're just goin' in the same direction instead of ridin' together," Venable suggested.

"Me and Tucker here talked to that tall cowboy," John Rowan said. "He said he was captain of Confederate cavalry and the other feller was a sergeant. It ain't likely they'd take to trail with two niggers . . . not of they own free will."

"They're headed to Brazos County," Bud Monroe said for the second time. "They're Johnsons, and they ain't goin' nowheres else but to Squaw Valley, where there's other Johnsons."

"Ain't nothin' says they got to," DeBow answered bluntly. "Any fool knows there's plenty country in Texas besides Brazos County."

"We wastin' time, Mr. Venable," Monroe said. Monroe's jealousy of Venable's preference for DeBow had been plainly demonstrated. Monroe exhaled deeply, impatiently, and said with obvious disregard for DeBow's opinion, "They's headed to Squaw Valley, Mr. Venable. Me and Tish here—"

"Nobody's holdin' you and Tish," DeBow broke in angrily. "You delivered Mr. Putterman's message. Now why don't you run on back like a good boy, and leave the rest to us."

Bud Monroe stiffened, as if a bucket of cold water had been dashed in his face.

"Quit it, you two!" Venable snapped. "Monroe, you and O'Callahan ride out front yonder and take us to Mr. Putterman."

"What about them?" Monroe asked, meaning the black men.

"If you can figger out which way they went, you lead us to 'em. Otherwise don't even bother to look back till I'm standing in front of Mr. Putterman, you hear?"

So Bud Monroe and Tish O'Callahan rode out front. At Monroe's lead they rode at a stiff pace, Monroe to prove to Venable he was a better man than DeBow, O'Callahan to avenge his dead brother.

An hour ahead of them, Berry rode in the lead. They trotted their horses in off the prairie, angling down into the wagon road that ran from Weatherford to Fort Richardson. They entered the bend the road took around an inexplicably large broken boulder. Berry checked his horse to a walk; Bodie did the same. Looking back down the road toward Weatherford, Berry told Bodie, "Comanches jumped me and Papa 'long in here. They come out of the rocks yonder."

"Good place for it," Bodie agreed, looking around.

"Part of the wagon's still yonder in the rocks," Berry said, looking off that way. "Papa whipped up the team and fought from there after he was shot twice."

"Musta been scary for a boy your age."

"I was scared," Berry confessed. "I didn't have no gun."

"Wadn't nothin' you coulda done."

They walked their horses toward the site of the battle. Abruptly Bodie drew up short. Something had his attention. He swung his horse past the broken wagon and rode into the brush. Stepping down, he picked his way through sagebrush and rocks, halted at the base of a large rock, pushed back underbrush, and exposed a piece of wood, a piece of the tailgate from the wagon. A grave marker.

"Papa?" Berry asked.

"Yeah." Straining his eyes at the carved letters, he

read aloud, "Britt Johnson," and carved under that was "July 1866."

"Boot and them musta come and buried him after them Comanches took me."

"That's likely." Stabbing the stub of wood back into the prairie sod, Bodie said irritably, "Let's go home."

They rode away from the site of the attack, Bodie in the lead, holding to the general direction Berry had kept.

As they skirted Elm Thicket, the faint smell of woodssmoke came to Berry on the prairie wind. Lifting his horse into a canter, he caught up to Bodie's side. Before he could say anything, Bodie told him, "Seen smoke from the woods up yonder. You know the place?"

"Elm Thicket," Berry said, struck by Bodie's observation of the thin column of drifting smoke that only a knowing man with a keen sense of the outdoors would have seen. "We'd be better off ridin' around."

"How come?"

"Papa always did. Said the woods was full of no-'count white men lookin' to make trouble."

Bodie glanced over his shoulder at Berry, and Berry explained: "Army deserters, draft dodgers, wanted men hang out in there. Papa always said they'd kill you for the socks you wore and wouldn't be disappointed if you didn't have any on. We always skirted the place, freight or not."

"That the quickest way home?"

"The best way, too."

"We'll take it, then."

Holding to the trail that led in front of Elm Thicket, they came toward the tendril of white smoke rising out of the elm branches and vanishing into the prairie sky.

In a clearing at the edge of Elm Thicket wood smoke from a branding fire curled away to the sky. Presently a dark-complexioned, thin-lipped man stood up from his haunches, his ears perked up to the sound of hoofs running toward him. Scanning the prairie in front of him, he found three riders as they left the prairie and took a beeline toward the clearing.

Holding the three men in his gaze, he deliberately returned the spoon to the plate of bacon and beans he had been eating, and wiped his right hand down the leg of the tight-fitting Mexican pants he wore. He took up the Winchester propped against the deadfall his chaps were slung over and moved away from the fire, setting the tin plate down idly, resting his right hand down to his side next to his six-shooter. "Don't give 'em reason," Boot said out of the side of his mouth to the other black man standing off to the side, his own plate poised in front of him.

"I ain't," Joe Ben said, looking out uneasily at the white men galloping down on them. "Putterman's men," Joe Ben said tersely. "They'll start trouble."

"Maybe not."

"They'll find reason to kick up a fuss."

Ed Blount, Tim Snowden, and Bill Gandy swooped down on the campsite, jerked to a stop in front of Boot, standing there, his Winchester held carelessly along his leg. Putterman had elevated Blount to leader of the men, since Bud Monroe had been sent off to bring back Klansmen.

Blount's eyes quickly swept the camp, pausing to look longer at the crude holding pen. Taking a mental inventory of the wild longhorns penned up there, he brought his gaze around to Boot and said coldly, "You was warned, Johnson."

"Unbranded critters free for the takin'," Boot answered smartly. "Ain't many white men would disagree."

"Last time we saw you," Blount said, "the law—"

"Heard you ain't got the law on your side no more,"

Boot cut in rudely, reminding Blount that Judge Semester had stripped Sheriff Willis of his badge.

"Don't matter," Blount said. "Law's still the law. Every beef you got penned there is rustled."

"Ain't a brand nowhere on none of 'em," Boot scoffed. "You can look for yo'self."

"Any cow that ain't wearin' a brand is fair game," Joe Ben added.

"There ain't a critter in Elm Thicket that's fair game," Blount said. "Not anymore."

"Putterman's land ends yonder," Boot said, nodding his head east where everybody knew Slash P holdings ended. "This is free range. Any man got a right."

"Old Ned's advice?" Blount asked mockingly. "Well, it ain't so," he stated. "I got a notion to land the both of you in jail for rustling." Blount made a show of softening his features, then said good-naturedly, "Ain't no use in that, though . . . unless you force it on me."

Blount took the silence that followed as quiet submission.

"Gandy, turn them beeves out," he ordered the man sitting the saddle next to him.

"You do and—"

Suddenly the fold of the prairie off to the left exploded. A burst of rifle fire rose up from across the prairie and a spate of bullets poured in, smashing sand and gravel against the horses' feet. All three mounts recoiled from the sudden assault, back-stepping and rearing fitfully.

At that instant, Boot swung his Winchester into action, firing as fast as he could lever the trigger, unleashing a seven-shot barrage of bullets that kicked up more dirt at the feet of the already startled horses, setting off a wild, rip-snorting melee.

Blount and his men could do nothing but let the horses

have their heads. They tore out of there as fast as their horses could carry them, riding for distance away from unseen bullets that struck at their horses' feet.

Suddenly it was over.

Boot stood looking for a time after Putterman's men, then shifted his attention across the prairie to the spot where the first burst of shots had come from, his Winchester held in his two hands. Two black men visible from the waist up leading their horses emerged from the dry wash. The older man was tall, dark, strongly built. The other was an easy-walking youngster wearing a fringed rawhide shirt, gliding forward effortlessly on his toes, something he had picked up from his Comanche captors. The older man was grinning a little.

Boot looked unknowingly out of the corner of his eye at Joe Ben.

"You know 'em?" Joe Ben asked.

"I hope to smoke I know 'em! Them's my brothers!" With a big half-moon grin on his face, Boot stood waiting as Bodie and Berry came toward them.

"Trouble, stranger?" Bodie asked in a serious tone.

"Stranger, my foot!" Boot replied sharply. "That young'un walkin' next to you is the only stranger 'round here!"

"I told you that was him," Berry said, grinning. "Them Mexican clothes didn't fool me none."

Joe Ben stood off to the side as the brothers he had only heard stories of got acquainted all over again. After a time of backslapping and handshaking, Boot told Bodie, "This here's Joe Ben."

"Hey, Joe Ben," Berry said.

Joe Ben nodded at Berry, and Boot told Berry, "Joe Ben's stayin' with us since you been gone."

"How come?"

"Gulch ain't a place where we welcome no more.

Him and some others was run out. Mr. Ned figgered it was only right to let 'em stay with us.''

"We earns our keep," Joe Ben said touchily. "Helpin' to make somethin' of the place.''

Talk fell off, each man thinking his own thoughts, then Bodie interrupted the pause: "If Papa was here, he'd be downright tickled at you, Boot,'' he said, and slapped Boot on the back again.

"You know about Papa?''

"Berry told me, and I seen the grave.''

Looking over at the holding pen, Bodie broke the serious conversation, adding lightly, "Never figgered you to be chasin' after cows.''

"He ain't exactly took to it like a duck to water," Joe Ben said sarcastically. "Don't be for me and the boys . . .''

"How's Bertha?'' Berry asked.

"Ain't changed a bit," Boot said, smiling. "She's bossier than ever. Worse'n any slave driver you ever heard tell of.''

"That's Bertha, all right," Bodie said, grinning at the memories.

"Joe Ben," Boot said, grinning, "you reckon Bertha would put up with two hardworkin' men like us sloughin' off the job long enough to bring her two brothers home?''

"I reckon she would," Joe Ben said, grinning too. "She'd be tickled to death to see the both of them.''

Hurriedly they picked up and straightened up around camp, then mounted and rode away toward Squaw Valley, holding to a good pace, passing few words as they rode. They swung around the flank of Rocky Hill where Slash P land ended and Lazy H land began. Lifting his eyes toward the Slash P ranch house, Boot slowed his horse to a walk and said to Bodie, "Ain't wishin' to put a damper on y'all comin', but there's trouble.''

"We got wind of it," Bodie said.

"Where?"

"Man at Colbert's Ferry. Way he told it, a feller named Putterman summoned Ku Klux men from Arkansas to come to Brazos County to see after some Johnsons." He added with obvious pride, "Seems these Johnsons was standin' up to a mighty big white man who wants to throw his weight over Brazos County."

"That's Putterman, all right," Boot said.

"Him and Papa never did see eye to eye," Berry said. "Papa always said Putterman wanted the whole valley to hisself, especially Mr. Ned's land. Papa always said one of these days it'd come down to a shootin' fight."

"Your papa was right mostly," Joe Ben said. "Everybody know Britt Johnson was a right thoughtful feller. If he was to tell you somethin', you could bank on it."

"He always did have a knack for seeing a thing in its true light," Bodie reflected.

"Wouldn't dispute the point," Boot stated.

Berry didn't have anything to say, so he didn't say anything.

They rode on, heading for the Lazy H.

Chapter Twenty-seven

It was an hour before noon when seven steely-eyed, tough-looking strangers walked their horses down the middle of Gulch's main street. Outwardly they saw indifferent glances, but behind their backs townspeople cast furtive, scared looks. Horses at the hitchrails along their way stamped and shifted nervously in their steps.

Four of the seven men rode inquisitively, panning their eyes around the new town as strangers will do. Two other men, Bud Monroe and Tish O'Callahan, rode high-chested and arrogant. They already knew the town; now they rode with men who would make the town know them.

The seventh man, Charlie Venable, rode with a serious purpose about him, his chin lifted, his eyes leveled ahead, careful to carry himself in a new town with that proper dignity expected of a man of high background from Virginia's slaveholding gentry.

They drew up at the hitchrail in front of the Bull Head

Saloon, the men closed around the man of obvious breeding, and they all dismounted. Venable carefully brushed the road dust from his coat sleeve, subtly looking over the town, a quiet, moving appraisal done with shifting glances from deep-set blue eyes.

"Mr. Venable, that vacant house is yonder," said Bud Monroe, nodding his head in the direction of Henry Parker's old house, which Putterman had made available for the Klan's use while they operated out of Gulch.

Venable looked critically at the dull, whitewashed frame structure just up the street. Passing his reins over to Tish, Venable said formally, "Mr. O'Callahan, see the place is clean and proper inside." Venable had been drawn to Tish undoubtedly because the Irishman's brogue brought to mind royalty, which Venable admired greatly.

"Yes, sir, Mr. Venable," Tish said respectfully.

"Mr. Venable," Monroe called out, and when Venable had taken due notice of the unpleasant look on Monroe's face, Monroe nodded his head across the street at Roy Willis, who had already been talked about distastefully by Putterman.

"The sheriff?" Venable asked.

"What's left of him," Monroe said, and smiled.

"I can see why Mr. Putterman would be worried," DeBow said, taking into account the careless, unhandy way Willis carried himself, the negligent way he wore his gun. "Don't seem like it'd take much to shove him aside."

"He's of no concern now," Venable said dismissively. "As long as he stays out of the way."

"What about that judge?" DeBow asked, his two palms resting over the butts of his guns sticking away from his sides. "That Judge Semester Mr. Putterman spoke of?"

"He's a different story altogether," Venable answered. "From what Putterman says, he ain't going nowhere. There's plenty of time."

Charlie Venable and his Klansmen made themselves at home in Gulch and set about making their presence felt, first in town, then in the whole of Brazos County.

Slowly Gulch came under the ruthless, cunning whiphand of the county's Grand Dragon, Charlie Venable, through intimidation, threats, and fear instilled by the heavy-handed, cold-eyed ways of Hinton DeBow and the men he commanded, coming and going at night mostly. Almost immediately their presence became known, then their reputation spread throughout Brazos County. No man, black or white, stood up to them. Klan rule became law.

On a dull-gray morning Judge Semester turned his horse off the valley floor and took to the wagon road leading up to the Lazy H. The judge was stymied by inaction at every turn by men of goodwill who drew back in fear as the Klan methodically took over Brazos County.

Ned squinted out at the coming rider from his rocking chair on the porch. Every morning since branding started Bertha had made him comfortable there while he watched the tough work of dragging up and branding maverick cows. It was being done at the ranch instead of out of a holding pen, as was the practice before Klansmen started riding the range, beating and killing.

"Gal," Ned yelled back over his shoulder down the dog run, "the judge is comin'."

Bertha joined him from down the breezeway. They both stood looking out from the porch as Judge Semester swung his horse into the ranch yard and headed toward them, his gaze averted to the corral where Bodie had a steer under his knee, Boot fixing to apply the Lazy H hot iron.

Boot stabbed the white-hot iron home. Cowhide sizzled and a trail of smoke rose away, the odor of burning hair lingering on the wind.

"Get it higher next time!" Semester called out. "Get that brand good and high on the hip so a man can see it from a distance."

Bodie and Boot lifted their eyes at hearing the voice. Boot waved a hand at the judge, who had become a known visitor to the Lazy H now. Bodie lifted his knee and released the critter, jumping clear as the steer bolted away. They both looked after the judge, Boot on his way to returning the iron to the coals.

"Judge ain't come all this way for nothin'," Joe Ben said from his saddle where he was gathering in a coil the rope he had just used to drag up the last maverick. "You ought to go hear what he come to say."

"He's right," Boot said. "The judge is a right savvy man. It'd do you good to hear for yo'self what he's come to say."

"Mr. Ned can tell me," Bodie said.

"That ain't the same," Joe Ben said seriously, looking from Boot to Bodie and back again. "All of us looks on you as the boss now. You got to start actin' like one."

"Go on, talk to the judge," said Boot. "Git the word straight from the horse's mouth. Anyhow, that's the last of the brandin'. Me and Joe Ben goin' to ride out to Rocky Hill, see if them old mossyhorns' gittin' the best of Berry or is he holdin' his own."

Bodie watched Boot and Joe Ben mount up, and when they rode out he mounted and started his horse toward the house. He drew their attention when he trotted his horse up to the porch where Judge Semester had dismounted, talking to Ned and Bertha. They all stopped when they saw him coming. Bertha smiled at him fondly; Ned looked at him approvingly.

"Place is starting to shape up," Semester said. "How many head you figure you got?"

"Close to two hunnerd," Bodie said.

"That's more 'n I expected," Ned said. "Or wanted. I always figgered the cattle business was a sight harder than it's turned out to be."

Looking seriously at Semester, Ned said, "Judge, the difficulty you spoke of in me signin' the place over to Gal here, I see no worry on that score now that Bodie's here."

"Me neither," Bertha said delightedly. "What Bodie don't know ain't worth knowin', ain't that right, Mr. Ned?"

"Ain't you got somethin' to do, Gal?" Ned asked, feigning exasperation.

"Coffee," Bertha said, smiling coyly. "Y'all need some coffee," she added, and hurried off.

"Some time ago Ned told me he wanted to sign the place over when the time was right," Semester said to Bodie. "Now's as good a time as any, but there's something you ought to know."

"I'm listenin'."

"New land commissioner is due in Gulch tomorrow. Like I told Ned, it'd be to his advantage to sign the place over before Venable and that bunch of his get sway over him."

"What about Putterman?" Bodie asked.

"The transaction's legal," the judge said. "There's nothing he can do."

"Only that Klan bunch we got to worry about," Ned said.

"That's right," Semester said. "They're a horse of a different color. That Venable is mighty canny. He'll stop you if he can. Last thing Putterman wants in Brazos County is colored landowners."

"You think he'll start somethin'?"

"He'll start something, all right. Only question is, what. Oh, by the way, they found Pierce's body on the outskirts of town." Semester's eyes came back around to Bodie's. "Hanging from an elm."

"The Klan?" Bodie asked.

"Undoubtedly . . . but there's no proof, or witnesses, as usual."

"Proof!" Ned scoffed. "Witnesses! Judge, me and you both know who's doin' the killin'. Question is, when's somethin' goin' to be done about it?"

"Until that new sheriff gets—"

"Look yonder!" Bertha yelled, coming down the breezeway toward them with a coffeepot and cups.

All three shifted their attention out across the valley where Bertha was looking, a sick, frightened look on her face.

Boot, Joe Ben, and Berry were walking their horses toward the ranch house, Berry riding slumped over in the saddle between the two of them. Even from that distance the amount of blood on his face and clothes told them he was hurt badly.

In one quick jump Bodie was in the saddle. He swung his horse away and took out at a dead run. Reaching them at the edge of the yard, he left the saddle, throwing the reins away from the horse's feet. The horse trotted to a stop off to the side.

"What happened?" Bodie asked, lifting Berry's bloody face and looking more closely.

"Damn cowards caught him workin' alone," Joe Ben said. "They took turns horsewhipping him with saddle ropes."

"That Klan bunch," Boot said angrily. "We got to do somethin', Bodie."

"We will," Bodie said. He ran his eyes over the bloody ridges of skin left by rope lashes across Berry's face and neck. "They'll answer just as sho' as God reigns," Bodie said grimly.

"Now!" Boot screamed, frustrated at their inaction so far. "We ought to see to it now!"

"Wadn't nothin' I could do," Berry said weakly. "Four of 'em jumped me."

Looking at the torn, bloody shirt hanging on his back, Bodie asked apprehensively, "You ain't gun-shot?"

"Uh-uh."

"Bring him on in the house!" Bertha scolded. "I can't see to him out there!"

Judge Semester and Ned looked on in silence as the others walked their horses on up to the porch. Boot and Joe Ben dismounted and carefully lifted Berry from the saddle. Draping his arms over their shoulders, they walked him down the breezeway into Bertha's room. Bodie stayed out on the porch looking after them, and when they had gone, Ned said critically, "Like I been tellin' you, Bodie, this trouble's got to be faced up to."

"It will be this time," Bodie said firmly.

"Look at it, Judge," Ned said. "Election is day after tomorrow, Gullytown was burned last week, Pierce is dead, now this. . . ."

"Bodie, it was Klan doin'," Boot said, emerging from the breezeway, a tight draw to his lips. "A man named Monroe was the one took the rope to Berry."

"There was a witness?" Semester asked.

"Naw. Berry says he heard the name called. And he says Monroe left word from Mr. Putterman that we was to forgit about the election, stay out of Gulch."

Judge Semester said, "Bodie, Ned here told me how you set out to find this family of yours when the war was over. Well, you found them." The judge stepped over to his horse at the hitchrail, lifted a toe into the stirrup, and swung onto the saddle. Looking over his shoulder, he said down to Bodie, "A man come into this

country better be willing to stand on his own two feet
... or git out.

"Gulch is two hours' ride from here," he said, and
swung his horse away. "You Johnsons take a notion to
ride in, I'll be there to see the law is done." He touched
spurs to his horse and trotted across the ranch yard,
Bodie watching him go.

It was deep in the afternoon when the clatter of a
ranch wagon passing in front of the Bull Head Saloon
got the attention of the bartender. Holly casually lifted
his eyes out over the batwings.

There was nothing unusual in seeing Old Ned handling the lines, the same black woman sitting the seat
next to him.

Holly resumed polishing the glass, smiling wryly at
the thought of seeing Old Ned finally mustering up
enough nerve to come back into town after all this time.
A black man wearing loud, show-off Mexican clothes
was riding alongside the wagon.

Abruptly Holly's head shot up as he recalled the com-
plete picture that had passed in front of the batwings: A
tall-riding black man wearing a high-crowned ten-gallon
hat and a flashy Mexican jacket, and riding a long-
legged Mexican pony, was alongside the wagon on this
side. And the black rascal even had a big heavy pistol
strapped on, Holly remembered. And a fighting knife
too.

Holly set the glass aside, staring blankly.

More details came to Holly's mind: Another man had
been riding on the other side, and a youngster wearing
buckskins was crouched in the bed of the wagon. Holly's
eyes flared as he was struck by the realization.

"Bud!" Holly blurted out.

"Yeah," Monroe answered from a table across the

saloon where he was sitting over drinks with Goodloe, Snowden, and Gandy.

"Old Ned just come in!"

"So?"

"Them Johnson boys y'all been tryin' to scare out of the county was with him, even that Gal."

Monroe gave Holly a stunned look. He shoved back his chair rudely, pushed up, and hurried over to the batwings. He saw the wagon moving away from him down the middle of the street, an armed outrider on each side, a youngster in the bed of the wagon. The gaudily dressed rider on this side Monroe recognized as the Johnson who had shot Lafe O'Callahan. Monroe yelled back to Goodloe at the table, "Ellwood, go tell Mr. Venable we got comp'ny."

"Who?"

"Them Johnsons."

"No need to bother Mr. Venable," Hinton DeBow said coolly, stepping around from the corner of the saloon where he had been quietly watching the Johnsons all the time.

He strolled up along the boardwalk, his palms resting on his gun butts, and drew abreast of the batwings where Monroe and O'Callahan stood. "We can handle this," he said arrogantly, and smiling across his shoulder at Monroe, said cynically, "Unless you two got somethin' else to do?"

Monroe stiffened at the insult as if he'd been slapped. "You calling me—"

DeBow chuckled lightly, amused. "Just funning, Bud. There's enough to go around."

"It's our fight too," Monroe said, calming down. "Me and Tish got a score to settle with them Johnsons."

DeBow smiled knowingly at Monroe's bluster and strutted on down the boardwalk.

Ned had drawn up the wagon next to Judge Semester's horse at the hitchrail in front of the land office, and he and Bertha had gone inside to meet the judge as planned. Bodie and Boot had taken up positions on the boardwalk at each side of the door. Berry was sitting the wagon seat and tending the lines.

Inside, the judge had attested for Ned to the new land commissioner that Ned was legally sound of mind and was taking the aforesaid action on his own free will.

Now, with the judge as witness, the new commissioner looked on as Bertha laboriously scribbled her name below Ned's on the quitclaim deed, lawfully relinquishing to Bertha Ned's claim to the Lazy H.

"Well, Gal," Ned said, relieved when Bertha had finally finished, "she's done. You got some land now. It's up to y'all and the Good Lord to make it pay."

"We will, Mr. Ned," Bertha said, smiling. "Bodie said—"

"They comin'!" Bertha and Ned heard Berry yell from outside.

They burst out onto the boardwalk and came to a sudden stop, searching around to see what was the matter.

"Git in the wagon," Bodie commanded them quietly. "There's trouble."

"Bud this here—" Ned started.

"Git in the wagon!" Boot shouted at them, stopping Ned from interfering in the fight that was shaping up. Bud Monroe was facing them at the side of Hinton DeBow, Bill Gandy, Tucker, and Ellwood Goodloe.

"You brought trouble, Ned," Monroe said sternly.

"Me? Trouble?"

"It's these . . . ," Monroe paused, searching for the right word, then continued derisively, "people . . . you keep around you."

"That's my business," Ned said testily. "Man's got a right—"

"This the one shot the Irishman?" DeBow asked,

smiling at the dandy way Boot was dressed.

"He's the one," Monroe said.

"Looks to me he ain't fit for nothin' but a Mexican whorehouse," DeBow taunted, spreading his stance menacingly. "Unless he can use that gun he's packin'." DeBow hovered his two palms over his gun butts, grinning a deadly grin.

Boot glanced uneasily at Bodie and raked his tongue over dry lips, unsure of himself. He knew that all the time he had spent practicing had made him quicker than he had been when he faced Joe Jones. Whether he was fast enough to go up against Hinton DeBow was a matter of speculation. And everybody did just that.

Bodie's eyes met Boot's, held for a second. Boot panned his eyes around at Bertha, then Berry.

They all knew Boot had to stand and fight now. There simply was no getting around it.

And he had no intention of trying to get around it.

He nodded his head slightly toward Bodie, as if he was saying, "I'm ready." Bodie took the cue and glanced over at Bertha. Bertha lowered the Creedmore's aim from DeBow's chest and stiffened her jaws.

Boot knew the matter was his alone to settle now. He squared his shoulders around, faced DeBow head-on, his jaw rock-solid, his forehead beaded with sweat.

DeBow smiled confidently, looked with twisted pleasure at Ned, then brought his eyes back to Boot, the smile gone from his face.

Nobody moved. It was quiet. Nothing could be heard except faint music coming from down the street at the saloon.

Ned and Bertha sat the wagon seat, Ned holding the gathered lines, Bertha at his side, the Creedmore down next to her right leg.

"He'll kill you, DeBow," Judge Semester said,

speaking quietly into the silence from the doorway where he had stepped unnoticed.

DeBow stiffened. Looking in the direction the voice had come from, he was shocked to see Judge Semester.

"Don't let that getup he's wearing fool you, DeBow," Semester said in a calm, measured voice. "He'll kill you before you clear leather."

DeBow knew that was preposterous; not even a white man could do such a thing. He looked unbelievingly at Boot, then back at the judge. But there had been something ominous, something worrisome in the way the judge had said it.

DeBow looked at Boot again, this time more closely. He saw something different in the armed black man this time: Boot's pistol looked big, sinister. Right at home, right where a man who knew what killing was all about would wear it. And it seemed a lot closer than normal to his hand, DeBow thought.

DeBow started to think twice.

Suddenly they could all sense DeBow start to doubt himself, start to question his own ability.

Even Boot sensed the change the judge's deliberate words had had on DeBow. Semester looked at Boot and could almost see Boot grow in confidence.

"Them sissy clothes can fool a man," Semester said to DeBow. And remembering what Ned had told him about the shooting when Boot had first come back, Semester added, "Ask Monroe here."

"Monroe?" repeated Bodie, the name ringing a bell. Shifting his attention to Monroe, he asked, "You the one that likes ropes?"

Looking from Bodie to DeBow, Monroe said boastfully to DeBow, "Like I told Mr. Venable, talking won't do no good with these Johnsons." Sidestepping away from DeBow's side, Monroe added, "They got to be killed out.'' To Bodie he said coldly, ''I'm the one horsewhipped him.''

Monroe never lived to draw another breath. Bodie shot him, shot him through the body without fuss or fanfare. He simply tilted his rifle muzzle up with his right hand, reached over with his left, centered the bore on Monroe's chest, and fired.

Bud Monroe died instantly.

The report of the Winchester shook Tish O'Callahan, standing there at Monroe's side. Even as he started at the blast, Monroe's body was torn away from his side. Tish was left like a man standing naked to the public's eye. He knew his name would be remembered in shame wherever white people gathered if he didn't do something this time. The last time, when his brother had been shot from the saddle by one of these same Johnsons, he had had no chance whatever against an aimed buffalo gun.

Tish reached for his gun.

Seemingly from out of nowhere a skinning knife zipped through the air, buried itself to the hilt in Tish's chest.

Tish's gun, which had cleared the holster, went off in the street. Then his grip went slack and he sagged to the ground heavily, clutching at the dagger in his chest.

Judge Semester was completely surprised by Bodie's unexpectedly smashing life from Monroe. Now Semester had seen the quick way Bodie's Winchester had come around on O'Callahan just as the knife had plunged home. The judge's mind recoiled at the callous way lives were being spent. ''Bodie, the law's got no say when a man settles his own troubles fair and square. But you shoot a man down in cold blood, you'll answer.''

''We didn't come lookin' for trouble, you know that, Judge.''

''I know that,'' Semester agreed grudgingly. ''DeBow,

take your men and clear the street," the judge ordered.
"The matter's settled."

"Can't," DeBow said. He glanced off to the side
where Gandy, Snowden, and Goodloe stood. DeBow
saw all three men watching him expectantly, waiting for
his response to the killings they had just witnessed.

"Don't be a fool, DeBow," Semester said. "The
land's signed over. The election's tomorrow. Mr. Putterman can't stop it. Nobody can."

"Maybe not . . ." DeBow said, and bringing his eyes
around to Boot, added, "then again . . ." DeBow's two
hands dived for the two pistols swinging from his sides.

Boot's six-shooter leaped into his curled fingers. He
squeezed the trigger, and squeezed it again. The first shot
struck DeBow six inches above the belt buckle, the impact jolting his body violently, freezing his two pistols
at the top of the holsters.

His next shot missed DeBow completely. The big
Creedmore had roared, sweeping DeBow's body out of
Bodie's bullet's path. And lost in the boom of the buffalo gun was the explosion of Bodie's Winchester,
smashing Debow's body yet again.

The guns fell silent. Bud Monroe, Tish O'Callahan,
and Hinton DeBow lay dead in the street.

"Bodie, you get these people out of here," said Judge
Semester. "You Johnsons have started a war. Let's hope
it stops here."

"You seen it, Judge," Bodie said. "They come
lookin'."

"That won't matter. This is going to stick in somebody's craw no matter how it's told."

Chapter Twenty-eight

The Johnsons rode out of Gulch. Judge Semester stood watching from the middle of the street until they turned off onto the prairie. Mayor Speed, Roy Willis, and other townspeople gathered around the dead bodies, each pressing upon the mayor his or her own particular version of what had happened.

Ellwood Goodloe, Bill Gandy, and Tim Snowden hurried back to Klan headquarters, and Goodloe, speaking breathlessly, told Charlie Venable that Hinton, Bud, and Tish had all been killed by the Johnsons.

Venable was shocked. "All three of 'em?"

"All three of 'em," Ellwood said. "Hinton was the last to fall."

"Hinton was no slouch with a gun. How'd they get him?"

"That Johnson Bud told us about that was dressed like a Mex, he beat Hinton to the draw."

"You're crazy!" Venable said in disbelief.

"Beat him fair and square," Ellwood said. "And the other one—Bodie, I heard him called—left word with the judge they'd be back in the morning."

"You sure?" Venable asked, toying with his neatly trimmed spade mustache, thinking.

"Yes, sir . . . the election, remember."

"I remember," Venable said, fighting back the cold fury inside him that wanted to come out. "They won't get the chance to vote," he said. "Tonight we'll settle with them Johnsons once and for all. When we get done with them there won't be a colored man left in Brazos County with nerve enough to show up to vote."

"I don't know, Mr. Venable, these Johnsons, I never seen the like," Goodloe said. "They don't scare like the rest of 'em."

"They're armed as good as white men, Mr. Venable," Bill Gandy added.

"No matter. We'll put 'em back in their places." Venable came around the corner of the desk and ordered, "Ride out to Putterman's. Tell him the time has come. Round up every man that's willing to stand up for a white man's rights. Tell every man that comes to disguise hisself in getup like we discussed."

"Yes, sir."

"Tell them to fix up real scary-like, the scarier the better. And Ellwood, let every man know beforehand, if it comes to it, there'll be hangin'."

Under a wan moon on a brittle fall night, eleven hooded men stealthily walked their horses up to the outskirts of the Lazy H ranch yard where homeless freedmen and their families led by the Johnsons from Lynchburg were struggling to get in on the emerging cattle business.

The men rode with a sense of mystery about them. For the first time the identity of each man was hidden

364

under a white sheet, only his eyes visible from two dark holes cut in a crude hood pulled over his head. Even their horses' faces were covered with demonic masks, only two fierce eyeballs visible to the observer. And one man had a four-foot-high wooden cross hoisted onto his saddle.

They came up like ghosts out of the night, then quietly fanned out facing the house. On signal the man bearing the cross ceremoniously walked his horse forward, dismounted, and erected the cross in the yard.

"What they doin', Mr. Ned?" Bertha asked, looking out one of the firing holes in the front wall of the ranch house that Ned had made for fighting Indians.

"Don't know, Gal," Ned answered, looking along his pistol barrel out the other slit. "What they up to is no good, that's for sure. Good thing Berry spotted them comin' like the judge warned they would."

"They might as well show theyselfs," Bertha said indignantly. "Them dressed like that ain't foolin' nobody." Resting the Creedmore out the slot, she added for effect, "Ain't nobody's doin' but Mr. Ben's!"

"Putterman figgers to scare the wits out of y'all," Ned said. "Old Ben hisself might be under one of them sheets," he added sarcastically, cutting his eyes at Bertha.

"This gun don't care who's under them sheets," Bertha stated.

Out in the half-light at the edge of the yard, the sheeted form of a tall, slender man wearing the only cone-shaped headpiece nudged his horse forward and assumed a lordly position, sitting his saddle next to the cross, facing the ranch house.

"That's him," Bodie whispered to Boot, looking over his shoulder from the corner of the barn. "He's the high-toned one that cowboy pointed out was sent to hang some Johnsons. I'd know that build anywhere."

"Look yonder!" Boot said in a low voice.

A torch had leaped into flames, touched off by Charlie Venable.

Venable rode along the line of hooded riders, lighting a torch each man held out. Venable turned his horse and touched his lit torch to the cross. The cross burst into flames, contributing its light to the ranch yard with that thrown off by the torches.

Venable walked his horse forward deeper into the yard, flames dancing eerily at his back.

"Now!" Bodie called out to Berry and Joe Ben over at the far corner of the barn.

Berry let out a bloodcurdling Comanche war signal, and out of the night every bondsman on the Lazy H appeared as one from concealment.

Surprised Klansmen ran their eyes around an unbroken semicircle of at least twenty crudely armed freedmen.

It was quiet. Nothing could be heard except the low squeak of the windmill and the ugly crackle of flames eating at the wooden cross, throwing out hissing cinders.

Bodie and Boot stepped away from their corner of the barn, Winchesters at the ready; Berry and Joe Ben stepped away from the other corner, Berry armed with a strung bow, an arrow notched in place; Joe Ben had the old cap-and-ball Colt pistol that he had shot Pony Harper with.

All along the crescent freedmen brandished weapons of every sort, anything to kill a man or maim him for life.

Ned came out the front door, his pistol in his hand, Bertha at his side, the Creedmore canted downwind.

The hooded men sat their saddles quietly, their burning torches held aloft.

Nobody said anything. Directly a horse stamped and blew, and a strawberry roan shifted restlessly.

Charlie Venable looked uneasily out the slits in his hood into the hollow of the semicircle, looked again from Bodie to Boot, taking note of the Winchesters they had.

"Who are you?" Ned asked from the porch. "What you want?"

Nobody spoke, as Venable had ordered. Hooded eyes looked from one to the other. Presently, a man thought better of it, threw aside his flickering torch, and sat his saddle idly.

Charlie Venable sensed doubts creeping into the hooded men's minds as they shifted restlessly in their saddles, unsure of their course.

"You men git off my land!" Ned ordered. "Clear out now!"

Nobody moved.

"Willis? . . . Tim?" Ned guessed at names of likely men, "that you? You got no right! Go on, git off Lazy H land!"

Shame overcame one hooded man. He looked around as if somebody important was watching him, then tossed aside his torch. Another hooded man brought a riderless horse to the man standing next to the burning cross and passed down the reins.

Venable knew his first robed Klan raid was coming apart, crumbling before his eyes. Against his own orders, he spoke: "Ellwood! Gandy! Fire the barn!"

"Mr. Venable, there's guns. Them Johnsons are armed," Ellwood protested.

"Fire the barn, I said!"

Ellwood looked helplessly out the slits of his hood at Gandy.

Gandy looked apprehensively across the gaping distance between them and the barn. Suddenly he jabbed spurs to his horse, sending him vaulting toward the barn door, the burning brand held aloft. Ellwood screamed out the unnerving rebel yell he hadn't hollered in a long time, spurring his horse into a run.

Gandy and Ellwood came out of torchlight into darkness, dim targets in a background of flickering torches and a burning cross at their backs. Halfway to the barn a crash of shots exploded after them. Ellwood left the saddle, the burning torch landing harmlessly in the yard.

Gandy took a bullet to the shoulder but kept his saddle, driving his horse on. Plunging through the open barn door, he twirled the torch overhead, starting to heave it into the hayloft.

A pitchfork thrown with deadly accuracy from up in the loft swept him from the saddle, the tines buried to the hilt.

A bondsman leaped down catlike from the loft and stomped out the burning brand before it could ignite the loose hay strewn over the floor. Gandy's horse trotted out of the barn carrying an empty saddle.

Venable knew he had lost two more men.

And Venable was undone. But there simply was nothing he could do about it. He swung his horse roughly, rode pass the burned-down cross through the opening his parted men made, and headed away from the Lazy H. His men turned their horses and followed after him, a solemn, sober procession.

The Johnsons closed around Ned and Bertha out in the middle of the ranch yard. Other freedmen came out in the open, stood arrayed around the perimeter, hearing hoofbeats of departing Klansmen and watching the dying flames of a symbol they would come to see much of in future years.

"Never seen the like," Ned said, shaking his head.

"What they wanted, Mr. Ned?" Bertha asked.

"Trying to scare us out," said Bodie.

"The election," Boot stated.

"That. And land," Ned said. "Property and wealth is

368

everything to a man like Ben Putterman.''

"Putterman,'' Bodie stated, ''Mr. Putterman's behind all the trouble.''

"It's him, all right,'' Ned agreed.

"Like the judge said, a man ought to see to his troubles,'' Boot said.

White men of Brazos County started filtering into Gulch a little bit after sunup on election day. Word had gotten around that hooded men had ridden the valley the night before. This morning was the last chance Putterman and his men had to stop the Johnsons from voting.

The morning dragged on. Gulch steadily filled up with white people from all around. They chatted among themselves, most agreeing that the Johnsons wouldn't show. Willis figured they would. He said as much. "The one I seen that come in from Mexico, he wadn't scared atall. They'll come.''

Time passed. Willis left Putterman and Mayor Speed in the mayor's office and went to the courthouse, making like he wanted to help Judge Semester set up the voting booth. Semester knew Roy's real purpose was to find out what the Johnsons were up to. Everybody knew the judge was thick as fleas with Old Ned and them niggers. Too thick, some folks whispered.

Willis left shortly, reported back to Putterman and the mayor that the judge had told him the Johnsons had said they would come in this morning to vote. When, the judge didn't say, Willis added.

"All right,'' Putterman stated resolutely. "That's the way they want it, that's the way it'll be.'' Looking at Willis directly, he ordered, "Get over to the saloon, tell Venable to see that the men are ready.''

The mayor started worrying, started to have second thoughts. "The army's not going to like this, interfering with the election. You sure there's no other way, Ben?''

"If there was, we'd take it," Putterman bristled. "Them Johnsons left us no choice."

It was almost nine o'clock when the ranch wagon first appeared out across the prairie, drawing the attention of a man on the boardwalk when it entered the ruts leading into the main street.

"They comin'!" the man yelled, and ducked into the saloon. A woman pulled a child to her skirts and ran off the street.

The wagon came on, Ned handling the lines, Bertha sitting at his side as usual. Bodie and Boot were riding on either side, Berry directly behind. At the head of the main street, Ned pulled up at the livery. Bodie, Boot, and Berry dismounted, gathered around Ned and Bertha on the wagon seat, looking down the street.

"Y'all wait here with the wagon," Bodie said to Ned. "Me and Boot'll go in on foot."

"Putterman's got men waitin' in front of the saloon," Ned said.

"I seen 'em," Bodie answered.

They studied the street carefully. Not liking what he saw, Bodie told Berry, "Keep an eye out. Anybody come up behind us, shoot 'em."

"How come I got to stay?"

"'Cause you ain't old enough to vote," Boot told him, grinning.

They started walking down the street, heading toward the courthouse, where Judge Semester had told them he would be waiting.

On they marched side by side, each man's eyes unblinking, taking in everything in front of them. When they got in front of the mayor's office a man said from the boardwalk, "I'm Mayor Speed. You Johnsons are causing trouble. I'm ordering you to turn around and go home. There'll be killing if you don't."

They drew up. "We ain't here for trouble," Bodie

answered. "We come to vote. Gov'ment says we got a right." Nodding his head toward the front of the Bull Head Saloon where Putterman and a half-dozen men blocked the street, Bodie said, "You tell them they step aside, there'll be no trouble."

"They won't listen," Speed said, looking out at the angry men Putterman had waiting in the street.

"The mayor's right," Ned agreed, calling down from where he had overheard the conversation. "Putterman won't listen, but the others might. They're all decent folks. Putterman's the one."

"Mr. Ned, you meanin' what I think you meanin'?" Bertha asked quietly.

"That's my meanin', Gal." Ned lifted his voice so Bodie and Boot could hear: "The way I figger it, you boys was to stand up to Putterman, the rest of these folks might go on home and abide by the election."

Bertha cut her eyes sharply over at Ned, and Ned added in undertones, "Mind you, I said might."

Thirty yards up the street in front of the saloon, Putterman stepped away from the others, his right hand moving his coattail back, exposing his pistol.

"That's far enough, Johnson," Putterman said. "Ain't no niggers votin' in this county."

"We got the right," Bodie answered.

Judge Semester stepped out the courthouse door into plain sight and said out loud, "I'm here to tally votes. The law says I'm to tally the vote of any qualified man that shows up."

"We qualified?" Bodie asked.

"Last I heard you was."

"What time the poll open?"

"When the first man shows up."

Bodie and Boot exchanged glances. As one they stepped off, heading down toward the courthouse.

"Damn you Johnsons!" Putterman screamed. "There'll be no niggers voting here!"

Ignoring Putterman's words, they came on.

They walked by Putterman, passing within ten feet of him. Putterman whirled around, screamed at their backs, "Goddamn it! Niggers will vote over my dead body! I'm warning you!" Bodie and Boot both froze. Deliberately they faced back around. "We been warned," Bodie said. "Now what, Mr. Putterman?" he asked soberly.

For the first time it struck Putterman that he was facing two men equally armed to kill, not two harmless pieces of property, as he had looked upon all of them before.

Suddenly Putterman needed assurance, needed a show of force. His eyes frantically searched the faces of men along the boardwalk, those in the street around him.

Nobody said anything. Nobody even blinked.

He looked out toward the courthouse where Judge Semester was standing.

Nothing. Semester's face was a closed book.

He stood alone out in public just as he had feared ever since Judge Semester had removed Sheriff Willis's badge, stripping him of cover of law. Nobody else wanted to chance the judge's brand of law and order.

"Ned!" Putterman demanded. "You tell 'em!"

"They got a right," Ned said quietly. "Law says they have." Ned nodded his head knowingly. Bodie and Boot turned away from Putterman, started walking down the street toward the courthouse where Judge Semester waited.

Putterman knew night riders behind sheets and hoods were of no use to him now. There was only one way to stop them.

He reached for his gun.

A Winchester went off from up the street in front of the stable.

Putterman's body jolted forward from the impact of a bullet slamming between his shoulder blades. He stumbled two steps, caved to his knees, then crumpled to the ground, his gun never leaving the holster.

The instant the shot sounded, Bodie and Boot whirled, each man's pistol coming clear of the holster even as they saw Putterman already stumbling to his death.

Now they swung their guns on Charlie Venable, Roy Willis, and five other men in the street. Each man put his gun hand conspicuously in plain sight.

Abruptly Judge Semester's boot heels rang out, coming down the boardwalk. He stepped down into the street in front of the saloon and called out stiffly, "Venable!"

Venable glanced quickly at Willis, then gave the judge his attention. The judge asked him flatly, "You got business elsewhere?"

"Maybe," Venable answered coolly.

"You've wore out your welcome in Gulch. The town could do without you."

"Who says?"

Semester pushed back his coat, exposing the Peacemaker. "I do."

Venable smiled cunningly, looking at the judge, a careful, measuring look. Every instinct told Venable he could beat the judge to the draw, beat him right out here in front of all these people. And Brazos County would belong to the Klan once and for all.

Long seconds ticked by, Venable weighing the matter carefully. Remembering something he'd heard about the judge, he thought better of his plan. Directly his smile broadened, spreading over his face. Calmly Venable turned, walked to his horse. Deliberately unhitching the reins, he stepped a toe into the stirrup and swung aboard. "You're right, Judge, I got business elsewhere," he said.

Swinging his horse away, he rode out of town.

While all attention was being paid to Charlie Venable, Roy Willis had quietly slipped away and mounted up. He had caught up to Venable's side by the time Venable got in front of the livery where Ned, Bertha, and Berry waited with the wagon. Venable and Willis slowed their horses, Venable looking across his shoulder at Berry holding the Winchester he had killed Putterman with.

"You Johnsons ain't seen the last of me," Venable promised, and kicked his horse into a canter, Willis following.

Word quickly spread that the Johnsons had cast votes in Gulch. By noontime every freedman of voting age at Gullytown and around had come in and voted. By sundown every black man in Brazos County had voted for the first time.

When the polls closed at dusk Judge Semester rode out of town with the ballot box, taking it to the county seat over at Weatherford. They found the judge's body lying faceup in a dry wash at the edge of Elm Thicket, a bullet in his back, the ballot box gone.

That spring General Forrest sent Charlie Venable and some more Klansmen back into Brazos County, where they remained during Reconstruction years. During that time blacks never cast a vote in Brazos County that was officially counted. And the census of 1870 counted not one Johnson in the county.

DON'T MISS OTHER CLASSIC LEISURE WESTERNS!

High Prairie by Hiram King. Cole Granger doesn't have much in this world. A small spread is just about all he can call his own. That and his honor. So when he gives his word that he'll deliver some prize horses to a neighbor, he'll be damned before he'll let those horses escape. And anything that gets between Cole and the horses will regret it.

____4324-6 $3.99 US/$4.99 CAN

Stillwater Smith by Frank Roderus. There are two kinds of men on the frontier. There's the kind who is tough with a gun in his hand, who preys on anyone weaker than himself. Then there is Stillwater Smith, who doesn't take easily to killing, but who is always ready to fight for what he believes in. And there's only so far you can push him.

____4306-8 $3.99 US/$4.99 CAN

Dorchester Publishing Co., Inc.
P.O. Box 6640
Wayne, PA 19087-8640

Please add $1.75 for shipping and handling for the first book and $.50 for each book thereafter. NY, NYC, and PA residents, please add appropriate sales tax. No cash, stamps, or C.O.D.s. All orders shipped within 6 weeks via postal service book rate. Canadian orders require $2.00 extra postage and must be paid in U.S. dollars through a U.S. banking facility.

Name_____

Address_____

City_____State_____Zip_____

I have enclosed $_____ in payment for the checked book(s).

Payment <u>must</u> accompany all orders. ❏ Please send a free catalog.

BRANDISH

DOUGLAS HIRT

FIRST TIME IN PAPERBACK!

Captain Ethan Brandish has finally given up his command of Fort Lowell, deep in Apache territory. But the vicious Apache leader, Yellow Shirt, has another fate in store for him. He and a group of renegade warriors attack a stage station and ride off just before Brandish arrives. But the Apaches are still out there—watching and waiting—and Brandish must risk his own life to save the few wounded survivors.

___4323-8 $4.50 US/$5.50 CAN

Dorchester Publishing Co., Inc.
P.O. Box 6640
Wayne, PA 19087-8640

Please add $1.75 for shipping and handling for the first book and $.50 for each book thereafter. NY, NYC, and PA residents, please add appropriate sales tax. No cash, stamps, or C.O.D.s. All orders shipped within 6 weeks via postal service book rate. Canadian orders require $2.00 extra postage and must be paid in U.S. dollars through a U.S. banking facility.

Name_____

Address_____

City_____ State_____ Zip_____

I have enclosed $_____ in payment for the checked book(s).

Payment <u>must</u> accompany all orders. ❑ Please send a free catalog.

BONNER'S STALLION
T. V. OLSEN

Winner of the Golden Spur Award

Bonner's life is the kind that makes a man hard, makes him love the high country, and makes him fear nothing but being limited by another man's fenceposts. Suddenly it looks as if his life is going to get even harder. He has already lost his woman. Now he is about to lose his son and his mountain ranch to a rich and powerful enemy—a man who hates to see any living thing breathing free. That is when El Diablo Rojo, the feared and hated rogue stallion, comes back into Bonner's life. He and Bonner have one thing in common...they are survivors.

___4276-2 $4.50 US/$5.50 CAN

Dorchester Publishing Co., Inc.
P.O. Box 6640
Wayne, PA 19087-8640

BREAK THE YOUNG LAND

T. V. OLSEN

Winner of the Golden Spur Award

Borg Vikstrom and his fellow Norwegian farmers are captivated when they see freedom's beacon shining from the untamed prairies near a Kansas town called Liberty. In order to stake their claim for the American dream they will risk their lives and cross an angry ocean. But in the cattle barons' kingdom, sodbusters seldom get a second chance...before being plowed under. With a power-hungry politico ready to ignite a bloody range-war, it is all the stalwart emigrant can do to keep the peace...and dodge the price that has been tacked on his head.

__4226-6 $4.50 US/$5.50 CAN

THE WHITE WOLF

MAX BRAND

"Brand is a topnotcher!"
—New York Times

   Tucker Crosden breeds his dogs to be champions. Yet even by the frontiersman's brutal standards, the bull terrier called White Wolf is special. With teeth bared and hackles raised, White Wolf can brave any challenge the wilderness throws in his path. And Crosden has great plans for the dog until it gives in to the blood-hungry laws of nature. But Crosden never reckons that his prize animal will run at the head of a wolf pack one day—or that a trick of fate will throw them together in a desperate battle to the death.

_3870-6 $4.50 US/$5.50 CAN

MAX BRAND

TROUBLE IN TIMBERLINE

"Brand is a topnotcher!"
—New York Times

Barney Dwyer is too big and too awkward to be much good around a ranch. But foreman Dan Peary has the perfect job for him. It seems Peary's son has joined up with a ruthless gang in the mountain town of Timberline, and Peary wants Barney to bring the no-account back, alive. Before long, Barney finds himself up to his powerful neck in trouble—both from gunslingers who defy the law and tin stars who are sworn to uphold it!

_3848-X $4.50 US/$5.50 CAN

WILL HENRY

JESSE JAMES
DEATH OF A LEGEND

Beneath the bandanna, underneath the legend, Jesse James was a wild and wicked man: a sinister and brutal outlaw who blazed a trail of crime and violence through the lawless West. Ripping the mask off the mysterious Jesse James, Will Henry's *Death Of A Legend* is a novel as tough and savage as the man himself. Only a great Western writer like Henry could tell the real story of the infamous bandit Jesse James.

_3990-7 $4.99 US/$6.99 CAN